MOONGLOW

Books by Michael Griffo

The Archangel Academy Trilogy

UNNATURAL

UNWELCOME

UNAFRAID

The Darkborn Legacy

MOONGLOW

Published by Kensington Publishing Corp.

MOONGLOW

THE DARKBORN LEGACY

MICHAEL GRIFFO

KENSINGTON PUBLISHING CORP.

www.kensingtonbooks.com

K TEEN BOOKS are published by

Kensington Publishing Corp.
119 West 40th Street
New York, NY 10018

ISBN-13: 978-0-7582-8072-5
ISBN-10: 0-7582-8072-6

First Kensington Trade Paperback Printing: March 2013
10 9 8 7 6 5 4 3 2 1

Printed in the United States of America

For Anthony and Bernice

Acknowledgments

I need to give a big thank-you to my agent, Evan Marshall; my editor, John Scognamiglio; and the entire Kensington team as we set sail on another exciting fictional journey.

And I must give a special shout-out to the entire Kensington design team for creating a book cover that is truly a work of art.

Thank you.

Part 1

The moon is dark and cold and light.
The moon commands our souls at night.

Alone, ignored, and ugly—she.
I am the moon,
the moon is me.

Prologue

Today

I am about to become a very bad person.

The change begins slowly, but not unexpectedly. Not entirely. There have been warning signs; I just didn't understand them. Until now. Now I know an enemy has been stalking me, watching me, waiting for the perfect moment to strike. When I scream I know that moment has finally arrived.

My screams tear through my body, gush out of my mouth, and infest the night air. They're the last sounds I hear before my world turns black. The last sounds I hear from when I was still good.

The first thing I notice when I wake up is that I don't feel any more pain. I no longer feel the burning. I no longer feel as if my limbs are being ripped out of their sockets, as if saws and teeth and knives are splitting my flesh open from the inside out. I no longer feel as if my body wants to kill me. That's the good news. The bad news is I have no idea what happened. The space between then and now is empty. One second I was happy; the next I was feeling worse than I ever thought humanly possible.

So I'm alive, but where am I? Forcing myself to remain calm, I take a deep breath, and the smell of grass and dirt and cold assaults me. I'm definitely outside, but exactly where, I don't know. I remember passing out when the pain got too intense, when I literally thought I was going to break into separate, unconnected pieces, but for how long? How long was I unconscious? And what happened to me while I gave in to the protection of sleep?

Now that I'm awake, I know that something is wrong. I can feel my body, and yet I can't; I'm both numb and tingling at the same time. Even still, I think I'm smiling because I'm thankful that I'm not dead. The thing is, I just can't believe that I'm alive.

I step on the sharp edge of a rock, and it feels like a knife blade has punctured the underside of my foot. The sting terrifies me because it reminds me of the original pain; if it starts again I don't think I can survive it a second time. How lucky can one person get?

I try to remember the prayer I used to say with my mother, but it's been too long since I've said those words, and anyway I'm distracted by the breathing. Loud, quick breaths, one after another after another, like panting. I don't know where the sound is coming from, but I don't like it. It sounds like a wild dog or worse, a coyote or a mountain lion, frightening. Whatever is making that noise sounds like it's right in front of me, staring at me, but I can't feel the breath on my face; I can only hear it. Before this change all I heard was laughter, Jess's and mine; now all I hear is breathing. But the worst part is that I can hardly see.

Someone's wrapped a plastic bag around my head—that's what it feels like, clear plastic, tight around my face—and whoever it is, is trying to suffocate me. I imagine what my face looks like pressed up against a plastic bag, my mouth and my eyes wide open, desperate to see and to breathe, and I shake my head because the image is too ugly; I want it out of my mind. I can't feel anything around my neck, and I don't feel anyone near me, so that calms me, but I cannot see right. Nothing is clear. Shadows and blurs, that's it, swirling around my head, making me dizzy, so I close my eyes again, but the blackness makes me even more unsteady. If I'm going to faint, I'm going to faint, regardless of whether my eyes are open or not, so I might as well keep them open and try to figure out where I am.

We were outside near the low hills, Jess and I, on our way to my house before this started, so maybe that's where I am now. But when I try to focus to remember more details, the breathing sounds faster, like whoever is doing it is hyperventilating. This anxious feeling, this sense of having no control grabs hold of me too, and I get dizzy again. I don't want to faint, but I don't know if you can prevent such a thing from happening. Focus and fight. I need to concentrate on specific things and not the swirls and the shadows that are making me unsteady. What do I know? What do I *know*? Think! Think of the simplest thing, the stupidest thing. My name. I know that my name is Dominy Robineau. My mother wanted to call me Dominique because she's French, but my father thought it was too fancy for a Midwestern girl, so they settled on Dominy.

Good, I feel better. Still a bit dizzy, but still conscious. My father's motto has always been "be grateful for what you have," and I finally understand what that saying means.

What else do I know? It's almost winter. Yes, that's right! But the air is more dry than cold, which is odd for Nebraska at this time of year, since it should be frigid and the ground should be invisible underneath the snow. However, the past few weeks have felt different, more like early fall, and I remember hearing people say that it was a relief and they wished it could last forever. That's a wasted wish because nothing lasts forever. Trust me.

One moment I was in control of my body, and now it's fighting against me. My head is spinning, my mind wants to shut down, and the only thing I can hear is the sound of that breathing! It's closer now, like someone's mouth is right up against my ear. My arms shoot up to feel if someone's next to me, but I only feel the swoosh of air. Vaguely, I see my arms moving in front of me, in slow motion so they look bigger, darker, but even though they're moving slowly, I can't get a clear look. Plus, I know I wasn't wearing a red jacket. I feel like I'm floating, wrapped tightly in a grass-scented plastic bag and floating, and it feels incredibly wrong. So wrong that my body rebels.

I fall, and the sound of my body crashing to the ground echoes in my ears, replacing the sound of the breathing for a few seconds. I taste dirt. Not that it matters, but I don't know if I'm lying facedown on the ground or if I'm kneeling, and I made dirt rise up in a little cloud and fill my mouth because I fell so hard. I give in to a strange impulse and start to claw at the earth, really dig in, and I can feel the coolness of the dirt underneath my nails. The sensation is calming, inviting, and I want to stretch out and roll in it, cover my entire body with cool dirt, but I hear a voice and freeze.

The voice isn't Jess's; it's coming from inside my head. Even more calming than the dirt, the voice belongs to my mother. Her slight French accent makes her words sound pretty, makes her sound as if she's singing.

Remember, Dominy, you are blessed.

The first time she said that to me was on my fifth birthday. Later, she wrote those words down in my card so I would never forget them. Yes! Now I remember! Today is November 29. Today is my birthday.

Slowly, instinctively, I lift my head to look up toward the sky and watch as the clouds separate to reveal a full moon. Magnificent. As welcoming as the unexpected return of a long-lost friend, as reassuring as a parent checking in on you as you pretend to sleep. Why have I never noticed how beautiful the moon can look until tonight? Round and radiant and perfect. But the moon is so much more than physical perfection. It has powers. Its glow is like a lifeline that connects my past to my present to my future. Every secret ever buried will be revealed when trapped within the light of the moon. All I need to do is accept the moon as my teacher, my guide, my master, and I can become powerful too.

A bright flash of light flickers on the ground like a lonely, restless flame, and I'm drawn to it. Scurrying closer to the light-dance, I almost laugh when I see what's creating such a commotion on the flat, dry land: my watch reflecting the glow of the moon. It's already begun. The moon is calling to me, offering a clue.

The powder-blue band is scuffed and smeared with dirt, the face is smudged and cracked, but I can see the numbers, and I can see that it's still working. The second hand ticks along, one second, two seconds, three, until it dawns on me that I can see clearly, no more shadows. Once again I know, somehow, that this change is the moon's doing.

I keep looking at my watch, waiting for it to do something special, and realize that it already has. The last thing I remember is standing next to Jess, her shoulder pressing into mine, her hair fragrant with the scent of cherry blossoms, and we were watching the second hand on my watch tick away until it reached 6:22 p.m. That's when I officially turned sixteen. Almost fifteen minutes ago. Why can't I remember what happened during that lost time?

I look up at the moon again because deep inside me, I know it's responsible. All the answers to my questions, even those I haven't yet asked, can be found in its glow, in its perfection. A large gray cloud with coarse edges slides across the face of the moon, changing its appearance. Radiance turns into something ominous. Could this be another clue? Or perhaps a warning that something even worse is about to happen? The revelation frightens me and, along with a renewed sense of fear come the shadows.

The world changes in front of my eyes, and sketchy black-and-white images return, but this time they're not alone. Accompanying them are noises, grunts and groans, sounds I can't recognize, but sounds that I can't ignore. Until I hear the screams.

These screams sound different than the ones I let loose into the air. These drip not only with the fear of the unknown, but also with the desperation and horror of knowing what lies ahead. They're unlike any sound I've ever heard before, and it's as if they're tainting the air with their fear. The screams are all around me, but I can't tell where they're coming from. Could be miles away, could be right next to me. It's like I'm in a sealed room, no doors or windows, but the sound is so loud that it can penetrate the walls. What makes it totally unbearable is that I can hear enough to know whoever is screaming is in serious trouble.

My heart pounds in my chest, and I hear the breathing again, wild panting, uncontrollable. Then I feel my stomach push out, contract, push out, contract, and I know that I'm the one making those sounds. I'm the one whose breathing is out of control. Fear grips every inch of my body and my mind; it has taken complete control of me, and I'm helpless. I can't even control my own breathing!

Another sound cuts right through the screams and the breathing, and it silences them both. The fear inside of me intensifies, because I've heard this sound before. It's a growl. And when you're outside near the hills, away from people and closer to the animals, hearing a growl is never a good thing.

Finally, my body starts to move. I feel the ground shift under-neath me as I run toward the screams. My vision starts to come back, maybe because I'm reclaiming control of my body, so I push ahead. Even though the moon resembles the midday sun, spreading light from its rocky, barren surface, I still can't see very well, and when I hear another growl, I turn my head too quickly, causing my eyes to glaze over, and I trip on some rocks. The ground shakes, or maybe it's just my body; I can't tell. But this time I know that my face is pressed against the ground. I taste the dirt, I can smell it, it's all over me, and I can feel filth burrow deep inside of me.

The growl is deafening, and I've got to move on. But when I push into the ground to stand up, the earth feels even more invigorating, and I can't, I need to stay right here, holding on to dirt and rocks, feeling connected to the soil. Suddenly, the fear is gone. I'm not scared anymore; I'm confident, vengeful. I look up at the moon and hear my voice turn into a howl. The sound is odd, but I know that it's mine. I howl again, this time holding the sound longer and letting it grow, so it be-comes louder, more powerful, more like my mother's.

Remember, Dominy, you are blessed.

All I want is for our voices to join together and become one, but we're interrupted. A louder scream erupts near me, and I recognize the voice. It belongs to Jess.

I've never heard her scream like this, and I've known her my entire life. She screams again. This time the sound pierces my ear; it's like she's right next to me, and her scream turned into a knife. Before I can touch my ear to feel if I'm bleeding, the growls start again, louder and more ferocious. Another surge of terror rips through me, grabbing my insides, and I feel my body shake violently; something's on me or in me, at-tacking me or Jess or both of us, I don't know, but I have to break free! This time when I fall I land on something softer, maybe some grass instead of the flat ground. I'm about to look down to find out what it is when an unfamiliar taste fills my mouth.

It's new, and it's bitter, and I like it. It tastes good, and when I swallow I don't even hear the growls anymore; it's like every sound has stopped, every part of my world has ceased to exist, and nothing has any importance except this new taste. It's heaven, and I have got to have more of it.

There's another scream, higher pitched, like Jess's voice is being strangled and made to disappear. I only want to concentrate on the taste in my mouth, but I have to find her; I have to figure out a way to help her. Despite the fact that I can taste and hear and even smell extremely well, better than ever before, my sight isn't good. I still feel like I'm inside a box or a sack. Like the plastic bag that I thought was around my head is now wrapped around my entire body. I can see outside, but it's all hazy and vague and warped. The world around me is filled with shadows, fast-moving shadows, and I wonder if it's the same for Jess. Or does she see everything clearly? Is the moon acting like a spotlight illuminating her whole world?

Oh my God. Maybe that's why she's screaming. Because she can see what's out there.

I'm holding something in my hand. I don't know what it is, but it's soft and hard at the same time. I think it might be a branch, thick and caked with dirt and mud that you find near the riverbanks. But I don't smell fresh water, and I don't hear the gentle flow of the current, so I know I'm not near the river. I must still be near the low hills, where I was when I passed out. Jess and I were running in the dried-up fields at the base of the hills, because I was going to be late and my father had told me to be home before the moon changes everything.

No, that isn't what he said. He didn't say anything about

the moon. I shake my head from side to side to trick my body into remembering. Now I remember; he told me to get home before it got too dark.

Once again, Jess screams my name, and I forget about my father. I want to scream back; I want to tell her that I'm here, that I can hear her and that I'm trying to help her, but I can't find my voice. It's gone. Furious, I squeeze the branch or whatever I'm holding in my hand tighter, squishing it, and the thing starts to move like it's trying to break free from my hold.

Jess screams my name, frantically, over and over again. My body trembles because I recognize something in her voice, something that horrifies me even more than not being able to see clearly. It's the way she said my name, shouted it, like she was afraid of me, like she was begging. She screams my name again, a sound that rises high and gets swallowed up by the night, the darkness, the moon, and then there's nothing. No sound, no Jess. It's silent and it's dark, but I'm warm and I feel good. Better than I have in months.

When I wake up I can see perfectly again. I don't need a watch to know that it's morning, very early because the sun is just starting to rise above the horizon. The air is chilly, but my body is still warm from sleep, so I don't shiver. I look down at myself, and the good feeling is gone, ripped from me, because I see that I'm covered in dirt and blood and I'm naked. Naked?!

My clothes are next to me in a heap, ripped and torn, even my sneakers. Quickly, I get dressed, pissed off that there's a huge tear in my good pair of school khakis from the middle of my thigh to just under my knee. Even my retro Pumas are ruined; the soles are practically torn off. Fear slowly coils around my heart and my mind as I contemplate what could have created such damage.

I collect the strips of material of my shirt to bring them together in an attempt to cover my exposed skin. When I look over to the left, all thoughts of my clothes and myself are gone. The horror and the shock and the agony in my screams remind me of the sounds I made last night. But these screams aren't made because I'm in pain; I scream because I see Jess staring at me. Her eyes are still wide open, but instinctively I know that she's dead.

I can't turn away, even though pieces of flesh on her arms and legs are ripped off and I can see her bones, smooth and pure white. I never knew my friend had marble underneath her skin. A breeze stirs her hair and makes her eyelashes flutter. Hope makes me gasp when I realize I could be wrong; maybe she isn't dead!

Reaching out to touch her, I gently shake her body. I desperately want to witness a miracle and see that she's still alive. Even if I knew the words, I don't think my prayers would be answered, because no one is listening and Jess doesn't wake up. I shake her harder, then let go as I watch her body move back and forth, back and forth until the momentum subsides and she's still again. I was right the first time; she's dead.

Her body's cold and hard, nothing like mine. I stare at my hand, not because I'm repulsed by having just touched a dead body, but because I see something. Pieces of someone else's flesh are wedged underneath my fingernails, and I know those pieces used to be part of Jess's body. I don't remember how this happened; it's just another instinct.

I clutch my stomach, and my knees fall onto the ground; the palm of my right hand slams into the dirt and digs into the earth to keep me upright as I vomit. I watch the rancid liquid spill out of my mouth to drench a cluster of rocks, and I feel the warmth finally start to flee my body, wanting no part of me. The stench burns my nostrils, and I turn away from the poison to look at Jess or what's left of her. I can't support myself any longer, and I collapse flat onto the ground.

Lying on my side I look over at Jess and I'm consumed by two thoughts that I believe to be facts: My best friend is dead, and I'm the one who killed her.

Chapter 1

Three Months Ago

"I am ugly!"

"You are not!" Jess yells.

"I am too!" I yell back. "Look at me!"

"I am looking at you," she replies. "And you look awesome as always."

"But..." I know Jess has more that she wants to say.

"There is no *but*," she fake-protests.

"Yes, there is!" I argue. "I can hear it in your voice. But *what?*"

Jess lets out a long sigh and puts her hands on her hips; it's her straight-shooter stance. She's about to give me her honest opinion instead of trying to make me feel good about myself by telling me a lie.

"But you have *got* to rethink that outfit," she says finally.

"Really?" I ask, looking at my reflection in the mirror.

"You're meeting Caleb's whole family for the first time; you cannot go looking like you just landed the starring role in a new Disney channel sitcom," she admits. "Okay, for sure that would mean you're going to be on TV and make a lot of money and stuff, but you look like you're wearing a costume. Matching belt, shoes, *and* scarf? It's way too much."

And that's why Jess is my best friend.

"I should lose one of them?" I ask.

"You should lose all three," she replies. "Whatever made you think you could pull off lemon yellow?"

"You look great in lemon yellow!"

"Because I am like a walking ray of sunshine!" she screams. "While you, Dominy, are more like sunset. You know, when the sky is all mixed up and doesn't know if it wants to be red, purple, or blue. Or purply-blue. Or if you just want to let nighttime take over and wear all black."

Though sometimes she can be a little hard to understand.

"That really doesn't narrow down my choices," I say.

"Sure it does!" she disagrees. "Stay away from really bright colors and go more sultry and sophisticated."

And sometimes she doesn't know me at all.

"I can't be sultry and sophisticated! I'm only fifteen."

"You'll be sixteen in a few months! It's high time you started acting like an adult," Jess reminds me. "Like me."

It's my turn to adopt my straight-shooter stance, so I tilt my head to the side and cross my arms. But before I can point out how incredibly off-the-mark her comment is, she points a finger at herself.

" 'Cause, you know, I'm such an adult!" Jess says, starting to laugh.

But Jess doesn't laugh; she cackles. Her mother is constantly reminding her that her cackling isn't ladylike, but Jess can't help herself. It's not intentional; it's just that she hasn't yet learned the fine art of subtlety.

She's cackling so loudly now it's like being inside a balloon when it's filled with helium; there's nothing else you can do except go along for the ride. And so I do.

The combination of Jess's cackling and my giggling—yes, I giggle, and I'm proud of it—fills up my room and my heart and makes me forget about my wardrobe trauma. Until I slip on the pile of clothes on the side of my bed, a pile that was created when I wildly rummaged through my closet to find the perfect outfit to wear to my boyfriend's cousin's wedding. It's her third marriage, but the first one since Caleb and I have been dating, so, for me at least, it's a really special event.

"I still don't have anything to wear next weekend!" I pout.

Jess surveys the pile of clothes on the floor. "Try on the pink wraparound dress one more time," she orders. "No matter what anybody says, redheads look great in pink, and a wraparound never goes out of style."

Grabbing the dress from the center of the pile, I know Jess's style advice is solid, but I already tried this dress on, and I looked like I was going out to meet the mailman, not my boyfriend's family. Holding it up in front of me, I'm about to protest, but Jess is firm.

"Don't argue with me, Robineau," Jess says. "The best friend knows best."

I've learned not to argue with Jess when she gets that "know-it-all" tone in her voice; all I can do is trust her, and more often than not I'm rewarded. Even when it looks like she has no idea what she's talking about. Just as I'm about to slip into the dress for a second time, Jess puts her hands up her T-shirt, shimmies out of her bra, and hands it to me.

"First put this on," she says. "Everything looks better in a Miracle Bra."

Looking at my fully dressed self in the mirror, I couldn't agree with her more. It is a miracle. I'm not ugly. I'm beautiful. And it's all thanks to Jess.

"Once again you've saved my life," I say, reaching out to squeeze her hand.

"That's why I was put on this earth," she replies, squeezing me back. "To protect my best friend from really bad fashion choices."

Now that we've solved my fashion crisis, we move on to home décor.

For as long as I can remember, my room had been painted pink, a few shades lighter than the dress. I grew up living inside a piece of cotton candy, soft and happy and comforting. Even the name of the paint, This Little Piggy, after the nursery rhyme, was comforting. Last month my father went on a painting frenzy because Home Depot was having a sale, and he repainted the inside of the whole house. My walls were stripped of their color and covered in off-white paint—I think the real name is Milkyway, which doesn't make any sense because the real Milky Way is black, not the color of milk, but whatever—so now they're blank, totally empty, and I feel like I have to start over. I don't want to. I want my pink back! I want to go back to living in cotton candy, back to being innocent. Luckily, Jess understands.

"By the way, Dom," Jess says while foraging through my jewelry box in search of the perfect accessories. "I really do heart your room!"

Or does she?

"What do you mean you heart my room?" I ask. "There's nothing to heart."

"Look around!" she commands, her arms opening wide to embrace the emptiness. "This room is the personification of you!"

Jess is sitting cross-legged on my bed; her arms are now outstretched and reaching forward, holding on to nothing. Her arms are as empty as my walls.

"Thanks a lot, Jess," I whine. "Guess that means I'm nothing."

"No, that's not what I'm saying!" Jess shoots back. "Your room is a blank slate." Jess jumps off my bed, toppling over the jewelry box so its contents spill out onto my bed, and runs to the wall next to my desk as if it's a magnet and she can't resist its pull. "These walls haven't decided what color they want to be yet," she declares, touching the wall delicately with her fingertips before turning around, eyes wide open, one index finger pointing at my face. "Just like you haven't decided what you want to be when you grow up."

Jess discovered philosophy this year.

"Is that so?" I ask.

"Buddha says listen to the silence of the walls, Dominy-san."

She's also obsessed with all things Japanese.

"Listen!" she instructs. "Listen to what the walls are saying."

For a moment I pretend to listen, but good old-fashioned American sarcasm cannot hold its tongue. "If the walls are silent, how can they say anything?"

"Because your walls don't need words to speak!" she pretend-scolds. "Now listen!"

"Sorry," I say, and try to pretend-listen better.

Jess kneels on the floor in front of me. She tosses the clothes I'm trying to fold to the side and grabs my hands. "Listen to the uncontaminated walls, Dominy, and you'll find your way," she instructs. "Then and only then will you be able to walk the path toward acceptance."

She drops her voice when she speaks, so it sounds deep and smooth and exactly like those people on talk shows who are experts in some weird branch of medicine or psychology, who think that if they speak quietly it'll make everyone who's watching at home forget that they're saying really horrific things. But Jess doesn't say anything horrific. She actually says something very sweet.

"Allow the energy to circulate," Jess purrs. "Attach your mind to its vibration and agree to become a passenger on its journey toward happiness."

Maybe it's the combination of fake voice and crazy babbling, but part of me thinks she's talking sense. That she chose those words specifically because I needed to hear them as I set out on a new journey. Maybe she's legit. A true Yoga guru who can transcend earthly shackles and see into the great beyond. Maybe she knows what I've been hiding from everyone, that I'm really very unhappy.

Could she know me better than I thought she did? She is my best friend, after all, and we've been close since before kindergarten. But does she truly know that I've been faking it lately? I've been acting like my normal self, when for some reason I've felt isolated and alone and uncomfortable even in places where I used to feel safe. Does she sense that I could use some guidance because I'm scared of losing my way permanently? Or wait . . . is she just having fun at my expense? When I hear her cackles bounce off my blank walls, I know my last thought is the correct one. It was all a joke.

That's when I hate her. I don't know if my expression is a perfect illustration of my emotions or if Jess can read my mind, but she knows how I feel.

"What is wrong with you?" she asks.

"Nothing."

"Oh stop lying!" she whines. "You got that look on your face again, Dom, like you want to rip somebody's throat out."

Again? So she has noticed.

"I mean seriously, I just gave you the bra off my back," she says. "Tell me what's going on."

How do I tell her what's going on when I don't understand it myself? I'm not a violent person; I'm not someone who gets off on insulting others, bullying them just so I can feel good about myself. But lately that's how I've been feeling, like I want to lash out physically and emotionally at everybody around me. The feeling comes over me unexpectedly and for no reason at all. Like right now. All I want to do is tell Jess that she needs to go on a diet because she's getting fat and that her blond roots are showing and her dyed black hair looks phony and ridiculous. Then I want to shake her hard and convince her that she has got to buy that Proactiv stuff online and have it delivered overnight because her face is breaking out again.

How can I share this with her? How can I even be thinking these thoughts about my best friend, the girl who I consider a sister? It's terrible and, worse than that, it's unlike me. I'm no angel, but I'm not a terrible person, but lately . . . lately I feel like I'm changing, and I have absolutely no idea why or how to stop it. But I can't share this with Jess. I can't share this with anyone, so I keep it to myself and make up an excuse.

"Sorry. You know how grouchy I get when I have my period."

"Dom, you must be having the longest period on record," Jess says, not really believing me.

"What do you mean?" I ask.

"You've been acting like a weirdling for months now," she admits. "Not just a few days at a time. Are you sure it's nothing else? You know you can tell me anything."

I do know that, but something's preventing me from speaking. Something is preventing me from being honest with my friend, and I don't know what it is. It's like someone has put a plastic bag over my mouth; I'm trying to scream, I'm trying to get somebody to hear me, anyone, but every attempt fails. Every time I open my mouth I just suck back my own breath and swallow it so it can reinfest my body, and each time I swallow it's making it harder and harder to breathe. Harder and harder to live. And harder and harder to look Jess in the face, so I turn away.

"Trust me, if it were something big and dramatic, I would tell you," I say, picking up my clothes and bringing them over to my closet.

"You can tell me the little, non-dramatic things too, you know," she says. "They have a habit of growing into really big, uncontrollable things if you ignore them for too long."

I get the sense that, whether I ignore what's going on inside of me or pay attention, the outcome is still going to be the same. Because the truth is I'm no longer in control; someone else has power over me; someone else is leading me on a journey into the unknown. Oh my God! If Jess could really read my mind, if anyone could, they'd think I was a lunatic. I have to fight this; I have to focus and take back the reins. My father taught me that the best way to take back control of your life when the world around you starts to get too complicated is to make one simple change. Something physical, specific, and uncomplicated.

"I have to paint that wall a new color," I say, pointing to the wall behind Jess.

She's back on my bed leaning against the headboard, and the white frame looks faded against the freshly painted walls. Could the best way to let go of the pink be to replace it? Or am I that afraid to live in emptiness?

"What do you think of teal?" I ask.

Kneeling on my bed, Jess does a 360-degree turn to take in the whole room and imagine what one teal wall would look like. It doesn't make the cut.

"Too much like turquoise," she replies. "And do you really want to sleep under a wall that's the color of reservation jewelry?"

She's got a point. "What about a bronzy brown?" I say, getting suddenly excited. My enthusiasm is not contagious.

"Dom, brown is great for eye shadow," Jess informs. "But on walls, it just looks like dirt."

Jess is getting on my nerves again. I don't understand it, I don't like it, but it's the truth. I know she's going to come up with a solution—she always has and she always will—but right now she is frustrating the hell out of me, and I have to fold my hands behind my back or risk slapping her across the face.

I mimic Jess and look around my room as if I'm appraising the area to come up with the perfect wall color. That's what she might be doing, but I'm just trying to keep my mouth shut so I don't say something bitchy.

During the silence a little slice of moonlight spills into the room. Its reach isn't long, but the tiny bit that lingers next to the window is strong and looks like a silver plank that leads from my bedroom to the moon itself. I feel a tug at my heart and wonder if the plank is sturdy enough to hold my weight, if I could walk on the moonbeam until I'm out of sight of Jess and everyone on earth. A warm sensation comes over me that reminds me of my mother's touch, and I take it as a sign that I should start walking, that I should begin my journey right here and now. Before I can say my good-byes, Jess crosses in front of me and blots out the moonlight, destroying my chance of escape.

These are the kinds of foolish, out-of-the-blue thoughts I've been having lately. I don't know where they're coming from, but these ideas ignite even more complicated feelings, feelings that are better kept hidden and not shared. Better to keep my thoughts simple and focused on finding a wall color solution. Finally Jess does.

"Orange!" she squeals.

Orange? Didn't I read somewhere that orange is the new pink? "That'll work."

"Of course it will. I'm a genius when it comes to design!" she squeals once more. "Just lose the banner."

"No!"

Over my headboard hangs the banner for our football team. Truth is, I know nothing about football, I don't really like the sport, but I'm the girlfriend of the quarterback, so it's my duty to keep a banner of our team in my room. But that's not the reason my reaction is so passionate. It's because of what is on the banner: a depiction of the team mascot.

Looking at the wall, I see the banner in full detail, maybe for the first time. Navy blue and white lettering spells out the team name, Weeping Water Timberwolves, while right in the center, the school mascot is depicted ripping through the material; its huge paw is outstretched, and its sharp nails are jutting out from its toes, as if it's clawing its way out of the wall.

Off in the distance I hear Jess rambling on about how she'll have to decorate around it, but I can't stop staring at the timberwolf's face. It's no longer a harmless school mascot, no longer a cartoon character, but a real live living creature. And I'm scared.

The whole room grows dark, and the only light is coming from the moon. The light is stronger now, and the silver plank has pushed itself farther into my room, illuminating my bed and the wall behind it. Glowing in the presence of the moon, the timberwolf looks like it's about to attack me; it's a creature that needs to pounce and feed. Its mouth is open and hungry and eager, its fangs ready to taste my flesh. Suddenly another one of those crazy, uncontrollable thoughts takes over my mind.

Part of me wants to jump on the silver plank and run out of my room to safety. Part of me wants to feel the creature's fangs plunge into my skin so the two of us can become one. The frightening thing is, I have no idea which part of me I want to win.

Chapter 2

The first day of school used to be so much fun. But all that's been ruined thanks to Bobby Worman's mother. Allow me to explain.

Jess, the rest of our friends, and I are decent students, not valedictorian material, but definitely college prep and definitely filled with a healthy dose of school spirit. To us, Weeping Water High School (henceforth referred to as Two W) was the perfect mix of educational institution, social club, and, of course, fashion show. Walking down the hallway used to be like walking down a runway. And we would be starting off sophomore year modeling this year's latest trends if Mrs. Beverly Worman read *Vogue* instead of the Bible.

Last year she bought her son, Bobby, a black T-shirt that spelled out the acronym OMFG in green velvet embossed letters because she thought it translated to "Oh My Fabulous God." Normal people know the *F* stands for something entirely different. But Bobby's mother is a "born again," very sweet, and she makes incredible brownies that Bobby brings to school on half days, but to her absolutely everything has a spiritual connection.

I remember the day Bobby—or The Worm as he is now officially known—wore that T-shirt to school. He couldn't stop bragging about how his mother bought it for him and that she had no idea what the *F* really stood for. Unfortunately, Principal Dunleavy (Dumbleavy to most of the student body as well as some of the cooler teachers) did. And since he overheard Bobby boasting about his mother's fashion faux pas of biblical proportions, he didn't believe The Worm when he tried to backpedal and say that the *F* was for fabulous and it was an expression of his religious beliefs. A week later we were informed that beginning the following year Two W would be adopting a new dress-code policy. And that's how our school uniform was born.

So instead of wearing an awesome eighties inspired top with shoulder pads and dolman sleeves in electric blue, vintage Jordache jeans, and Candie's high-heeled clogs, I stand before my mirror in a white, short-sleeved polo shirt with two navy blue *W*'s embroidered on the left chest pocket, paired with navy blue khakis, and simple navy flats. I look like I tighten screws into engine parts in an automobile factory. Or like I bowl. Neither of which I ever have any intention of doing.

This morning when I got dressed I didn't even know how to accessorize. What goes with bowling attire? A wrist brace? After much deliberation and rummaging through my jewelry boxes, I opted for simple sapphire studs and a matching necklace and, in homage to my new wall color, a bunch of bracelets in various shades of orange. Stymied, I kept the hair and makeup to a minimum. I'll have to live with this new outfit for a while before I feel brave enough to experiment.

Luckily, I don't have to do much with my hair for it to look good. Despite the fact that my mother has blond hair and my father's is brown, I'm a redhead. Some distant relative must've had the red hair gene for it to land in my DNA.

And it's a pretty red, closer to auburn than Little Orphan Annie. Thick and bouncy, so even dressed like I'm the poster child for Androgynous Anonymous, I still look like a girl, though I'm not sure I'll still be the prettiest girl in the world like my boyfriend, Caleb, always says. Thanks to The Worm and his mother I may have to settle for top ten.

As I grab my navy blue and white cowhide-print back-pack—I had to find some way to self-express—and turn to run so I won't miss my bus, I see the timberwolf eyeing me. I still don't know if he's friend or foe, but in the early morning sunshine he doesn't look as menacing, nor does he instill in me feelings of dread and anxiety and fear. I must have been caught up in a moment the other night; why else would I be so freaked out by a stupid mascot?

I don't know; maybe it's a phase I'm going through. Maybe these negative feelings are all a result of being stressed out, thanks to my subconscious quest to make a good impression on the first day of school. I mean, sophomore year should be better than freshman, right? But last year I became a football player's girlfriend, made the cheerleading squad, and if it hadn't been for my B in algebra, I would've made the honor roll. Freshman year is going to be hard to top, so there's a lot of pressure on me to impress the masses.

On the bus ride into school, I change my mind and I swear all my problems have to do with Jess. Before I even sat down in the empty seat next to her, I felt my stomach clench and my throat tighten; just looking at her pissed me off. What is wrong with me? So what if she didn't adopt my less-is-more approach to hair and makeup. It's her look, not mine, and usually I think she looks great. Why is her face infuriating me this morning?

Obviously she got up in the middle of the night to re-dye her hair to get rid of her blond roots and straighten her curls so the color and style will be as close to Japanese as she'll ever get. It's also clear that she spent another hour polishing her nails a deep burgundy, the same color as her lipstick, and topped it off with plum eye shadow and mauve cheeks. She looks like she's ready for a night out in Tokyo, not a day at Two W. I could warn her that Dumbleavy may make her scrub all the color from her face before first period, but I don't trust myself to say it nicely, so I keep quiet. And honestly, it's kind of hard to say anything to Jess, nicely or otherwise, when she just won't shut the hell up!

Oh my God! On and on and on she's been rambling, hardly taking a moment to breathe, telling me yet another stupid story about her stupid boyfriend. Normally, I thrive on this stuff; I'm a very social girl, and my friends' social trials and tribulations are mega-important to me. But today I just can't take it. I don't think I can listen to another entry in the disappointing saga that is her relationship with Napoleon Jaffe.

They've been dating for most of the summer, practically since he came to town with his mother and sister after living in Connecticut his whole life. When Jess explains his backstory, she makes it sound way more interesting than it is, but the basic facts are that his mother grew up here, got married, and moved away to the East Coast, became a widow, and returned to Weeping Water with her two kids to live with her mother-in-law. Unexciting. But Jess has convinced herself that he's led a wildly dramatic life that is movie-worthy. It's not even TV-movie worthy. I told her that she's gotten overly excited because he has an unusual name.

"Why would any parent name their kid after a short, maniacal emperor who was always scratching his chest?" I asked.

"Your parents named you Dominy," Jess replied.

Score one for the best friend.

Watching her fiddle with the cheap ID bracelet he bought

for her spelling out her full name—Jessalynn—the same crappy piece of jewelry she swears she will never, ever, *ever* take off, I swear I can feel my blood start to boil.

"Can you believe it?" she asks.

What I can't believe is that I haven't scratched her eyes out. Since I haven't been listening to Jess, but daydreaming about ways to silence her long-winded, tedious, and oh-so-boring story, I have no idea what her question is relating to, so I fake a reply.

"No, Jess, I can't."

Her second question is even more unbelievable. "Don't you think after all this time he should've tried to go a little bit further with me?"

I'm still not completely certain, but I think Jess is talking about sex.

"So you haven't done anything except *kiss* all summer long?" I venture.

Jess slaps my knee and yells, "Will you keep your voice down!"

She looks around the bus to make sure my question hasn't drawn the attention of our fellow riders and only looks at me when she's satisfied no one has overheard and is currently eavesdropping. "Last week we had a very long, French-kissing make-out session," she says.

"Well, that makes sense," I reply. "Napoleon's French."

She slaps me again on the same knee only harder this time. "This isn't funny," she whispers. "That was the high point of our two-month, one-week, and three-day relationship."

There's so much I want to say, but so little that I know Jess wants to hear. I've already told her that I think she's more attracted to the guy's name than to the guy himself, but she told me that was ridiculous, even though her notebooks are already filled with the name Napoleon written in every conceivable manner and configuration. Print, all caps, all lower-case, script, bubble letters. Followed by pages of heart drawings that are filled with *Napoleon and Jessalynn*. She used her full name because, she informed me, *Jessalynn* has the same amount of letters as *Josephine*, who was the real Napoleon's wife back in the day. She believes it's karma; I told her it's coincidence.

The real glitch is that Napoleon's only outstanding feature is his funky name. He isn't too tall or too short; he isn't too fat or too thin; he's got a normal haircut, normal IQ, normal everything. I want to tell Jess that Nap is the dull mayor of Dullville and she should be grateful that he's really not into her so she can break up with him and find a cool guy who really likes her and who's a lot of fun. But I'm not in the mood to be a straight shooter, so instead I tell her what she wants to hear.

"I don't know what the problem is," I say, sneaking a glance out the window to watch the world fly by. "Whenever I see the two of you together, you look like you're in love."

"Really?" Jess asks. In the reflection, I can see her blue eyes bulging at me.

"Yes!" I reply, turning to look at her. "You're grosssweet."

"What?"

"A little gross and a little sweet," I explain. "Both at the same time."

I'm staring into Jess's eyes, but I see her hand move. Before she can slap my knee again, my hand springs out lightning fast and grabs her tight around the wrist. Jess tries to break free, but my hold is secure, and after a moment of struggle Jess gives up.

"Let go of me."

"Do not hit me again."

I could let go of Jess's wrist, it's what I should do, but I don't. I like how my fingers feel wrapped around her skin, and I like how her tiny bones feel pressed against my flesh, delicate and vulnerable. If I made the choice I could probably snap them into little pieces. No, not probably, definitely. I know it, and Jess knows it. It's what I want to happen; I want to twist my hand so her bones shatter, break through her flesh so we're both stained with her blood. The thought of it makes me want to squeeze her hand harder. Just as I'm about to, the bus goes over the speed bump into the school parking lot and shakes me in my seat. The spell is broken. While Jess rubs her wrist and looks at me warily, it gives me enough time to think of a lie.

"I think you gave me a black-and-blue!" I say, massaging my knee. "I couldn't risk another assault."

True to her nature, Jess chooses to embrace the good and believes my story. She would never hurt me physically—she would never entertain the idea—so how could she think for a split second that I would want to do the same to her? Before this morning I would've felt the same way. Now I know differently.

I almost forget the incident until I run into Archie Angevene, who after Jess is my second best friend, and feel the need to replay the entire story so I can get a reality check and find out if I overreacted.

"Archie!"

"Hey, Dom!" he replies. "Heard you almost ripped Jess's arm off."

Guess Jess beat me to the punch. So to speak.

"Arch, I don't know what's wrong with me," I confess. "I just couldn't stand listening to her anymore, and all of a sudden I grabbed her and wouldn't let go."

"Let me guess," he says, shoving a book into his locker. "She was filling you in on another riveting chapter of Nap 'n Jess's 'not-so-in-love story' and you snapped?"

"Yes!"

Thank God, Archie gets me. And thank God, he's gay. If he weren't, we would probably date, break up, and I would lose my best guy friend forever. Things are so much better this way.

"FYI she's not upset with you," Archie says. "But I think she's upset with me now."

"Why?" I ask.

"She kept asking me if it was normal that a guy would only want to French-kiss a girl after almost three months of going out," he relays. "I finally told her I don't know why any guy would want to stick his tongue down a girl's mouth in the first place. Everybody knows that girls got cooties!"

"Which is why I got my vaccine," I reply, playing along.

Turning around I see my boyfriend, but he seems happier to see Archie than me. Maybe I do have the cooties?

"Winter!" Caleb exclaims.

"Bells!" Archie shouts back.

Let me explain their nicknames. Besides being gay, Archie is an albino, and when he was a kid he wore his white hair straight and long, which reminded Caleb of the Winter Warlock on his favorite Christmas special. Meanwhile, Archie says Caleb's high-pitched laugh reminds him of church bells. So Archie is Winter and Caleb is Bells and together they're Winter Bells. At moments like this I think they make a better couple than Caleb and I do.

"Can we talk later?" I ask. Caleb, unfortunately, doesn't hear me.

"Winter, did you get the new playbook?" he asks.

"Just picked it up," Archie replies. "Why?"

"Coach has got some cool new plays for us," Caleb informs him. "There's this one . . ."

Besides being gay and albino, Archie is also on the football team. Back in junior high he was in love with Johnny Saretti, a gorgeous Italian kid in our class. Archie was convinced he could snag Johnny as a boyfriend if he could only make a good impression; so when he heard Johnny was trying out for football, Archie tagged along. Jess and I watched from the stands, ready to dial 911, convinced Archie was going to break every bone in his then-skinny body. An ambulance was called, but for Johnny, who suffered a major asthma attack on the field. Archie made the team as a wide receiver, whatever that is, and two months later Johnny and his family moved to the more arid climate of Arizona for health reasons. Today, Archie, along with Caleb, is one of the stars of the team. And most of the time I love the fact that my boyfriend and my best guy friend are buds, but not right now.

"Caleb," I interrupt. "Archie and I need some girl time."

"Sorry, Dom," Archie says. "I have to get to chem or else I'll be late. Catch up at lunch. Later, Bells!"

"Later!" Caleb cries out.

Caleb high-fives Archie so hard Caleb's blond hair bounces and his bangs fall into his eyes. Usually, the look makes me smile, but now I'm feeling exactly the way I felt on the bus with Jess. Like my insides are going to shoot out of my stomach.

"Oh I almost forgot," he says. "I can't come over tonight."

Now I feel worse. His broad shoulders shrug slightly, and the right side of his mouth lifts up into a smirky smile that I know from previous experience is a look that he thinks is sexy. It doesn't work this time. The hand that isn't carrying his books reaches out to me, presumably to touch some part of my face, and his mouth opens again to speak, but before I'm assaulted with any more words, I do something I've never done before: I hit my boyfriend.

I slap his hand away before he can touch me; the back of my hand hits his palm and makes a loud smack. What is wrong with me? I mean seriously, what am I doing? Because I've never hit him before, Caleb is more startled by my action than I am. The strange thing is, a part of me feels completely normal.

"What do you mean you're not coming over?" I seethe. "We have plans."

Now his lips form a real smile; he clearly doesn't realize how ticked off I am. "I know, but I have homework."

"Nobody has homework on the first day of school!"

I hit him again, this time a punch in the chest. The sound it makes isn't as loud as the slap, more like a muffled thud, but the impact is greater. He stumbles and falls into the bank of lockers to his right; the flesh-to-metal crash creates a noise louder than I could ever create, so I'm not disappointed. In fact, I'm really happy because I know I've hurt him and he deserves it. But something's wrong; Caleb isn't acting like he's in pain.

"Don't laugh at me!" I shout.

Caleb is taller than me, bigger than me, but at this moment I know that I'm stronger than he is. I sense that he's starting to comprehend this new fact as well. The feeling of power that's racing through my body, making my veins pulse and tingle, is unlike anything that I've ever known before. The sensation is extraordinary and mind-boggling and unexpected, and I know that it's always been waiting for me to reach out and grab hold of it. Just like I want to reach out and grab hold of Caleb's throat and squeeze it tight so his laughter turns to begging.

Instead, I punch him in the shoulder, and his body flinches; he's not in that much pain, not yet, but at least he's stopped laughing. My fist whizzes past my face again, but stops when it collides into Caleb's waiting hand. He wraps his fingers around my fist and holds me tight. For a few moments we're motionless, staring into each other's eyes. His are confused; mine are triumphant. My fingers dig into the palm of my hand, and I'm glad Jess and I just gave each other manicures or else my nails would be cutting into my flesh. The thought makes my mind wander and my heart beat a little faster. No, I wish my nails *were* long enough and sharp enough so I could dig them into Caleb's face and peel away his lips and all of the flesh around his mouth, so he could never laugh at me again.

"Stop!"

The voice comes from behind me, but I refuse to listen to its command. Ever the obedient student, Caleb does, and releases his hold on my fist. His mistake. I let my arm fall to my side, but only for an instant before I throw another punch that lands on Caleb's forearm. I was aiming for his shoulder again, but he must have sensed that I wasn't ready to give up and at the last second he raised his arm to block my punch. Now we're just staring at each other. I have no idea what my face looks like, but his forehead is scrunched up like he's trying to figure out my next move or his next move. The next move actually doesn't come from either one of us.

"Dominy Robineau! I told you to stop!"

This time the voice is too loud and demanding, and once again the spell is broken. I feel light-headed as I whip around to see Mr. Carbine staring at me with an expression similar to the one Caleb is wearing. At the moment I can't remember if Mr. Carbine teaches science or gym; doesn't matter, he's a teacher and that means that he can get me into trouble. And no one, not even Caleb, is worth being sent to detention on the first day of school.

"Everything okay over there?" Mr. Carbine asks.

He's a complete fool if he thinks everything is okay, but I understand that he's giving me a chance to escape a trip to the Office of School Security and Discipline, so I grab it. I smile, perfectly and beautifully, the embodiment of everything Caleb thinks I am. "It's all good," I reply. "Just fooling around." Then I turn to Caleb. "Right?"

Dumbfounded would be the correct adjective to describe Caleb's expression. I have to repeat my one-word question to get Caleb to speak, but he proves he's loyal to me and still my boyfriend when he agrees.

"Yes," he says in a strong, flat voice, nothing like the sound of his laughter. "Just fooling around."

Mr. Carbine tells us to knock it off and get to class. Caleb looks concerned as he asks me what's wrong. I ignore them both and run off to the ladies' room.

I hear the class bell ring just as the bathroom stall door slams behind me. I lean back against it and press my foot into the side of the toilet bowl and kick it a few times. Nothing's working, and the adrenaline and tension and whatever else is locked inside my body won't relent; it won't disappear or even subside.

I start to walk from one side of the stall to the other, then in circles, like a caged beast, like a wild animal that's just been caught and is trying to make sense of its new surroundings. Even though the stall isn't enclosed and there are openings at the top and bottom, I feel like I'm suffocating. I kick the door open, and when I catch my reflection in the huge mirror that takes up the entire wall, I freeze. I don't know who I'm looking at. I don't recognize this girl. She doesn't even look human. I close my eyes, and when I open them I'm staring back at myself.

I've returned.

And now it's become official: The first day of school sucks.

At lunch it gets worse. I explain to Jess and Archie how Caleb not only broke our date for tonight, but lied to me as well.

"He didn't lie to you, Dom," Archie says.

The tater tots on my tray are about to make a new home on Archie's face, but I take a deep breath. I take another one, slower this time, and the urge to hurl food dissipates. My anger at Caleb does not.

"Yes, he did! He said he has *homework*. Nobody has *homework* on the first day of school!" I pound my fist on the table, and Archie's milk carton jiggles; it doesn't fall over, but some white liquid spills over the spout and onto Archie's fingers. I'm mesmerized by the sight of white spilling over onto white. I'm so focused on watching the milk dribble over and in between his fingers that I don't realize he started talking again. "What?"

"He didn't lie," Archie explains as he wipes the white milk off his white fingers with a white napkin. "Mr. Lamatina gave us homework in world history."

First Caleb, now Archie. Why is everyone lying to me? "I had world history third period, and Lamatina didn't give us homework!" I respond.

"You have regular history," Archie says softly. "Caleb and I have honors."

I have no response to this logical explanation, so I remain silent, which Archie takes as permission to keep talking.

"We have to write a paper comparing the end of the Vietnam War to the end of the Iraqi occupation," he explains. "Five hundred words, due tomorrow."

"Five hundred words?" Jess asks, utterly appalled. "In one night?"

"Ladies," Archie replies, raising his milk carton, "that's why they call it honors."

Simultaneously shaking her head and chewing on tater tots, Jess replies, "I loves me my school, but I'm so glad I'm only *slightly* above average."

All the energy, the good and the bad, leaves my body. I'm no longer angry or passionate or outraged; I'm just empty. I don't feel stupid or foolish; I'm curious. I feel like an observer, like I'm someone watching my life, not the person living it. People make mistakes, but I don't feel like I made a mistake with Caleb; I feel like someone made the mistake for me. And according to Jess, it was a big one.

"You really went ballistic on him," Jess says, now chewing on a fish stick.

"How do you know?" I ask.

Jess stops chewing and stares at me, her expression all surprise and skepticism. "Because I was standing next to Mr. Carbine," she informs me. "You didn't see me?"

"I can't believe I missed it!" Archie shouts. "I would've totally bailed on chem if I had known you were going to fine-tune your Roller Derby skills."

Ignoring them both, I shove a slightly burnt fish stick in my mouth. I reply, "Guess I overreacted."

"You guess?!" Jess exclaims. "Dom, it was reality TV, live and in person. And the good reality TV, like a train wreck. I was totally looking around for the camera crew."

As Archie and Jess engage in a debate over what constitutes good reality TV, I'm overcome by a huge sense of grief that far outweighs the event by which it was inspired. I'm sure I hit Caleb in a fit of unwarranted fury, but I didn't kill him; I doubt if I even really hurt him. I'll apologize, he'll cringe when I blame it on my period, I'll let him cop a feel, and we'll be over it. He's a guy; he isn't complicated. But I get the feeling I'm another story.

After school, locked in my bathroom, I try to push the events of the day from my memory, but I can't, so I decide to face the enemy head on. My reflection stares back at me blankly, and I wish my mind were as uncluttered as my expression. Lying to my teachers isn't the end of the world, but it's unlike me, and physically assaulting both my best friend and my boyfriend and then wishing I could do them even greater harm is completely unacceptable. The first day of school didn't suck; it was a disaster. Of epic proportions. It's like someone took my body hostage and went to school in my place.

Could this be the start of a whole new me? Is this how people turn bad and go crazy? They start by doing little things that are easily explained and quickly forgotten and then catch everybody by surprise by bringing a machine gun to school or a shopping mall and opening fire on strangers. Then they kill themselves before they have to explain their actions or take responsibility for the horror they've caused. Is this what I have to look forward to?

My reflection is too difficult to look at, and I shut my eyes tight. I clutch my head and run my fingers through my hair; the pressure feels good against my scalp, calming, and I keep doing it for a few minutes. I stare into the mirror, my hands still holding my hair away from my face, and I see a few wispy strands of red hair growing by my ears where a guy's sideburns should be. The hair is soft to the touch and there isn't a lot of it, but I don't think it was there this morning. No, I'm sure it wasn't.

What the ef is happening to me?! I can't look at myself any longer, but I can't turn away. Jess was right; I am a train wreck. I drop my hands to my sides, and my hair falls down, covering the new strands, but I still know this new, unwelcome growth is there. Not only is there possibly something wrong with my mind, but now there's possibly something wrong with my body too?

I watch the tears well up in my eyes, and they look like the sky during a rainstorm. Gray with only the slightest hint of blue. Despite how I feel about myself, I can't help but notice how beautiful my eyes are, only because they're just like my mother's. If only she were here. If only she could tell me that everything was going to be okay. I close my eyes and feel the tears run down my face. Her image appears before me, and she looks as radiant as always, but her presence isn't soothing, and I'm not comforted; if anything I'm more disturbed and more agitated. Because the truth is that she isn't here, she isn't coming back no matter how badly I want her to, she'll never help me again, and I simply have to accept that fact.

My eyes spring open, and I look as frightened as I feel, because even though I don't have a whole lot of proof, I know with complete certainty that something is majorly wrong with me. My body starts to shake as I cry even harder when I realize that I'm going to have to figure this one out all on my own.

Chapter 3

Morning isn't always better; sometimes it's just morning.

I open the medicine cabinet door so I can brush my teeth without having to look at my face in the mirror, then take a quick shower and dress in about fifteen minutes. I think it's my new personal best.

Downstairs in the kitchen my brother is pouring milk over his cereal, which looks like some super-sweet mix of artificially colored chocolate and several types of sugar. At fourteen, Barnaby is little for his age, short and scrawny except for his nose, which is huge. Everyone keeps telling him he'll grow into it; I keep telling him that'll never happen because his nose is going to grow along with his body, so even if he defies the odds and grows to be over six feet tall, his nose is still going to be too large for his face. It's a big sister's job to make her kid brother's life miserable, and I take my job very seriously. Unfortunately, Barnaby has learned from the master.

"Did you use the last of the milk?" I ask, holding the refrigerator door open.

"Somebody had to," Barnaby replies, shoveling a spoonful of brown mush into his mouth.

I peer into the fridge and look behind the orange juice bottle and the pitcher of de-chemicalized water, thinking that a gallon of milk is going to miraculously appear. Furious, I pull open the drawer where we keep vegetables and the other one that's filled with cold cuts, knowing full well that I'm not going to find milk in there. But hiding a brand new gallon of milk in the most inappropriate place is exactly something that Barnaby would do. I fling open the freezer, convinced I'll find milk among the ice cube trays, frozen meats, and the box of baking soda, but nothing.

"What am I supposed to do now?!"

My father walks in right when I shove Barnaby in the shoulder. It's not a big shove, but he's so small that he teeters on his chair and has to grip the edge of the table to keep from falling over. Chewed up chocolate cereal spills out of his mouth so it looks like he's throwing up mud. He looks like a little brother should: pathetic and at my mercy. I forget that I'm pissed off that there's no milk for my cereal and laugh at my brother wobbling in his chair. I'm so preoccupied I'm not surprised that my father hasn't screamed at me yet. Until Barnaby reminds me that his silence is unusual.

"Aren't you going to say something?!" Barnaby demands.

Chocolate milk is still dribbling down my brother's chin, but now I'm more interested in my father's non-reaction. I know he saw me hit Barnaby, and that's grounds for a lecture. He hates when we hit each other, which is understandable; his silent gaze is not.

"Earth to Dad!" Barnaby shouts. "Your freakazoid daughter hit me! Do something!"

Despite the screech of my brother's voice and the fact that I was caught red-handed, so to speak, my father doesn't do anything. And since my father is the sheriff and an action-oriented kind of guy who responds quickly to the scene of a crime, it doesn't make sense that he's staring at us like he's an immobile deer and his children are a pair of headlights.

"Dad!" Barnaby shouts again.

At last the sound flicks the headlights off so my father can respond.

"Apologize to your brother," my father instructs.

"I'm sorry," I say immediately.

Barnaby recognizes the insincerity in my voice. "You don't mean it!"

No, I don't, but that's all he's going to get out of me, and he knows it. He also knows, like I do, that my father didn't handle the situation very well.

"If that's the way you serve and protect," Barnaby snipes, "you're lucky there's never any crime in this town!"

Something's definitely wrong with my dad, because he, like me, takes his job very seriously and has never allowed anyone to belittle his profession or his abilities, especially not his kids. Barnaby knows this too and shoots me a look as if to say that he can't believe he got away with his comment. Nothing like a peculiar parental moment to create a bond between squabbling siblings. Unfortunately, this does nothing to rectify Milkgate.

"I still don't have any milk for my cereal thanks to you!" I whine.

"My fault. I forgot to get some yesterday," my father says quickly. "I'll pick up a gallon on my way home tonight."

And now he's taking the blame for the whole episode. I pour myself a glass of orange juice and drink it slowly to give myself some uninterrupted time to think about the last few weeks. This isn't the first time my father's acted strangely and out of character. He's been preoccupied with something, absent-minded; in fact one night he left his gun on the kitchen table, out of its holster. First time that's ever happened in my entire life. Being sheriff of a sleepy town is still a stressful job, but until recently he's handled it without any noticeable repercussions. Maybe the stress is getting to him? Maybe I'm not the only one going through a rough patch.

"Everything okay, Dad?" I ask.

I don't get the response I was expecting. He looks at me like he's never seen me before, like I'm a stranger who has no right to ask such a personal question.

"Daaaaad . . . is anything wrong?" I ask again. And again I get an unexpected response.

"Everything's fine," he mumbles as he turns from me.

Everybody in the room knows he's lying, but since up until this moment he's been a man of his word, we accept his response at face value. That doesn't mean I give up trying to uncover the truth. Digging into some strawberry yogurt—a poor substitute to the cereal I was craving—I watch him as he shuffles around the kitchen, pouring juice into a glass, spilling a little on the counter, wiping up the spill, and I examine his face and his body for signs of illness, but he looks the same. His eyes aren't bloodshot; he's not pale or sweaty; his body isn't hunched over like he's carrying the weight of the world on his shoulders or even the weight of our family; he looks as strong as ever, which makes me even more concerned. Something must be really wrong if he's going out of his way to hide it from us.

Barnaby's freshman-only bus comes first, and he grabs his backpack and runs out of the house shouting a good-bye to our dad just as he slams the front door shut. As a little brother, being annoying comes naturally; as a son, being disrespectful doesn't.

Being alone in the kitchen with my dad is unusually tense. I'm not used to this feeling. We don't agree on everything, we have our spats, we yell at each other from time to time, but my dad is a good guy and, most important, he's accessible. Whenever Barnaby or I need to talk or vent, he listens. On the flip side, if something's bothering him, he'll share it with us. He may not offer up the version that's rated A for adults only, but he'll share enough details with us so we feel like we're a part of his life. I'm not used to feeling like an intruder, and I'm not used to my father acting like someone other than my father. So of course when I see him open his mouth to speak, I act like a jerk.

"It's a bit too early for a father-daughter chat."

I throw my spoon in the sink, grab my bag, ignore my dad's woeful expression, and escape.

For the rest of the day I feel guilty for acting inappropriately when the whole thing was my fault. I was the one who was wrong, so I guess I'm the one who's going to have to make it right.

The police station is walking distance from Two W, so after school I ditch the bus and walk over to see my father so I can apologize properly. The weather doesn't know if it wants to be summer or fall; it's still warm, but every once in a while a breeze floats by and brings with it cool air that's an indication of things to come. Nebraska weather isn't always predictable, but more often than not it's severe. When it's hot, it's scorching, and when it's cold, well, let's just say that it's hard to maintain any fashion sense when long johns and a parka are required clothing.

Today I don't even need a jacket, and the air feels good on my arms. The walk is so quiet, it's almost meditative. Most of the kids have either taken the bus home or stayed late to practice some sport or extracurricular activity. Caleb and Archie have football practice, and Jess is the president of Broadway Bound, the school's theater group. I haven't committed to anything other than cheerleading, and practice doesn't start until next week, so until then I'm a free agent.

I leave the main road to take a shortcut into the center of town. I'm hardly the first to do so, and even if I had never taken this route before, if I was a foreigner and not a townie, I still wouldn't get lost. There's a well-traveled dirt path that leads from the end of school grounds, from the edge of the baseball field, directly to the back of the Super Saver, Weeping Water's one and only supermarket. On either side of the makeshift walkway are grass and weeds, more weeds than grass actually, some tree stumps, garbage that keeps piling up despite the town's many litter-prevention initiatives, and halfway in between the two locations a town landmark—a lone tree in the middle of a clearing that we all call The Weeping Lady.

Huge oak, about twenty or twenty-five-feet tall according to the locals. Remember, I'm not that great in math, so I'm taking them at their word. This time of year The Weeping Lady still looks like she's in her prime; her thick, sturdy branches are the home for rows and rows of hearty-looking leaves. Come late November she'll look old and bare, like a fading monument in a patch of parched earth. Today she looks grand and deserving of both solitude and admiration.

The Weeping part of her name is obvious—it's a tribute to the town's name; the Lady part not so much, unless you're looking at the tree at night. When the moon shines through the tree, a cluster of branches on its right side creates the silhouette of a woman. Nobody believes it until they see it; then they still can't believe that nature conjured up something that looks man-made. The branches on this little cluster weave and ripple, so it looks like the Lady has long, wavy hair that covers most of her body; when the tree is covered in leaves like today, her hair looks soft and billowy and the most beautiful shade of green. Her profile faces the other side of the tree; what she's looking at, no one can agree on. Some say she's gazing at her long-lost lover, some say she's looking into the eyes of God, while some others think she's waiting for just the right moment to hang herself. Guess you interpret her action depending upon your point of view of the world.

The sun shines through the branches of The Weeping Lady, surrounding it with a yellowish haze, making her leaves look less robust and secure and more like a string of light. The woman's outline isn't as pronounced as it is in the moonlight, but I know it's there, so I can make it out. Up until now I never gave her much thought; I never fell into one camp or the other about the origin of her mythology. I took the practical approach and just considered her a tree. But now I can see The Weeping Lady for what she is: lost.

She's hanging in between two worlds. She can't quite touch the earth and make a home and a life for herself here, but she also can't return to where she was born. I don't know if that's the sun or the moon or some distant star, but wherever it is she can't get back there. On the one hand she's doomed, forever crying because she's destined to straddle two worlds, neither of which she can ever call home. On the other hand she's free, shedding tears of joy because she can travel wherever she wants without feeling the need to put down roots and settle. Suddenly, I feel a connection to this woman, this carving, this image. I feel a breeze pass through me; it's warm and it feels good, but I don't know if the wind is agreeing with me or if it's trying to pry the idiotic thought from my mind.

I walk diagonally across the Super Saver parking lot, weaving in and out of the parked cars to make my way to Robin Boulevard. Don't get the wrong idea; there's no connection between the boulevard and Robineau, my last name, even though I used to think it was named after my father's family. After all, his ancestors came here from Canada in the middle of the nineteenth century to make their fame as fur traders, so Robineaus have been living in Weeping Water for as long as Weeping Water has had people living in it. But no, Robin Boulevard didn't get its name to honor a prominent local family, but rather to honor a prominent local bird.

A long time ago, when they were naming streets, this stretch of land was home to an insanely large number of birds. And by home I mean cemetery. Robin sounds like such a pretty name, conjures up an image of a cute red-breasted bird perched on your finger chirping a happy tune like something out of an animated Disney movie. Truth is real robins are more like something out of one of those *Saw* movies, incredibly aggressive. Don't know why, but if a robin were perched on your finger, he'd probably peck at it until your finger was as bloody as its breast. When I found that out, it kind of ruined *Snow White* for me.

From what I've heard, at some point there must have been some kind of robin bird war, because this patch of land was covered with the corpses of hundreds of robins, bloodied and decapitated and wingless. Rotting corpses strewn across the land, one lying next to the other to create a robin boulevard. Get it? I'm sure in reality there were like five birds that got into a deadly spat over who was going to eat the last chunk of bread that fell from some fur trapper's satchel, but truth usually doesn't become legend. Fantasy does. So kudos to the forefathers of my hometown for creating such an interesting, and completely unbelievable, fairy tale. Because fairy tales are supposed to be unbelievable, that's the only reason we believe in them anyway.

Even without a connection I still think it's pretty cool that my name is almost the name of the largest street in town. At the end of the day it doesn't mean anything, my family doesn't have any ownership of the street name, but it reminds me that no matter how crazy and disjointed my mind gets, I still have a place in the world. A place that can sometimes feel very, very small.

At the stoplight is Jess's mother in her bright yellow Nissan Xterra, which is almost as vibrant as Mrs. Wyatt. Sitting next to her in the passenger seat is Misutakiti, Jess's German shepherd and her pride and joy. Loosely translated his name is Japanese for Mister Kitty; he's named after one of that country's most famous exports and Jess's all-time favorite pop-culture icon, Hello Kitty.

Misutakiti sees me, but Mrs. Wyatt doesn't, because she, as usual, is talking on her cell phone, with her hands pointing and gesturing and flying through the air. Misu isn't moving; he's up on all fours facing the passenger-side window, staring in my direction. On second thought maybe he hasn't seen me yet, because when he does he flips out, knowing he's going to get the best belly rub ever. His tail starts to wag frantically, and he runs in circles, his tongue flopping out of his mouth. Now he looks different.

His ears are pointed straight up and look like two motionless, multi-colored teepees, black on top, gradually turning to brown at the base. His entire body, in fact, is stock still, and his beautiful eyes—one blue, one black—are staring straight ahead.

"Hello, Misutakiti!" I say in my singsongy voice, reserved for when I'm talking to dogs and babies, even though I know he won't be able to hear me from where I'm standing.

He might not have heard me, but he does respond. Just not in the way I expected. Bam! One huge paw hits the window. Bam! The other huge paw hits it even harder. His paws start to move quickly, pounding against the glass as if they were clawing at dirt and he was on a mission to bury a bone. The only reason I can't hear his nails scratching against the window is that he's barking too loudly. I stop waving when I realize this isn't Misu's typical "Hello, rub my belly" bark; this is his "I want to get the hell out of this car and attack you" bark.

"Misu, it's me, Dominy."

Personal identification doesn't temper Misu's barking; if anything, it intensifies it. Despite the sound's being muffled by the car windows, I can still hear how gruff and deep and hostile it is. And the dog's posture matches his sound. He's not his usual flopsy-mopsy self; his body is rigid and ready to pounce. But why would he want to pounce on me? He loves me almost as much as he loves Jess. Probably even more because I bring him people food all the time.

A quick look around shows that there isn't a stray deer behind me or a lost rabbit nearby that Misu would like to turn into an afternoon snack; the area's deserted. No, Misu's rabid barking is directed at me. I can see Mrs. Wyatt's hand motions change, and now she's slapping Misu on his backside to get him to shut up. Oh that must be it! He must want me to help him get out of that car because he's tired of hearing her yak on the phone.

"Hi, Mrs. Wyatt!" I shout.

I wave back, but not nearly as wildly as she's waving at me. Her mouth is moving, but I can't hear her and, of course, I'm not sure if she's talking to me, Misu, or the person on the other end of her cell phone line. Doesn't really matter because the only thing anyone can hear is Misu's harsh barking, which hasn't diminished in intensity since he started. Poor thing, he really wants his freedom. When the light turns green and Mrs. Wyatt pulls away, Misu leaps into the backseat, his body rigid and unwavering, his mouth opening and closing in a steady barking rhythm, begging me to rescue him. Sorry, Misu, unfortunately your place in the world is next to a woman who never shuts up.

My father's place in the world is directly across the street, in the police station. It stands right on the corner, but the entrance to his office is in the back of the building, so I make my way around to the rear. When I hear my name, I stop underneath the window.

"I'm worried about Dominy," he says.

"Why? She do something wrong?"

The other voice belongs to Louis Bergeron, his deputy. Another local of French Canadian ancestry, but with some Creole mixed in, so his name is pronounced without the "s" at the end. Louis is loud and fun and not at all an authority figure, but he's my dad's best friend, so I guess that's how he became the deputy. His daughter Arla is pretty much the same way, loud and lots of fun, but as one of the best athletes on our little high school campus, she cuts a more authoritative figure at school than her father does in town.

"No, she hasn't done anything wrong," my father says, "but I . . . I just think she might."

The drawer of a filing cabinet slams shut. "Of course she will," Louis replies. "She's a teenager; that's what they do."

No one's talking now, and I stupidly press my ear up against the brick on the side of the building, as if that's going to help me hear their conversation better, like putting my ear up to a glass on an apartment wall, which I don't think works either, by the way. Acting more logically I walk around the back and see what I had expected, that the screen door is closed, but the main door is wide open. Standing just off to the side of the screen is a much more effective way to listen in on their conversation.

There's a high-pitched whistling sound that I figure must be from the wheels of my dad's chair rolling across the hardwood floor. "Not the usual stuff, something more," my father says.

This is how he spends his day? Imagining that I'm going to do something terrible?

Now there are some clinking sounds that get drowned out by Louis's voice before I can identify them. "One job isn't good enough for you?" he asks. "Now you want to be the town psychic too?"

"It's just a feeling I have."

My father speaks slowly, choosing his words deliberately. He's lying, hiding something like he was this morning. It's more than just a feeling; he knows something.

"Mason, do yourself a favor and don't make things up," Louis says. "My Arla can be a handful sometimes, don't I know it, but she and Dominy aren't gonna screw up; they're both good kids."

"Dominy is good," my father replies. "For now."

"What's that supposed to mean?" Louis asks.

"Yeah, Dad, what's that supposed to mean?"

The screen door slams behind me. I didn't plan it, but it makes my sudden entrance that much more dramatic. Jess would be proud. My father isn't; he looks the same way he did this morning, like I've caught him doing or thinking something that he wants to keep far away from me.

"Dominy," he says. "What are you doing here?"

His tone of voice doesn't match his expression. Mildly inquisitive doesn't equal frightened.

"Hey, Dom," Louis calls out, raising his cup of coffee. My eyes involuntarily shift to take in the coffeemaker, and I know what was making the clinking sounds. One mystery solved.

"I asked you a question, Dad." The fact that I don't cringe even though I sound as whiny as Barnaby did this morning makes me realize that I'm madder than I thought. After the way I acted yesterday and this morning, my father's proven to be a pretty good psychic; in all probability I am destined to do something seriously bad. But I don't want logic; I want an answer. "What do you mean I'm good . . . *for now?*"

My father is fifty-two years old, much younger-looking than Louis, who is a decade his junior and much younger looking from what Jess and Arla tell me, but now he looks impossibly young. It's not a physical thing; it's more an emotional state. He looks innocent and pure, the way I should look and feel, but don't. There isn't a mirror in sight, but the one feature I know we have in common is that we both look scared.

"I didn't know you were there," he replies. His voice is

meek, and I know that down deep I love him, but right now I can't stand him, because he's acting like a jerk.

"That's not an answer!" I tell him.

I'm completely focused on my father, so I don't notice Louis has moved until he's standing right in my line of vision, and it's not a pretty sight. His rough features—an oddly bent nose, and an array of scars on his cheeks and chin that are tiny but highly visible on his dark black skin—seem grossly exaggerated as his face reels back in shock. I guess my voice is kind of loud and out of control. I'm not acting the way a sheriff's daughter is expected to act. Or sound.

"Barnaby was right," I growl. "If you act the same way as sheriff as you do as a father, you suck at your job!"

Voices trail after me, but I can't make out any words because the screen door slams so loudly behind me the noise blocks them out. Sends the birds scattering too. If there are any robins around, they can go claw themselves to death and leave a bloody trail from their war zone straight to my father's desk. And there won't be any need for them to worry because he won't say anything about the mess.

Two hours later and I'm still staring at the same page in my textbook. Nathaniel Hawthorne's writing is incomprehensible. If he were here in my bedroom right now, I'd write the letter *A* on a piece of paper and staple it to his chest, tell him he wasted his time being an author, and then push him out the window. I'm about to fling the book across my room when someone knocks on my door. Has to be my father; Barnaby has no manners.

A part of me melts when I see my father standing in my doorway. A part of me is always going to be his little girl, the one who still wants to hold his hand or turn around to make sure he's nearby and watching me, no matter where I might be. Another part of me wants to slap him across the face.

He closes the door behind him. It's a slow, deliberate move, so it comes off as awkward. "Can we talk?" he asks.

"I tried to do that earlier," I reply. Of course I didn't fill my reply with enough sarcasm; have to compound it. "Did it take you this long to come up with something to say?"

He sits on the edge of my bed and places his hands on his knees. The backs of his hands are very smooth, completely unlike the palms, which are calloused and rough. He's never been in a fight, not on the job or off, but he's worked outside most of his life, building houses, chopping down trees for firewood, planting crops even, and his hands tell an intricate story. But he likes to keep that story hidden and only let the world see the smoothness outside, let the world believe in his perfection; that way he thinks he's the only one who can see the cracks in his armor. Unfortunately, I see them too.

"I'm sorry," he says. That's it. Sorry that he thinks his daughter is some kind of bad seed waiting to blossom into full grown evil.

"Doesn't really explain your comment."

"I know," he agrees. Well, that's good; at least I know I'm right to be pissed off.

I want to try a different tactic and keep quiet so he will divulge the real reason behind his words, but I'm too angry and I can't keep my mouth shut. "That's all you've got? Sorry? Why would you say such a thing about me?"

My questions don't seem to make much of an impression until my father lifts his head. He's been crying. His eyes are still red and a little wet. I want to take back everything I said and just run into his arms, because I can remember the last time I saw my father cry, and my heart still hasn't completely mended from the sight. He's not the jerk; I am, because despite how I feel I can't manage to lift myself off the chair and embrace him like I know he wants me to. I stay put.

"It had nothing to do with you, Dominy," he says. "It has everything to do with me."

He doesn't say another word; he doesn't offer up any more information to convince me that what he's saying is the truth, but he doesn't have to because I believe him. I don't understand it at all, but I believe every word of it. Just as he's leaving my bedroom, I see some flecks of gray hair at his temple that I never noticed before; they're like the hair by my ears, sudden and wrong. Walking out of my bedroom, hunched over, my father now looks old, not the young man I saw in his office this afternoon, and for the first time I realize he's going to leave me someday. And I instantly hate him.

I run to my door with every intention of opening it up and screaming after him to tell him that, but I can't. He's always said you don't kick a man when he's down, and my father resembles a man who got tossed in the gutter. How he got there doesn't matter, but he's lying there in the dirt, the water that flows into the sewer trickling past his face, some drops latching onto his lips, slithering into his mouth, and poisoning his body. Instead, I shut the door tight.

Roughly, I grab a framed photo of my father and me from a few years ago at some police function, I can't remember which one, but it was during the summer, so we're wearing T-shirts and shorts. My father looks so handsome and young; his brown hair doesn't show a trace of gray, and it's cut short against his face, a face that's clean and unwrinkled, nothing like Louis's. His blue eyes are alive and happy and looking at me instead of the camera. He's smiling at me, but is he also waiting for me to do something wrong? Did he know then that I would make every one of his bad dreams come true?

It takes me a few seconds to realize that I'm pacing my room like an animal, like my bedroom is a cage, not a sanctuary, and it's a place from which I want to break free. But where would I go? I feel as lost as The Weeping Lady, straddling two worlds, at home in neither, and because I'm angry at the world I fling the picture frame against the wall. My aim is perfect, and it crashes into the center of the banner.

For a second my father and I are caught in the mouth of the timberwolf and surrounded by fangs that have one purpose. My knees buckle because I instinctively understand what that purpose is: to devour, to destroy, and to kill.

Chapter 4

One look at Caleb and I forget the world can be anything but beautiful.

Even from a side view, he is still one of the best-looking guys in school. In the entire town for that matter. He's got extra long eyelashes (longer than any girl's I know) that are the same shade of blond as his unkempt hair, brown eyes that make his blond hair look blonder than it actually is, and a superhero-style square chin. And unlike my brother's, Caleb's nose is perfect, regal looking according to Jess, which is why she's dubbed him Prince Caleb. It's a perfect nickname for a perfect boyfriend.

In the beginning we took things slow, probably because we didn't know we were in the middle of a beginning. We didn't talk to each other at school; we hardly noticed each other despite the fact that the population at Two W is only slightly larger than the population of Weeping Water itself—and no, I'm not showing off my inferior math skills; we bus in kids from neighboring towns that are even smaller and more isolated than we are.

Of course I was aware that Caleb was a starter on the football team, but he was a sophomore and I was a lowly freshman; there was no reason for our worlds to intersect. Until my dad made them collide.

"What about that Bettany kid?" my father asked one night during dinner. "The one on the football team."

I had to think for a moment. "*Caleb* Bettany?"

"Yeah, didn't I read in the *Three W* that he won a prize in some math competition?"

My precise response escapes me, but I'm sure I shrugged my shoulders and said something like, "Yeah, I usually skip articles on arithmetic."

"No, I'm sure of it; he won third prize," my dad insisted. "He'd be perfect. I'll look up his number tomorrow at the station and give him a call."

Barnaby couldn't resist making a snarky comment. "Praised by the sheriff *and* the *Three W* in the same week. You might be out of luck, Dad; he probably disconnected his number to avoid the paparazzi."

I definitely know I laughed at that. The *Weeping Water Weekly* or the *Three W* as it's more commonly known is our local paper, filled with all the town news and gossip, and has come out every Thursday since 1957, a fact proudly stated on the front page of each issue. Since the paper's debut there's only been one editor, Lars Svenson, who does double-duty as sole reporter, churning out issue after issue by himself on some ancient machine in the basement of his house.

The article my father was referring to was undoubtedly written by Mr. Svenson, but was less an article and more a photo opportunity, just a picture of Caleb holding a trophy, surrounded by some official-looking men in bad suits and worse haircuts with a blurb underneath. When Caleb's mother showed me the clipping, the first thing that struck me was his smile; it was genuine and not at all forced. This football player was proud to be receiving a prize that celebrated his intellect and had nothing to do with his athletic skill. So much for stereotypes. Luckily I keep them alive and thriving. Despite the progress my gender has made in what are known as the hard sciences, I do my part to uphold the statistics. I'm a girl, and I suck at math. Which is why my father had the brilliant idea to get me a tutor.

The trophy Caleb won was for third place in the Nebraska State Mathematics Competition, justifiable cause for my father to think he'd make a suitable instructor to coach his daughter in the finer aspects of algebra. I had to agree with my father. Since they used math's full and proper name in the title of the competition, I assumed it was a very prestigious event, and even though Caleb only came in third it was still an impressive showing. I never guessed he was übersmart in addition to being überathletic, but his prize was proof that he was worthy of the job. When I told Caleb this he laughed. Later on he admitted that's when he realized he wanted to be my boyfriend as well as my tutor. I'm glad to report he excels at both. It's not every guy who arrives within fifteen minutes when his girlfriend calls unexpectedly on a Wednesday night saying she needs a ride.

Before I asked him to play chauffeur, I apologized for hitting him, and he accepted, no questions asked, like I knew he would. For a smart guy, he really is simple and uncomplicated. When I called him a little while ago he was finishing dinner and planning to write out a chemistry lab. But when I told him where I wanted to go, he said he'd come right over. Again, no questions asked.

We drive in relative silence until he pulls his Chevy Equinox into the parking lot of The Retreat, then he asks his first question. "So, Domgirl, do you need me to come in with you?"

Even though I think Domgirl sounds like "dumb girl," it's Caleb's sometime nickname for me because Dom—the more popular shortened version of Dominy—is a boy's name, and according to Caleb I'm too pretty for that. Now that's my kind of logic.

In response to his question I shake my head. "Do you mind waiting for me here?"

Caleb isn't put out; he knows my reasons and understands. He's also come prepared. "No prob," he says, reaching into the backseat to grab some books. When he raises his arm I smell a mixture of sweat and cologne, nothing too strong, just the normal guy smell. "Brought my chem book just in case." Simple, but smart. And even directly underneath the near-blinding glow of the lamplight, wildly handsome. My heart flutters a bit, and I'm not sure if it's because of him or the person I'm going to visit. Probably a little bit of both.

We kiss each other on the lips, and while we're still connected, he says in the low voice that he thinks is sexy, "The Sequinox will be waiting." His voice *is* kind of sexy, but his comment is funny, and funny trumps sexy most of the time, so I laugh. His Equinox is silver, so of course Archie dubbed it the *Sequinox,* and, like most of the things Archie says, Caleb thought it was hilarious and the name stuck. I swear if Caleb didn't kiss me the way he does, I'd set him up with the albino. They'd make a sweet couple.

Walking away from his car, I notice as I always do that from the outside The Retreat looks like a regular hospital. But it isn't; it's the local sanitarium. Combination state-run mental hospital and nursing home, The Retreat is where people go if they're insane, if they need electric shock therapy, or if they're unlucky enough to be really old or really sick and have nowhere else to go.

It's built on several acres of flat land, and, tucked in the middle of a spray of bushes that serve as deliberate camouflage, is a weather-beaten sign made out of heavy-duty plastic that's supposed to resemble wood. Engraved black letters spell out the hospital's official title—SOUTHEASTERN NEBRASKA STATE INTENSIVE CARE CENTER AND NURSING HOME. The Retreat, my personal nickname for the place, sounds so much more inviting.

The structure itself is more horizontal than vertical, made out of solid brick like a lot of the state buildings in town, and decorated with rows of windows, some normal sized, some floor-to-ceiling, but none functional. They merely provide light into the facility; they can't be opened. The overall look is formidable, like a friendly fortress, which I guess is what a hospital is supposed to look like.

Inside, the décor is equally foreboding and the fluorescent lighting in the main entrance area does nothing to enhance the look. The floors are made out of some kind of linoleum in a design that looks like a team of hyperactive kids dipped paintbrushes into cans of gray, white, and black paint and sprinkled them all over the floor. I've studied them for years and have never found any discernible pattern.

Most of the walls throughout the building are gray, though some have a thick horizontal stripe of black that cuts the wall into two unevenly sized gray blocks. I'm not a specialist in color therapy, but I can't imagine anyone thinking that the combo of black and gray creates a cheery atmosphere.

The receptionist's desk is bathed in an even more severe fluorescent light show and manned most of the time by a woman who should really stay out of the light. Essie looks like she's past retirement age but still part of the workforce. Lucky for her the state's employment standards are low, as she has not kept her job because of her uplifting disposition; she's about as lively as the color of the walls. I guess she keeps trudging on due to financial necessity or the fact that if she stops working she might actually bore herself to death.

"Hi, Essie, can I have a pass?"

She looks up from her celebrity magazine as if her head is connected to her neck by a rusty hinge. "What room are you going to?"

The same room I've been going to for the past four years. "Nineteen."

Like she does every time, she writes the number on an index card and hands it to me. The only difference with our routine is that today's card is green. They rotate colors so you can't save your card and come back with it another day; that way there are never more than the allotted number of people in a room at one time. It's about as high-tech as The Retreat gets in terms of its customer service.

I haven't even turned the corner of the receptionist's desk and Essie's neck has lowered back down; once again she's buried in her magazine. Reading about the lives of the rich and famous is obviously much more important than making the lives of visitors pleasant and less nerve-wracking. But in Essie's defense she probably thinks I'm used to the routine by now. She's wrong.

The only real patch of color comes from the hallway. The long, narrow stretch—that I've dubbed The Hallway to Nowhere—is lined with faded gray doors on either side, the same color as the gray on the walls, but outside each door is a chair made out of purple fabric, more orchid than purple pizzazz if I remember my Crayola crayons correctly. The cushions on the back of the chair, the seat, and the armrests are all the same shade; the rest of the chair's frame is silver chrome. They're from a standard issue, industrial-strength office furniture collection, but they're better than nothing. I contemplate sitting on the one outside of Room 19, but before I can commit I see Nadine.

"Dominy," she says, a bit startled. "Hi."

"Hi, Nadine," I reply, not nearly as startled, but not particularly thrilled to see her roaming the halls either.

We stare at each other for a few seconds, but since we're not close friends it seems longer. I blink my eyes, and when I open them my focus zooms in on a cluster of pimples on her chin. Zits for me are like Japan to Jess, sort of a weird obsession. I think it's because my skin so far has been pimple-free. But I'm not a fool, and I know that puberty is unkind and unpredictable; I could wake up tomorrow with a face that looks like the "before" photos in a dermatologist's office.

Nadine's pimple cluster reminds me of a mountain range—snow-capped peaks towering above a reddish-brown valley. It's disgusting and fascinating at the same time. If she were Jess I'd trace my finger all over it like her chin was a topographic map and I was interested in geography. But Nadine isn't Jess, so I keep my hands to myself.

"Haven't seen you here for a while," Nadine finally says.

"No real need to come," I respond. "Never any change."

Nadine fiddles with her clipboard, switching it from one arm to the other, and clicks her pen a few times nervously before smiling. The smile is not genuine like Caleb's from his award ceremony photo, but the situation is much different, so I cut her some slack. At least she follows up her attempt at friendliness with honesty. "No, there isn't."

And she follows up her honesty with an old nursing home chestnut: "At least no news is good news, right?"

Wrong. But again I cut her some slack since I caught her by surprise. Visiting hours are almost over, and even when I used to come regularly, it was usually right after school or on the weekends. A weeknight visit at this hour is unusual for anyone; for me it's extraordinary. This rare circumstance finally hits Nadine, and her eyes bug out despite her extensive volunteer training to always conceal emotion.

"Did someone call you to come?" she asks. "I wasn't told there was an emergency."

I wave my hand in front of our faces, and the green index card I'm holding creates a little breeze between us. "No emergency, just felt the need."

Now her response is genuine; she's relieved that a patient isn't going to die on her watch. Nadine may only be a volunteer, but she considers her position a step toward her ultimate goal of becoming a nurse and then, of course, ruler of The Retreat. That last part is merely assumption.

"Oh that's good to hear."

Another boring platitude and I'm reminded how similar Nadine and Napoleon are, which makes sense since they're twins. They both spout these clichés that are perfectly acceptable and ones that everyone uses, but for some reason out of their mouths the clichés come off as phony and even a little condescending. Maybe it's their East Coast accents; they're not wildly exaggerated, but Nadine and Napoleon do speak differently than most of us. And I'm not above condemning someone based on how he or she speaks.

I guess *condemn* is a harsh word. I let out a deep breath so it looks as if I'm doing a self-help exercise to prepare myself to enter Room 19, but it's really to remind myself that at least one of the Jaffe twins is cool. From the little bit I know, Nadine's friendly, smart, and driven, all noble qualities, and more than that Jess and Arla like her, so I vow to myself right here and now to give her a fair shot.

I glance at my watch; it's a quick gesture, offhand, but it prompts Nadine to touch me. Well, touch my watchband, but I flinch when I see her fingers glide over the smooth powder blue band and fall onto my wrist. It's a fleeting moment, but odd in a way that I can't explain. Other than a slightly sticky sensation, probably the result of Nadine's being overly reliant on hand sanitizer, there wasn't anything creepy about her action. But something about the connection, of Nadine's fingers on my flesh, feels deliberate and makes my spine twitch. Maybe it's because I'm very close to exiting The Hallway to Nowhere, and part of me would rather stand still then keep moving. The other, more take-charge part of me, takes over.

"I better get inside before Essie hunts me down for loitering," I lie.

Nadine leans in close to me, and I fight the urge to lean back. "The world as we know it could begin to implode, and

Essie still wouldn't get off her chair until her shift is over," she whispers. "Stay as long as you need to."

This time I'm prepared for contact, but none comes. Obviously, our relationship hasn't entered the touchy-feely stage, and our brief encounter truly was accidental. Nadine just smiles and starts to walk down the hall, the clicking of her pen creating a steady counter-rhythm with the squeaking of her sneakers. Suddenly, I'm overwhelmed with the desire to follow her to wherever she's going, go on "rounds" with her, visit some other patient that I don't know, but Nadine turns right at the end of the hallway and disappears. I miss my chance. Guess I'll have to visit my mother as planned.

The room smells like it always does—a mixture of antiseptic cleanser and cheap perfume, both compliments of the hospital staff. If my mother's sense of smell is working at all, I can't believe the appalling aroma hasn't roused her from her coma by now. I reach into my shoulder bag and take out the small bottle of Guerlinade, the perfume my mother always used to wear, and spray a very tiny amount of the scent into the air like I always do. I only spray a little bit, because my father gave this bottle to my mother shortly before she fell into her coma, and it's rare and expensive. But whoever made this stuff knew what they were doing. Even after all these years it's as fresh as the first time I smelled it, a delicate blend of lilacs and powder. When my parents were going out to a party, she would spray a little extra on her body and I'd walk right behind her inhaling her scent and make believe I was floating on my own private cloud over a field of flowers. Originally I sprayed it in her room because I thought she might be able to smell it and it somehow would act as a link to bring her back to me from wherever she's hiding out. Now, I just spray it so I can remember how the air smelled when she was alive instead of sleeping.

I've been coming to The Retreat since I was six years old,

and I still can't relax. My mother's been in this particular room for the past four years, so by now you'd think that there would be some level of home-away-from-home, but every time I come here it's like I'm coming for the first time. The sight of my mother lying motionless in this hospital bed, covered in thin white sheets stamped with the facility's official name in blue ink, ink that's faded from being washed a thousand times to erase germs, blood, and disease from the endless parade of patients who check in either voluntarily or because they no longer have free will, turns my stomach.

So what that she looks as beautiful as I remember, as beautiful as she does in her wedding picture, the one in the ornate gold frame on my father's bedroom dresser. So what that she looks like she's sleeping or dozing off in front of the TV. Looks don't matter, not in my mom's case. She's in what countless doctors and specialists have diagnosed as an irreversible coma, the aftereffect of a possible stroke. Possible, because all the kazillion tests those same countless doctors and specialists performed on her all came back inconclusive. The only thing the brilliant medical practitioners can agree on is that even though she's my mother and she's right here for me to touch, she's farther away from me than if she were dead. If only she were that lucky.

I drag a chair next to her bed; the cushioned parts of this one are mostly gray with only some blue circles in different sizes randomly placed throughout. I sit next to my mother, take her hand, and wish that she were dead. That way she'd be in the ground in a coffin, done. The happiest scenario would be that her spirit would be free to travel the world or visit us—and if those were her two choices, there's no doubt in my mind that she would visit us every day. Worst case, she would definitely be out of pain, and The Retreat would have an available room. But with her in this state of suspended unanimation, the only choice is for us to visit her, sit by her side, and wonder if she can hear a single word that we say or if she can even feel our presence. It isn't that I resent coming here, that I resent having to squeeze visiting my mother into my social calendar. Hardly. I resent that her choices have been removed, that someone is running her life for her and it isn't fair.

Her hand is as soft as it was the day before she was rushed to the hospital, the regular one and not this halfway house between life and death. A thought brings tears to my eyes: Maybe it's part of Nadine's job to rub lotion on her hands. Could she truly be so kind and compassionate? She does want to be a nurse, and such a profession requires empathy. Tracing the lines on the palm of my mother's hand, I wonder if I would have the strength to touch the hand of another child's mother, rub cream on her skin so it would remain smooth and wouldn't start to crack. I hope I have that much kindness inside of me, but lately I'm not so sure.

"Hey, Mom, how are you?"

That's always my opening question. It's stupid and lame, but it helps me find my voice to begin a conversation, which come to think of it is really a smart thing to do, since the only dialogue we're going to have is one-sided. I call it the coma-logue. Bad at math, pretty good at making up new words. So if I can't find my voice, the comalogue will never get started, and we'll be trapped in silence. Tonight, the thought of that possibility is unbearable.

"Looks like they're treating you okay," I say, examining the insides of her fingernails. "You look clean."

When I realize what I've said, I shake my head. From everything my father's told me and from everything I've heard people say who knew her, telling my mother she looked clean would have been an insult. Suzanne Robineau didn't strive to look clean; she aimed to look perfect. And based on our photo albums, she achieved her objective every time.

"And beautiful," I add quickly. "Your hair looks terrific; I think somebody cut it." Gently, I run my fingers through her hair. It's soft and shiny and looks like it's just been washed. A few strands fall out when I pull my hand away, and I watch them fall to the floor. The blond hairs lie on the dark mahogany floor, looking like pieces of spun gold. "A bit shorter than you used to wear it," I say, "but you're older, so shorter hair comes with the territory."

That comment is not at all insulting. My mother had no problem with aging; my dad told me it was a French thing. In France, older woman don't sprint to the nearest plastic surgeon like many American women do when they turn the big 4-0 or at the sight of the first wrinkle. Instead, they embrace their age and consider every facial line well-earned and the narrator of a fascinating story. I used to agree with that way of thinking, but that was before I found hairs growing on my face where hairs are not supposed to be. I may be French, but I'm clearly not *that* French.

"It, um, seems like *I'm* having a minor hair problem," I say. I glance at the door to make sure no one is peeking through the vertical windowpane and then pull my hair up to show my mother my latest imperfection. And my mother opens her eyes.

"Mom!"

My half-dead mother is staring right at me, and I can feel all the blood inside my body start to warm up and my breath escape me. It's an amazing feeling, and now I know that there was a reason why I came here tonight; there was a reason why I had to see my mother. Because she had something to tell me. That something, however, isn't good.

Slowly her eyelids close, her beautiful gray-blue eyes that we share once again hidden, separated from the rest of the world and me the way they've been for almost a decade. But before they closed I saw how they looked. They were frightened. Not for herself, but for me.

I sit back into the hard cushion of the chair and feel the

warmth leave my body and wait for my breath to return.
There's no reason to press the button for the on-call nurse;
my mother's back to her normal state, and anyway the nurse
would just tell me what the doctor told my father when he
decided to take her off of life support, that even while in a
coma the body will involuntarily move. Sudden spasms, fluttering eyelids, facial tics are all common physical traits
among coma patients; they're not the beginnings of resurrec-
tion.

But I know this was different. What happened here was direct communication between my mother and me; she was
telling me that we're the same. My problems, just like hers,
lie beneath the surface. Outwardly, we look fine; it's what's
happening inside of both of us that's all screwed up. Involuntarily, my body shivers, and I'm suddenly ice-cold. Something
inside of me is changing, shifting, and it's doing it on its own,
the same way some unknown disease or ailment took control
of my mother's body and took her away from us.

Looking at my mother is like looking at myself, at my future, and it terrifies me. And down deep, lost in whatever
world she's living in or being held captive in, it terrifies her
too. Because we both know my life is about to get much,
much worse.

I press my mother's hand against my cheek, and her touch
is so warm that I wish I could cover myself with her skin and
wear it like a coat so I wouldn't be so cold. "Why won't you
wake up?" My whisper is soft, but it seems to bounce off the
walls because the room is so quiet. Why won't she just open
her eyes again and keep them open and tell me in her
singsong voice that I have nothing to worry about, that I'm
making mountains out of molehills. Despite the fear that's
beginning to cling to my skin, I laugh through my tears and
accept the fact that it's contagious; prolonged exposure to
The Retreat makes one speak in clichés.

Sitting in the Sequinox, back in the real world, I feel more conflicted and anxious than before, and I wonder if my visit helped at all. What was I looking for? Comfort, advice, absolution? In a very distant part of my mind I hear a little ping, like someone flicked a finger into the mushy wall of my brain to get my attention. My mother can no longer offer those things, but what she can do—what she just did—is give me confirmation and strength. She's not completely dead; whatever has taken over her body, whatever wants full and complete control still hasn't won. So whatever is trying to take over my body will only succeed if I let it. If I fight, like my mother's still fighting after all this time, refusing to give in to whatever outside force is her enemy, I can be just as worthy an opponent, just as determined, just as skillful. Like my mother I can survive.

I look over at Caleb, and he's already looking at me.

"You have a good chat with your mom?"

A new sensation overcomes me, and I can't speak. Is this real love? Or am I still caught up in my revelation about my mother and how I can fight whatever unnatural presence is creeping into my body and my heart and my soul? Unsure, I just nod my head and allow Caleb to brush away my tears. It's such a tender moment and he's so sweet that I can't believe I ever wanted to do him any harm.

I take his hand like I took my mother's, and it's not nearly as soft or as warm, but it feels even better because it can touch me back. I place it on my neck and kiss his thumb, my lips hardly touching his skin. Caleb sighs, and even though my eyes are closed I know what his face looks like: The hard edges are softened, his creamy complexion is now pink with heat, and his eyes are half-closed.

We move closer to each other, his textbook wedged between us, and I slide his hand down until it reaches the top of my breast. With my fingers on top of his I trace the inside of my bra until we reach the middle of my chest. Suddenly he stops.

"Looks like I can finally touch our invisible string, Jane," he whispers.

Between his warm fingers is a thread, a frayed piece of cotton hanging off the little bow in the center of my bra. I blush and rest my cheek against his.

"Which must mean our connection is real, Mr. Rochester," I say, my voice just as hushed.

The invisible string is a reference to our favorite novel, *Jane Eyre,* and the undeniable and unbreakable bond between Jane and her employer and future husband, Mr. Rochester. A classic story filled with epic romance, life-threatening obstacles, even supernatural elements, and, happily, a happy ending. In our mushiest moments, Caleb and I consider ourselves a modern-day Jane and Mr. Rochester, though of course we're both better-looking than the originals.

Neither of us knows if our relationship, like theirs, will stand the test of time, but right now we believe it wholeheartedly. And so we act accordingly.

He's kissing me deeply now, and I can feel his tongue against mine. I open my eyes, not that I have to, just because I want to see his face. His skin is on fire; it's almost glowing in the light of the moon, the light that is so bright it burns a little, and I know what's he's thinking; he wonders how far I'll let him go tonight.

Not very. Just far enough to remind him and myself that, at least for tonight, I'm exactly like my mother. That nothing and no one else but me is in control of my body.

Chapter 5

I want to break Jess's skull into two separate pieces and toss her lifeless body on top of my teacher's desk.

Think I'm exaggerating? Guess again. Here's what happened: Last night she came over to my house so we could study together for the first geometry test of the year, which we were told was going to be all about triangles, because a long time ago some loser teacher decided that triangles are an important part of our world. And by important I mean complicated and completely un-understandable.

"I don't get it!" I had yelled.

We were both sitting on my bed, textbooks open, staring at our notebooks filled with diagrams and scribbles and numbers, trying to turn these indecipherable symbols into pieces of knowledge. Isosceles, scalene, obtuse, Pythagorean theorem, Euclidean space, all these words and their definitions and their practical applications were going to be on the test, and Jess and I were expected to understand them, be able to identify them, and answer math problems based on their principles. Right. And Weeping Water, Nebraska, is going to be named the host city for the next Winter Olympics.

"*Chottomatte!*" Jess shouted, in her stupid Japanese. "I think I have it."

"You got it?" I replied. Never imagining her answer would be yes. But it was.

"Yes! If you take out this side of the triangle," she started.

Then I knew she was as lost as I was. "You can't take out one side of a triangle," I reminded her. "Because then it's not a triangle."

"I know that," she said dismissively.

"No, you don't," I corrected. "You just said to take out one side!"

"Don't yell at me!"

"I'm not yelling!" I yelled. "You're being stupid."

"*I'm* stupid? You can't even follow what I'm saying!"

Jess's little nose was all crinkled up like I suddenly reeked of b.o., and I knew that it didn't matter if she unlocked every geometrical mystery for me and was able to explain them in terms that I could understand; I was still going to think whatever she said was stupid. That was the mood I was in. Or more precisely, the mood that overcame me. Once again, like with Caleb, I felt as if I were watching my life and not actively participating in it. Like I was losing control, giving up the reins that connect my mind to my body to a stranger without question or resistance or care. One second we were sitting on my bed bonding, jointly commiserating that it was the night before we were going to fail the first math test of the year, and then it was like a switch in my brain went off and I felt separated, alone, and as if Jess were the enemy. An enemy who had to be hurt and defeated.

Jess spoke again. "Just ignore this one side of the triangle."

"Now I should *ignore* the side?" I mocked. "And how is that better than taking it out?"

"Are you going to keep interrupting me?" she asked, super frustrated.

"Nice zit."

"What?!"

"On your lip," I said. "Well, right next to it."

Believe me, I was trying to listen to what she was saying even though everything that came out of her mouth sounded like she was the slow kid in special ed, but I was distracted by a new pimple that had sprouted on the side of her mouth, right in the crease where the top lip meets the bottom, a whitehead that hadn't been there when she had arrived, so it must have been conceived, developed, and born while we were studying. Amazing how fast these things work.

Jess touched the left side of her face. "The other side," I corrected. "Can't you feel it? It's huge-ungous."

Jumping off my bed, Jess ran to the full-length mirror that hangs over my closet door and inspected her face. "Gross!"

"Yeah, it is," I said, confirming her assessment.

Fingering the thing she turned to me. Remembering it now, I think she looked hurt by my comment. Well, I know that she was hurt, but at the time I thought she looked pathetic, standing there on the verge of crying and touching her pimple.

"You don't have to be such a bitch," she said.

Yes, I did. She just didn't know I had no other choice.

That feeling in the pit of my stomach came over me again, the same feeling I felt when I thought Caleb was lying and more interested in talking to Archie than with me. It felt like someone was taking a stick, churning my insides, and then pulling them out the same way honey is pulled out of a jar with a spoon. The honey doesn't want to leave the jar; it puts up a good fight, it clings to its home for as long as it can, but the fight is futile, the spoon is stronger and always wins out. The interesting thing is that even though it loses, a little honey is always left in the jar—it's impossible for the spoon to get every drop—so the jar is never completely empty; remnants are left behind to remind anyone who looks into it that it once held honey. That's exactly how I felt staring at Jess. I knew I was looking at my best friend only because a tiny part of me, the real me, remained in my body, but there wasn't enough of me left to stop myself from hurting her.

So much for my mother's inspiration. It had worked for a few weeks, me being in control, but there I was feeling the same way I had the last time I lashed out at Jess. The same way I had when I hit Caleb and my brother. A brief, victorious interval followed by the familiar feeling of failure.

"Tell me, how does one say 'you look disgusting' in Japanese?" I asked. And yes, my voice sounded as vile as my comment.

Jess was as shocked as she deserved to be. "Dominy!"

I wanted to take back my words, tell her that someone else made me say them, but who? Confess that I suddenly had a split personality? That's not the truth. If it were, I wouldn't remember saying or doing these things, but I do. I remember everything. And even if I'm being controlled or giving up control to somebody or something else, I'm still participating, I'm allowing this to happen. Which means that no matter how you look at it, I'm the only one to blame.

"What the hell is wrong with you lately?!"

A completely valid question. Also direct and easy-to-understand, and yet I didn't have an answer then or now. I kind of have an excuse, a reason for my behavior, but nothing specific or satisfying, so I remained quiet. Jess did the opposite.

"Seriously, Dom, you're like this nasty *jerk!*" she screamed. "No, not like, you are! And don't think I'm the only one who's noticed; everybody has!" Anger left her face and was replaced with an expression that was close to concern. "Oh my God! Are *you* not straight edged? Are you smoking something?"

This made me laugh. Jess always has to look for the drama in a situation. I can see her grabbing Archie and Arla, whisking them into an empty classroom, and whispering, "I know why Dominy's been an a-hole; she's shooting up heroin, snorting crack, and popping pills." The laughter seemed to help me break free long enough so at least I could respond. "No, Jess, I am not on drugs."

Her look of concern turned into disappointment. "Too bad," she said. "At least that would explain your attitude."

For a split second I wished I were on drugs too so at least I could check myself into The Retreat, into a nice room next to my mom's, and have a clear-cut enemy to defeat. But I'm not, and because I still didn't know who to strike out against I zeroed in on the only other person in the room.

"I don't have an attitude," I snapped. "You just don't like hearing the truth. You need to do something about your face!"

By this point Jess had already stuffed her books back into her bag and was lacing up her sneakers. "I don't have to take this grade-A crap from you," she huffed. "You want to be an a-hole, be one, but you're not going to do it in my shirt."

I had no idea what she was talking about until I looked down and realized that I was wearing one of her Hello Kitty T-shirts, the white one with purple sleeves and a picture of the cat on the front holding a purple balloon that doubled as a thought bubble with the word "Hi" in it. She had left it here after a sleepover a few weeks ago, and I had put it on thinking Kitty might bring me some luck while studying since she's from Japan and those Japanese kids are math wizards. Didn't do the trick. In fact the only thing it seemed to have done was make Jess even madder.

"Give it back! *Sugu ni!*" My blank expression forced her to translate. "Immediately!"

I stood up on my bed, and out of the corner of my eye I could see the timberwolf's face breaking through the banner, and it was like we were twins. I ripped off the T-shirt and flung it at Jess. She tried to grab it with her free hand, but missed and had to bend down to pick it up, which made me laugh. Standing on my bed in just my bra and sweatpants, I threw my head back closer to the wolf in the banner and caught a glimpse of the orange wall, recently painted, glowing behind us like sunlight, illuminating two godlike creatures who were misunderstood and persecuted because the rest of the world was jealous of our strength. That was the craziness that was going through my head at the time. And even more craziness followed.

Jumping to the floor, I grabbed Jess by the arm, flung open my bedroom door, and shoved her out into the hallway. She was mumbling something about me hurting her, and I still don't know if I really was or if she's just so weak she gets injured if you touch her. I do know that I wanted her out of my sight, which is why I gave her a jump start and shoved her right into my father's waiting arms.

Thanks, Dad! Come to my friend's rescue and leave your daughter to fend for herself. He must have heard us arguing and was on his way to break up the fight or stand there all fatherly-like and think that his presence was going to scare me into submission. Think again. The only thing he did was catch Jess before she fell over the banister and crashed onto the stairs below. If that had happened it wouldn't have been my fault, although I'm sure everyone would have thought it was. So I shoved her? She's the one who lost her balance and stumbled. Not that it mattered because my father saved her from toppling over to her death or from spending a lifetime cruising around town in a wheelchair, while at the same time he stared at me with fear in his eyes. But not just fear by itself, fear mixed with knowledge. Looking into his eyes was like crawling inside my father's brain; he knows something is going on, and he's afraid of it, more afraid than I am if that's possible. Even if I hadn't seen his face I would have known he was frightened, because after he drove Jess home he didn't come back into my room to yell at me, and I was up waiting.

I was waiting for Jess to yell at me too, but that never happened. She avoided me all morning, and during geometry her eyes were fixated on anything else but me. At Mrs. Gallagher—our new teacher who replaced old Mr. Winslow who retired last year—as if she were giving out instructions on how to survive a nuclear holocaust; at the back of Danny Klausman's head like she was trying to count his dandruff flakes—impossible, I've tried; or at her test as if she understood the questions.

I kept stealing glances and felt my stomach spin out of control again watching her pencil fly across her test, hearing the scratching sounds as she filled in the blanks with sentences, circled answers to multiple-choice questions. She didn't look baffled at all; she looked nothing like me. I looked down at my test page, and I saw nothing that made sense. It was like staring into a mirror.

After we handed our tests in, I heard Jess brag to Danny that she had done really well on the test because she had had a breakthrough last night. A breakthrough that she didn't bother sharing with me. And that is why I want to break her skull into two separate pieces.

When the bell rings signaling the end of class and the three-minute countdown to the next, I clutch the back of my own skull. My thoughts are irrational I tell myself. These images of violence that are popping up in front of my eyes with more frequency and in Blu-ray detail are not normal. I want them to stop; I need to make them stop before I start believing full-time that they *are* normal, but I don't know how. How can I make something disappear that appears without warning? How can I make something stop when I don't know how it starts?

"Dominy, are you okay?"

Mrs. Gallagher's question does what I couldn't; she makes me stop thinking.

I look up, and I see an image of my mother looking down at me. Her beautiful features marred by worry and concern.

I'm about to say, "No, Mom, I'm not okay," when Mrs. Gallagher's face comes back into focus. The only thing they have in common is their hair color, and that's not enough to get me to tell the truth.

"Yes, I'm fine."

When I'm asked the same question a few more times by my friends and some other teachers, I repeat the lie, and by lunchtime I almost believe it. Of all days, Archie has to skip lunch to attend an impromptu football playbook meeting, which means Jess and I are left without an intermediary. She's already seated and eating, so I tentatively place my tray on the table and sit across from her. I don't apologize—I can't find words that would be suitable or adequate—but Jess doesn't break the silence by leaving to sit elsewhere, so I take that as a positive sign. Unfortunately, her good nature alone won't bail me out this time, and I'm definitely going to have to make amends if I want to salvage our friendship. Which I absolutely want to do. Just not right now. Now I want to eat my spaghetti and meatballs, even though it tastes about as Italian as my last name sounds. So I do, and so does Jess. While we eat we both know that if we're ever going to speak to each other again, I'm going to have to be the first one to talk.

After school I have the urge to catch the early bus home, but I resist and slip into the crowd heading over to the football field for the first home track meet of the season. There's no way that I can ignore Jess, because she's sitting next to Archie and his white hair is like an oasis; no matter where your eyes look, they get drawn back to the patch of pure white in a sea of color. I've been repeating to myself what I want to say to Jess for the past few hours, but when Archie moves over so I can sit between the two of them, I feel like somebody shoved sandpaper down my throat, and I can hardly breathe let alone talk.

Buying time, I fake-cough, preoccupy myself with adjusting my backpack under the metal stadium bench, and finally mutter something that resembles a greeting. By the way Archie launches into a tirade about how Coach Emerson ignored his suggestions for a new game-play strategy, it's clear to me that for once Jess hasn't filled him in on our fight. Not a good sign because that means she doesn't need any support to be mad at me. I'm the one who needs support, and once again it comes from an unlikely source.

Bounding up the bleachers to our row, Nadine sits in between me and Jess without asking either of us to make room. She's wearing the same white sneakers she wears while volunteering at The Retreat, and when she shifts her weight to adjust her position, I notice that they squeak when she moves. I find it odd that the sound isn't specific to The Hallway to Nowhere and odder still that my mind is filling up with such nonsense when I should be forming an opening statement to beg Jess's forgiveness. Luckily, Nadine does it for me.

"What's going on with you two?" she asks.

Okay, maybe I've misjudged this one; she might be super insightful. If Jess didn't fill Archie in on what happened last night, there's no way that she told Nadine. They're friendly, but after me, Archie is Jess's closest friend.

"If I had a Ginsu, I could cut the tension up into two easy-to-serve slices," she says.

When the three of us—me, Jess, and Archie—look at her in silence, the tips of her ears start to get red, a shade or two brighter than my hair, and she tugs at her shirt. I assume it's another nervous tic like the pen clicking, and I figure it's time to find my voice, if for no other reason than to help Nadine relax. After all, she isn't the one who did anything wrong. I am.

"It's my fault," I start. Jess doesn't add anything to my confession, so I know she agrees with me. "I flipped out on Jess the other night because . . ." Because why? That's what I don't understand. Since I don't have a real answer, I say something that sounds logical. "I was frustrated that I couldn't figure out the geometry."

Then I decide that if I'm going to apologize I should do it right and stop talking to the bleachers under my feet and look Jess in the eye. "I'm sorry." Jess doesn't look away. "I was a complete, total, and undeniable jerk."

Jess purses her lips as if to tell me that my description falls a little short.

"Okay, I was a stark-raving bitch," I amend, and then I get a little lost. "I . . . I really don't know what came over me, Jess. I just got so . . . *angry*, really, really angry at not being able to comprehend what I was reading, angry at . . . just everything, and I needed to take it out on someone, and you were right there."

Jess hasn't stopped looking at me, and I can tell that she's been listening to every word I've said. She doesn't understand it any more than I do, but she wants to. That helps me reach across Nadine's lap to grab her hand. "I'm sorry, Jess; I didn't mean to hurt you. I would never do that."

My vision is blurry from the tears stinging my eyes, so I only feel Jess's arms embrace me. It's enough for me to know that she believes me, but it feels even better to hear her say it.

"I know you wouldn't," she says, her voice muffled because she's crying—even harder than me naturally—and her mouth is buried in my hair. "I know you didn't mean it. You're my *simai!*"

"You're my sister too!" I cry.

"Ladies!" Archie shouts. "I feel like I came in at the tail end of the movie. What've I missed?"

We're both crying like fools, so Nadine speaks for us. "I think they had a spat."

Shaking my head, I disagree. "It was a more than that. I pushed her, Archie, for no reason. I threw her right out of my bedroom because I'm an idiot when it comes to math."

Archie makes a joke, but he isn't smiling. "Dudette, mathematically challenged doesn't equal spontaneously violent."

Despite his comment, Archie doesn't appear to be as surprised as I think he should be. But I guess I've given him reason to expect this of me.

"Seriously, you really need to fine-tune your Roller Derby skills," he jokes. "You can hip check your aggressions out on total strangers and wear cool, retro mini-shorts. We'll film it, and you'll be an online sensation."

We're all laughing so hard that we don't notice Nadine hasn't joined in until she speaks. "I know exactly how you feel," she says, staring down at her feet, at the very spot I was fixated on a few moments ago.

"You have a video that went viral too?" Archie asks in a totally serious voice.

Just as serious as Nadine's. "I lost a parent too."

Yup, she could teach Gut Instinct: 101. She's comparing her father's dying with my mother's being in a coma because she knows exactly how I feel.

"I know how hard it can be," she tells us. "The day starts off and you're fine, endorphins are flowing and you're perfectly happy, but before you know it you're angry, filled with rage that you can't control or deny, and you don't feel better until you hurt someone in order to bring them down to your level."

It's like she's reading my mind.

"It doesn't matter if you hurt them with your fists or your words, as long as you make them feel some of your pain," she continues. "Even if that person is your best friend."

At that very moment Nadine Jaffe, basically a stranger to me, knows me better than anyone on the planet. She has one more thing to add. "Truce?"

Jess and I reply as one, "Truce."

Our hug is interrupted by Caleb's arrival. I don't want him

to sever our physical connection, so I hit Archie's knee with mine and he moves over to let Caleb in.

"What's up, Winter?" Caleb asks Archie, holding out his fist.

"Not much, Bells," Archie replies, bumping his fist into Caleb's.

By the time the first race begins the air surrounding us is tension-free and filled with chatter and laughing. Jess is back to her old self, talking quickly in both English and Japanese and jumping randomly from thought to thought.

"Archie, you reminded me that we have got to go online later," she says.

"Why?" we all ask.

"MAC uploaded another one of their makeup tutorials!" she sings rather than states.

"With our favorite Brit diva?" Archie asks excitedly. Gotta love Archie. He's so comfortable with himself that he can go from fist-bumping with Caleb to cosmetic-chatting with Jess.

"None other than Saoirse!" Jess squeals. "And her gaysian sidekick of course."

Saoirse Glynn-Rowley is this really funny girl from England who does these videos online showing people how to properly use MAC cosmetics. She pronounces her name *Seersha,* but spells it with so many vowels I have no idea how the two are connected. But I looked it up, and it's an old Irish name, so it's legit. Anyway, she's always joined by her friend Nakano Kai, who's Japanese, gay, and her demo model. We laugh; we cry; we get great makeup tips.

"Is this a follow-up to funktastic Asian eye-shadow tricks?" I ask.

"No," Jess replies. "This one is all about the squoval."

"The *what?*" Caleb asks.

"Caleb Bettany, you are way too heterosexual!" Jess chastises.

"No, he isn't," Archie teases.

"It's a new fingernail technique," Jess goes on to explain. "Not quite a square, not quite an oval, therefore it's called a squoval."

"Ah, now I get it!" Caleb says. "That's why you had a breakthrough in geometry."

For a second a hush falls over our little group; no one's quite sure how Jess and I are going to react to Caleb's unwittingly tactless comment. We react exactly the way two best friends who had a huge fight and recently made up would react. We start to cry all over again.

"Oh, Jess, I'm sorry!"

"No, I'm the one who's sorry," Jess replies. "I'll study with you all weekend so you can experience the same breakthrough I did. It'll change your life. At least geometrically speaking."

"*Subarashi!*" I cry, using the Japanese word for awesome that Jess taught me.

"*Shin yu eien ni?*" she cries back.

"Absolutely!" I reply. "Best friends forever!"

Caleb's shaking his head, and I see him throw his hands up in mock desperation; he doesn't get what's going on, and as the boyfriend he's not supposed to. But as my former math tutor he feels like he's let me down.

"Domgirl, why didn't you tell me you were having trouble in geometry?" he asks. "Bronze medalist here."

"I didn't want to bother you," I say. "And I really thought I could master this one on my own."

He smiles, and the sun catches his brown eyes, lightening them so they look like two circles of gold. "When are you going to figure out that you can't live without me?"

The entire group except for Caleb lets out a huge moan, but not in response to Caleb's mushy remark, in reaction to the end of the latest race.

"Dammit! Nap is going to be more like his namesake than ever!" Nadine yells. "He'll be pure misery to live with."

"Want to switch places?" I ask. "I'll take Napoleon over the obnoxious midget."

We're moaning because my little scrawnfest of a brother, Barnaby, beat Napoleon in the hundred-yard dash. Correction, he beat everyone. He's not even supposed to be a freshman; he doesn't turn fifteen until January, but my father pulled some strings years ago when he was just starting out on the police force and got Barnaby to start kindergarten a year early because even as a toddler he was the smart one in the family. Now he's also going to be the athletic one.

The surprises continue up until the very last race of the meet. In an attempt to bridge the gender gap and eliminate any sort of battle of the sexes, the Weeping Water Athletic Board has initiated coed relay teams this year. Barnaby is the lead man, and, watching him crouch down in his starting position, skinny right leg bent, skinnier left leg extended behind, both feet pressing into the starting blocks, I have to say I feel a surge of pride. I know he'll do something tonight to tick me off, but right now I'm blown away by his talent.

On the other side of the track in the final position for the team, Arla Bergeron is pacing, shaking her wrists and legs, keeping her body warm, waiting until it's her turn to run. Her close-cropped Afro is dyed a chestnut brown, and she is glistening in the sunlight. In between Barnaby and Arla are another girl and guy in second and third positions around the track, looking as anxious as Arla for the race to begin. Barnaby is the only member of the team who looks calm and eager to attack.

The starting pistol is fired and immediately my brother takes the lead. We jump to our feet as one collective cheering squad and don't stop cheering until Arla crosses the finish line several strides in front of her closest competitor.

Later that night in Arla's living room, the excitement still lingers. I felt a little awkward going over to her place, because I hadn't seen her father since I barged into the police station, but his macaroni and cheese is the stuff of legend, so my hungry stomach trumps my reluctant mind. When he says hello to me, he's uncharacteristically discreet, avoiding any mention of my outburst. My father chose him as a best friend for a reason; he comes through when you need him to. While we gorge ourselves on the mac 'n' cheese and some pigs in a blanket—a true meal of champions—the chef retreats to his bedroom to watch some grisly crime show about a real Los Angeles police squad.

"It makes him feel like a real cop," Arla explains.

Why I have a hot boyfriend and Arla doesn't is a mystery to me. Caleb thinks the reason she's unattached is because she might take after her mother. I told him lesbianism isn't hereditary.

Truth is she could have any guy she wants. She's pageant pretty with a knockout body thanks to years spent running track and swimming, and she's got a better personality than I do. I've got a tendency to go emotionally goth while Arla is pink and bubbly 24/7. Plus she's got mix 'n' match hair. As an athlete she likes to keep her hair really short, but she's also a girlie girl like me and Jess, so she sports wigs for fashionable versatility and so she doesn't miss out on indulging in the latest hair trends. Today's offering is a pixie cut in a range of colors that looks like someone put a s'more in a blender. I think Arla's single because she's amazingly secure and doesn't need a guy to make her feel complete.

Looking at Caleb I wonder if that's what I'm doing, if I'm dating him to make myself feel whole. But then he smiles at me, and all my doubts leave me. I like him; it's that simple. What's not so simple is why Napoleon is ignoring Jess and won't leave me alone.

"Your brother was *subarashi* today."

How dare he speak Jess's adopted language to me?!

"Could've been a fluke," I reply, not because I believe it, but because I don't want to agree with him.

Of course he doesn't detect the goth-like sarcasm in my voice. "No way!" Nap stresses. "He was awesome. I really think he can go all-state if he keeps it up, probably get a scholarship, definitely be able to compete on the college level."

They may be twins, but Nadine and Napoleon are polar opposites. Suddenly, I get this weird image in my head that they're like a bee and a butterfly. The bee flies under the radar, collects its pollen, and flies away. It has no desire to sting you unless you get in its way; otherwise you don't know it's there. That's Nadine.

Napoleon, on the other hand, is the butterfly. Fluttering and flitting and flying all around you, unsure of where to land, desperately trying to distract you with its presence. But if a butterfly doesn't have colorful, ornate wings, it's just a mutant fly. Napoleon's wings are not pretty to look at. I know he's doing his best to make a good impression with me by complimenting my brother and latching onto the one thing that we have in common, but he's annoying me. Thankfully, before I yawn in his face or, worse, say something that I know I'm going to regret, Jess and Caleb approach us from either side.

"Nap," Jess says, grabbing his hand, "you've got to try this punch."

I turn to face Caleb to make it virtually impossible for Nap to protest, and it works. Free at last.

"Doesn't he realize you're my girl?" Caleb asks. "Or do I have to remind him?"

When I take Caleb's hand in mine, he doesn't flinch like Nap did when Jess grabbed his; instead he welcomes the touch and lets his fingers find their way in between mine. "I think Nap's got 'new kid on the block' syndrome, just trying too hard," I whisper. "He's harmless."

Caleb presses my hand into the small of my back and swings me around, an impulsive move, and I feel like we're on a dance floor. His other hand never spills the non-alcoholic beverage in the plastic cup that he's holding. "Don't you watch the movies I take you to?" he asks. "The harmless ones are always the guys you have to worry about."

I shake my head and scoff. "The dude couldn't even beat my brother in a race!" I remind him. "There is absolutely nothing to be worried about."

Then I look over Caleb's shoulder and see Napoleon staring at me intently while Jess is talking to him. I hold Caleb more tightly to my body as I realize the butterfly might not be so harmless after all.

Chapter 6

A half-moon is a perfect geometrical shape. Guess that's why I'm filled with hate at the sight of it.

The past few weeks have been awesome, totally *subarashi*. I've kept my feelings under control, no violent outbursts, no desire to hurt the people I love or to hurt anyone at all for that matter. The urge to insult and mock and wound—all gone—and I felt like my old self again. Like I was back inside my body and not next to it. But now I know the feeling isn't going to be permanent. From my bedroom window I see mostly darkness; the stars are either in hiding or dead, and all that's left is a semicircle of glowing white.

Hanging alone in the blackness, the half-moon reminds me that good things don't last; change always comes, and it usually comes unexpectedly and with long-lasting effects. A mother is taken away from her children and brought to a hospital where she falls asleep and never wakes up. A father makes a comment about his daughter that he can never take back and can never fully explain, even though the pain in his eyes makes it clear that he understands exactly what he's said. Life, like the moon, never remains all white, never remains all good, never does it stay the same. Life changes, and rarely does it change for the better.

My stomach makes a noise, a little gurgle, and an image fills my head: A spoon is scraping against the top of a jar and letting the last, uncaptured bit of honey slide back to the bottom. The honey slithers slowly down the side of the glass, an unrushed journey to a place that is familiar, a place where it can feel safe. When I see the honey land at the bottom of the jar, I let out a deep breath and clutch the windowsill to steady myself. I allow myself this moment of peace, but I'm far from calm, and I don't feel safe. I look at my hands, and my fingers are grasping the sill so tightly they're as white as the piece of the moon that's burning me with its light. If half a moon can make me feel this uncomfortable and agitated, I think a full moon might push me over the edge. Make me want to replace my fingers with my feet, stand on the sill, look away from the moon and down at the ground as I let myself fall. Pray that the fall snaps my body in several places so it can't be repaired. Pray that my brain stops working. Pray that I never see the moon in any of its many ugly shapes ever again.

The moon is the enemy.

It's a crazy, insane thought, and yet I feel that I've uncovered a secret. Maybe I am right, because I get a mental picture that some more honey has spilled back into the jar, coating the glass walls, staining them gold, filling the emptiness. Before I can truly enjoy my newfound peace, I'm interrupted.

"Your boyfriend's here!"

Barnaby's voice smashes into my head and shatters the calm. My brother is always such a help.

Before I put my jacket on, I take one last look in the mirror. The outside looks untouched by the turmoil underneath. The new conditioner has made my hair look even shinier, and the silver-blue eye shadow Jess made me buy does exactly what she said it would do: It makes my eyes look more beautiful than ever, like puffs of London fog.

My legs look good in these dark blue jeans that accentuate the curves that seem to become more pronounced every day. They're cropped so they fall a few inches above my ankle, allowing for maximum emphasis on my black pumps, the classic ones with the three-inch heel that were my mother's. Might as well take advantage of the fact that there's still no snow on the ground to wear heels instead of boots.

I'm wearing the top Jess got me for Christmas last year. It's a V-neck green thermal, like a boy's undershirt, but lightweight and clingy, with just a little bit of lace above the v. It's a look I call mascufeminine. Jess thought it was sexy without trying too hard, the perfect style for me. Caleb agrees.

"You're wearing my favorite shirt," he says as I jump into the Sequinox.

He likes it because he says with my red hair it turns me into a real live Christmas present. "Which is why I wore it," I tell him. And then I kiss him on the lips.

"Yum, cinnamonny," Caleb says, licking his lips. "Another one of my favorites."

I've been trying to do things that I know Caleb likes to make up for freaking out and hitting him. He hasn't brought it up again; I'm not sure if he really thinks about it or thinks that it was significant, but I do, so I guess I'm trying to compensate. Which is why I told Caleb we didn't have to go to Nadine and Napoleon's day-after Thanksgiving party if he didn't want to. The party, however, is in honor of the last football game of the season (which Two W won, by the way), so Caleb thought it would be rude not to go. He's also constantly hungry, and the latest rumor flying through school is that the twins' mother cooks even better than Arla's father, so I'm sure that helped sway his opinion.

"Archie said Mrs. Jaffe makes this thing with lobster, crab, and artichokes, that makes Mr. Bergeron's mac 'n' cheese taste like dog food," Caleb says on the way to the party.

"What kind of thing?" I ask, touching up my makeup job in the drop-down mirror.

"Who cares, Domgirl?" Caleb replies. "It's got lobster in it!"

When I taste the culinary concoction, it's like the first time I ever tasted food.

"It's so good!" I gush with my mouth full. "You don't even taste the artichokes!"

"*Nanite koto!*" Jess exclaims.

"Hey, geisha girl, can you translate?" Arla asks.

"Oh my God!" Jess interprets. " 'Cause this is what food tastes like . . . *in heaven.*"

We're hovering over the bowl of heavenly dip like malnourished pigs over an overflowing trough when Mrs. Jaffe comes downstairs with a refill. She looks strange. Nothing at all like her kids or vice versa, because kids should really look like their parents. Guess the twins take after their father, though I can't be sure because I've never seen a picture of him. Melinda Jaffe does, however, look like my mother.

When she stands next to me to replace the nearly empty bowl of her signature dip with a new one, I'm startled by their resemblance. If I look hard enough I can see my mother's face in most any woman; some characteristic, some physical feature is always shared. With Mrs. Jaffe there's more than just one.

She's around the same age as my mother, in her forties, and has the same short, blond hair cut in a shaggy bob. Both their faces are wrinkle-free with high-set cheekbones that either have a natural glow or she's found the most natural-looking makeup on the market. All traits that millions of women share, but when I look closer, I see the reason why the twins' mother reminds me of my own; they have the same nose. Weird, but true. Inches from my face, I zero in on Mrs. Jaffe's nose as she leans over the table, and it looks as if my mother is hosting the party.

Her nose is small, but wider at the tip so it looks a tad thicker than it actually is. Just like with my mother, it's this slight imperfection that makes the rest of her face look even more beautiful. What makes their noses truly different, and truly similar, is the cleft, a little indentation that starts in the middle of the nose and runs down the center of the nostril. It's hardly noticeable unless you're looking at her face as closely as I am right now. Once you see it you can't ignore it; it's part of her. Them. And it makes me happy and sad at the same time. Happy, because a little piece of my mother is living in this woman and sad that the feature isn't unique. But if my mom has to share it, why not with a woman who's beautiful, looks rockin' in a yoga pants and hoodie combo, *and* is an incredible cook. Could be linked to somebody a lot worse.

"Mrs. Jaffe, this dip is amazing!" Archie says.

"Heaven must be missing a recipe," Jess adds, obviously still in a religious mode.

"Is the recipe top secret?" Archie asks. "Not that it matters 'cuz I'm really good at cracking codes."

Using a large clear plastic spoon to transfer the last bit of the dip from the old bowl into the new so as not to waste a precious drop, Mrs. Jaffe laughs. "Just an East Coast specialty," she says. "I'm glad all you kids like it."

"Like it? I love it!" Archie replies. "If this dip was a guy and we were in Connecticut I'd marry it."

I'm not sure if the twins told their mother that Archie was out and proud, but his comment doesn't seem to surprise or offend her. In addition to all her other attributes, she's also cool.

"Well then, remind me never to let you taste my crème brûlée," she whisper-jokes. "The two of you will up and run off together."

Make that very cool. Maybe it's because I'm imagining how my mother would embrace Archie and how she would tease me because Caleb is so cute and how she would spend hours talking about fashion and makeup with Jess, but I'm startled when Mrs. Jaffe speaks to me. Or maybe it's just because her comment is so creepy?

"Isn't the moon beautiful tonight?" she asks.

Although she's looking out the window and not at anyone in particular, I know she's directing the question at me. How does she know I've been practically daydreaming about the moon lately? Swooning over it? She smiles and looks like my mother again, and I don't want to think there's anything dangerous about her or her question, but suddenly I have the feeling that this woman, like her son, is more than she appears.

"I actually think it looks kind of ugly," I reply.

"Really?" Mrs. Jaffe says, her fingernails clicking against the bowl she's holding. The sound reminds me of Nadine's pen clicking at The Retreat. "It's a perfect half-moon."

Jess is right by my side. Could she have sensed I need backup? Whatever the reason my best friend is here, and she's overheard every word, but she doesn't comprehend the truth about what's been said. "And also a perfect semicircle," Jess adds. "Dominy and geometry do not get along."

"That's unfortunate," Mrs. Jaffe says. "You should learn to love the moon." Instinctively, I know that's never going to happen, but I'm also curious, so I remain quiet to see what other stupid thing she'll say.

Mrs. Jaffe's fingernails have stopped clicking against the bowl; she's cradling it in her arms, her index finger stroking the bowl lazily. No, she isn't stroking the bowl; she's writing a word on it with her finger. *O, r,* followed by some other letters I can't figure out. *Or?* Why would she write the word *or?*

"The moon holds so many mysteries," Mrs. Jaffe states,

her eyes dreamy. "So many unconquered mysteries that we here on earth will never be able to understand."

An extra hard squeeze of my hand and I know that Jess finally gets it. The twins' mother might be beautiful and a great cook, but she could also be a patient in the psycho section of The Retreat. Maybe that's why Nadine volunteers there? To get her mother a discount.

"Oh my God, that is so interesting," Jess says, adopting her best fake-interested look. "Like borderline profound."

We'll never know what Mrs. Jaffe's response would have been, because just at that moment a loud screech comes from the other side of the basement, ricocheting off the dark paneled walls. It's Arla. My guess is that Archie said something hilarious as usual that Arla found hysterical. Her laugh is even higher-pitched than Caleb's and so infectious that others always join in. But sometimes they join in too loudly.

"Keep it down, gang," Mrs. Jaffe says. "Grandma went to bed early; she isn't feeling well."

Her mother's footsteps can still be heard on the uncarpeted wooden stairs that lead into the main part of the house, but Nadine doesn't care; she's already griping. And sounding nothing like a nursing home candy striper. "Why the hell can't my grandmother live in a senior citizens' home like a normal old woman?!"

For a moment I think I'm going to hear Nadine's mother's footsteps stop, turn around, and march back down the stairs to yell at her daughter, but I'm wrong. Amid the laughter Nadine's uncharacteristic response elicits, I hear the basement door click shut. Once again it's an adult-free zone where teenagers can speak their minds.

Arla is the first one to do so. "Oh you can't mean that; she's your grandmother."

"So?" Nadine replies, her voice calmer now as she begins to tidy up the room, but just as irritated. "The woman is old and needs round-the-clock care."

"Do you have a nurse come in?" Archie asks.

"She refuses," Napoleon adds, eager to join in on the conversation.

"Face it," Nadine says, shoving some plastic plates into the overstuffed garbage can. "The reason everybody loves their grandparents is because they live elsewhere."

I've never known my grandparents, so I can't agree or disagree. I would do anything to have my mother live with us again, but a grandmother, I'm honestly not so sure.

"My nan, my mother's mother, lived with us for a few years when I was much younger, before my mother, you know, ran off to be a lesbian," Arla says, in her typical straightforward manner when talking about her mom. "All I remember is that she was sick all the time and in and out of hospitals."

"It's because they're selfish!" Nadine declares.

"Lesbians?" Arla inquires.

"No!" Nadine corrects. "Old people. They've lived their lives, but they refuse to move out of the way so you can live yours."

"She isn't the selfish one," Napoleon whispers almost under his breath. "You are."

The clock seems to tick louder as we wait in silence to see how Nadine will respond to her brother's comment. I want to stop staring at Nadine's face; I want to look away, at the collection of ceramic owls on top of the bookshelf, at the side table filled with half-eaten pizzas and salad, even at the black velvet map of the solar system that hangs from a wall behind the bar, but I can't. Something is compelling me to look right into Nadine's eyes. They're angry and guarded, and they remind me of myself. When Nadine snaps back, her nasty whisper reminds me of myself too.

"No, Nap, I'm not selfish; I'm a realist," she hisses. "Your problem is that you're a dreamer."

It's as if the rest of us aren't there. If Nadine had lasers for eyes, her brother's head would be burnt to a crisp and would fall off his shoulders in a spray of black ash. She starts to walk toward Nap, oblivious that there are people all around her.

"You like to live in your little fantasy world, don't you? You like to see the world as a happy little daydream. You think you see the best in everything and everyone." She doesn't stop talking until she's about an inch from her brother's face. "Wake up!"

Peripherally I can see Archie and Jess on either side of me trying to get my attention, but the tension, the magnetic pull between the twins is drawing me in, and I'm transfixed. Even though they're in the middle of a party, surrounded by people they hardly know, they're acting as if they're alone, having a private argument. It's revolting, but must-see viewing at the same time.

None of us really knows the twins that well, even Jess, and she's dating one of them, but if a poll were taken to find out which one is the stronger of the two, Nadine would be the unanimous winner. Standing in front of her brother, her body is like stone, her face is unflinching, and her words are like daggers. Napoleon, in contrast, looks like a feather in front of a fan.

"And then after you wake up, Napoleon, do us all a favor and grow up!" she screams. "I'm tired of being saddled with a baby for a twin."

Napoleon's lips press together, and he wants to form a word. His lips start to open, but then close and press against each other even tighter. He does this twice more. I don't know if he's trying to choose the right word or if he's frightened. Might be a combination of the two.

"What, Nap? Baby don't know how to talk?"

By this time the crowd is speechless, and it's evident by the way Nap's eyes are darting around the room that he wishes they would start screaming or laugh about some dumb joke, anything to silence the silence. He catches my gaze and I don't know why, but I seem to give him strength. At least the courage to speak.

"Better than having a bitch for a sister!"

Thrilled that her boyfriend finally showed some spunk, Jess squeezes my hand. I squeeze it back, but I don't turn to face her. I have to see how Nadine responds. I never expect to hear her laugh. Deep and hearty.

"I'm a bitch because I want my grandmother to be in a facility where she can get the help she needs?" she asks rhetorically. "You would say something that idiotic."

"No, you're a bitch because you want our grandmother dead!"

And just like that, Nadine's laughter stops. She tosses the dirty cups she was holding back on the table, causing them to fall over so a little soda river spreads out until it reaches the edge of the table and drips onto the floor. Moving even closer to her brother, Nadine forces Nap to take a few steps back until the backs of his legs crash into the wooden end table. Nap stumbles to the side in an attempt to get out of his sister's path.

"When did I say I wanted her dead?" she asks. "When did I say that?"

I can tell from the way Nap's looking at her that he's wounded, not physically, but emotionally. The way they go at each other reminds me of how Barnaby and I can sometimes argue. Instantly, I'm grateful that Nadine has come into my life; I've witnessed firsthand that I'm not the only girl in town who's filled with anger. Jess will never be replaced as my best friend, but Nadine is becoming something of a soul mate. Which is why I feel like I have to help her out.

"Nadine," I say, "I don't think that's what Nap meant."

She's so upset with her brother that when she turns to face me the anger remains on her face. It takes a few seconds for the harshness to recede, but then her face softens, and I can tell that she's grateful for my comment; it's helped her return to reality. Her lips start to move; they press against each other, a spot-on imitation of her brother, but she doesn't speak; she can't find the right words. The twins might be different in some respects, but they're still twins, and they have similar characteristics.

"Thank you, Dominy," she says finally.

While I've been noticing that I have no reason to feel isolated and alone, others have noticed that the party is no longer a celebration about youth and its victories, but a debate about the elderly and their inevitabilities.

"Um, I thought this was a party for the football team?"

Leave it to Caleb to be able to sidestep the furious argument taking place right in front of him and make everybody laugh again. Almost everybody. Nadine looks like she's going to scratch my boyfriend's eyes out. I don't blame her or get upset, because I know the feeling quite well. I also know that it'll pass.

"Sorry, Caleb," Napoleon mumbles, trying to control his anger. "You have a sister?"

"Two of them," Caleb replies.

"Then you understand," Nap says. "And you have my sympathies."

It looks like Napoleon is about to engage Caleb in some intricate male-bonding handshake 'n hug ritual that I know my boyfriend would rather skip, when Jess once again comes to the rescue. By screaming at the top of her lungs.

"What's wrong?" I ask.

"Nothing."

Lie of the century. Clearly she's lying because she's staring at me, bug-eyed, and I'm afraid her eyelids are going to expand and her eyeballs are going to pop out and dangle from their sockets.

"Jess, seriously, what's wrong?" I repeat.

By now everyone is facing Jess, and her expression is getting more fearful by the second. Part of me wants to shield my face because I really think her eyes are going to launch themselves into the air. The other part of me is growing very concerned.

"I, uh, I thought I saw a mouse," Jess explains.

And this is the announcement that officially ends the party.

"Vermin?!" Arla shrieks.

There's a noise, sounds like cardboard pizza boxes being crushed and shoved into the garbage can. I know the harsh sound is connected to Nadine even before she speaks. "We do not have mice."

"I . . . I just saw *one*," Jess stutters, as if one mouse is so much better than two. "And it was little, but still it kinda freaked me out."

Whatever reprieve I might have helped create is gone; Nadine is back in angry mode and doesn't take this contradiction very well. Her voice is calm, but I doubt her insides are. "I don't care what you think you saw, Jess, we do not have mice or any other kind of *vermin* in this house."

Knowing Jess, chances are good that the mouse was a product of her imagination. A quirky shadow, one of those black squiggly lines you see in your eye from time to time, and she made the rest up. The nonverbal consensus is that everyone believes Nadine when she says her house is vermin-free. Everyone except for her brother and my boyfriend. Her brother because I'm guessing he's still anti-Nadine and doesn't want to agree with his sister regardless of whether she's speaking the truth and my boyfriend because I know that he has a fear of all things that fall under the rodent umbrella. Rats, squirrels, hamsters, guinea pigs, and, of course, mice. He's frightened of them all, kind of his phobia. Whenever he sees a squirrel he unconsciously clutches my hand and scrunches up his face into this grimace. It's actually a cute look. So I completely expect it when he tells me he has to leave.

"C'mon, we have to go," he says, his voice shuddering.

"No!" Jess screams, turning me to face her. "I need her to stay with me."

"I need her to come home with me!" Caleb shouts back. It's like he's forgotten he's a guy and a football player and my boyfriend, and he's become my little sister or something.

"Sorry, Caleb," Jess whines. "I really need Dominy to walk me home." Frantically, Jess's eyes dart around the room until she lands on a solution. "Archie'll drive home with you. The party's over anyway."

"C'mon, Winter," Caleb says, his voice still shaky.

"Sure thing, Bells," Archie replies.

Caleb's already got his jacket on. "Sorry, Dominy, you know how I get."

I do. "No big d," I tell him. I try to give him a kiss good-bye, but he's racing up the stairs with Archie right behind him. "Call me when you get home!"

Outside, Jess, Arla, and I are walking, but Arla's the only one doing any talking. Jess is still shell-shocked from whatever it is she thinks she saw, and I'm trying to peel back the complicated layers that make up the Jaffe household. I've barely scraped the surface of the matriarch when Jess makes us stop. She clutches Arla's hand, and they both face me. I feel the moonlight bathe my face, and I feel exposed.

Jess bends her head close to Arla and whispers, "Look at her."

Baffled, Arla follows orders and looks at me. In less than three seconds she gasps.

"Oh my God!" Arla screams. "How did I not see it? It's ... it's ..."

"What?!"

"Guh-ross!!"

Involuntarily, I look behind me, around me, thinking that I misheard Jess's instruction and something nearby is the object of their disgust. But I'm wrong; the gasps of horror are directed at me. Okay, I admit that I'm vain, but I sort of have a reason to be. If I were taller I could model. Then I realize it has to be karma, cosmic revenge. I made fun of Jess and Nadine's pimples, so now my face has gotten hit with a new crop of zits. I probably have red, blotchy skin, littered with white spots. My face must look like a slice of the pizza that we just ate. Unfortunately, it's even worse.

"What do you mean, I'm gross?!"

"Sorry, Dom, it just slipped out," Arla apologizes. "But . . . and it hurts me to say this, but gross really describes it quite well."

I feel the moonlight on my face and the rage churning in my stomach; I've had enough. "Show me!"

Jess's and Arla's heads snap toward each other, and if I wasn't so pissed off I'd think it was comical.

"Should we?" Arla asks.

"We have to," Jess replies.

Arla digs into her purse for, presumably, a compact, and Jess launches into a speech that is supposed to calm me down, but it has the opposite effect. "Remember that most things like this are temporary; they never last very long, and no matter what you may look like, Dominy, we still love you. And we will help you get over this, we promise!"

I yank the compact out of Arla's hand and flip it open. The glow from the moon is blinding, and I can't see myself; for a moment I don't exist, but then I come into focus and a second later I scream. "I have a moustache!"

Jess looks like she's going to cry. "Yes, honey, you do."

"Nadine was right," I say, putting the pieces together. "There wasn't any mouse; you were creating a diversion!"

Now she really does cry. "What else would a best friend do?!"

I look at myself again, and I start to cry. No, I don't really have a full-grown moustache, but I have hairs all along my upper lip, deep red, which makes sense, but then at the corners of my mouth the hair is darker, almost jet black, and thicker. Suddenly, I feel faint. My heart is racing, and I feel sweat forming on my forehead. How can this be happening? How can I look so disgusting?

"I *am* guh-ross!" I shout.

"No, you're not," Arla protests.

"You said I was!"

"Temporarily! Temporarily guh-ross!" she repeats with even more conviction.

Standing is no longer an option. I grab onto their arms so the girls can lower me onto the curb. The three of us sit there, me in the middle, and try to make sense of my situation.

"My face was fine when I left my house," I remember. "When did you notice I was little Miss She-ape?"

"Right after Nadine and Napoleon were fighting," Jess admits. "You calmed Nadine down and turned around. I swear on the eternal soul of Siddhārtha Gautama, the Buddha, that I almost lost my shiz right then and there."

Arla shakes her head. "It couldn't have happened that fast," she says. "It had to have been there all night, and we just didn't see it."

No! There's no way my sudden hair extensions could have gone unnoticed.

"The lighting in their basement isn't really that good," Jess adds. "And, Dom, you always get dressed so fast you hardly take a good look at yourself before you leave your house."

Normally that's true, but tonight was different. "I did, Jess," I tell her. "I looked right in my mirror to make sure my outfit looked good for Caleb since I haven't been the best girlfriend lately."

"That explains it then," Arla says. "You did a quick wardrobe check and ran out. You were so focused on your outfit, you didn't notice your extra hair."

My head is spinning. I hear Arla, I know she's probably right, but my instinct tells me she's completely wrong. "I . . . I

don't know," I stutter. "How could Caleb not have noticed?
He didn't say a thing."

Once again Arla has an explanation. "Even if Caleb did
notice, how in the world do you expect him to tell you that
you have unsightly hair growth on your upper lip?" she asks.
"You slapped him around when he broke a date with you.
He was probably afraid you'd go postal and pull a gun on
him."

"Not helping, Arla!" Jess cries.

"How are you going to help me?" I shout. "I can't go to
school like this tomorrow. Every classroom has *fluorescent
lighting!*"

Sheer terror envelops the three of us. There is no way that
I'm going to be able to hide my face from the harsh glare of
the high wattage that exists throughout my entire school.
There's only one thing I can do; I'll have to quit. My father
will have no other choice but to homeschool me, even if that
means he has to give up his job; that's the only solution. That
is until Jess saves the day.

"There's a woman."

"What woman?" I ask.

"A woman who works at the salon my mother goes to,"
Jess conveys. "She's old, but she's beauty royalty, a magician
when it comes to hairy women treatments."

"I'm a hairy woman?!"

Jess wraps her hands around mine; this is the stuff she lives
for. "You got a hairy upper lip, Dom; this is how it starts,"
she enlightens me. "But don't worry. My mother will make
an appointment with Vernita for first thing in the morning
for a mega-wax. You'll be girlie-girl smooth again before the
morning bell."

"And while she's there, make sure they clean up her arms
too," Arla suggests.

"My arms?!"

"Oh, Dominy, tell me you haven't noticed?" Arla asks.

"You have more hair on your arms than most boys have on their legs."

I tear off my jacket and pull up my sleeves. I sense a chill swarm around my exposed flesh, but I'm warm from fear. Arla's right. Have I been ignoring it? Have I been subconsciously pushing the reality out of my mind so I wouldn't have to deal with it?

I look down at my arms, and I see dark auburn hairs all over my skin. An image pops into my head of a fur coat, and I see my arms encased with disgusting red fur, matted down, wet and dirty. I shake my head and choke down a scream. Refill the jar with honey; reclaim what's left of my insides. This is some sort of cosmic joke, some physical ailment that can be easily explained and rectified. Tomorrow I'll go to this Vernita person, and she'll take care of me; she'll make me look like I'm supposed to; she'll make me normal again. Even though I know that's what will happen, I can't stop myself from asking out loud, "What's wrong with me?"

The question stumps Jess and Arla, just like it stumps me. None of us have an answer, so my friends embrace me under the light of the moon. We cling to each other all the way home, and the only thing Jess says to me when they drop me off is that she'll call me in the morning.

Just as I'm about to enter my bedroom, my father comes out of the bathroom, and we look at each other. I'm standing right under the ceiling light in the hallway, the one with the super bright bulb, so I know he can see every detail on my face. He sees the hairs that are growing on my face. He sees how ugly and disgusting and unexplainable I am, and he doesn't say a word.

He clutches the banister and starts to cry.

Chapter 7

My father reminds me of a half-moon. Split in two, part witnessed, the other part invisible. I want to know what he's feeling, but at the same time I'm frightened to find out the truth.

He didn't say a word when he looked at me and cried. The only sound that disturbed our silence was the banister creaking in protest under his weight. His crying was quiet, just tears skimming down his face, no sniffles, no muffled whimpering, nothing extra; it was like he was prepared for this moment and it didn't catch him by surprise.

We stood facing each other without saying a word for far too long, way too long at least for a father and daughter to be alone in each other's presence without speaking. When I could no longer look at him, when I needed a distraction, I zeroed in on one tear that had spilled out of his left eye and watched it travel down his cheek. I lost it for a few seconds when it entered the dark stubble underneath his lips, but then it reappeared like a bubble, holding on to his chin, clinging to my father like I'm trying to cling to my innocence, to my better self, until the tear lost its grip, succumbed to gravity, and fell. It landed on his T-shirt, right over his heart, and turned the light red cloth a darker shade. He looked like he was bleeding.

When he turned away from me, the banister creaked once again, but this time in relief. He walked back into his bedroom and closed his door by pulling it behind him without turning around. Because he was simply unable to look at me anymore.

What is happening? I mean seriously, what the ef is going on? Why is my father acting like this, like he sees, but he's blind? I know he knows everything that's going on with me, and yet there's this concrete wall encircling him, separating us. It's rooted deep into the ground, and it rises so high that there's no way I can scale the cinderblocks, reach the top, and find my way to him. Physically we're living in the same house; emotionally it's like we're on separate continents.

Under the covers I held open my mother's old compact mirror and stared at my ugliness, for how long I can't remember, but the entire time I traced the intricate design on the cover of the case with my fingers. It's a jeweled tapestry, an image of Little Bo Peep alone in a field; only a smidge of her face can be seen in profile, but she looks worried, because everyone knows she's lost her sheep. Night has just begun to fall, so the sky is a shimmering purple with only a smattering of stars, and a halo of light adorns Bo Peep's head like a crown, making her look angelic, even though it's because of her irresponsibility that her flock is in danger. The border of the mirror is silver, the same color as the stars, and smooth in contrast to the raised, embossed cover. It's a beautiful piece, more jewelry than necessity, and it was a gift my grandmother gave my mother when she was a little girl. My mother once said my grandmother and I looked alike, and if I looked hard enough in the mirror I'd see Grand-mère looking back at me. That's the comfort I was searching for, and that's exactly what I couldn't find.

After I fell asleep it was my father's face I saw in a dream.

I could only see the left side; the other half was gone, lost to me. It was either snatched by someone, or he was deliberately hiding it from me. His one visible eye was no longer crying; it was dry and smiling at me, reassuring me that everything was going to be okay even if everything at the moment felt wrong. I wanted to believe him; I wanted to trust in his confidence and compassion, but like Bo Peep I knew better. Not all her sheep are going to return home safe and sound, and no matter how optimistic my father appeared I knew he was lying. When the moonlight that spilled into my room invaded my dream and revealed my father's entire face to me, I had proof. On the right side of his face were scratch marks, long and deep and red. Like an animal had taken a swipe at his face because he had gotten too close while trying to capture or tame it. Even with that raw, unhealed scar he was smiling, or trying to. He was trying to hide what he truly believed, but I only had to look into his eyes to see the truth: that my world was about to change irreversibly; that the clock was ticking, the fuse was lit, and the bomb was set to go off. The little sleep that I finally had was restless.

The next morning I hid out in my bedroom feigning illness until the house was empty. I looked at myself in the mirror only once, foolishly hoping that maybe it had all been a nightmare. No such luck. Should I smash my face against the glass? Aren't people more sympathetic if you're scarred instead of just repulsive?

Before I could do anything that would upgrade my appearance from seriously ugly to unfixable, Jess and her mother arrived to drive over to the Hair Hut. Good thing I already know that Jess's tendency to be a drama queen is not self-taught, but inherited, because Mrs. Wyatt stole glances in the rearview mirror to look at me during the entire ride, each time her expression growing more and more concerned, until you would have sworn she was witnessing a massacre. I expected her reaction. Since Jess had had time to absorb the shock of my very shocking appearance, she had ventured into stage two—acceptance—and was relishing her role as my savior. That title, however, belongs to Vernita.

Overweight, with short, spiky hair in seven different shades of white that makes her look younger than she probably is, a long brown cigarette dangling from her mouth, Vernita greeted us at the door, stirring what looked like honey in a coffee cup. I took it as a good sign. Until she gasped.

"Praise be, St. Martin!" she shouted the second I entered the salon.

"Who?" Jess asked.

"St. Martin de Porres," Vernita replied. "Patron saint of hairstylists everywhere."

"Oh my God!" I cried. "You're going to need divine intervention to fix me?"

Waving me toward the back of the room, she dripped honey on the floor and shook her head. "Relax, baby-doll. Vernita and her magic potion will have you back to looking female in no time."

Turns out, what I thought was honey was really her magic potion, a secret concoction of wax, some other hair removal depilatory solutions, and something that smelled like pumpkin pie. When she leaned over me and started to apply the hot, sticky mixture onto my upper lip, I realized the smell was coming from the clove cigarette she wouldn't stop puffing. Obviously, herbal cigarettes don't violate Nebraska's anti-smoking law.

Next she placed a strip of cool linen over the hot wax and told Jess to hold my hand.

"On the count of three, baby-doll," Vernita said, her cigarette bouncing up and down. "You're gonna become a woman."

Wrong. On the count of three I was still a girl, only one who was in agonizing pain.

"Ahhhhh!!!!!" I screamed, twisting Jess's hand in mine and making her shout along with me. "That hurt!"

But my pain wasn't over yet.

"Do her arms next, Vern," Mrs. Wyatt commanded as she flipped through a magazine in the corner of the salon.

"Maybe I should make another appointment," I suggested, not sure if I could endure the amount of pain two much larger body parts would cause.

Vernita ignored my request and glopped more wax onto my arms. "I'll tell you the same thing I told Sophia Loren when I waxed her from head to toe," she said. "Baby-doll, beauty hurts."

"Hurts like hell," Mrs. Wyatt seconded.

"Who's Sophia Loren?" I asked.

"I don't know who she is either, but she is beyond beautiful!" Jess replied. "Look!"

Shoving her smart phone in my face, Jess showed me the picture she had found online of this Sophia woman, the most incredibly gorgeous woman I have ever seen.

"She doesn't have hair in any of the wrong places," I observed.

Covering my arms completely in the sticky solution, Vernita replied, "Should've seen her before I performed my magic."

The magical feeling remained with me for the next few days, and it wasn't just a physical thing; I felt the difference inside. My thoughts felt softer; I didn't feel like this piece of hard glass that had been broken in several places, leaving behind jagged edges. I felt like my real self again, not that imposter who considered lies, insults, and physical violence normal and necessary. I wanted to make up for all the times I had made everybody around me feel less than spectacular.

That's why I made Barnaby breakfast. I didn't even get mad when he asked before he took his first bite if I had added pepper to the pancake mix. I deserved that. My father said they were the best pancakes he'd ever had, which we all knew was a lie, but it was a lie that he believed, so we didn't question him. Sometimes questions are unimportant and ir-relevant and don't need to be asked, which I assume is why my father didn't ask me how I got rid of my facial hair. What did it matter how it had disappeared? The unsightly, un-wanted mess was gone. The important thing was that I was happy again.

My father only said one thing to me after that breakfast. "Thank you." I don't know if he was referring to the meal I had cooked or thanking me for not mentioning the fact that he had cried in front of me. I decided it didn't matter which and replied, "You're welcome."

I carried the goodness I was feeling with me like a brand-new purse. I clutched it close to my body, swung it by my side, and stared at it with pride and admiration. It was mine, and I wanted to show it off. After school I surprised Caleb with his favorite snack—marshmallow Peeps. Immediately I made the connection with the picture of Little Bo Peep on my mother's compact and felt like she was giving me her bless-ing: She had never met Caleb, but she approved of him.

Caleb's eyes lit up like a little boy's; he was thrilled by the simple gesture and amazed by his luck. He bit into the sugary soft green marshmallow and stretched it until it was about a foot long, then popped the other end into my mouth. I made a mental note to remember that this was the first time in my life that I felt sexy. All the times before when Caleb and I had kissed or fooled around, I had felt nervous or at least self-aware, not completely at ease, probably because I had known what was coming and I had known what Caleb was hoping our kisses would lead to. When we had our moment with the Peeps—or the Peepscapade as I christened it—it was sponta-neous and impulsive, and I felt a warm tingling in my stom-ach and a bit lower that I had never felt before. I wasn't scared of what was happening or what our actions might lead to; I wasn't thinking about anything except how happy I felt.

Later on when I told Jess, Archie, and Arla, they all shrieked appropriately, asked for specifics, and forced me to recount the entire scene, which really just amounted to Caleb's and my eating an entire package of Peeps and kissing the sugar off our lips.

In geometry, Jess leans over to me and whispers, "You do understand that the Peepscapade is a direct result of your recent beauty treatment?"

Yup, she's self-congratulating, but she's kind of right, so I can't dispute her train of thought.

"If one waxing can change your world like this, you have got to sign up for monthly treatments!" she exclaims. "Vernita will give you a discount."

It's my chance to do something that could truly make up for how crappy I've been acting toward Jess lately. "Let's do a birthday makeover!"

I have to cover my ears when Jess cackles. "Oh my God!! I cannot wait until your birthday tomorrow!!"

Her cackling is infectious, and I add my gigglaughs—which are the heartier version of my regular giggles—to the sound. In between cackles and gigglaughs, I tell her that I can't wait either, but that we have to shut up before Mrs. Gallagher comes into class or else we'll both spend my birthday with the after-school-special delinquents.

"Dominy Robineau," Jess announces, "your sixteenth birthday will be one you will never forget!"

She has no idea how right she is.

"Happy birthday, sis."

The next morning I find Barnaby sitting at the kitchen table eating cereal, a square box wrapped in bright red and white paper that upon closer inspection is revealed to be a collage of pictures of different-sized candy canes in front of him. Barnaby must have gotten the paper from the attic, since it's the same paper my father used to wrap our Christmas gifts last year. Ah well, it's the thought that counts.

"Thanks, Barn," I say, the words coming out of my mouth slowly, cautiously. "I can't believe you actually remembered."

Munching on a huge mouthful of Frosted Flakes, he replies, "Dad reminded me."

Jerk. Well, semi-jerk. He did get me a gift after all.

"Open it," he commands, jutting his spoon into the air in the direction of my gift.

A voice inside my head tells me to give in to my emotions, give in to the excitement and joy that my brother went out and bought me a gift with his own money. I tear off the paper, and I want to silence that voice forever. Silence all the voices around me that tell me to do stupid things like be joyful and be nice to people and not to hurt anyone. A putrid smell starts to ooze out of my body, like rotting flesh, a smell of garbage, decaying meat, and I'm heartbroken to discover that the goodness I've felt lately was never meant to be permanent, never meant to be mine. Barnaby's gift is a shaving kit.

"I thought you could use it," he says, milk dribbling down his chin. "Ape Girl."

First the cereal bowl crashes to the floor, then the table, then Barnaby with me on top of him. My hand is wrapped around his tiny throat, and I can feel the muscle and veins and bones underneath his skin. He's trying to speak, but his sounds are meaningless, and I ignore them. With wonder I watch his skin change color from pink to red to purple. It's fascinating to me how quickly life can be extinguished; one little concentrated effort, and it's gone. Apply a bit more pressure on the sides of his scrawny neck and the purple will intensify until Barnaby's face turns blue, and then his entire body will stop moving. I press down, harder and harder, not stopping until my father rips me off of my brother, severing our sacred connection, and infuriating me because I'm not going to see Barnaby in his final transformation; I'm not going to see him get what, in this moment, I truly believe he deserves.

"Dominy, stop!"

My father's command fills up the kitchen, but it's as if he's shouted at me from a mile away. I hear a whisper, a snippet of his anger and his fear.

Looking at Barnaby on his side, his legs twitching, his bony fingers shaking and clutching the throat that I just held, stroking the now-red skin, it's like I'm watching a movie that I directed. I'm not part of the action any longer, even though I'm the one who set it in motion. I feel normal again.

"She tried to kill me!" Barnaby screams.

I remain silent because I can't disagree.

"Ape Girl tried to kill me!"

My father steps in between the two of us when Barnaby lunges at me even though I don't take a step toward him; I don't flinch. It's as if I'm not in the room, although I can hear and see everything.

"What the hell happened?!" my father asks, crouching down so he and Barnaby are on the same level.

"She flipped out again! Like some . . . rabid animal!"

My father drops his head, and his eyes examine the floor. I have no idea what's so enticing about the linoleum, but he can't lift his head for a few moments. Finally he turns toward something on the floor, and I feel my head turn in the same direction. He sees Barnaby's gift. He then looks back at Barnaby, his expression eager for an explanation.

"T.J.'s grandmother works at the Hair Hut," Barnaby explains. "She had to do a wax job on Dominy 'cause she's sprouting hair like some mutant dog!"

When my father slaps Barnaby across the face, it's the first time I've seen him hit one of his kids. This is more sinful than my actions; nothing is right in our house, in our family. I close my eyes, and slowly I feel them shifting back into focus in the darkness. When I open them I can feel my body again.

Barnaby is on the verge; I don't know what he's going to allow his body to do: cry or lash out. He does both.

"Why'd you hit me? She's the one who tried to kill me!"

I can't see my father's face, but I know that he's weary. His body shifts, and his knee hits the kitchen floor; he has to press his hand into the tiles so his whole body doesn't topple over. All the while Barnaby is slapping his hands against my father's shoulders, his arms, his head, and my father lets him, lets Barnaby give him the punishment he feels he deserves, until Barnaby is exhausted and stops. At first my brother's arms are limp as my father hugs him, but their embrace grows tighter, and soon Barnaby relents; he gives in and accepts my father's grip and his apology.

"I'm sorry," my father whispers into Barnaby's ear. "Please forgive me."

There's silence as the two of them continue to hug and contemplate the flurry of emotions filling their minds and hearts. I know exactly how confused they must feel, but they're also lucky; they have each other to hold on to; I just get to watch.

Watching my father as he kneels in front of Barnaby, I can see his face now; he isn't crying, but he's ashen—his handsome features are drenched in gray. He holds Barnaby tenderly around his neck, the neck that I tried to snap a few minutes ago. "Your sister didn't mean it," he says. "It wasn't her."

Neither of us really understands what he's saying.

"It's . . . it's her birthday and you . . . you hurt her," he stammers. "It was wrong of you to do that. You know that, don't you?"

Barnaby nods his head. I see his lips move, and I know that they mouth the words "I'm sorry," but I can't hear them. They're only meant for my father anyway.

"Now let's clean up this mess."

We follow my father's orders like robots, silent and mechanical. We don't look at each other, but somehow we work as a team to make the room look normal again, as if rage hadn't devoured it moments earlier. Maybe this is what a family does during times of crisis? Cleans up their messes in silence. But the silence doesn't last long, and when my father is making noise throwing away some broken dishes, Barnaby leans in close to my ear, deliberately ignoring my face, and whispers, "Don't think I'm ever going to forget what you did."

He runs off to catch his school bus before I can tell him that I doubt I will either.

"You'll be home tonight?"

My father's voice sounds like the kitchen now looks. Serene, but startling.

"I was thinking of doing something with Caleb and Jess," I reply, even though I hadn't made any such plans. The thought of being alone in this house with my father and Barnaby any longer than I have to is suddenly unbearable.

"I thought we would have a quiet family dinner for your birthday," he says. "Just the three of us."

I watch him make circles on the kitchen counter with a sponge.

"Can I invite some friends?" I ask.

He presses down harder onto the surface; there's a stain that simply won't come out. "No, let's make it a family celebration."

My father looks at me, and his face is no longer gray; it's the face I remember. He's handsome and young and filled with hope. His quick changes are confusing me; I don't know who my real father is and who is the imposter. Something is so wrong. It feels like a turning point, but it doesn't feel like my birthday.

"Let's not invite anyone else until . . . until the weekend, and then we can have a party," he says. "Just make sure you come home before dark."

He tosses in this comment casually, to make it sound like he hadn't wanted to say it since the conversation started, but I know better. He throws the sponge into the sink and leans into the counter, his back to me, and I see his shoulders rise and fall. He's breathing deeply, searching for courage or warding off fear. "I have to work later tonight, and I want to make sure . . ."

He turns around to face me, and the sight of me makes him lose his concentration, erases all meaning from his mind, and he stops speaking. Whatever he wants to say to me, whatever words he wants to share with me remain unspoken, remain his alone. The stone wall is back up; I can barely see my father standing right in front of me.

"Make sure what?" I ask.

"That . . . um . . . that you're home for our celebration."

I desperately want to ask him what's going on, but I'm desperately afraid that he's going to tell me the truth, so I keep quiet. I nod my head as I grab my coat and bag so I can leave, get out of this house, finally get outside where I can gulp in the air.

"I love you, Dominy."

The words stop me from leaving. I have one foot out the door; I can feel the fresh air on my face, but I can feel my father's love like sunshine on my back. Pushed and pulled into two different directions. I want to reply; I want to turn around and look my father in the eye and tell him that I love him too, but the words won't come. Something is holding them back, keeping them from finding their voice, keeping them trapped inside my mind and my heart. It's the same thing that's pushing me outside into the unknown and away from my father.

The door slams behind me, and I still can't breathe. I feel as if I'm completely alone in the world.

*   *   *

When I wake up next to Jess's dead body, I no longer simply feel as if I'm completely alone in the world. I know that it's true. Because that's how you feel when you become a very bad person.

Part 2

The moon is gone and I am lost
My body, mind, and soul
are tossed
Into a prison, no longer free
The warden moon holds the key.

Chapter 8

The Day After

Remember, Dominy, you are blessed.
The sky doesn't look normal without the moon. Where's the black velvet? Where's the silver circle? Where are the things that fill my heart with hope and gratitude?

A chilled breeze wraps itself around me, and a few seconds later I shiver. I'm a different person. I don't have to look down at Jess's body to know this; it's a certainty that something inside of me has changed. Yesterday the moon was the enemy, and now I'm seeking it out, begging for it to arrive. I'm like a vulture circling above a bleeding animal, willing it to turn into a carcass so I can carry out the tasks I was born to perform. Jess's lifeless body reminds me that I've done just that.

"Jess!"

My voice is rough and sore and hollow. I wait for a response, although I know she won't answer. She's dead. My best friend is dead.

Her ravaged body is two feet from where I'm standing,

and the reality starts to drill into my brain and into my mind and into my heart, until it can no longer be ignored. No! This can't be real! Close my eyes; open them. Nothing's changed, except everything has. And it's all because of me. But no, it can't be! I can't possibly have done this. Could I? Could this . . . *horror* . . . be my doing?

I reach out to hold on to something, anything to steady myself, but there's nothing. I'm alone. My bare ankle scrapes against the pointy edge of a rock, and I feel blood trickle out of my body. The shock steadies me, and I look down to see a stream of red trickle over my anklebone and onto my sock, staining the white cotton material pink. The color reminds me of yesterday, of my innocence and my youth—everything that's been taken from me and everything that I will never have again.

Another breeze, another shiver. This time they both attack my body with more intensity. There is no yesterday; there is no innocence and youth, only today and this new life that I've chosen or that's somehow been forced upon me. Whichever one it is, I know that it's a life from which I'll never be able to escape.

I hear a rustling in the distance, and my body takes over, interrupting my thoughts. I crouch down, all fours on the ground, and my head jerks to the side to search the area for intruders. This position feels odd and familiar at the same time, like I was a marine or something in another life and the memory was lost to me until now. I twist my head around to look behind me and back again. Nothing. I'm disappointed because I was hoping to see a wild animal staring at me, watching me from the entrance of the hills, which makes absolutely no sense because if that did happen I'd soon be as dead as Jess. But maybe that's my wish? Pray for death by attack from a cougar or a mountain lion, so the world will think that Jess and I died the same way, so I can take my secret with me to the grave.

The rustling sound catches my ears again, and my back stiffens. Once again my body takes over. My body is certain; my mind is hazy. I don't want to die; I want to fight. How disgusting can I be? The survival instinct has already kicked in, and while my mind may want to convince me that I wish I were dead, my body clings to life. My eyes shift to the left, the right, while my head doesn't move, and my opponent is finally revealed; it's not an animal I heard, just my jacket rolling in the dirt. There's no immediate danger, no chance for death, and for some sick reason I'm disappointed.

Sliding my arm into the jacket I notice there are tears in the left shoulder; it looks like a claw ripped through the material. Now I really am confused. *Was I attacked?* Did Jess and I stumble upon some lone creature on our way home? Did we disturb some *thing* that was hungry and on the hunt? It would be a rare occurrence, but not unprecedented, as there have been such reports in this area before, an area well past the town border that the locals call Dry Land. Once or twice I've heard about someone being attacked, but usually there's a scuffle and the animal retreats back into the hills to feed. Could it be that the food supply in the hills has dried up? Or were we just unlucky?

The material of my jacket, a kind of lightweight parka, is covered with dirt and weeds. I look closer, and they're not weeds, but hair. Could be strands of my own hair, but they're not long enough. Short bristly strands of hair that are a deep red. Against my green jacket they remind me of Christmas, candy-cane wrapping paper, Barnaby's gift, and home. Home. I've got to get home before my father and brother wake up. The only way I'm going to make it is if I stop thinking and start acting.

I'll never be able to carry Jess home with me, but I can't leave her here on display either. Out here in Dry Land, she'll be exposed. Some early morning hiker might find her, or worse, the wind will carry her scent, and it'll be picked up by an animal just waking up in the hills or stir one out of its sleep with the promise of breakfast. If anything can lure an animal out of the comfort of its home hidden deep within the dense foliage of the hills, it's the smell of blood. My only choice is to conceal the corpse.

I wince when I touch Jess's skin. It's already inhuman; it feels like ice. There's loud shouting going on in my head: *Don't think about what you've done, could've done, might have done! Don't think; just get on with the job.* I grab underneath her calves and start to drag her over to a fallen tree, no longer suitable to provide shade, but perfectly suitable to provide camouflage.

I place the tree's fallen branches over her body, and she disappears; her life is gone, and now her body is too. Almost. Peering out from underneath the branches that crisscross to create a natural lattice, Jess's blue eyes are staring at me. I've been so careful not to look at her face, to focus only on her body, her new weight, that I don't recognize them at first; I think they might be stones or absurdly, two birds in a nest that I accidently covered up. But they're not; they're parts of Jess, parts of my friend. Her eyes surprise me; they aren't filled with accusation or judgment; they're kind. I wonder if they know that they may be looking at their killer.

My fist bangs against my forehead, once, twice, three times in an attempt to jostle my brain back to the past and remember exactly what happened, but my memory is unclear; it's like the night brought with it a fog that refuses to fade away. Why would I have done this? Why would I want to kill my best friend? Think! Think! There has to be a more plausible explanation than the one that keeps clutching at my heart. But what other explanation can there be? Yes, I have some scratches on my body and my clothes are torn, but that's nothing, *nothing* compared to what happened to Jess.

My hand navigates its way in between the zigzag of

branches until it finds Jess's eyes. Two shaking fingers touch her eyelashes. They don't feel natural; they're hard like the bristles of a toothbrush. One finger is poised over each eye, and I hesitate. The warmth of my tears feels good against my cold cheeks, and I grab my wrist with my free hand to steady myself. I'm not ready to say good-bye; I'm not ready to close Jess's eyes and cover up the blue forever, but I have to do this; I have to close her eyes so Jess can move on. If we do have some kind of spiritual afterlife, I don't want Jess's soul to be lured into staying inside her body because she can still see the physical world. I want her to escape, move on, and go to a much better place. A place that I may never be allowed to enter.

"Good-bye, Jess."

The blue is gone, and I hear a sound come out of my throat that I've never heard before. I don't recognize it, but I understand what it means. It means that somewhere inside of me lives the filth. All my fears over the past few months, all the suspicions I've had were not just coincidences; they weren't just creations of my own imagination. They were clues. The sounds coming out of my throat grow louder and angrier and sadder, and I feel my fists banging against the dirt and my body. Striking out against everything and nothing at the same time.

Finally, the wild fury takes its toll on me, and I slump over exhausted, my forehead pushing into the ground, my body rocking back and forth. All I can hear is my breathing, strong and loud and steady; it's like a code that triggers something in my brain. I've heard this sound before. I can't remember when or where, but it strengthens my conviction; none of what I've been feeling lately is my imagination. For months something has been forcing its way inside of me to take control. For months something has been trying to turn me into something unrecognizable, and it's finally succeeded.

Who am I?

What am I?

I have no idea. All I know is my life has changed. Why and how I'm determined to find out, but for now all I know is that Dominy Robineau has been turned into a new person.

And it's definitely not a blessing.

Chapter 9

My house is quiet. The only sound comes from the clock ticking in the kitchen. Even the voices that often fill my head are silent, taking a much-needed rest and leaving me alone. I would like nothing more than to stop, stand still, and melt into the silence, lose myself in the absence of sound. But I can't. I don't have that luxury. I'm still visible, which means I can still be caught.

Standing in the living room I close the door behind me, careful not to make a sound. The sun hasn't fully risen yet, so only a dull light penetrates the curtains, illuminating the lower half of my body; the rest of me remains in darkness where it wants to be, where it belongs. Slowly, I walk up the stairs, thankful my father either forgot or was too busy to follow through on his promise to pull up the carpet. My footsteps are cushioned; on hardwood my arrival could not be kept secret.

I pause at the top of the stairs when I see a light peeking out from under my brother's door. He's awake. All he has to do is open his door and I'm screwed. One step, two steps, only a few more until I reach my bedroom door, until I can retreat into my own privacy and start to put this nightmare behind me. My hand hovers over the doorknob, and I watch it shake. I'm a fool. This nightmare isn't ending; it's only just beginning. With one eye on Barnaby's door, I grip the knob and turn it. I don't want to be caught unaware at the last second. I push; I'm inside; I'm free. I'm not.

"You are in so much trouble."

In the shimmerlight I see Barnaby sitting on my bed. He's fully dressed; his ankles are crossed. He's been waiting for me, waiting for this moment since I strangled him or perhaps since the moment he realized that as his big sister I would always make him feel inferior. Now he has the upper hand to watch me squirm under his superiority and beg for his silence. Sorry to disappoint him, but he's waited in vain.

"Get out of my room."

My voice is unraised, but unwavering.

"Dad's been out looking for you all night," he says. His hands are holding the sides of the mattress, his crossed legs lifting up, then down, up, then down. It's like he's on a swing and enjoying every moment of his ride. "Where were you all night long?" Barnaby asks. "Doing it with Caleb?"

I hate to spoil my brother's fun, but I need some alone time. I grab him by the shoulder and pull him off my bed. He wriggles, trying to break free of my hold, and I jerk forward, my jacket opening up to reveal my torn shirt underneath. Barnaby loses his bravado; I'm still his flesh and blood, and he turns as white as three-quarters of my walls.

"What happened to you?" He can't take his eyes off my chest, and it's not because he's trying to get a quick look at my bra. He's frightened.

"Nothing," I reply. A stupid thing to say, but it's all I've got.

"What do you mean *nothing?*" Finally Barnaby looks me in the eye, and he looks more concerned than I've ever seen him look before. Looks like my nightmare is going to be

shared. "Your shirt's all t-t-torn up," he stutters. "And . . .
and you've got scratches."

"Shut up, runt!" I let go of Barnaby so I can cover myself
up. "I told you it's nothing."

"Did Caleb do this to you?" he asks. "Dominy, did Caleb
hurt you?"

Three wrinkles appear on Barnaby's forehead, the exact
same wrinkles that appear on my father's forehead when he
asks a serious question. If nothing else my father and brother
will be forever connected by three squiggly lines that appear
on their flesh. They'll never be able to deny each other like
they're going to want to deny me.

"No, I wasn't with Caleb."

"Then who were you with?" Barnaby insists. "Who did
this to you?!"

His voice catches with fear, and now he not only looks like
my father, but he sounds like him too. He's afraid something
terrible has happened to me. If he only knew the whole truth
his expression would change, but he can't; he can't find out
what really happened. No one can.

"It's none of your business!" I scream. "Get out of here!"

I want him to stop asking questions that I can't answer; I
want him to stop staring at me with my father's face; I want
him out of my room. One strong shove and I get my wish.
Barnaby stumbles backward and falls onto the floor; shock
and pain register in his eyes. I slam the door and lock it. I
hear him scramble to his feet, then I hear him bang on the
door.

"Dominy!!"

Between the ferocity of his voice and his fists, I expect the
door to splinter into millions of little pieces. I step back because I seriously don't think the door stands a chance against
Barnaby's rage, and I am about to crouch down behind my
bed to take cover from the inevitable flying shards of wood

when the banging and the yelling suddenly stops. The silence is deafening, and I can't hear a thing; it's when I venture closer to the door that I hear his voice.

"Dad, she's home!"

I don't think—I don't have time—I just act. I kick off my sneakers and grab some dirty but untorn clothes from my bedroom floor, fling open my door, startling Barnaby, who's standing right on the other side holding his cell phone, and run to the bathroom. The lock clicks shut just as I hear Barnaby shout.

"Come home now, Dad!" my brother squeals. "Something bad happened!"

I laugh out loud when I hear that. I guess my killing Jess could be described as bad. It can also be described as insane, unconscionable, "twenty to life" in state prison. All of the above. Laughing turns to sobbing, and I can feel my body shake; I think I'm pacing the tiled floor of the bathroom, but who knows? I could be standing still; I could be jumping out the window. It's like my body and my mind are disconnected, like those skew lines we learned about in geometry, living independent of each other, destined never to connect.

My knees crash to the floor, and the skew lines are given a jolt. Suddenly my mind and my body crash into each other, and I crawl to the toilet bowl just in time to throw up my guts. My legs feel like hundred-pound weights that are being pulled away from me, and I clutch the side of the bowl, closing my eyes so I don't have to see the mess, the vile disgust that's rupturing out of my body. But I can taste it, and I recognize it. It's the bitter taste from last night, and a sick, twisted part of my mind wants to swallow because I remember how much I liked it. Violently, I shake my head to prevent that from happening, and I can hear myself scream while retching.

Somewhere off in the distance I can hear my brother calling out to me, telling me that my father is coming home, that it's all going to be okay. *It's never going to be okay,* I want to shout. Nothing, not me, not him, not this family is ever going to be okay again after what happened. He sounds like he's crying, and I want to tell him to save his tears for someone who deserves them.

I spit once more into the toilet then flush away the foul contents. Looking in the mirror, I'm startled because I look normal. A little pale, but otherwise completely normal. Until I take off my shirt. Across my chest, just below my neck, are four scratches, four more perfect skew lines that will never connect but are forever linked. They're brownish, littered with small crusty blotches of dried blood that are even darker, and they run about six inches long. Not very deep, hardly life-threatening, but a reminder that Jess fought against me before I took her life. A symbol of my guilt. Then I remember that they are connected, not to Jess, but to my father. My scars are exactly the same as the scars on my father's face in my dream.

I can't look at myself anymore so I bury my face in my hands, which only makes me feel worse because my fingernails are still chock-full of Jess's skin. Luckily, my stomach is empty, so when I lean over the sink I just gag; nothing comes out.

Furiously I wash my hands until I think they're going to bleed. I rummage through the drawers underneath the sink until I find the brush with the soft ivory bristles that was given me by an aunt years ago, but that I have never used, and start scrubbing my fingernails. I stop when they feel raw. Tentatively I look at my fingers and let out a deep sigh; I let out the breath that I've been holding in. They're clean.

"She's in the bathroom!"

My brother's voice echoes off the tiles as if he's in the room with me. I hear my father bounding up the steps; sounds like he's taking them two at a time. He's as eager to see me as I am not to see him. Quickly, I take off my clothes and put on new underwear and jeans. Just as I'm putting on the T-shirt that I swiped from my bedroom floor, my father bangs on the door.

"Dominy, open up!"

One last look in the mirror and it's remarkable; I look fine. I can do this. I can look my father in the eye and lie that nothing bad happened last night. No cover story is formulating in my brain at the moment, but I'm sure when the time comes inspiration will strike. Before I can turn to unlock the door, reality strikes first.

Decorating the sink are tiny pieces of Jess's flesh. Pieces of pink staining the otherwise white porcelain. She won't leave! She won't stay away from me. It's like she wants to remind me that I can't run from what I've done. I've taken her life, and she's prepared to haunt me for the rest of mine.

"Dominy!"

I've never heard my father scream at me like this. I've never heard him scream at anyone like this before. Sounds as if we're all entering new territory.

"Open this door right now or I'm breaking it down!"

I twist the water faucet and watch Jess's flesh begin to swirl around the sink in a clockwise motion. Round and round and round and round. I don't have time to wait, so I help it out and push the pink clumps into the drain. When my father bursts into the bathroom, the sink is empty; there's not a trace of Jess to be found. Except in the vibrant silence that separates me from my father.

We stare at each other. I'm so preoccupied with my own thoughts and emotions that I have no idea what's going on inside my father's head. He looks like he hasn't slept; he looks like he's been out searching for me for hours, but he also looks incredibly grateful that he's finally found me alive.

His hand reaches out to grab the counter. I think he's going to fall, but he only needs strength to speak, to ask the question he doesn't want to know the answer to.

"What happened last night?"

Before I can stop myself, I cross my arms in front of my chest. I know I look defensive, but I can't help it. Could be that I'm still just self-conscious and trying to hide my fingers from his view; I don't know. I also don't know what to say. Inspiration has not come; it's abandoned me. So without a plan B, I answer my father's question with the truth. Well, part of it anyway.

"I don't know."

My father doesn't need to use the bathroom counter as a crutch any longer; he's got his strength back. "That's not good enough, Dominy," he says. "You were supposed to be home before dark so we could celebrate your birthday. Now tell me, where were you?"

The force of my father's question makes me take a step back, but my shoulders hit the tiled shower wall that juts out from the counter. There's nowhere for me to go. I feel trapped; the feeling is uncomfortable and unnatural, and I don't like it. Unfortunately, my father is standing in front of the only exit, and Barnaby is right behind him, so it's the feeling I'm stuck with. There's nothing I can do to change things.

"I was out," I reply, trying to sound casual, but coming off defiant.

"Where?!"

Oh my God! If he's so insistent to know the truth, I'll tell him. "By the hills!"

A wave of panic spreads across my father's face; he wasn't expecting this. Clearly he was hoping I was going to say something else, like that I *was* doing it all night with Caleb. That's not how a father wants his daughter to spend her sixteenth birthday, but better to lose her virginity than begin a career as a homicidal maniac. He takes a step closer to me, and it looks like he's wading through water; it takes effort for him just to move his leg. "Why?" He's exerted so much energy, he can only utter one word before he has to regroup to be able to speak again. "Why were you by the hills?"

The smooth tile feels like a series of sharp needles jutting into my back, and I can't stand still. This interrogation has gone on long enough. Darting to the right I try to get around my father, but despite his tired, weary appearance, he's too quick for me. He is a cop, and he's used to dealing with antsy criminals who freak out when they're cornered.

"Look at her shirt!" Barnaby cries. "It's all torn up."

It doesn't matter that Barnaby is trying to do the right thing, that he's trying to help me by offering my father proof that something terrible happened last night; when I look at him all I see is my spiteful little brother who's only motive in life is to get me into trouble. A low grunt escapes from my lips as a reminder to him that I will make him pay.

"Show me," my father commands. He's existing somewhere in between being a father and being a cop. Face filled with fear, voice dripping with authority. There's absolutely no way I'm getting out of this one, so I bend down to grab my ripped T-shirt from the floor and hand it to my father. He takes it from me and holds it tenderly in his hands like he just delivered a newborn. His eyes fill up with wonder and amazement; he's acting as if my T-shirt, like a baby, is a product of destiny.

"How did this happen?" my father asks, his voice now barely a whisper.

Once again I don't know how to respond, but it doesn't matter; Barnaby answers for me. "She was in a fight."

My father doesn't even turn around to acknowledge Barnaby; he keeps staring at me. His eyes lock with mine, and he holds my gaze until I speak.

"Maybe," I say, sounding like an idiot.

"Maybe?" my father replies. "Were you in a fight or not?"

"I don't remember!" I clutch my neck to prevent any of the scratches on my chest from becoming visible.

Something in my father cracks, and his patience is lost, possibly sucked into whatever world is holding my memory ransom. He bangs his fist so hard on the bathroom counter the three fake marble containers holding Q-tips, cotton balls, and our toothbrushes topple over.

"What do you mean you don't remember?!"

"Just what I said!" I scream. "I don't remember much of what happened last night!"

Damn it! I hear the slip of my tongue just as it comes out of my mouth, but there's no way I can take it back.

"Then tell me what you do remember," my father demands.

Fine! He wants to know everything I know, then I'll tell him. "We were on our way home, taking the long way, it wasn't dark out yet, not really, and I remember seeing the moon." An image of a full moon pops into my head, and its beauty disrupts my thoughts. What was I saying? Was I talking about the perfect roundness of the moon, a halo hanging over all mankind? *A halo hanging over all mankind?* Maybe I am on drugs.

"Dominy!"

My father's voice brings me back to reality. Where was I? "Then . . . then the next thing I remember is waking up near the hills, with my clothes all torn up!"

My father's steady, slow breathing reminds me of my own. "What do you mean 'we'?"

That's his takeaway? I tell him I can't remember what happened to me during the night and that I woke up on the outskirts of town with my clothes ripped and that's what he asks.

"Dominy, who else was with you?" he insists.

It's hard to speak while sobbing, but I finally answer his question. "Jess."

If this news comes as a shock or if this was the information my father expected, I have no idea because my vision is distorted by my tears. My hearing, unfortunately, is fine.

"Where is Jess now?"

I feel as if I've been carrying this secret around with me for a lifetime instead of a few hours. My chest feels like it's going to cave in, like a huge weight has been laid on top of it; it's incredibly hard to breathe, and all I can see is Jess's face dangling in front of me. She sways for a bit and then sits on the bathroom counter, watching me talk to my father, wondering what I'm going to say next. Her face and body keep changing: She looks like my best friend; then she looks like my best friend's dead mutilated body; then she's my best friend again. I can't take it anymore! I need help. I need my father!

"She's near the hills!"

"Why? Dominy, why is she still there?"

I can't see anything except Jess's bloodied face, and I feel like I'm going to fall. But this time when I reach out my hands, I'm not alone; I feel something. I hold on to my father's arms, and they feel strong and steady, and he doesn't move away. He's going to help me; my father's going to make it all right so I can tell him the truth. My knees buckle when I confess. "Because I killed her!"

I was wrong.

Instinct has proven more powerful than unconditional love, and my father rips his arm away from me. Doesn't want to be infected by the poison that he knows I am. My body twists in reaction, and my hand hits the bathroom wall a second before my face does. The impact is cushioned, but still severe. As I steady my body, I examine my father. Thoughts and ideas are being calculated in his head. I've seen this look before; whenever he has to make an important decision, he

cocks his head to the right, and the skin around his eyes
wrinkles. Since this is probably the most important decision
he'll ever have to make—how to deal with his homicidal
daughter—this might take a moment. But sooner than I expect, he speaks.

"Barnaby go to your room," he says firmly. "Don't get on
the computer, the TV, or your phone. Just stay in there and
read a book until I get back."

"But I have to go to school," he replies quietly.

"Not today!"

When my father turns to face me, he can't look me in the
eye right away. I don't blame him; I can hardly look at myself
either. "Give me all the clothes you were wearing last night,"
he orders.

Scooping up my jeans I place them on top of the ripped
shirt he's holding. Silently he follows me into my bedroom
where I add my jacket to the pile. When he turns around, his
face is stern, not completely devoid of compassion, but he's
in action-hero mode, and everybody knows an action hero
only has time for compassion after the dirty work is done.
My father's dirty work is just about to begin.

"Go take a shower, then change your clothes and stay in
your room," he says. The instructions continue. "If the
phone rings do not answer it; that goes for your cell phone
too," he orders. "No texting either, no communication what-
soever until I get back." He sees something out of the corner
of his eye. "Where are your shoes?"

Wordlessly, I look around my room until I see my ruined
Pumas, one resting on top of the other, underneath my desk.
Picking them up I'm surprised to find the soles are caked with
dirt, a multicolored clump clinging to each bottom. Brown,
beige, red. I hand them to my father, and he adds them to the
pile of clothes he's holding. Using my jacket as a towel, he
bends down and scoops up some dirt and debris that's fallen
onto the carpet. As he kneels before me, I'm reminded of

when I was little and he used to bend down to tie my shoes for me. That seems like it happened to another person.

Something on my face must alert him that he needs to include some fatherly piece of wisdom along with his authoritative instructions. "Everything is going to be all right, Dominy," he says. As an afterthought he adds, "I promise."

His words are empty. There's no way he can follow through; we both know that. But we both want to believe he can, so we remain quiet. I watch him race down the stairs, and when I hear the back door slam, my body starts to shake.

Afraid of being alone, I take the fastest shower on record, ignore my image in the mirror while I change into some clean clothes, and go into my brother's room. I lean against the wall for a bit, then slide down until I hit the floor. Barnaby's on his bed, not lounging or sprawled out, but sitting on the edge of the bed, the palms of his hands on his thighs, his feet barely touching the ground. His legs aren't swinging back and forth; his life is no longer a playground. The kid's in shock, and I don't blame him. I am too, but at least I'm responsible for my condition; he's had his thrust upon him.

He's so far into his own private world that he doesn't hear my cell phone vibrate yet again with another text message. I look down at the carpet between my legs where I've placed the phone and see that it's another one from Caleb: **Im wrried call me**

It's his fourth text. The first one asked me if he could come over for my birthday; the second assumed that my father didn't want to have any company; the third asked if I was sick or mad at him for some reason; and now this one asking me to call him. *If I called you, Caleb, and told you what happened, you'd be even more worried. No, in this case silence definitely is golden, and the only way to prevent you from being an accessory to my crime.* Our silence, however, is interrupted when Barnaby and I hear a car pull into the driveway.

Barnaby is the first one downstairs to greet my father when he enters the kitchen through the side door that leads to the garage.

"Why'd you park in there?" he asks, oddly out of breath for a track star.

"Don't ask questions," my father says, his voice kind, but firm. "Just go upstairs and leave us alone."

I can see the muscles in my brother's neck and all around his jawline clench and twitch. He understands that these are unusual circumstances; he understands that my father is trying to handle a crisis; but he doesn't understand why he has to be left out of the action. What he's missing is how lucky he is to be able to leave the room.

When we're alone, my father ushers me into the garage and closes the kitchen door behind us. The windowless garage door has been pulled down, so we're completely alone, unseen. We're surrounded by bikes, patio furniture hibernating for the winter, boxes filled with junk that we'll never use but that have sentimental value so we'll never throw them away, and now my father's police car, so there's very little room for us to move, which is kind of good because I feel my strength slipping away from me every second I'm in my father's presence. Movement will only make me weaker.

"I know about Jess."

My head nods slowly; I don't know if I'm making it move or if I'm on autopilot. Against all odds, I still must be in control, because I start to talk, and I actually sound rational.

"I've been thinking about it, Dad, and I must be wrong," I start. "There's no way that I could've killed Jess. She was my best friend! It had to be somebody else or . . . or a cougar, a coyote or something!"

"No, Dominy, it was you."

My father's words have a finality to them, as if he knows

exactly what happened without even being there. As if he knew this day would come, as if he's been planning for this day my entire life.

"What?" I whisper. "How can you be so sure?"

He places his hands on my shoulders, but I toss them off of me. I don't want a father who believes I'm a murderer; I want one who can erase what just happened.

"I can explain everything," he tells me.

Well, why don't you start?! "Where'd you go?" I ask. "And what . . . exactly do you know about Jess?"

Calmly, too calmly, he opens the trunk of his police car, and Jess is lying there, wrapped in a dirty gray flannel blanket, with only the side of her face and her shoes visible. I open my mouth to scream, and my father pulls me in close to him so I can bury my face in his chest and scream so no one can hear me. His touch is repulsive; his touch is salvation. I feel his chin resting on my head, and I scream even louder, holding him so tightly that when my body shakes uncontrollably his does too. It's like we're the same person.

Screams tumble out of me, ram into my father's chest, struggle for life, and die. One after the other until the raw sound subsides and turns to soft whimpering. The scents of sweat and dirt and cold air cling to my father, and I breathe in deeply. A whiff of decay overwhelms and excites me. Abruptly, I pull away and look up at him. I may no longer be innocent, but I feel younger than I have in my entire life. "How could I do such a thing?" I ask.

Before my father can answer, a loud garbled sound fills the garage and then a voice. It's his deputy Louis calling on his police walkie-talkie.

"Chief, we have a missing person's case," Louis says, his voice bookended by bursts of static. "Jessalynn Wyatt. She's friends with Arla and Dominy."

My father puts a finger up to his mouth, silently ordering me not to speak. "I know who she is," he replies.

"According to her mother the kid's been missing since yesterday afternoon. Arla said Jess might have gone over to your place last night 'cause it was Dom's birthday. That true?" Louis asks.

There's nothing in his voice to indicate that his statement hides a deeper meaning, but it still sounds like an accusation to me. My father agrees. There's a slight pause, and then I watch my father lie to the man who he trusts with his life. "No, we were just going to do a family thing, but Dominy got sick so we even canceled that."

"Got it. Think the kid could be a runaway?" Louis asks. "I don't know her that well."

This time when my father lies he has to close his eyes. "Could be," he answers. "Check the bus and train stations and tell her mother . . ."

"Chief?"

"Tell her mother we'll do everything we can to find her."

"Will do."

When static once again fills up the garage, my father slowly closes the trunk of the car, pushing on it until we hear the lock click shut. Jess and the static and Louis's voice are gone, and once again it's just my father and me. Or this man who's standing before me who resembles my father, but whose actions I don't recognize. "Why did you lie?"

He still can't look at me. He presses down on the trunk again to make sure it's securely locked and walks to the front of the car. I tug at his arm like I'm five years old and want ice cream. "Where are you going?"

"To get rid of the body," he says flatly, getting into the driver's seat.

The door slams shut; the engine turns over; my father puts on his seat belt. What is going on? Why isn't he completely freaked out, surprised? Why is he acting like he had "cover up all traces that my daughter committed murder" on his to-do list for today?

"Daddy!!"

I have to bang on the window three times before it starts to descend, eliminating the barrier between us.

"Why did you lie to Louis?"

Finally he looks at me, and I shudder. I have never seen him look more apologetic and anguished and helpless than he does right now.

"Because this is all my fault."

Chapter 10

Where's Jess?

Why am I surprised when I see that Jess's seat is empty? Did I really expect my father to bring her body to geometry and prop her up in a chair? Shove a pencil in her hand and make it look like she was waiting for the bell to ring so class could start? Am I losing my mind?

Yesterday was like a dream. Barnaby and I spent the day home from school, each allegedly suffering from the same twenty-four-hour bug, while my father spearheaded the search for my best friend after secretly burying her body in a location that he hopes will remain secret. Around lunchtime he came home and spoke to us in a sort of shorthand as if the house were bugged. He never mentioned Jess's name or the specifics of where he'd been or what he'd been doing all morning; he just gave us the go-ahead to text our friends in an attempt, we both implicitly understood, to make it appear to everyone outside our family that life in the Robineau household was still normal. He did caution us—very firmly—to keep our texts simple and short, let our friends know we were staying home sick. Refrain from including any details about my disappearance the night before or murder or evidence tampering or crime scene contamination, or, of course, Jess.

Dutifully, Barnaby and I played along. And if it hadn't been for my father's last comment to me before he drove off with Jess's body wrapped in a dingy blanket in the trunk of his police car, I would have thought he was just doing his fatherly duty: protecting his daughter. But his words make me think that he's also protecting himself.

This is all my fault.

That's what he said. He didn't explain what he meant; he didn't elaborate on his comment. He just drove off and ignored it when he returned home. As confused as I am about my father's motives, I want to protect him as much as he's protecting me, so when Danny Klausman asks if I heard from Jess, I do as my father taught me. I lie.

"She sent me a bunch of birthday texts," I say as casually as if I were telling the truth. "I had to cancel my dinner 'cause I must've caught a stomach bug or something; my brother had it too."

I prove to be a good liar, and Danny believes every fictitious word I've told him.

"Could've been food poisoning," he suggests. "I had that once when my mother tried to make Mexican. Her chili was rancid or something. The whole family was going from both ends if you know what I mean."

Sadly, I got the picture. Danny really is disgusting though, and for once I don't feel bad for dubbing him The Dandruff King.

"Did that happen to you?" he asks with an expression that can only mean he's hoping my answer is yes.

"Just throwing up," I say. "But Barnaby wasn't, so I don't think it was anything we ate, just a dumb virus."

It is so easy to lie. I never really did it before, never saw the point to it unless, of course, it was a way not to hurt someone. But it's also hard to keep a lie straight. Now that I've mentioned that Barnaby didn't throw up, made that part of our fake scenario, I have to make sure that's what he tells people or I'll be proven a liar. And if I can lie so effortlessly, chances are an eager assistant D.A. will make the case that I can commit murder with the same ease. Now I know why I rarely lie; it's hard work. I have never been more thankful to see Mrs. Gallagher walk into class, because for the first time in my life geometry doesn't seem so complicated.

Getting through lunch, however, is going to be like getting through one of those laboratory mazes. I'm a mouse in search of a piece of cheese, and I simply don't know which way to turn to find my reward.

"Domgirl! I can't believe you were sick on your birthday," Caleb declares.

Do I turn to the left or to the right? Do I stand still? Do I let the guilt that's clawing at my insides break through my skin and confess, or do I maintain my made-up innocence?

"Total bummer," I tell him sheepishly. Fake innocence wins.

"So what up?" he asks. "You were feeling okay when I saw you during last period. Something happen after school?"

An inner voice tells me that "Lying is another word for protecting." It's exactly the reminder I need to get me to open my mouth and speak.

"No, I wasn't feeling great all day, but I thought it would pass," I say. "It did, but only a day later."

"Well, this weekend we'll do something," Caleb says. "Just me and you."

Smiles are contagious, and in spite of what I'm hiding in my heart, I look harmless, one half of a smiling couple. I'm just a girlfriend enjoying a sort-of-intimate moment with her boyfriend at a lunch table in the middle of a normal school day. Like a bad omen the scratches on my chest tingle; I'm about to discover this is a day that's about to become anything but normal.

"Ohmigod, ohmigod, ohmigod!" Arla whisper-shouts as she sits at our table in an empty chair next to Caleb and across from me. Not quite sitting actually; her leg is tucked under her so she's sitting on her calf, and her body is leaning across the table. She's acting like one of those special ADD students whose parents are unsuccessfully trying to wean them off of Ritalin. Her body is bouncing slightly, so her long crystal necklace isn't just dangling from her neck; it's swaying, the crucifix at the end of the necklace swinging toward me, then retreating as if salvation were just out of my grasp.

"Did you hear about Jess?"

Her hand feels warm on top of mine. I look down, and I have to fight back the tears. *Don't give yourself away; don't give them any reason to question you later; keep lying; keep acting as if you don't know anything.* That's what I tell myself, but it's hard when I see Arla's hand, because it reminds me of Jess.

Not in the color or texture, but in the fingernails. They're painted Jess's favorite color, lemon yellow. The MAC name for it is Sunblind, and the shape is the squoval that Jess just introduced us to. Only last week we piled on her bed to re-watch—for about the fifteenth time—the online video starring Saoirse demonstrating how to achieve the square-meets-oval look on her friend Nakano's hand. Jess so adored Nakano that she e-mailed him to tell him he should branch out and do his own spinoff videos. He wrote her back and thanked her, but said he's happy just being Saoirse's sidekick.

I'm so lost in absurd thoughts about Arla's fingernails and Jess's online friends that I see Arla's mouth moving, but I don't hear what she's saying.

"Rewind please?" I ask.

She runs a squovalized fingernail through the bangs of her

wig. Since it's Thursday, she's sporting her goth-black, shoulder-length, straight-haired wig with bangs that tickle the tops of her eyebrows. It's Jess's favorite for the obvious racial implications. Just as Arla shifts in her chair and lets go of my hand, I start to shake. I can't help it; all I'm doing is thinking about Jess, seeing her face in front of me, the "before" and the "after" looks, and now I have to listen to Arla talk about her.

"My father told me that Jess disappeared," Arla repeats.

"What?!" I say. It's only one word, but I say it with such conviction that I hate myself.

"Like vanished?" Caleb asks.

"Poof," Arla replies, snapping her fingers. "Into thin air."

"Oh come on," Caleb says, shrugging his shoulders. "That's ridiculous."

"Tell that to her mother," Arla replies. "She never came home after school and that was two days ago!"

Words and ideas are forming in Caleb's mind; he's trying to digest this information and make it palatable. He's got innocence and an optimistic spirit on his side, so he should be successful. He is.

"She's probably being all dramatic about something stupid and took off. They'll find her," Caleb says confidently. "She can't be that far, and nothing ever happens in this town anyway."

Cupping her chin with her hand, Arla presses one lemony-yellow squoval-shaped fingernail against the side of her light brown cheek. The color combination is like something out of a design magazine. Her words, however, are right out of the police blotter.

"Remember Mauro Dorigo?"

"Who?" we both ask.

"Fat bully a few years ahead of us," she clarifies. "About two years ago he up and disappeared right around Thanksgiving too."

Recognition seeps into Caleb's face, but not into mine. Clearly, Arla is much more informed as the daughter of the deputy sheriff than I am as the daughter of the man in charge.

"Whoa! I do remember hearing about that," he exclaims. "He was a runaway right?"

Arla's eyebrows rise so high they get lost amid her bangs. "That's what they told the press," she explains, knowing full well that we know "they" means "her father." She drops her chin and her voice. "But there was no note, no family problems, nothing that would indicate he'd want to run away," she confides. "And there hasn't been a trace of him ever since."

I have to ask. "So your father doesn't think Jess ran away either?"

She grabs my hand again, but by now I'm so cold she can't warm me up. "Oh, Dom, I'm sorry, I thought your father would've told you already."

I can only shake my head.

"Should've known," Arla replies. "Your father's professional; mine's got a big mouth." She waves her hands to make us lean in closer to her so she can finish her story. "They don't know anything yet, but my father said the first twenty-four hours, which we're already passed, are the most crucial and so far they don't have a clue."

"What about Napoleon?"

I try not to look as shocked as Arla and Caleb when I ask the question. My goal is to make my face look like I've made a valid deduction, not like I'm casting blame on someone else. "I mean, you know," I stutter, "he is her boyfriend; maybe she's with him."

"They've already talked to him," Arla says, shaking her head. "Anyway, Dom, you know that Nap would rather be with you than with Jess."

Even if I didn't agree with her, even if I were the Helen

Keller of Two W, I'd still have to protest. Remember, I'm sitting across from *my boyfriend*. The same boyfriend I've been trying to convince that he has no rival.

"Oh that's ridiculous!"

"Dominy Suzette Robineau! You cannot tell me that you haven't noticed the way that boy looks at you?" Arla asks.

"And just how does *that* boy look at *my* girlfriend?"

"Nap looks at Dom the way he should be looking at Jess," Arla replies.

"I knew it!" Caleb explodes. "I've had just about enough of this d-bag!" Caleb stands up, and his eyes scour the cafeteria in pursuit of his nemesis. I look at Arla with a scrunched up expression that silently asks, "Why'd you have to spill the beans?" And she responds with an equally scrunched up expression that silently says, "I'm sorry; I thought he already knew."

"Where is he?" Caleb asks, his neck twisting side to side. "It's time I taught twinboy a lesson in how to behave."

Arla and I twist our necks as well, hoping to find Napoleon before Caleb does in order to prevent the inevitable fistfight.

I search for the sweetest, most girlfriendy voice that I possess. I find it. "C'mon, Caleb, forget about Napoleon," I practically purr.

"Not until he understands the rules," Caleb seethes. "You're my girl, so hands off!"

"Caleb," I say in that same sugary voice, "he never put his hands on me." I'm hoping this piece of information will placate him, make him stop acting like a Neanderthal. It has the opposite reaction, even though his vocabulary expands by a few centuries.

"I'm speaking figuratively!" he shouts.

The only thing that prevents Caleb from leaving the table to search for Nap in every classroom throughout Two W is Archie's arrival. I can sense that something's wrong while

Archie's still two tables away. Gone is his bouncy walk, gone is his trademark smile, and when he sits down next to me there's no funny greeting, no fist bumping with Caleb, just a dour expression and silence. His gaze is unfocused; he's staring at something on the table, and he wears sadness as if it were a perfectly tailored jacket.

I'm not sure if it's biologically possible, but he looks whiter than usual; in fact, the only color in his face is coming from his eyes. Spreading out from the outer rim of his deep purple irises, a common albino trait, are spindly red spider webs, so numerous and thick that they threaten to wipe out the white parts of his eyes. Archie's been crying, and he looks as if he's about to start all over again.

"Winter, what's wrong?" Caleb asks.

Slowly Archie looks up at us. He wants to speak but has lost the ability.

"Dude, tell us," Caleb says kindly. "What's going on?"

When he speaks, his voice is hoarse and shaky. "They found Jess."

This is what it must feel like for people who are about to hear a jury's decision or the results of a biopsy; they exist in a kind of suspended animation. Not breathing, not really living, just waiting for a signal from some more intelligent, exterior force as to how they should react. Should I sigh in relief? Should I squeak in delight? Or should I remain quiet and ponder how I'm going to die?

If they have found Jess's body, it's only a matter of time before they connect her death to my father or me; either way the truth will be revealed, and I'll have to pay for my crime. Doesn't matter that I can't remember committing any crime, that I had absolutely no motive; I'm still going to have to pay. And the three people sitting at the table with me will want to see that happen.

"Why don't you sound happy about that?" Arla asks nervously.

Archie's focus returns to the table. "Because . . ."

When it's obvious Archie can't find the right words to continue speaking, Caleb interrupts him. "Because what?"

"Because they only found part of her."

The significance of that statement doesn't penetrate right away. *Part of her.* What's he talking about? That phrase doesn't make sense. Until Archie takes his iPhone that he's been clutching and places it on the table so we can read the news bulletin on the screen.

> A girl's right arm has been found in the brush near the hills in Weeping Water; it looks to have been bitten off by a wild animal. The only identifying mark is a bracelet the victim was wearing spelling out her name—Jessalynn.

"The gift Napoleon gave her," Arla says out loud.

Archie nods his head, and it's like a domino effect. It starts slowly; first Arla reacts and then Caleb and then one person after another after another in the cafeteria starts to scream. Screams mixed with words. One word, actually, as Jess's name echoes throughout the cafeteria, jumping from one table to the next. Obviously Archie isn't the only one to have uncovered this news, and anguished voices fill the lunchroom, mine among them. The only difference between me and everyone else is that they're screaming for their friend; I'm screaming for myself.

Within seconds our principal's voice comes over the loudspeaker, instructing the students and faculty to report to the gym immediately for an assembly. I watch the crowd start to move in clusters, slowly, bodies hugging awkwardly, arms wrapped around shoulders, foreheads pressed together, and I wish I were blind. I hear the choked sobs, the wailing cries of disbelief from the students, and the stern, solemn orders from the faculty to keep moving, and I wish I were deaf. I feel

Caleb and Archie and Arla grab me, hold me, clutch me close to them so our individual grief can fuse together to become one giant broken heart, and I wish I were invisible. I can't be a part of this charade. My father was wrong. This isn't because of him; this is because of me. I'm the cause of everyone's pain; I'm the cause of everyone's sorrow, so I can't be a mourner as well.

I'm not proud of what I do, but I use Caleb's jealousy of Napoleon to ensure my freedom. I see Nap enter the cafeteria, like a salmon swimming against the tide, and when he's a few feet away, he stops to stare at me as usual. This time, however, I maintain his gaze. The tears I've been holding back are given their independence, and they stream down my face. As expected, Napoleon is at my side in seconds, his thin arms around me, his hands stroking my shoulders, brushing my hair off my wet cheeks, to comfort me in my time of grief. He really does feel like a butterfly, soft, wispy, and unable to keep still. A few seconds after his butterfly-touch, and Caleb is pushing Napoleon off of me, shouting, "Keep your hands off my girlfriend!" Boys really can be so predictable.

During their scuffle, I back away, and without worrying if anyone sees me, I run out of the cafeteria in the opposite direction from where the crowd is heading. I have no choice. There is absolutely no way I'm going to be able to sit in the bleachers surrounded by my shell-shocked classmates and listen to Dumbleavy and his team of lame counselors guide us through the labyrinth of our difficult-to-navigate emotions. The best way I know how to deal with these feelings that are eating away at me is to talk to someone who can't talk back.

For once Essie's poor job skills are to my benefit. She doesn't ask me why I'm visiting The Retreat during school hours; she merely hands me an index card with the number nineteen written on it in black Magic Marker. Today's index card color is orange, so I'm reminded of Halloween, which I think is highly appropriate since I'm masquerading as the heartbroken, innocent best friend. Well, two out of three adjectives isn't bad.

Inside my mother's room I can let the mask fall; I can be myself, whoever that person really is. I follow my usual routine so I can relax. Pull the chair next to my mother's bed, sit down, repeat my opening line: "Hey, Mom, how are you?" There's no response, which I've come to expect, but there's no calmness either, which I've come to rely upon. I take a deep breath to slow down my racing heartbeat, and when I exhale for the third time I realize the problem: I've forgotten her perfume.

Instead of filling up with lilacs and powder, the scent of her favorite Guerlinade, my lungs fill up with antiseptic and some other heavy scent that I don't recognize. Must be some cheap perfume from a nurse or maybe a housekeeper, not sure, but definitely from someone who can't handle the smell of sickness all day long so she bathes in some musky cologne. I hate the smell, but I can't blame her; it's no different from what I do.

I grab my mother's hand, and thankfully it's as smooth as ever; it's good to know some things don't change. The back of her hand feels so warm against my cheek, it's like I'm sitting in front of a roaring fire. I close my eyes, and I can see the flames dancing, orange, red, and yellow pieces of fire interwoven, leaning and bending, destroying all that's bad, all that needs to disappear, and leaving behind only remnants of sorrow, so it's easier to move forward; it's easier to keep on living. That's what my mother shares with me, the ability to move on. In the crackling of the flames I can hear her voice, the voice that I remember, the voice that reminds me I can share anything with her and she'll love me unconditionally and she'll always be able to make my world perfect again. The sound is like a lullaby, crackling and hissing and squeaking. Squeaking?

I whip my head around, but no one's there. I remain quiet for a few seconds, straining my ears to discover an intruder, but none appears. The crackling and the hissing and the squeaking are all gone. Guess that's what happens when you lose yourself in a daydream: You begin to hear things.

Turning back to my mother, I stroke her hand and am overcome by the desire to hear her once more. I want to hear her singsong voice answer my questions. Who cares what she says; who cares if she doesn't have the answers. Her voice will be enough.

"What's happening to me, Mom?"

Silence.

"Why am I different?"

More silence.

"Why am I changing?"

Suddenly, my mother's face starts to glow. It's like there's a light shining from within her body, illuminating her face to let me know that she can hear me. I'm not fooled. I know that I'm going insane; I know that this is impossible, but I find it so comforting that I ask more questions.

"Why can't I put an end to this, Mom?"

The light emanating from my mother grows softer, more like stardust floating around an angel's wings. It's impossible, but she's responding to my voice. Maybe it's because she can sense that I'm desperate to make some kind of connection, I don't know, but instead of analyzing it, I continue to talk.

"I don't like what's happening to me, but I can't do anything to stop it," I admit. "I don't understand any of it, but my body and my mind are not the same, and they haven't been for months!"

The stardust lifts, and the light around her face is twinkling. I look away and focus on the small wooden desk in the corner of the room, focusing hard on it, and then turn back to my mother. She's still glowing. It's real; it isn't my imagination. I have absolutely no idea what's happening, but I don't care. I don't want an explanation; I just want an answer, and I'm convinced she can give me one.

I lean in close to her, an inch from her face. I'm wrapped in the glimmer of light and hope and love that is pouring out of her. "Mom," I whisper. "Why did I kill Jess?"

For the second time in very recent memory, I see my mother's eyes. But this time they're different; they're alive. They open, and they're like two gray rainclouds with the promise of a clear blue sky behind them. They're beautiful, and they're looking at me with a kind of love I barely remember. Instinctively, I squeeze my mother's hand tighter, and I feel more than warmth; I feel movement. The light was only the beginning; my mother's starting to come alive. My temples are pounding with such excitement and surprise that I almost don't hear her speak.

"Ask your father."

The sound of her voice stuns me so sharply that I fall back in my chair and let go of her hand. Once our physical connection is lost so is she. Her eyelids close, and her face is shrouded in shadow once again. No!!

"Mom! Mommy, come back to me!" I shout, grabbing her hand.

There's no response, only the emptiness I'm so used to. I'm left looking at a sleeping woman who looks like my mother. Where did she go?! Why did she speak to me and then leave?! And what did she mean?

Ask your father.

Maybe if I can revive her, she'll explain what she meant. Frantically, I press the button at the side of her bed and shout into the intercom for a nurse to come. I'm still holding the device when I hear squeaking behind me again and turn around. This time I see the source of the sound.

"Nadine?!"

Somewhere in the distance I swear I can hear the buzzing of a swarm of bees.

"Is everything all right in here?" she asks.

"What are you doing here?" I ask.

"I heard you scream and came right in," she explains.

It's a logical explanation, but my body isn't listening to my brain, so disbelief registers on my face. As a result Nadine explains further.

"I have work-study here twice a week," she continues. Another logical explanation, but still there's something about her calmness, something about how she's standing in front of me like a statue, her face frozen instead of curious, that convinces me she's lying. But why would she lie to me? And why would she be spying on me? Before our conversation can continue any further, a nurse I recognize bursts into the room, followed by a doctor whom I've never seen before.

"My mother woke up," I say.

The nurse looks at me like I'm crazy, while the doctor ignores me and walks to the other side of the bed. He opens one of my mother's eyelids with his thumb and shines a light into her pupil and then repeats the task in her other eye. Roughly, he presses his finger onto the mini-flashlight's clicker and the little beam of light disappears.

"She spoke to me," I add.

Now it's clear that the doctor agrees with the nurse, because he's looking at me like I should fill out a new patient form. Nadine, however, appears to accept every word I've said as fact. At least someone else in the room believes me.

"Miss Robineau?"

The doctor is very tall, way over six feet, so when he talks to me he looks down even from the other side of the bed. It makes what he has to say sound even more condescending. "I'm sorry, but there's no change; your mother's vital signs are the same," he informs me. "She's still in a coma."

"You're not looking hard enough!" I cry. "She opened her eyes. She looked right at me and spoke."

"And what did she say?"

Now all three of them look exactly the same. They're all staring at me, anxiously waiting to see how I'll respond to the doctor's question.

"She, um, she called out my name," I lie.

This time the doctor doesn't even try to make his tone sound anything but patronizing. "I'm sure that's exactly what you've wanted to hear her say for years."

The doctor makes a hasty exit. He's followed by the nurse, who doesn't even bother to say anything; she just offers me a pity-smile and bows her head on her way out, leaving Nadine alone with me and my mother in the room.

"I'm sorry," Nadine says. Her voice is filled with so much compassion, I realize I must have misjudged her. That is until she turns to leave the room, and the sound of her shoes squeaking makes my breathing stop. I wonder how much she heard of what I said.

But I can't worry about her right now. I have to get out of here and do exactly what my mother told me to do.

"Dad, we have to talk."

That's the first thing I say to my father when he comes into my room. I knew if I skipped dinner and stayed in my bedroom he would eventually come in to see how I was handling the latest news about Jess. When I share with him *my* latest news, he doesn't seem the least bit surprised. I can't take his nonchalant attitude any longer.

"What is wrong with you?!" I blurt out. "You're not freaked out that Mom woke up and told me to ask *you* why I killed Jess?!"

"No, honey, I'm not."

"And why the hell aren't you?!"

I watch my father's Adam's apple rise and fall as he swallows. "Because I've known you would do something like this from before you were born."

I remember the conversation my father had with Louis, the one I overheard, when he assumed it would only be a matter of time before I did something wrong. And now this comment.

"How?" My voice is cautious, and it takes a moment to find its strength. "How could you know that I would kill my best friend?!"

My father doesn't move; he just stands at the foot of my bed, his arms dangling at his sides like they're too heavy to lift. "I didn't know who you would kill, but I always knew that you would kill someone." His voice is not quite boastful, but he does sound as if he's saying he always knew I'd get into a prestigious college or that I'd marry a doctor and not that he knew I'd commit murder. "And I've always known you would do it on your sixteenth birthday."

My body slumps on my bed, and I grab onto my flower pillow, clutching its softness with my fists. This is all too much. My father is a freak, a lunatic. He's one of those crazy people you hear about on the news. He's hidden it all these years, but finally it's come out.

"Daddy, please," I say, tears falling from my eyes. "You're scaring me."

"I'm sorry," he says, and he almost sounds normal. "I wish I didn't know about any of this. I wish it weren't coming true, but it is." He sits on my bed, and I pull my legs away, tuck them under myself so I'm practically sitting on my knees. We're both aware that I want to keep a wide space between us so he doesn't move any closer. "It's all happening like I knew it would."

"What?!" I scream. "What's happening?!"

My father's lips move, but it's like I'm deaf, so I have to ask him again.

"What? Daddy, what's coming true?!"

This time I hear him loud and clear.

"The curse."

Chapter 11

"The *what?!*"

I could not have heard what I thought I heard. My father did not just tell me that the reason I've been acting strangely lately, the reason that I don't feel like myself, the reason that Jess is dead is because of some curse. We live in Nebraska! This isn't the jungle; chickens aren't beheaded and sacrificed on Saturday nights in the town square for God's sake!

"Dad, what are you talking about?"

"I know it's hard to understand," my father replies, sounding like one of my teachers.

"There's nothing to understand," I shout, sounding like a very ticked-off student. "Curses aren't real."

He shifts his body and bridges the gap that separates us by a few inches. I stop myself from leaning backwards. I'm not sure how close I want to be to my father right at this moment, but he is my father after all; he isn't really some crazy person. Is he?

"I used to think that as well," he says, his eyes completely consumed with sorrow. "I used to believe that curses were just made up, parts of legends." He can't or won't look at me; he's looking at something, I'm not sure what it is, but I know it's not in my room. He's looking at something from his past, a memory; whether it's real or fake, I have no idea. "But now I know I was wrong."

My father places his hand on my bed next to my knee. He wants me to reach out to him, to clasp his hand to make a connection, but I can't. This conversation has stopped being ridiculous and is starting to become frightening. I don't want it to become sentimental as well. Have to keep my heart out of this and only listen with my mind.

"I should've prepared you; I should've warned you," he says, the words tumbling out of his mouth angrily. "But I did nothing . . . and now the curse has come true."

"Dad, listen to me, curses don't exist," I start. "They turn princes into frogs and apples into lethal weapons in fairy tales. But they have nothing to do with real life."

Ironically, my father's smile is even more patronizing than that a-hole doctor's in my mother's hospital room. He's the one claiming that curses are real, and I'm the whackjob.

"I know that you're looking for an explanation for what happened, for what's going on," I say, keeping my voice as even and rational as possible. "But the only way we're going to do that is to logically figure out what's wrong with me."

My father's not paying attention to me. He's looking down at the ground again, shaking his head. I have got to get him to listen.

"That's the only way we're going to be able to put an end to it," I plead. "So nothing like this ever happens again."

Still no response. Just his head shaking slowly from side to side and then suddenly stopping. "No," he says finally.

His response so infuriates me that something inside of me is triggered, and I hear screams in my head that have no voice. For a split second I'm back at the hills, back with Jess when she was still alive. I'm not imagining this; it's a real memory. I see a paw covered in red fur slice through the air, slice through Jess's arm, ripping away her flesh. There was an animal; there was something with us out there. Blood gushes, Jess screams, a flood erupts in my mouth, and that taste is back. Bitter and familiar and delicious. I'm back in my room now, and I look at my father. He has to help me. Together we have to figure this out.

"The only way we're going to put an end to this is to break the curse," my father declares.

This is how my father plans on saving me? By executing a plan to break some nonexistent curse?!

My feet pound into the floor when I jump off the bed. They keep pounding as they take me from one end of the room to the other. Once again the walls, three white, one blazing orange, are like a cage. I wish the painted wall could erupt into flames, devour the entire house and me and my father with it, let Barnaby escape. He can be a jerk, but there's no reason he should die for my crimes and my father's stupidity.

"You're drawn to it, aren't you?"

My father's question startles me out of my wish-trance, reminds me that walls can't spontaneously combust, but once again I have no idea what he's talking about. And my confusion reads all over my face.

"The wolf," he says.

I look up at the banner on my wall and see the timberwolf, the Two W mascot, staring back at me, his paw reaching out, ferocious and tender, in a desperate attempt to make some kind of connection. He reminds me of my father.

"Seriously, Dad, you are freaking me out."

My father looks weary, as if he's used up every trick in his arsenal and still can't make his obstinate child behave. Suddenly, he lowers himself to the floor and leans back against the footboard of my bed. Clasped hands resting in his lap, crossed legs, a sweet smile. He's the perfect daddy. Except this daddy's got a terrible secret.

"I need to tell you a story."

"I was your age, just sixteen, when it started," my father begins.

I want him to stop. I don't know where his story is going to lead, but it can't possibly have a happy ending.

"I thought I was a man, wanted to be one anyway. I was tired of being a boy, always having to do what I was told, always having to be instructed and not make my own choices, always having to wait for something exciting to happen." He looks down at his hands resting in his lap, so I look at them too. We're both expecting them to do something magical, but nothing comes. Just ten fingers interwoven and motionless. "I had no idea that my life was about to change forever."

This time when he looks down at his hands, his thumbs spin around each other. Slowly, they turn a few times and then reverse direction. He seems fascinated by this action, as if he's not controlling it, as if his thumbs have little thumb-minds of their own. Only when they stop moving does my father start to talk again.

"My dad and I used to go hunting," he says, picking up the story. "Just the two of us, deep in the hills on the outskirts of town, sometimes for the weekend in the Sand Hills or near Lake McConaughy. We hunted deer mostly, on occasion pheasant or wild turkey. Once, my dad shot a moose, I have no idea what it was doing around here, must've gotten lost and strayed too far south, but my dad killed it." Lost in his memory, my father laughs. "Whole town ate moose steaks for a month."

Normally, the thought of eating a moose would disgust me. Now for some reason it doesn't.

"My father promised that we would go on a special hunting trip for my birthday, my sixteenth, all the way up in Montana," he remembers. "Bucks up there weigh almost seven hundred pounds, antlers five feet wide, majestic creatures, and I couldn't wait to hunt them down with my new rifle. Show them that they were no match for me."

The little boy still living inside my father comes out, and he sounds boastful and bold and unashamed at the prospect of teaching some innocent animal that he's the stronger species. Not because he's naturally superior, but because he's smart enough to hunt with a rifle.

"Friday after school I ran home after spending the entire day telling my friends that I wouldn't be around for the weekend because my father was taking me on a trip, just the two of us," he says. "I knew something was wrong when I turned the corner of my block. My dad's pickup was parked in the driveway, right outside."

My father grew up in this house, so I feel like I'm with him, standing right next to him in his memory. I get a mental picture of a dust-covered pickup truck where my father's police car is usually parked, probably a red truck, tires covered in mud, and I know exactly what my father is thinking as a kid standing in front of his house. Something has to be wrong because fathers are never home right after school.

"He came home sick from the factory with stomach pains," my father explains. "Turned out to be a gall bladder attack, but I didn't care what it was, didn't care if it was the flu or some fatal disease. All I knew was that my dad screwed up everything and my birthday hunting trip was canceled."

When my father laughs this time, I smile along with him. I don't find what he's saying to be funny; it's a reflex.

"But it was my birthday, and I wanted to celebrate by killing some deer," my father remembers. "So the next morning that's what I set out to do."

"Without your father's permission?" I ask.

"Without anyone knowing I had left," he replies. "I took my dad's treasured Winchester though, instead of my brand new Remington, so it would feel like he was coming with me."

It's hard for me to imagine my father being so irresponsible and reckless. I've never known him to go out hunting for food or for sport; I can't recall his ever mentioning that it was something he did with his father. I lean my head against the wall for support. This is not the man I know. Sure, my father grew up to be a hunter of sorts—he's a cop, he hunts down criminals—but that's like a peacekeeping effort, not murdering a defenseless animal.

"So you snuck out in the morning with a rifle to go hunting solo?" I ask.

"And I wasn't coming back until I had shot the biggest buck I could find," he adds. "My family was going to have a venison feast thanks to me."

Once again I wait for my stomach to turn as I imagine my father cooking up a deer, a meat I've never tasted, never dreamed of eating, but I find the concept natural. I'll dwell on that later; now I have to urge my dad to get to the point. "So you're out in the hills by yourself," I repeat. "And . . ."

"And my life changed," he says quietly.

My body shudders. And I'm not being figurative; I literally shake. It's like a ripple that starts at my toes, runs up the length of my body, and doesn't stop until it escapes out the top of my head. Whatever happened to my father all those years ago, this thing that he's labeled a curse, has affected him deeply. Now it's my turn. I look at him, and it's like I'm looking at myself. We both had similar experiences at the same time in our lives in the same place on the planet. I've got to hear more.

"Daddy, please just tell me," I say. "How did your life change?"

He runs his fingers through his hair, revealing a thick layer of gray underneath the brown. Really, he's a lot older than I think he is.

"There was an accident."

My father's voice has aged. It's somber. No, not somber. Scared.

"About thirty yards away I saw a beautiful deer," he continues. "Female, sandy coat, her chest spotted dark brown, and she was standing still, looking right at me." He's pointing straight ahead, and I swear he can see the deer in my room. "It's as if she's giving me her permission to shoot."

His hands unclasp, and he raises them as if he's holding a rifle. Tilting his head, he shuts his left eye and looks through the little view thing in the gun, whatever it's called, and he's eyeing the deer that he saw over thirty years ago. He has no idea that he's sitting on the floor in my bedroom.

"My heart was racing," my father says in a whisper. "I had never shot a deer without my dad by my side, and then they were young does, hardly worthy opponents, but this was going to be a huge victory, a huge kill, and my dad was going to be so proud of me."

I've never heard my father speak so callously, so cavalierly about a life before. This is the man who helped me bury my pet hamster in the backyard when I was nine. We had a funeral for Whiskers. How did this bloodthirsty little boy grow up to be so gentle?

He fake-shoots the rifle and slightly raises his arm, which I guess is like the aftershock you feel when you pull the trigger. He repeats this movement twice more in quick succession and then after a moment's hesitation one final time. Four shots for one deer.

His hands are dangling at his side, the rifle is gone. I don't know if he's out of bullets or out of the past, but there won't be any more shooting today. A glimmer of sweat has appeared on my father's face, and he looks pale and ghostly. No, he was just out of bullets, because he's still lost in his memory, and whatever happened in the past is happening now.

"I killed him."

Him? "I thought you said it was a female?" I ask.

"The deer got away," my father replies. "I killed *him*."

One bead of sweat slithers down the side of my father's face. He doesn't move a hand to wipe it away; he gives it freedom and lets it slide down his skin and fall to the floor. The natural order of things has taken over. I have to do the same thing to my voice, give it freedom and let it ask the questions it wants to.

"What do you mean killed *him?*"

"I-I didn't see him. I was focused on . . . on the deer," my father stammers. "He . . . he must've been crouched near her, hidden in the brush, hoping to take her down the same way I was."

Suddenly, my room shrinks in size. My father gets up; it's his turn to pace in the cage. Problem is he's bigger than me and more powerful, so it's frightening to watch him lumber from one side of the room to the other, his fists clenched and slicing the air. Every other step his head twitches to either get rid of the memory or make it come into focus.

"I tried to tell her that I didn't see him, but she wouldn't believe me!" he shouts. "I tried to tell her that it was an accident!"

He's talking to me as if I had been there, as if I understand what he's saying.

"Daddy, who?" I ask. "Who did you tell?"

"The wife . . . the wife of the man I killed!"

Briefly my father stops pacing, but watching him bent over, his hands gripping his hair, is almost worse. I get the feeling that this is the first time he's ever said these words out loud, or at least to another person.

"She came running up to us, and she saw me standing over his dead body."

I look down to where my father is staring, half-expecting to see a corpse lying there in a pool of blood.

"Two holes in his chest. I hit him twice out of four shots," he remembers. "I didn't even see him; I was aiming at the deer, but his wife . . . She saw me, and she saw my gun, and she saw her husband. . . ."

No matter how many times you watch your father cry, it's never an easy sight. You want to know that he is sensitive enough to feel so deeply that tears are the only recourse, but you don't want to bear witness to it. You want him to be strong and cry in private, when he's alone, not tarnish your ideal of him. Even though I would prefer to look away, I can't. I watch my father as half man, half boy cry over something that happened decades ago but clearly is as real to him as if it took place this morning.

"She tried to stop the bleeding, but it was too late; he was already dead," he says. "Only when she stood up did I see that she was pregnant."

He grabs his stomach as if overtaken by intense pains.

"Her belly was huge and swollen, and her dress and her hands were covered in her husband's blood. She didn't have to say a word; I knew the truth without it ever being spoken," he says. "This is all because of me."

There are those words again. *This is all because of me.* Now they make a little more sense, but just a little. Okay fine, I get it, he killed this man by accident, but what does that have to do with me?

"She put a curse on me," he says through the last of his tears. "For what I had done to her husband and to her, she cursed me. And that curse has finally come true."

Oh my God, he believes this. He believes that there's a connection between these two deaths, this unlucky hunter and Jess. Just because they both were killed in the general vicinity of each other hardly links them. This woman, this angry wife screwed up my father's mind, I mean royally screwed it up big time, if because of her he truly thinks these two events are related.

"I know you think it sounds crazy. You must think I've lost my mind," my father says, accurately summing up my thoughts. "Trust me, for the longest time I thought it was just the ramblings of a bitter woman."

And *certifiably insane* I want to contribute.

"I remembered all the stories I had heard growing up about how the Indians believed in stuff like that, in curses, witchcraft, the supernatural," he adds. "So this was just a woman turning to her beliefs in a moment of despair. Like we prayed when Mommy got sick."

The hair on the back of my neck stands up at the mention of my mother's name. How dare he compare this vindictive witch with my mother?!

"She was doing what she had been taught to do," he says. "Avenging her husband's death."

"The man you shot . . ."

"The man I *killed,*" my father corrects.

It might be accurate, but I can't say the word so I ignore it. "He was American Indian?"

"Yes."

"Which tribe?" I have no idea why I ask that question, but I want some simple information, nothing about curses, just a fact I can hold on to. A fact that my father can't recall.

"I have no idea," he answers. "I assume they were native to the state, Plains Indians, I guess. They must have lived in the hills. I had never seen them in town before, and I knew practically everyone. Still do."

"So who is this woman?" I question. "Do I know her?"

Even though this occurred when my dad was a kid, most

people his age and older never leave this town, born and raised and proud of it, so the odds that this crazy Indian woman is still a Weeping Water resident are pretty good.

"No, after that day I never saw her again," he replies. "But I'll never forget what she looked like. Jet black hair, perfectly straight, and skin the color of milk."

That doesn't make sense. "Then she couldn't have been an Indian," I say.

"Her features, her bone structure were pure Native American," my father confirms. "Just her skin color was different, very pale; she must've had some European blood in her family."

So how does one chance meeting turn into a lifetime of regret? "So you meet this woman once and yet you believe she's manipulated your life for all these years?!"

"Yes."

The tables are turned, and I'm the parent now. "Well, that's not good enough!" I scream. "You need to explain everything."

I'm no longer afraid. I'm angry, so I'm now standing in front of my father, my face inches from his. "You don't believe in rituals and curses; you never have," I continue. "I get that you want to protect me, but the only way I can protect myself is for me to confess what I've done."

"But you didn't do anything!" he insists.

"Yes, I did!" I scream. "I don't remember it, but there's no other explanation."

"Luba put a curse on my firstborn!"

Luba?

"The Indian woman," my father replies, answering my silent question. "She clutched her swollen stomach and knelt down in front of me. She placed a hand on the blood that was still pouring out of her husband and then lifted it up to the sky."

My father mimics the crazy Luba woman's movement and raises his hand.

"It was a beautiful spring morning, and I'll never forget how the blood glistened in the sunlight; it made the sky look even bluer," he says. "I was so amazed by the sight of her hand dripping with blood that at first I didn't understand what she was saying. Not until she said 'I curse you.' "

His hand turns toward something, something that doesn't exist in my room, but only in his mind.

"She turned her hand toward the moon," he explains. "It was faint, pale gray, but it could be seen against the blue sky. Unusual, but I'd seen the moon during the day before. Now I couldn't take my eyes off it."

For some idiotic reason the mere mention of the word "moon" makes me uncomfortable, sick. I want to run out of my room, but my father's blocking the door. And anyway, I know, deep down I know that I have to hear this.

" 'By the light of the moon I curse you,' she said. 'I curse you and your firstborn child.' "

With his free hand, my father clutches his stomach. He's no longer in the present; he's no longer my father; he's a crazy, curse-wielding woman from his past. I'm amazed by the transformation, and when he speaks again I can hear the woman's evil voice.

" 'When your firstborn is the age you are now, it will become an animal, like the animal that lives deep in your soul, and transform into a werewolf.' "

A werewolf?

The word bounces inside my head, inflates larger and larger, so no other word or thought has any room inside me and it's the only word my brain can recognize. Then it breaks free and ricochets off the walls of my room. The word has come alive, and it's all around us. I turn and see the Two W mascot looking at me. My father was right; I have been drawn to it, but no, no! That's crazy!

" 'The full moon will possess your child and steal its soul like you have stolen my life,' " my father says, repeating the pregnant woman's words. Then he begins to cross himself, his right hand touching his forehead, his stomach, and both sides of his chest. " 'In the name of my husband, my child, and the moon . . . I curse you.' "

When my father looks at me, it's like he's coming out of a trance. His cheeks are red, and his hair is wet against his forehead. He looks so tired I almost tell him to lie down, sleep until he forgets everything, but he's not done with his story.

"I didn't believe her, Dominy. I thought she was mad, vengeful, lashing out at me for killing her husband," he says. "I ran home and put the rifle back with the others in my dad's gun cabinet. He was still sick, so no one even knew I had been gone." His breathing quickens; the little boy is in full control of my father's body. "Shortly after I got home, my mother called for an ambulance. They went to the hospital, and my dad had his gall bladder removed," he explains. "I stayed home with my Uncle Jacob and waited and prayed to God to save my father. I told God that if he let my dad live, I would never shoot a gun again. That night I was sitting next to my dad; he was fine, and since that day I have never hunted again."

A touching story, but with one very big, gaping hole to it.

"You're a cop, Dad," I say. "You carry a gun every day."

"A gun that doesn't have any bullets," he replies. "The only time I shot a gun after that was so I could pass my police exam test and get my badge."

I had no idea. And now that I know, I wish I didn't. Weeping Water is hardly a hotbed for criminal activity, but we have our share of crime. A cop carrying an unloaded gun is just asking for trouble. Maybe my father is insane. But before I can convince him to go back on his word to God, he once again answers my unspoken question.

"I made a pact, and I'm not about to break it," he says. "Even now that this curse has come true."

Again with the curse!

"Daddy, listen to yourself," I say. "I am not a werewolf, and I'm never going to become one."

"That's what I tried to tell your mother," he says. "Suzanne, I said, it's an old wives' tale; our baby isn't going to grow up to be a werewolf."

"Mommy knew?"

Somehow this makes his story real.

"She found out while she was pregnant with you," he explains. "By that time I had forgotten about it. The man's body was never found, so I never had to admit to anyone what I had done. I kept it a secret, and after a while I tricked myself into believing it had been nothing more than a bad dream."

"But Mommy," I say. "How did she find out?"

Unease etches across my father's face like he's reliving the moment my mother discovered his secret.

"Nothing stays buried, Dominy," he says. "I tried to forget, but the thought always nagged at me, which is why I didn't marry until I was older and then I convinced your mother that she shouldn't get pregnant right away, which is what she wanted to do."

"What made you change your mind?" I ask.

For the first time my father looks at me and smiles. "I loved your mother," he replies. "She wanted a child, and I couldn't deny her such joy. The curse seemed like something in the past, something that could no longer hurt me or my firstborn, so I gave in."

Still not answering my question.

"But how did Mommy find out?"

"She had a difficult pregnancy, all throughout. About a month before she was due, she started having pains that kept her up all night, so she started to clean the house to have something to do," he explains. "I tried to stop her, make her see that it would only make her feel worse, but doing something physical actually took her mind off of the pain. Until she found my box."

"Your box?"

"When I was younger I had done research on werewolves, curses, Indians, and I had put everything I found in a metal box," he tells me. "I thought I had gotten rid of it, but she found it in the closet in Barnaby's room when we were using it for extra storage."

Once again my father is lost in the past, in a distant memory, but this time with another woman. A woman we both know and love.

" 'Mason, what is this?' " he says, repeating my mother's words. " 'Why do you have a box filled with such terrible things?' "

He sits on the chair next to my desk and leans forward, his hands clasped and hanging in between his legs, as I imagine he might have done when my mother asked him those questions, when they had that first conversation.

"It's junk. *Then why was it locked? I had to break the lock, Mason.* I didn't want you to ever find it. *Why?* Because I didn't want to worry you. *But you have worried me. Why do you have these things?* Because I've been cursed. And so has our child."

My mother's words to me have added meaning. *Remember, Dominy, you are blessed.* She completely believed the curse was real; that's why she said that to me.

I imagine she must have felt the way I do right now, that the man who has always been so rational, so steadfast and trustworthy, no longer exists. He's been replaced by a liar, a rambling fool. But I'm wrong. My mother didn't think anything he said was foolish.

"She started to scream at me in French. I had no idea what she was saying, but I knew she hated me at that moment," he says. "You see your mother was from a small village in France, outside Lyon. Her family was very superstitious. If I thought this curse could possibly be real, she knew it was inevitable. She went into labor right there, and on the way to the hospital she almost died."

I can't believe I've never heard this before. My mother believed in curses and witchcraft. She almost died before I was born. Both my parents are strangers to me.

"She recovered, of course, and you were a healthy baby. We forgot about the curse, and soon Barnaby was born," my father says, recapping our early family history. "But a few years later while she was working at The Retreat she started having nightmares."

My father doesn't have to say another word. I know exactly what kind of nightmares she had. They're all about me.

"About werewolves and killings," he describes anyway. "The nightmares got worse. They started to plague her while she was awake, and one day at work she collapsed, fell into a coma, and hasn't woken up since."

"Until today," I correct him. This comment triggers my father to turn his back on his past and to return to me completely.

"Yes, until today," my father agrees. "And that's why I know the curse has come true."

He may be convinced, but I'm not.

"This is a really interesting story, Dad, but I'm not buying it," I say. "I am cursed, I'll give you that, but only because I killed my best friend!"

For the first time my father touches me; his hands grip my shoulders tightly so I stop moving, stop shaking.

"This is why you've been changing lately. Your aggression, your outbursts, the physical changes, they've all been leading up to your final transformation," my father explains. "It wasn't a coincidence that there was a full moon on your birthday."

The pieces fit together neatly; it's just that the picture they create is so obscene I can't look at it. My father forces me to.

"That's why I wanted you home before dark, that's why I wanted to be with you—to prevent something bad from happening."

"Well, something bad did happen!" I scream. "What am I supposed to do now? Tell everyone that I turned into a werewolf and couldn't help myself from killing my best friend?!"

"You don't say anything! Do you hear me?!" my father commands. "Dominy, you didn't kill anyone."

"But Jess . . ."

"Was killed by an animal, not you!" my father stresses. "You have got to understand that!"

"Even if I do . . . even if I do believe that, Dad, how do I live with myself?" I ask. "How do I live like this?"

My father's arms feel so good around me. So comforting.

"I promise you, I'll figure a way out of this."

So suffocating.

"You've already had sixteen years to figure a way out of this, and you failed!" I spit, breaking free from his hold. My actions are so quick and harsh and final that my father doesn't try to reconnect; he simply stares at me in shock and then leaves my room without saying a word. That's it? He drops a bombshell of supernatural proportions on me and just leaves? I'm about to chase after him when he returns carrying a metal box, olive green, rectangular, with a broken lock. He places it on my bed.

"Maybe you'll have better luck."

"What is this?" I ask.

"This is everything I've accumulated so far," he says. "There's a clue in there about how to break this curse; I've just never been able to find it. Maybe you can."

This time when he leaves the room he shuts the door behind him; he won't be coming back tonight. I sit motionless for a few minutes, but curiosity wins out, as it often does, and slowly, I open the lid. I'm no longer looking inside a box; I'm looking into a mirror. A picture of a wolf is staring at me. Its fur is a glorious shade of red; its eyes are ice-gray; its fangs are bared, but it doesn't look menacing, not at all.

It just looks like an animal.

It just looks like me.

Chapter 12

Jess would definitely approve of her casket.

It's pale pink, and whatever material was used is shiny, lacquered I guess is the right word, so it has a glossy finish and looks like one big fingernail that's been drenched in several coats of pink nail polish. Instead of having the traditional carved roses on all four corners, the coffin has an embossed ribbon of cherry blossoms wrapped around the entire base. Very Japanese. Very joyful. Very Jess.

But as much as her offbeat send-off fills my heart with a bittersweet warmth, the rest of my body is shivering. It's beyond cold outside.

Inside St. Edmund's Church, where her funeral has just taken place it was like a sauna. Jess's death—or *unexplained murder* as Lars Svenson dubbed it in the *Three W*—attracted a huge crowd of mourners, gate crashers, and curiosity seekers. It was S.R.O. And the heat was on extra high because outside the temperature had finally dropped, at last making it feel like December. At least one thing feels normal.

As I sat in a pew in the front of the church, my father on my left and Caleb on my right, I felt like I was dreaming. This can't be happening, I told myself. Why was I listening to Father Charles talk about Jess as if she were dead? Didn't he know that the church doors were going to fling open any second and Jess was going to race down the aisle to sit next to me? Not that we're regular churchgoers, but when we do attend—on Christmas, Easter, and of course Ash Wednesday, the only day that you can advertise to the rest of the world how holy you are—Jess is always late. At one point I actually turned around when I heard a noise in the back of the church. Wasn't Jess. Just some other late arrival.

Now that I've had a week to consider and reflect, I know I couldn't have killed Jess. File it under *I* for Impossible. We must have been attacked by a wild animal; I blacked out, and Jess was killed. An unfortunate tragedy, a senseless act of violence, but not willful murder. It has to be that simple; there can't be any other explanation, especially not my father's hypothesis that I'm the victim of some family curse, even though it's a theory so wild and over the top that it would get Jess's approval. And so what if the wolf in the photo in my father's treasure chest and I share the same hair and eye color and look like we could be featured on *Separated at Birth: The Cross-Species Edition*? It's all nothing but a series of ludicrous coincidences.

I believe this Luba woman—or, as I've dubbed her, Psycho Squaw—said some mumbo jumbo to my father when he was a kid that freaked him out, and since he got away with accidentally killing her husband, he's given her words power as a way to pay for his crime. His guilt is his self-inflicted punishment, and that's what makes him believe this curse is real, even though there isn't a shred of tangible evidence.

And even though there's no real proof linking me to Jess's death, I need to get a better handle on sustaining my father's lie. Barnaby too. If we don't, my father will probably be tossed in jail for a number of highly criminal offenses, and we'll become orphans, wards of the state. I've convinced Barnaby that, even if he wants to tattle on me and expose my role in covering up the details surrounding Jess's death, he has to understand that his squealing will have far-reaching ramifications that will cause him to suffer just as much as I would. The look of fear on his face was guarantee enough that he'll keep quiet. Now if only my father were as easy to handle.

Ever since he confessed to me that he accidentally killed a man when he was my age and tried to convince me of the subsequent fairy-tale curse thing, he hasn't let me out of his sight. Constantly watching me, constantly texting me, constantly picking me up from school or the library or Caleb's house. But because every other parent in town thinks some sick maniac or wild boar is on the loose and their kid is going to be killed next, his actions are perceived as perfectly normal and to be emulated. They all think he's doing his duty as a father. I wonder what they'd think of him if they knew he's the real reason Jess's casket is empty. And I wonder what they'd think of me if they knew I was the last one to see Jess alive.

At one point during the service I felt Caleb's hand on my knee. I thought he was trying to console me, but he was just trying to stop my leg from shaking. Even when I'm not aware of it, I'm reacting to losing Jess, to lying about it. Too bad I don't know how to meditate, transport my mind and soul to a happier place, maybe a place where Jess and I can be together again and swap clothes and give each other makeovers. Too bad, because that skill would've come in handy so I could have tuned out the parade of speakers during the eulogy marathon.

First Dumbleavy spoke as a representative of Two W and painted a picture of Jess as the model student. It was laughable. Even her parents knew he was embellishing. Jess was a solid B student, a rah-rah girl, but only in the subjects and clubs she was rah-rah about. He did score points when he announced that this year's play, *Miss Saigon,* would be dedicated to Jess's memory. Vietnam is sort of like Japan, so I know Jess was thrilled by this news.

A few more teachers spoke, and then the mayor droned on. Finally, Archie took the podium, and I could listen again. He misses Jess almost as much as I do, and as expected he choked up a few times. Unexpectedly, he proved to be far more thoughtful than anyone imagined and ended his piece with a Japanese proverb, *kishi kaisei,* which he explained meant "wake from death and return to life." If only.

Some relatives, cousins I think, spoke next and relayed some anecdotes of Jess as a little girl. They described someone very different from the Jess I grew up with, but I figured that was because she acted one way around her family and like herself around me and her friends. They spoke of a girl who enjoyed playing baseball with her brothers and who staged impromptu arm-wrestling tournaments with her uncles. I have absolutely no idea who that girl is. Unless the prize was an all expense-paid trip to the Hello Kitty factory or free MAC products for life, there was no way the Jess I knew would ever do those things. Could it be that Jess was hiding a whole other side of herself from me? Maybe we're all like that, two separate selves living in one body. I could swear I heard Jess whisper to me that I was correct, that everybody has a secret self, but the voice disappeared when Father Charles called my name. It was my turn to speak.

Standing in front of Jess's family and our friends, I felt as empty as Jess's casket. The honey jar had finally been scraped clean, and there was nothing left inside. What could I say to these people that would make them feel better? What could I say that would make me feel like less of a fraud? Nothing. And so for about half a minute that's what I said. And half a minute of silence in church when the congregation isn't joined together in silent prayer feels like an eternity.

I looked out at the sea of faces, and they were all staring at me, willing me to speak, but I refused. Gazing at their expressions, I could tell no one knew if I had stage fright or if I was about to break down. Neither. I just didn't have anything to say. Until I saw the Jaffe twins.

They were sitting next to each other about five rows back on the opposite side from where I was seated. The only reason I noticed them was because unlike everyone else they were talking. They were looking straight at me, but their mouths seemed to be moving in unison; I guess they were talking to each other, some sort of twin-code thing, barely above a whisper. I imagined it was their private form of communication. Whatever they were doing or saying was inspiring, and finally I found the perfect thing to say.

"I'd like to tell you the story of the bee and the butterfly," I began.

Instantly, Nadine's and Napoleon's lips stopped moving, as if they knew I was talking about them.

"A long time ago on a beautiful summer day God created two creatures—the bee and the butterfly—and let them loose upon the earth," I began. "Even though they shared the same birthday and were both creatures of the wind, they didn't like each other. The bee found nothing in the butterfly that it could respect, and the butterfly found nothing in the bee that made it smile. They were furious that God had given them the same birthday, binding them together for all time."

Another glance over at the twins, and it was like they were illustrating my story perfectly. Nadine was sitting at attention, with perfect posture, while Napoleon was slouched, head tilted, as if lost in a dream.

"The bee found a place to live immediately, a well-built hive where she could live with other bees and where she found a purpose, and so she was content," I continued. "The butterfly wasn't so lucky. He flew for miles scouring the land for a place to settle, and although many places intrigued him and looked beautiful as he whizzed past, no place felt like home."

Now the twins sported new expressions. Napoleon looked heartbroken, while Nadine just looked pissed off. If I hadn't been so intrigued—along with the rest of the congregation— by where my fable was going, I would've laughed out loud at how angry she looked.

"One day as the bee was gathering pollen for her colony, she stumbled upon the butterfly. He was perched on a red rose and was enjoying the view," I said. "By now the bee was convinced that the butterfly had followed her, and she was driven mad by the prospect of having to spend the rest of her life with such an inferior companion. So while the butterfly fluttered happily on the petal of a rose, the bee stung the butterfly and watched it fall to the ground, watched its fluttering stop, and watched it die."

I honestly don't know if the tragedy of my story touched Nadine personally or if she was upset over Jess's death, but she was greatly disturbed by what I had said. Once again her lips were frantically moving; I guess she was trying to engage Nap in a dialogue, but he wasn't playing along. His lips were shut tight.

"Overcome with grief about her heinous crime, the bee picked up the butterfly with its little claws and carried him back to her hive," I finished. "And the bee stayed with the butterfly until the day she died."

Later on I told everyone that I was describing Jess and how she was really two people. She was the no-nonsense bee who had a strong foundation in Weeping Water and a deep connection with her family. But she was also the whimsical butterfly, someone who wanted to travel the world with her friends, experience new cultures, and have amazing adventures. No one knew that I had been describing Nadine and Napoleon. Except maybe the two of them.

"That was a beautiful story you told back in the church," Caleb tells me, his hand gently cradling my elbow. "Where'd you read it?"

"I made it up," I say as I toss a cherry blossom on top of my friend's casket.

"You did not," he protests.

"Did too," I reply. "I had no idea what to say when I got up there. Why do you think I stayed quiet for so long?"

The icy dirt crunches underneath our shoes as we walk back to the Sequinox.

"I dunno," Caleb replies. "I thought you were collecting your thoughts, summoning up the courage to speak in front of everyone."

I shake my head. "Nope, just searching for inspiration."

We both turn back as Jess's shiny pink casket is lowered into the ground.

"Kinda cool that Jess helped you out when you needed it," Caleb ponders, incorrectly assuming Jess was the source of my inspiration. "Guess she's your guardian angel now."

A violent wind rips through the cemetery, the scent of cherry blossoms swirling in the air like a fragrant cyclone, and we hurry into the car. Inside the Sequinox the wind is banging against the windows; it's as if Jess is trying to break through the glass, break through all the physical barriers, and make contact with me. I'm not ready yet. Not until I know exactly what happened the night she was killed. Not until I know if Jess is trying to break through so she can protect me or just the opposite.

An hour later at the repast I'm still not ready to make contact with Jess; I'm not really ready to make contact with anyone. I'm back to hiding my feelings, keeping the truth to myself, and choosing my words in my head before speaking them out loud. It's tedious, and it doesn't feel natural, but I understand it's the only way for me to keep my family and me safe.

I know this house like I know my own, so I head for the one place where I know I'll be safe on a day like this: Jess's bedroom. I'm wrong.

"Guess we had the same idea," Napoleon says as the door closes behind me.

I try to grab the door before it shuts, but I'm too late; I'm stuck. Stuck in Jess's bedroom with the butterfly.

"Yeah," I say. "Needed a little quiet time."

"Me too," Nap replies. "I've never been to one of these things before. It's harder than I expected."

He really is like a butterfly; it's amazing. He's standing still, and yet it's like I can see his flesh ripple. Like there's a layer of energy just underneath his skin that can't be controlled. He would rather be anywhere but here.

"I didn't even want to come," he confesses. "My mother made me."

Suddenly I can't fight the urge to prove that Nadine isn't the only one who has a good gut instinct. Or who knows how to put her brother in his place.

"That's a horrible thing to say," I tell him. "Why didn't you want to come? You were Jess's boyfriend."

Napoleon picks up one of Jess's many stuffed animals, a porcupine with raised needles all along its back that are merely wires wrapped in black velvet. He runs his hand over the porcupine's back, and the needles bend and snap back into place.

"Can I tell you a secret?" he whispers.

I'm not sure if he's asking me or the porcupine, but since Porcy's not going to respond, I answer for both of us. "Sure."

"I never felt like her boyfriend," he admits. "I liked Jess a lot, don't get me wrong. She was a real sweet girl, real sweet, but . . . but I just didn't like her that way." He tosses the toy carelessly onto Jess's bed with the rest of her stuffed menagerie then stares at me. "Do you know what I mean?"

Only too well. "I think I do."

Slowly, he starts to walk around Jess's bed, his long, skinny index finger tracing the curves of her footboard. I don't know if he's checking for dust or trying to be sexy.

"You see, there's somebody else," he starts, "who, you know, I really like."

"But this somebody else happens to be in love with yet another somebody else," I finish.

My voice startles Nap, maiming his confidence, since he probably thought his secret was just that, secret. He abruptly stops at the corner of her bed and clutches the wooden frame. His lips are moving again, but no sound is coming out, and I wonder if downstairs Nadine can hear him.

This time when he speaks, he can no longer look at me or even at Jess's stuffed animals; he has no courage or confidence, just words. "I'm not really sure about that."

Oh really? It sounds like the butterfly has been too busy flying all over town and not paying attention to what's going on right in front of him. Before I can say something cryptic yet obvious enough so he understands that I'm Caleb's girlfriend and have no desire to break up with him to start a new relationship with Jess's ex, the door flies open and we're interrupted.

"Here you are. Mrs. Wyatt is looking for you guys."

Archie stares at us, and because I know him so well, I know he's thinking of something to say about me and Napoleon being together behind closed doors. To prevent him from making an awkward situation even more awkward, I roll my eyes, and thankfully Archie gets the hint.

Downstairs, Mrs. Wyatt puts a plastic storage box on the dining room table. The black plastic box looks out of place amid trays of food and her good china, but she tells us that she wants to give us some of Jess's things. She knows we don't need mementos to remember her daughter, but she wants each of us to have a keepsake. When she looks into the box she starts to cry. No one makes a move toward her; she's looking at her dead daughter's possessions, so this is expected. It would have been nice if Mr. Wyatt had been at her side to put his arm around her shoulder or gently press his head against hers so she knew she wasn't alone, but he's sitting in a chair in the corner. He's clutching his tumbler of Scotch—at least I think it's Scotch—so tightly and his eyes are so glassy, it looks as if he doesn't know there are other people in the room.

Composed, Mrs. Wyatt shakes her head, giving her teased hair a little bounce, and tugs on her black dress so the hem stays below her knee. The first gift she pulls out is for Arla. It's a box of MAC cosmetics.

"Jess loved her beauty products," her mother says, beaming with pride.

"Yes, she did," Arla agrees. "I'll think of her every time I mix 'n match my eye shadow and my lip gloss."

"That's my girl!"

Mrs. Wyatt hugs Arla tenderly. I push the thought from my mind that she'll never again get to do that to her own daughter.

Next, she gives a whole bunch of theater paraphernalia to Archie. Playbills from shows Jess and her family saw on Broadway when they visited New York, posters, articles, CDs, even a *Phantom of the Opera* sweatshirt. *Phantom* is Archie's favorite musical because, as he once told us, he and the phantom are a lot alike. They're both oddities and do their best to blend into the shadows of the world to remain unseen. It's an out and out lie—Archie doesn't hide from anything—but we let him have his moment and never questioned him.

Finally she pulls out a bunch of bags and hands them to me. They're filled with Jess's Hello Kitty collection—dolls, stuffed animals, key chains, a lunchbox, T-shirts, hair clips, pencils, stationery.

"Jeremy!" Mrs. Wyatt shouts. "It's time."

Jess's older brother enters the dining room carrying his sister's prize possession, a Hello Kitty wheelie suitcase that she would use whenever she slept over my house. I'm speechless. Not because I'm moved by the gesture, but because I know I don't deserve such kindness. Not from anyone and especially not from Jess's mother. And Jess's dog agrees.

Underneath the chatter a sound bubbles and rises to the surface. I know that sound very well; it's a growl. Standing in the archway is Misutakiti, Jess's German shepherd, looking exactly the way he did when I saw him in Mrs. Wyatt's car, motionless, but ready and eager to pounce. And his eyes are glaring right at his target: me.

Slowly the crowd notices the canine intruder and his disposition, and the chatter becomes hushed, then silent. Misutakiti walks toward me gracefully, each step deliberate, each step a warning, and he doesn't stop until he's right in front of me, his eyes peering into me as if he knows what role I've played in his beloved owner's disappearance. As if he knows more than I do. And whatever he knows calls out for revenge.

The growl deepens, and white foam appears around his mouth, seeping out the sides. Suddenly Misu jumps forward and lunges for me, paws clawing, mouth open and teeth bared, eyes glaring with murderous intent. I scream and jump back, sending a lamp flying through the air. Misu falls into the wall next to me as a glass bounces off of him and shatters on the floor. Mr. Wyatt's Scotch spills across the hardwood. Before Misu can get his footing and stage a repeat attack, Jeremy grabs his collar and drags him out to the backyard, the dog growling and barking the entire way.

Mrs. Wyatt apologizes and says Misu must have smelled Jess's scent on me and gotten upset and confused. Maybe what he really smelled was the scent of Jess's death that still clings to me.

My run-in with Misutakiti has unnerved me. Maybe it takes

an animal to recognize the presence of another animal. Maybe Misu singled me out because he knows what I've been thinking about. Maybe Misu is a lot wiser than everyone else in this town.

Ever since I got home from the funeral and the repast I've been wondering if I can confirm that I'm a . . . a . . . I can't even say it! The word clings to my throat so it can stay hidden and not face the world. But it has to come out of hiding so it can be made real and either become accepted or be proven a mere myth. I have to say the word out loud so I can hear it. And so I do.

"Werewolf."

I wait for something foreboding or important to happen, but nothing does. Disgusted with myself for giving in to such an idiotic thought, I jump off my bed and trip over my father's metal box that's jutting out from underneath my bed. Frustrated, I kick the box, and the contents spread out on the floor. Great, now I have to clean up this mess. I'm about to leave my room to get a drink when something catches my eye. It's a calendar caught in the glow of the moonlight that's streaming into my room. Picking it up I see that it's current, a calendar my father must have recently added to his collection that plots out the phases of the moon.

Sitting on the floor I look at the drawings—half-moon, crescent, gibbous, full. The full moon. It's a black-and-white drawing, so the moon looks like it does in the old horror movies Barnaby and I used to watch snuggled together in my bed. A round circle, its surface decorated with swirling gray shadows, hanging motionless in a deep black sky, unmoving but filled with some kind of power.

Staring at it is like being lured into a trance, but I'm not frightened because this is a familiar feeling. I've felt this before, right here with the moonlight invading my room and while walking near the hills with Jess on our way to my house to celebrate my birthday, a celebration that never took place. The moon uses its power and makes my body start to burn. It doesn't feel like scorching flames or as if I'm on fire; the feeling is more like I'm glowing from within. The moon has switched on a light inside of me, and I've suddenly been turned into the person I was born to be. The frightening part is that I don't know if that person is someone good or someone evil.

My windows rattle as another violent wind erupts outside. The glass of the windowpanes shuddering in fear or delight, I have no idea. What I do know is that the truth is close to being exposed; it's trying so hard to be unlocked, recognized. I look at the calendar and see that the next full moon is in three weeks.

The metal box clinks loudly as I shut it.

Three more weeks.

Let the waiting begin.

Chapter 13

Patience is highly overrated.

It's a prerequisite for saints, a learned skill for archeologists, and a bonus for people waiting in line at the DMV. But for people who want to find out if some crazy woman put a curse on their heads, patience is elusive. I thought I was going to absolutely lose my freaking mind waiting, but "three more weeks" has finally turned into "three more days." Three more days until December 26, the night the full moon returns. At least that's the day *after* Christmas; otherwise I might find a very different kind of gift hiding under my tree.

Even though I told my father it would be in poor taste to have a tree this year, he insisted. Surprisingly, Barnaby agreed with me. Jess always made a fuss over him, treated him like an equal and not like her best friend's annoying little brother, so I guess he wanted to honor her death in a small way. But we lost the battle.

"Christmas, after all, was Jess's favorite holiday," my father reminded us. "If we don't celebrate, it would be like we were forgetting her."

I could've argued that point with my father, but I let it slide. No matter what I do, I can't forget Jess. Staring out the window of the school bus, I see Jess waiting on every corner. I turn to the empty seat next to me, and I can see her there fiddling through her school bag, looking for something that she probably never put there in the first place. No one has sat next to me since Jess died because they all know they can't take her place. Archie and Arla live on the other side of town and take a different bus into school, so I'm alone until I get into class. Only one more half day before our Christmas break. About four hours. If I can survive that long.

I know that I'll see Jess walking down the hallway and sitting in geometry. I have since the day she died. In fact, she's the first thing I think about when I wake up and the last thing I think of when I fall asleep. She's in my dreams; she's in my conversations; she's in the pauses when I'm not speaking. It's like she's inside of me and I can't separate myself from her, like a possession, like I'm being haunted.

Hunched over the toilet in the girls' room I lift the lid of the bowl and grip it tight with two hands. My eyes shut as I feel my face stretch, and my breakfast splatters into the water. The second time the mixture of bile and partially digested food erupts from my stomach, my throat burns from the acid, and my body shakes uncontrollably. The third time I wretch, nothing comes out of me. My eyes are filled with water, so when I open them my vision is blurry, but I can still see a thin strand of saliva extending from my lips to the contents of the bowl. There's no doubt about it; I'm connected to this filth. We're one and the same.

With one hand I flush and watch the disgust that was once part of me disappear. I wish it meant that now I'm clean, but I know that isn't true.

Still hunched over, one knee pressing into the hard, cold tile of the bathroom floor, I pull on the roll of toilet paper, and, without tearing off a piece, I wipe my mouth. I rip off some paper and wipe the sweat off my forehead and the back of my neck, then toss it all into the bowl and give it another flush.

The mirror over the sink takes up the entire length and width of the wall, so I have no choice but to look at myself. I expect to see a tarnished version of myself, uglier, unkempt, like I got carried away and spent the night partying. I don't expect to see a wolf.

It only lasted a second, but it was there, either a reflection of my true spirit or my screwed-up imagination. The animal looking back at me was majestic and powerful and familiar. It was covered in a coat of thick red fur the same color as my hair, and when it tilted its head and looked directly at me, I could see that our eyes were the same unusual shade of blue gray. But the eyes of this animal were more different than just their color would suggest; they had powers. They pierced right through me, and this wolf knew the truth about me that I've yet to discover.

The cold water feels good splashing against my warm skin, washing away the image or my memory and making me return to reality. After I turn the faucet off I let my head hang, let the water drip off my face into the sink, watch the single droplets connect with one another to create something larger so they don't have to travel down the sink alone. So they have someone to be with when they enter the darkness. I want that. It hits me like a hard, unexpected slap to my face that I cannot do this alone. I know I have my father, but he's my father; I'm supposed to stand behind him as he paves the way for me or he's supposed to watch me run off into the world from a safe distance behind me. He's not supposed to walk with me by my side, and that's what I need now, now that time is running out. I silently count to three and promise myself that at the end I'll stand up and look in the mirror at the only person I can count on, the one person who will come with me on this journey wherever it may lead.

"Nadine!"

She's in two places at once, in the mirror and behind me to my left. Just like the wolf, she's staring at me, not in surprise or in judgment, and I think I may have found a travel companion.

"Sorry," she says. "I heard you in the stall and was trying to give you some privacy."

My eyes glance down to the floor, not because I'm embarrassed, but because I want to see if she's wearing those orthopedic white sneaker-shoes she wears at The Retreat. Thankfully, she's swapped them for a pair of fleece-lined suede boots. Could be UGGs, but I don't see Nadine as the trendy type, so I'm pretty sure they're knockoffs. They're cute though, sort of a pale blue, a few shades lighter than her blue khakis.

She's tucked her pants into her boots, and she's wearing a body-hugging sweater, almost the same blue as her boots with white snowflakes on it. Her frizzy hair is pulled back into a ponytail, and her face looks fresh and unblemished and inviting. She looks different. Or maybe it's the first time I've really looked at Nadine for who she is and not the person I judged her to be.

"Yeah . . . having a rough morning," I confess.

Nadine smiles, but doesn't say anything. With her fist she bangs on the hand towel dispenser twice to produce a sheet of the brown, heavy-duty paper, holds it under the faucet in the sink, the one next to the one I just used, and wets it. She folds it twice then turns to me.

"Hold still," she says.

I don't have a chance to move before Nadine folds the wet towel around some strands of my hair and runs it down to the tips. She holds my hair away from my shoulder, careful not to get my shirt wet. I have no idea what she's doing, but she's doing it with such command that I don't consider interrupting her.

"Hold your hair back next time," she says, brushing my

hair back into place. "You might be aiming for the bowl, but vomit has a mind of its own."

Gross, but honest. And that's exactly what I need right now.

"Thank you," I reply.

Without moving closer to the garbage can, Nadine tosses the rolled up wet paper and makes a perfect shot. As she washes her hands, her eyes bounce off the mirror and look right at me. "Dominy, I don't want to pry into your business," she starts, "but is this something you do often?"

"I'm too vain to be bulimic," I laugh. "All that constant puking turns your teeth gray."

"And puffs up your cheeks so you look like a very industrious chipmunk on the last days before hibernation," she adds.

Leaning into the counter, Nadine laughs and looks so much younger than the matronly girl who squeaks down the hallways of The Retreat, clutching her clipboard to her chest. So much more like someone who could be a friend. And who doesn't need a friend who isn't too squeamish to wipe off stray vomit from your hair?

"It's because of Jess, isn't it?" Nadine asks.

I nod my head. "I know you didn't know her that well," I reply clumsily.

"Just because I volunteer at The Retreat doesn't mean I'm used to people dying," Nadine states. "No one ever gets used to that."

"I didn't mean to imply that," I say defensively. "It's just . . . oh God I don't know what I meant. I'm sorry."

"Nothing to be sorry about. I'm the new girl; I totally understand I have to earn my keep," she responds. "And your trust."

Do I tell her what I'm thinking? Do I confide in her? Do I share with her all the impossible thoughts and ideas banging around inside my head? Yes. I just told the universe that I didn't want to take this journey on my own, that I needed a trustworthy companion, sort of a nuJess, and the next thing I know Nadine pops up. Can't be coincidence; has to mean much more than that. Yes, I want to take this leap and share everything with her, unburden myself so I don't feel so sickeningly alone. I open my mouth to speak, but before the words come out we get company.

"Archie!" Nadine cries. "This is the girls' room!"

"I know!" he replies. "The lack of urinals kind of gives it away."

"Just because you're gay doesn't give you carte blanche to burst in here without any warning!" Nadine roars.

Ignoring Nadine's protest, Archie walks right up to me. "Are you all right?"

"Yeah, I'm fine, thanks," I answer.

"I saw you come in here, and I've been waiting outside for like fifteen minutes," he sputters. "I know it takes you girls forever to go and, you know, freshen up and do the lady thing, but seriously how fresh do you need to be? It's only a half day!"

I look at Archie and then Nadine. They're perfect.

"Could the two of you meet me after school?" I ask.

"Are you going to keep me waiting again?" Archie shoots back.

"Shut up," I say. "Yes or no?"

Archie's response comes immediately, Nadine's a few seconds later, but they both consent to my request.

"Good," I reply. "Meet me in the library after the final bell."

"Ooh, that sound positively clandestine," Archie jokes. "Like you're going to lure Nadine and me into some crazy web of mystery and intrigue."

He has no idea how right he is.

At two minutes after one I'm sitting in a far corner of the library tucked away in the reference section that no one uses anymore. Who needs a vintage encyclopedia when you have access to the Internet? The sounds of eager students leaving the school ready to start their Christmas vacation fill up the halls and spill into this secluded area. Their happy sounds are muffled, not part of my life, not until my waiting period is over. But hopefully in a few more minutes I won't have to wait alone.

Archie arrives first, acting as if he's auditioning for a spy movie. He slowly comes around the corner and then presses his body close against the wall, every few seconds whipping his head to the left, as if convinced that he's been followed.

When he approaches the table, I say, "Will you sit down?"

"With my back to the door?" he replies in a faux British accent. "Do you take me for an amateur?"

Before he sits down, Nadine appears, looking a bit nervous and nothing like a wannabe spy. Her lace is a lot straighter than ours, so she's afraid of getting caught. She hasn't yet figured out that Mrs. O'Delia, the head librarian, is almost completely deaf and takes her hearing aids out before the school bells ring. Nadine also doesn't know that Mrs. O'Delia retires this year and refuses to stay at her post a second longer than necessary. She's put in forty-seven years of service, and she's done.

"Ma'am, you can chillax," Archie says, speaking in his normal voice again. "Nobody tailed us."

"Sorry," Nadine replies. "I get nervous when I break the rules, though it isn't like we're doing anything that could get us into trouble. Right?"

I shake my head. "Not unless reading is no longer fundamental," I say, holding up a thick volume of the *Encyclopedia Britannica*. "I just wanted a place where we wouldn't be overheard."

"Should I do a sweep for bugs?" Archie deadpans.

"Quit it with the spy talk," I say.

"Yes, ma'am."

"And stop calling everybody ma'am," I add.

"Yes, sir."

Finally, Nadine laughs, and I wonder how long it will take for me to turn her laughter into gasps of horror. Maybe I should back out? Maybe this was an incredibly stupid and foolish idea? Thinking that anyone other than me and my father could even entertain the idea that supernatural forces are at work right here in the heartland of America. But no, I made the decision to confide in them; I have to follow through. Enough of this back-and-forth ambivalence; I have to choose something and stick with it no matter what the outcome.

"Thanks for meeting with me," I start. "I, um, have something . . . extremely important to share with you."

"Me too," Archie interrupts, pulling something out of his backpack. "Want a brownie?"

"Archie, please!" I cry.

"Oh I'd love one actually," Nadine says, grabbing one from Archie. "Did you make them yourself?"

"Nope, The Worm's mother always bakes brownies on half days," he explains. "Dom?"

"No, thanks, I'm not hungry," I reply. "I'm trying to share some important news with you."

Jovial expressions turn serious and then confused when I hold up the encyclopedia volume.

"Today's secret meeting is brought to you by the letter *L*?" Archie asks, chewing on a huge chunk of brownie.

I open up the volume to the page that I previously earmarked so they can see the word that I'm not yet brave enough to say out loud in their presence.

"You want to share with us the history of Lycra?" Nadine asks.

"Oh my God, I love Lycra!" Archie shouts. "I bought a pair of jeans with just five percent Lycra in them. Ladies, you have no idea the difference five percent of Lycra can make; it's like getting away with wearing leggings without the rest of the school beating you up."

"Not Lycra!" I scream. "The word before it."

Nadine and Archie peer in closer to the open page, scouring the text to figure out what I'm talking about.

"Lycanthropy?" they ask simultaneously.

A deep breath escapes from my nostrils. I'm so tense my lips are clamped shut. I inhale and exhale rapidly a few times, because I'm nervous and I need to work up the courage to speak. "Yes."

"Why did you bring us here to discuss . . ." Archie looks at the page again. "Lycanthropy?"

"Because . . . because that's what I have."

Archie looks perplexed, but I can tell that Nadine understands. At least she understands the words I've just spoken.

"You think you're a werewolf?" she asks.

"A what?!" Archie cries.

"I'm not sure," I say meekly. "But there's a very good possibility that I am."

After a slight pause filled with ear-shattering silence, the conversation resumes.

"Dom, that's ridiculous!" Archie cries. "And not even that funny. Is there like a punch line that I'm missing? Some really obscure eighties movie reference or something? 'Cause I just don't get it."

"There's no punch line," I reply. "Just the truth about who I am or at least who I might be."

I know it's only my imagination, but it sounds as if the clock in the library is actually a ticking time bomb. Someone or something is going to spontaneously combust if I don't make them understand everything, and quickly.

"It all has to do with the curse," I blurt out.

My two friends, one old and one new, look at each other, their expressions changing rapidly and ranging from disbelief to fear. They look exactly how I feel. That is until Nadine starts to laugh again, louder than I've ever heard her.

"Now I get it! This is some hazing ritual you guys perform on the newbie," she declares. "Where's the webcam? This is being streamed live to everybody's e-mails right? Or do you have a fan page on Facebook where everybody can download you pulling a fast one on me?"

I reach out to grab Nadine's hand, but when I do she flinches. Can't blame her; she thinks I'm playing her, setting her up to be Two W's latest fool. "No, Nadine, I swear to you this isn't a joke," I say. "I'm serious. I think someone put a curse on me."

"Dominy!" Archie finally says. "Since when have you become delusional?"

"I know it sounds crazy."

"Crazy?!" Nadine cries. "Talk like this will get you thrown into The Dungeon."

Okay, now who's talking crazy? "The dungeon?"

"Official name is the First Ward," Nadine shares. "But unofficially the staff at The Retreat calls it The Dungeon, complete with initial caps."

"Part of me seriously doesn't want to know why," Archie says. "But the other part will absolutely not rest until I know how the First Ward got its nickname. Spill it, Jaffe."

She's reluctant to reveal classified information, but she relents. "Three floors below the main level is an area reserved for the true, well, the truly disturbed," she explains. "The criminally insane, mega-violent patients, they all live down in the proverbial padded cell that's locked with a deadbolt so the psychopaths can't get in contact with the, um, more normal population."

For a moment I don't believe Nadine. I've been going to The Retreat for years; certainly I would have heard about such a place. But she isn't laughing or smiling or amending her comment with a lame "just kidding." She's serious.

"Right below where my mother sleeps is a dungeon?"

It's Nadine's turn to sigh deeply before she speaks. "Figuratively speaking, yes."

"Oh my God, have you ever been down there?" Archie asks the same question I'm thinking.

She shakes her head. "Strictly off-limits to volunteers and visitors," she replies.

Before I can dwell any further on the secret lair that lies underneath my mother's hospital room, Archie gets us back on track.

"So, Dominy, let me get this straight," he begins, once again speaking like a Brit. "You asked us here so you can confess that you think you're a werewolf because someone put a curse on your head?"

"Correct," I confirm, not even bothering to tell him to drop the accent.

"Absurd," Archie counters.

"Let me explain, and you won't think it's so absurd after all."

Crossing his arms, Archie leans back in his chair and scrutinizes me harshly before speaking. "What do you say, Nay?"

Shrugging her shoulders, Nadine replies, "Well, we already missed the bus."

That's enough for Archie. "You got three minutes, Robineau. Go."

A minute ago I didn't think I'd have the courage to share everything with them, but now my father's story pours out of me as simply as if I had lived it. Uninterrupted, I convey what my father told me—secret hunting trip, accidental shooting, vindictive pregnant woman, curse of the firstborn. I can't tell if they believe me or think that I'm still playing some sort of practical joke.

"And that's why she put a curse on my father's head," I say, wrapping up the tale. "A curse on his firstborn child, me, so she could destroy his child's life the same way he destroyed hers."

When I'm finished we're all speechless. Did I just make the biggest mistake of my life trusting these two? Did I just ruin any chance I had of convincing them to join me on this journey to wherever it might lead? Did I just seal my fate and condemn myself to being known as the village idiot?

"That is absolutely the best story ever!" Archie exclaims. "It should be front page of the *Three W!*"

Or did I just become Lars Svenson's next headline.

"No!" I shout. "No one can know about this except us."

"Unless we change all the names to protect the innocent," Nadine suggests.

"Dom's the only innocent one in the story," Archie points out. "Her father's a juvenile delinquent, and prego is a vindictive bitch! Seriously Joan Crawford and Joan Collins all rolled up into one."

Clearly Nadine doesn't get the specifics of Archie's gay references like I do, but she gets the gist of his comparison. She also gets the gist of the crazy woman's actions.

"Well, can you really blame this woman?" she asks. Even if it wasn't intended to be a rhetorical question, it turns into one, because neither Archie nor I respond. "C'mon, think about it! You're pregnant, out with your husband on a hunting trip, and before you know it he turns into the day's bounty instead of some deer. What mother-to-be wouldn't want some kind of revenge?"

This is amazing! I'm not going to have to go through this alone. "So you believe me, you believe that I'm cursed!"

"No, not at all," Nadine replies. "In fact, it's the stupidest thing I've ever heard."

So much for finding a new soul mate.

"I understand why this woman would put a curse on your dad's head, and she probably imagined that she was successful," Nadine explained. "But no, I do not believe that you really are cursed. That stuff's not real."

She sounds just like me when I first heard the story. I bet in a day or so she'll come around. Archie, of course, comes around a lot sooner.

"I believe it," Archie declares.

"You do not!" Nadine scoffs.

"I do too! For the past several months Dominy hasn't been acting like herself. She's been angry, aggressive, violent, not the frilly Domgirl we all know and love," Archie details. "And let us not forget the hair spurt incident."

"So her hormones were out of whack and she got some unsightly hair on her upper lip," Nadine says. "Big deal."

"You both know about that?!" I shriek.

"It happened in my house," Nadine reminds me. "The lighting's not great in my basement, but, Dom, you practically had a moustache. If Caleb hadn't been so freaked out thinking we had a rat infestation, he would've noticed it too."

"So you see it really does make sense," I declare. "My body was starting to change as the day of the curse got closer."

"And when exactly was that day, Dominy?" Archie asks.

Here comes the tricky part. Asking them to believe in a wild story is one thing. Asking them to accept that it may be connected to Jess's death is another.

"My sixteenth birthday," I reply warily. "The same age my father was when he killed that man."

Before Nadine speaks, I can feel the silence invade our space. It's not just that we're probably the only three students left in the school; it's the feeling you get just before your innocence is taken away, just before you hear your first bad word or the first time you see something sexual in a movie. You can never go back; you can never return to who you were before you were soiled. That's how I feel right now. And that's how Archie and Nadine are going to feel once she asks the question she's contemplating.

"Isn't that also the same day Jess was killed?"

There's no backpedaling; there's no starting over or calling
for a time-out. I have to move forward. That's the only way
I'm going to reclaim my life and my sanity.

"Yes."

It takes a moment for the implications of this one word to
sink in. But soon they do.

"Dom, what are you saying?" Archie asks in a soft, scared
voice.

I close the book in front of me. If I'm going to continue, I
have to do it on my own. Even if Archie and Nadine and
everybody else in the world turn their backs on me and leave
me to fend for myself. I owe it to my best friend.

"I killed Jess."

"Dominy!" Archie screams. "That isn't possible!"

I reach out to grab his hands, but he slaps my hands away.
Awkwardly, I fold my hands and place them on the table.
"Archie, I think it's the truth," I plead. "I don't remember
much about that night, but I do know I was in the hills with
Jess on our way to my house. Then it all gets cloudy, and the
next thing I know I'm awake and Jess is lying next to me . . .
dead."

Fists clenched, arms stiff, Archie jumps up. Nadine has to
grab the back of his chair to stop it from toppling over. He
talks while circling the table. "That . . . no! That can't be
true! You're just upset because she died on your birthday,"
he stammers. "The police said an animal killed Jess."

"And who's in charge of the police, Archie?" I remind
him. "My father made it all up because that animal was me."

Suddenly I'm reminded of geometry class because the three
of us—me, Archie, and Nadine—are forming a triangle. I
have no idea what kind; that's not important. What is important is that we're three separate people who have been joined
together by the same continuous line. They may not believe
what I've said, they may hate me, but they know as much as

I know, so that means we're all connected. Which means the next few days will be bearable.

"So your father actually believes this curse is true?" Nadine asks.

"He does."

"But there's part of you that still doesn't," she adds.

Like I've always said, she's got incredible instincts. "Even if I am this thing, this werewolf that this woman cursed me to become before I was born," I reply, "I just don't think I could do something so horrible to my best friend."

Suddenly, I'm yanked up out of my chair. Archie lifts me up by the shoulders. "That's it!" he cries. "If you are this thing, this she-wolf or whatever, then *you* didn't do anything. This creature did."

He sounds just like my father. "I know, Archie, I get that, but regardless, Jess is still dead."

My tears come at the same time as Archie's. Four lines of silent sadness. "I know, Dom, but at least we'll know what happened to her and . . ." Before I can interject, Archie cuts me off. "And we'll know that you had nothing to do with it. It wasn't you; it was this curse."

We hug tightly, and I'm acutely aware that Nadine is watching us. She doesn't look jealous, but I don't know exactly what she's feeling or thinking. When she speaks, she makes her thoughts very clear.

"If this is true, and that's the biggest *if* in the history of ifdom," she says, "you do realize that being a werewolf isn't a one-time event?"

My fingers graze over the hard cover of the encyclopedia. "I'm fully aware of that, Nadine," I reply.

"And when's the next full moon?" she asks.

"Day after Christmas," I reply.

"So the werewolf inside of you could rise up and strike again," Archie announces.

"It could," I say.

Even though I'm in the company of these two, I've never felt more alone in my entire life. Maybe this was just a colossal mistake; maybe I should have weathered the storm on my own? Maybe I should have just kept my mouth shut? No, very little is accomplished alone, very little can be achieved when you act like you don't need help or guidance or support. I did the right thing. And once again Nadine does something that offers me confirmation.

She comes around the table and grabs both Archie and me by the hand. The triangle has become a circle with no beginning and no ending. "Well then, in three days we'll find out if this Indian woman's curse really has power and has indeed come true," Nadine says firmly.

It's only later that night as I'm about to fall asleep that I realize I never mentioned Luba by name or that she was an Indian.

Chapter 14

"I don't trust Nadine."

Archie can't respond immediately because he's too busy chewing two-thirds of a snowman cookie. He brought over a tin filled with an assortment of holiday cookies his mother made for our private Christmas Eve gathering. Gingerbread men, sugarcoated snowflakes, Santa and Mrs. Claus, and, of course, vanilla-dipped snowmen complete with chocolate top hats. She also made oatmeal raisin reindeer cookies, but Archie picked those out of the tin thinking it might be kind of weird to eat reindeer in light of the story about my father and the curse. When his mother asked why he was taking out the reindeer, Archie said that I was a vegetarian. His mother is a member of PETA, so she totally bought it.

When he swallows he finally answers. "What do you mean you don't trust Nadine?" he asks, waving the plump bottom-third of the snowman cookie in my face. "She's part of Operation Big Red."

Now I can't respond immediately because I don't know what Archie's talking about. "What's Operation Big Red?"

"You," Archie replies.

"Me?!"

"Yeah," he says as if his comment made sense. " 'Cause you're half Little Red Riding Hood and half the Big Bad Wolf. Operation Big Red."

Makes a lot of sense actually. But where was I? "I don't care if Nadine's a part of . . ."

"Operation Big Red." Archie finishes my sentence and the snowman cookie simultaneously.

"Yeah, that," I say. "I don't trust her."

Sitting on the bar stool at my kitchen counter, Archie swivels from left to right. In the middle of the return trip, he stops himself only long enough to look at me and ask, "Why not, Domino?"

"Because of what she said," I say.

Another swivel to the right and back again. "What did she say?"

This time when he's facing me, I reach across the kitchen counter and grab his wrist. I get a flashback of when I grabbed Jess, when I was so close to breaking her wrist. Ashamed, I let go of Archie so he can keep swiveling and hope that he doesn't realize what memory was just floating through my mind. Since he just popped a whole snowflake in his mouth, I'm guessing he doesn't.

Chewing, Archie asks, "Are you having second thoughts about confiding in her yesterday?"

Sitting on the stool next to Archie, I turn him so he's facing me. "Yes," I reply. "But only because I think she's hiding something."

"Maybe it's just that you'd rather be, you know, a lone wolf?"

"Archie!" I shout, slapping him on the shoulder.

"Sorry, Dom," he says, laughing. "I'm still not convinced that this curse thing is legit. I mean it's fun in a bizarre 'you might be suffering from post-traumatic stress' sort of way, but I just don't see you as the wolf type. Perhaps a peacock—you do pride yourself on looking pretty."

I used to also pride myself on my conviction. Once I made a decision, I stuck with it; I didn't flip-flop like some shifty politician. But my opinion of Nadine is constantly changing. I think she's freakish; I think she's cool. I think she's my soul mate; I think she's my enemy. I don't know what to think about her. So I'll let Archie decide for me.

"What did I tell you about the woman who put the curse on my father?" I ask.

"That she saw her husband get shot, she was pregnant, and she put a curse on your father's head," he recaps.

Good, just what I thought. But I need to be sure before I continue. "What tribe was she from?"

"Tribe?"

"Was it the Arapaho?"

"Oh! Pregnant curse lady was a Native American Indian!" Archie exclaims. "You never mentioned that."

Perfect! "Then how do you explain what Nadine said before she left?" I ask. "She referred to the pregnant woman as an Indian."

"She did?"

"Yes!" I scream. "Right before you both left, she said something like, 'In three days we'll find out if this Indian woman's curse really has any power and if it really will come true.' I heard it."

"I didn't," he replies.

Not so perfect! "What do you mean you didn't hear it?"

"Just what I said," he replies, reaching for a gingerbread man. "I didn't hear her say that."

"Well, she did," I confirm. "And how could she possibly know that the woman who cursed my father was an Indian if I didn't mention it?"

"Well, c'mon, Dom, what else could the woman be?" he asks, biting off a gingerbread leg. "Think about it. We're surrounded by reservations; Indians are superstitious people.

Nadine is smart; she put two and two together and came up with four."

More logic. Quickly followed by speculation.

"But are you sure you didn't mentally slip the word into her sentence yourself 'cause you want a reason not to like Nadine?" Archie asks.

I'm shocked. Not because Archie is off the mark, but because he may have hit a bull's-eye.

"Archibald Angevene, why would you say something like that?"

"Because, Dom, I wouldn't call you a mean girl," Archie says. "But you are pretty and popular and pert."

"Pert?"

"I needed another *p* word, and that's all I could think of."

"Will you be serious?" I ask. "Do you really think I'm looking for a reason not to like Nadine?"

Before Archie can contemplate reaching for another cookie, I shut the lid on the container. No more distractions, just answers.

"It's possible," he hedges. "I mean, she's an outsider, she's super smart, and she's closer to the 'before' pictures in a 'before and after' makeover photo spread, and, let's face it, that's kind of icky to a girlie girl like you."

Can Archie really think I'm that superficial?

"Plus there's the whole Napoleon thing," he adds.

Nope. He was just leading up to the more substantive material.

"We all know Jess loved Nap; Nap's into you instead," Archie spells out. "So you're protecting Jess by not liking Nap and by extension not liking—or not trusting—his twin, Nadine."

Hmm. Napoleon does annoy me, especially after he told me that he had to be convinced to go to Jess's funeral, so maybe I'm displacing my dislike for Napoleon onto Nadine because I don't want to give Napoleon the satisfaction of knowing that he irks me. Kind of complicated, yet straight-forward at the same time.

"You're right. Nadine must've drawn her own conclusion about Luba's ethnicity. How else could she know anything about this crazy woman?" I decide. "Who, by the way, I've dubbed Psycho Squaw."

"Holla!" Archie beams. "Love the label even though it's très politically incorrect."

"I don't mean to be offensive or, you know, malign an entire race or anything," I protest. "Just denounce one mentally unstable woman."

"And from what I've heard about this Luba woman, your nickname is spot on," Archie says. "So anyway, it looks like Nadine made a lucky guess, end of story. Can we *now* exchange Christmas gifts?"

Archie pulls my gift out of his bag and places it on the counter. The wrapping is as swanky and nontraditional as I've come to expect from him. Fuchsia metallic paper and a hot pink bow that looks quite expensive. The gift does not.

"Wow, Arch, um, this is . . . nice," I stutter. "I mean what girl wouldn't want a notebook for Christmas."

Shaking his head and tsk-tsking rapidly, Archie smiles. "I knew you'd think that!" he chastises. "It's not a notebook."

I pick up the notebook and open it so the blank pages are staring Archie in the face.

"It's filled with lined paper, and it's got a spiral binding," I tell him. "It's a notebook."

"No," he insists. "It's a *journal*." Semantically different, but literally the same thing.

"With all the, you know, issues you've been having lately, what with Jess's death and this curse thing," he whispers, "I thought you could use a journal to write down all your feelings so they don't, you know, overwhelm you."

A cheap gift, but a thoughtful one. And practical. I have been bombarded by thoughts and feelings and emotions lately, ranging from anxious to hopeful to despondent, and until I have some real answers maybe the best thing to do is to write down how I'm feeling, sort through all the confusion with a pencil as armor. This $1.99 gift may be my salvation.

"Thank you, Archie," I say, my voice catching unexpectedly with gratitude. "It's perfect."

The combination of my words and my tone makes Archie blush. He's silent for a moment as he searches for the right way to respond.

"Now where's my gift?" he asks.

Excellent! Sentiment is useful, but only when underused.

Archie's present is tucked underneath our tree, so we move into the living room so I can retrieve it. I have to kneel on the floor and rearrange some other gifts to find it, and suddenly I'm hit with one of those powerful emotions: guilt. It seems so wrong that we should be celebrating, that we should be doing anything except mourning Jess. This should not be a house of cheer; it should be a house of remorse.

When I stand up I lose my balance and teeter a bit to the side before bracing myself by grabbing the arm of the couch. Archie's not concerned; he probably thought I was stepping out of the way so I didn't step on the ornament I dislodged from a branch when I grabbed his gift. The ornament that also happens to be my mother's favorite.

A gold satin ball with its insides scooped out to hold a family photograph. I bend down to pick it up, and the joy wafting off the photo cuts right through me; I can feel how happy we used to be, all four of us, so long ago. Tracing a finger along the black velvet bow on top of the ornament, I remember my mother saying that as long as you have happy memories, you can have a happy life. It's the first time I think my mother was wrong about something.

"I'm waiting!"

Standing behind me, Archie's got his hands on his hips, only half-serious, and I don't blame him. He deserves some

Christmas cheer even if I'm not fully convinced I'm worthy of it.

Flopping on the coach, Archie rips the gift out of my hands and proceeds to rip off the wrapping paper. Of course this is when I get second thoughts that it was a totally stupid idea. Up until now I thought it was brilliant. In fact, I picked it out in September, and I've been holding it ever since. Too late now to find something else.

"A key?" Archie asks. "To what?"

I hold up the brass key, about twelve sizes larger than normal, and tell Archie that it's the key to the town of Weeping Water. As sheriff, my father gives them out to outstanding citizens, those who have exhibited bravery or charity or creativity; I'm giving it to Archie to remind him that he possesses all three.

"It's so you'll always know that you have a home and that you belong here," I say.

Archie's mouth opens, but no words fall out. I follow his lead and don't try to fill the silence; I give him whatever time he needs. Finally, after about a minute he knows what he wants to say. It's not what I expect.

"Right before junior high I almost ran away," he admits.

I had no idea. "Why?"

He tilts his head to the side and smiles. "Think back. Do you really have to ask?"

Archie is incredibly self-assured and well liked for an out-of-the-closet albino, but thinking back I do remember a time when he was considered by a huge number of our classmates to be nothing more than the freaky-looking gay kid. He's become so much more confident since we first became friends in grammar school, I forget about that unhappy part of his past.

"I'm sorry, Archie. I'm shocked," I reply honestly. "What made you change your mind and stay?"

"The day before I was going to run you invited me to your

end-of-summer Labor Day party," he says. "It reminded me that I had friends and I wasn't alone."

"Well . . . I'm glad I got you to change your mind," I say, trying unsuccessfully not to cry.

Holding up the key, Archie replies, "After that invite this is the nicest gift anyone's ever given me."

Our hug is everything a hug between friends should be, easy, comforting, and safe; it's nothing like the hug my father gives me later on when he comes home. His is awkward, rushed, and disturbing. Almost as disturbing as how easy it is for him to lie.

"I'm not lying for your sister, Barnaby," I overhear my father say. "I'm protecting her."

One inch closer and I'm at the edge of the living room. They're both sitting on the floor surrounded by a crinkled sea of ripped wrapping paper, the result of opening up some Christmas gifts early. My father's back is to me, and, if Barnaby were looking straight ahead instead of at the floor and the new electronic gadget, PS 20 something or other, he just got from Santa, he would see me. But he's too upset and confused to make eye contact with anyone.

My father's voice is gentle and firm, and still Barnaby doesn't meet his gaze. "I've already questioned Dominy, like I would question any potential witness," he says. "But she can't remember anything about that night. It's a blank."

My father brushes away my brother's bangs with his fingers, and their resemblance intensifies. I remember seeing photos of my dad when he was a kid, and Barnaby looks just like him. Same brown hair, same blue eyes, same wrinkled forehead. Now there are so many wrinkles on his forehead it looks like it might explode.

"But she already confessed to killing Jess!" my brother shouts.

"Of course she did," my father answers in an eerily calm

voice. "Because that's the only thing that made sense to her at the time."

The wrinkles slowly disappear, and I can tell that Barnaby is trying to accept what my father just told him. As much as he sometimes hates me and as frustrated and scared as he is right now, he doesn't want to believe that his big sister's capable of killing someone.

"Then what happened out there?" Barnaby asks.

I see my father grab Barnaby's hands and hold them tight; they look so small next to my father's. "We just don't know, Barnaby," he lies.

Fighting the urge to cover up the nativity scene under the tree to protect the residents of that holy barn from such blasphemy, I retreat into the kitchen. My father was so convincing I almost believed him. Sadly I realize that since he's been lying since he was my age; he's become a master. Not only a master at lying, but at upholding tradition as well.

My father never wanted us to spend Christmas at a nursing home—and I'm sure my mother would second that decision—so we always visit her on Christmas Eve. An hour later that's where we find ourselves. And as I've said The Retreat is a first-rate facility, a go-to stop for those who need rehabilitation of the body and the mind; but it is what it is, and what it isn't, is a happy place to be on a holiday. By the look on Essie's face, she shares my opinion.

The bulk of the holiday decorating budget seems to have crash-landed on her desk, which makes for a particularly frightful sight. Sloping strands of braided garland in neon red and green hang from the edges of her desk, which itself is covered in a layer of fluffy cotton in an attempt to create a snowy panorama. Amid the puffs of cotton are lopsided trees, dancing elves, forest critters, snowmen and their snow families, and an endless variety of reindeer. Obviously Essie isn't a member of PETA. The deer make me think of my father, so when I see a few toppled over, half-hidden in the cotton drifts, I don't think that they're simply exhausted from too much holiday cheer and resting; I presume they've become some teenage hunter's bounty. Such happy thoughts fill my head. Where the hell are the sugar plum fairies this year?

The wall behind Essie's desk has been turned into a giant present. It's covered in red construction paper, with two lines of black masking tape, one horizontal and one vertical, and a green bow stuck on at the point where the lines intersect. But the most miserable-looking decoration is Essie herself.

Sitting at her desk Essie is wearing a Santa hat and a green sweater that depicts a gingerbread family all holding hands, frolicking in a winter wonderland underneath a star-filled night sky. The largest star actually twinkles, so I can only assume she's stuck a battery in her bra. The problem is Essie looks like she was held at gunpoint when she got dressed to come to work.

"Hi, Essie," my father says. "Merry Christmas."

"Will be when my shift's over," she replies.

The three of us can't help but laugh at Essie's comment, but she isn't looking for any positive reinforcement. When she hands us our index cards, she looks especially surly, or perhaps it's just the contrast between her sourpuss face and the card's holiday redesign. Tonight's index card has been cut into the shape of a snowflake, and the one is written in green sparkly marker, the nine in red. There isn't a Christmas bonus large enough to make Essie do any extra work, so I'm guessing Nadine and her fellow volunteers spent hours cutting index cards into holiday shapes.

Entering my mother's room is like entering a monk's hideout after spending time in the Vatican. The only decoration on display sits on the windowsill. It's the angel that used to perch on top of our tree when my mom was alive. Well, really alive. Like my mother, the angel has blond hair; unlike my mother she's wearing a red sequined gown.

During our brief visit, my father and I take turns holding my mother's hand while Barnaby remains seated the entire time. He's never touched my mother, not once in the whole time she's been at The Retreat. He was only four when she was brought here, so his memories of her are dim and beyond his reach; to him our mother is really just a woman in a bed, nothing more. There's little connection between them, and I'm sure today's mandatory visit is a nuisance to him, not a selfless and necessary activity. Funny, I'm only two years older than Barnaby, and yet I remember my mother vividly. Honestly, I'm not sure what's worse: to be like me and miss her terribly or be like Barnaby and not remember her at all.

Less than thirty minutes later we leave. Essie is the most animated I've ever seen her in my life, I'm guessing thanks to the rum-smelling eggnog she's drinking. In between sips she hums along to some guy over the loudspeaker who's singing a very melancholy version of "White Christmas." His voice is deep and sad, as if he were trying to burrow a hole into the ground with his notes so he could hide from the holiday.

"I miss Bing, don't you?" Essie asks.

Barnaby and I look at her with blank faces.

"Bing Crosby," my father mutters to us. Then he responds politely to Essie. "He sure did have a beautiful voice."

His voice could only be considered beautiful if you want to spend the Christmas holiday with the dying. And then I get a fit of the gigglaughs so uncontrollable I can't stop, not after Barnaby shoots me a dirty look, not after Essie and my father stare at me sternly, trying to telepathically remind me that such an outburst of laughter is inappropriate. But it's incredibly appropriate; they just don't get it.

Since my life may be over in two more days, I understand that Bing in his deadly serious voice is singing his sad, pathetic song just for me.

Chapter 15

From the moment it started I wanted Christmas to be over, but it felt like the day that wouldn't end.

We all got up around the same time, not too early and not too late, and my father cooked us our traditional Christmas breakfast of French toast and Canadian bacon. Edible. I know we talked at the kitchen table, but since Barnaby carried most of the conversation, it consisted of the latest technology gadget news and how he had to keep training over the holiday break in order to keep his edge as rising star of the Two W track team. Boring.

Then we moved from the kitchen into the living room where we sat in front of the Christmas tree willing ourselves to feel the joy of the season. Failure. After accepting that this Christmas was never going to crack the top ten list of Favorite Robineau Family Holidays, we proceeded to open our gifts.

I didn't get anything spectacular or worth mentioning. Well, that's not true, I might have, but I honestly can't remember what my father and Barnaby got me. All I kept thinking was that this would be my last day on earth where I wouldn't know the truth. Tomorrow all would be revealed. Either the full moon's glow is going to transform me into something subhuman, or I'm going to have to confess to the world that I possibly committed a subhuman act without any supernatural intervention. Like I said, it was not a good day. Luckily my boyfriend has the uncanny ability to know exactly when I need him.

His kisses feel wonderful. Tender and hot and when I wrap my fingers around his bicep I can tell that he just spent an hour working out in his basement. Maybe I am inappropriate—we are in my kitchen after all—but I want to lose myself in Caleb's kisses and his touch and his body. I want to run upstairs, lock my bedroom door, and give myself to him right now. For a few seconds while Caleb responds to my deep kisses, I contemplate taking him by the hand and secretly leading him upstairs. I know that Caleb would love the idea, but I'm not sure if he would give in to the passion I know is churning in his stomach. I am the daughter of the sheriff. Though he might think he had a fighting chance if he knew Sheriff Daddy's gun shoots blanks.

"Merry Christmas, Domgirl." He sighs.

"Merry Christmas, Bells," I reply.

Caleb pushes me away and scrutinizes me like I've done something wrong. Turns out I've said something wrong. "That's Archie's name for me," he says. "You can't use it." I forgot that my boyfriend kind of has a boyfriend too.

"Didn't know Archie had dibs on it."

His expression lies somewhere between sincerity and sarcasm. "He does, so you just have to call me something else," he informs me.

"How about Christmas Bells," I declare.

I can tell from his expression that he'd prefer I come up with something more original, but luckily Caleb knows when he's going to lose a battle. He doesn't fight me; he just lets me have my way. It's nice to know that I can count on him to be stable when my world is wobbly and disorienting.

We join my father and Barnaby in the living room, and I'm

tricked into thinking we're an ordinary family. Twinkling lights on the tree, crackling Yule log on the TV, and munching cookies on the floor. We're downright traditional.

Sitting next to Caleb, his arm brushing against mine every so often out of need and not by accident, I can tell that he wants to be alone with me. My father gets the hint as well, though it takes a bit of conniving to get Barnaby to get in step with the rest of us. Finally, my father convinces my brother to join him upstairs so they can install the new wireless router he bought for us. Barnaby is reluctant to give us some privacy, but in the end he can't resist the lure of superior technology.

When we're alone, Caleb stiffens instead of relaxing, and I wonder if he's going to break up with me for acting like such a weirdo these past few months. But no, he would never do that, not on Christmas Day. Would he?

"Merry Christmas, Dominy," he says softly, handing me a beautifully wrapped box.

Green velvety wrapping paper with a piece of red string instead of a bow. Sort of Christmas meets *Jane Eyre*.

"It's beautiful," I reply.

"You're not supposed to say that until you open it," he reminds me.

As carefully as possible, I open up the package, trying my best not to damage the wrapping. It's silly I know, but it looks so pretty, it would be a crime to just tear it. When I see what it's concealing, I know I acted appropriately.

"Oh, Caleb," I gasp. "It really is beautiful."

A circle of diamonds on a beautiful silver mesh chain. Probably diamond chips, but I don't care. It's the first piece of jewelry Caleb's ever given me, the first piece of jewelry any boy's ever given me, and I know immediately that I'll treasure it forever. Just like I want to treasure this moment. And I will, but for all the wrong reasons.

"I was going to get you the one with three stars," Caleb

admits. "But Napoleon has a tattoo like that and no way was I getting you a gift that was going to remind you of him."

"Napoleon has a tattoo?" I ask.

"Yeah, three stars on his leg," Caleb explains.

"How come I've never seen it?" I ask.

"You better not have seen it," he replies as he puts the necklace around my neck and fastens it. "It's way up his left leg, top of his thigh. I've only seen it once when he was changing after gym."

I try to get a mental picture of nerdy Napoleon with an edgy tattoo, but the image doesn't materialize; the idea is ridiculous.

"I think he's embarrassed by it though," Caleb continues. "He's always trying to cover it up. Anyway, I just didn't want anything to link the two of you together."

The first kiss is quick, but the next one lasts much longer. "You have nothing to worry about," I tell him.

Reaching behind me I find my gift for Caleb and give it to him. It's not as exquisite as my necklace, but he loves it just the same.

"How'd you know I wanted a David Humm football?"

"Because you've been dropping hints since July!" I remind him.

I don't even know who this David Humm person is, but if his autograph on a football makes my boyfriend happy, it was worth all the money I spent on the thing. Watching Caleb grip the football and make believe he's going to toss a touchdown-winning pass causes the insides of my stomach to flutter. He's so handsome and sexy and mine, and I want him to know that; I want him to know without a doubt that he's loved and appreciated. Instead I prove that I'm daddy's little girl and lie.

"Can't believe I have to go on a road trip with my dad tomorrow."

To ensure that our mid-holiday absence doesn't arouse any

suspicions, my father came up with the story that we're driving to Iowa the next day to look at colleges, when in reality we'll be camping out in the wilderness to see if the full moon has any power. I'm only a sophomore, but my father is anal-retentive and a planner, so Caleb—and everyone else we told—totally believed the story.

"You really think you might go all the way to Iowa for school?" Caleb asks, as if Iowa were Indonesia.

"Doubtful," I reply. "I mean Bethany is a good school."

"And it rhymes with Bettany," Caleb says, "so you can't forget me."

I blush a little at his comment, but I'm trying too hard to follow the logic of my lies; I don't dare return his flirt. "Briar Cliff's good too, but I don't think I'd get into either."

Caleb can't hide his relief at my hypothetical academic short-comings. I don't take it as an insult, since he isn't focused on my chances of getting a highly regarded higher education, but on the fact that if I cross the state border, I'll be lost to him forever. He has no idea that there are other borders that once crossed make it much more difficult to return to the world and the life that you leave behind.

"I didn't want to disappoint my dad," I elaborate. "He's mega looking forward to this daddy-daughter road trip so we can bond."

Caleb rubs his fingers along the nape of my neck, and the unexpected movement lifts the chain of the necklace, making the diamond circle travel over my skin. It's like he's lit a match; a current of pink heat encircles me, and I sigh. Of course Caleb takes this as further confirmation that I have no intention of ever leaving him or living outside of the Weeping Water town limits. He has no idea that it's because my lies are like a fire and are about to consume me. Always on cue, Caleb is ready with the extinguisher.

"At some point on the drive you can slip in that Big Red is a good school," Caleb teases.

"What?!" I exclaim, suddenly feeling as cold as ice.

"Big Red," Caleb repeats. "David Humm is one of their legendary quarterbacks, and it's my dad's alma mater, so it's probably where I'll end up going too."

For one horrifying second I thought I had misjudged Archie and he had told Caleb all about Operation Big Red, but Big Red is the nickname for University of Nebraska, which is in Lincoln and therefore commuting distance from Weeping Water. Merely Caleb's way of suggesting that we can attend college together and never be apart. Both suffocating and sweet at the same time, but at least it isn't confirmation that Archie can't be trusted.

Caleb's hand feels so soft on one side and so rough on the other. I hold it in my hands and wonder how much longer I'll get to do just that. How much longer would Caleb want to be touched by a freak? Or worse, a murderer?

"I'll definitely slip Big Red into the conversation," I say as if I mean to keep my promise.

Truth is I never thought much about college or leaving town or leaving Caleb for that matter. I like my life the way it is—well, the way it was—so I was in no hurry to make any changes. Yes, attending college is a given, but since Weeping Water is a small town, there are really two choices you can make: become a townie or escape. As the daughter of the town sheriff I guess everyone, including myself, always assumed I'd never break free and that I would commit to walking down that unbreakable path by attending a local college. And I guess now, as the town's youngest girl murderer, I'll never break free from my inevitable death-row prison sentence.

"You have to go," I blurted out.

"What?" Caleb said, his voice all little-boy squeal.

"I'm sorry," I replied. "It's getting late, and all this college talk reminded me that I still haven't packed."

Now it was Caleb's turn to laugh. "Gonna take you all

night just to fill up your makeup bag," he said. "You and Jess carry around so much makeup all the time, you make the lunch table look like one of those makeover counters at Dillard's."

It's not until he stops talking that we both realize he used Jess's name in the present tense. There's nothing left for us to say, nothing that Caleb thinks he can say that will make me forget Jess is no longer alive, and nothing that I can think of to say that will make me forget that I'm responsible.

On my doorstep, the cold wind does its best to separate us and pull us apart. I lie to Caleb once more and tell him that I'll be fine, that I'm not upset by his mentioning Jess, that I had been thinking about her all day. That part was true; I just didn't tell him in what context. He kisses me softly on my lips, the warmth emanating from him desperately trying to win out over the cold, but the wind and the fear churning in my stomach are too much competition. I don't think he knows that he lost out. He's too innocent to believe such a thing could happen, and I'm just the opposite.

After I unplug the Christmas tree lights, my necklace is the only thing left sparkling in the room. When I turn around I'm surprised to find my father staring at me. I shouldn't be surprised, but I am. I know exactly what he's thinking; it's the same thing that's been in the back of my mind all day long. Tomorrow may be my last day of peace. When the full moon comes tomorrow night, if this curse really does control me, what kind of a life am I going to have? How will I ever live knowing each month I'm going to turn into some kind of monster? And why is Caleb knocking on our front door.

"Tell your boyfriend it's getting late," my father says, his voice no longer sweet and pleasant.

"I'm sure he just forgot something," I say.

But it's not Caleb knocking on the door; it's Nadine. Is she not only smart, but psychic too? Does she somehow know about my conversation with Archie and want to explain her unexplainable comment? Or does she really have a knack for showing up when least expected?

"May I come in?" she asks before I can even say hello.

"Sure," I reply, because I can't think of anything else to say.

I'm not sure who's more surprised when they see each other, my father or Nadine.

"Sorry, I thought I might find you alone," she stutters. Her lips continue to flutter nervously after she stops talking. The bee is a bit more like the butterfly than I thought.

"Don't mind me," my dad says, starting upstairs. "But remember, Dominy, we have a big day tomorrow."

When we hear my father's bedroom door close, Nadine finally speaks. "That's why I'm here," she whispers. "To talk about tomorrow."

So no explanation about her comment, but I'm about to get an invitation.

"If this *thing* happens like you think it might," she starts, "you're going to need a safe place to hide out."

"We thought we'd go down to The Retreat and shake things up," I joke.

"What?!"

Clearly Nadine doesn't think I'm funny.

"I'm kidding," I tell her. "My father has a plan to get us out of town. I'm not sure exactly where we're going, but we're camping out somewhere."

"You're going camping?" Nadine asks, justifiably flabbergasted.

"I know!" I reply. "Do I look like a girl who even knows how to unzip a sleeping bag?"

"Well, as my Christmas gift to you let me save you from sleeping under the stars," Nadine begins. "I think you should use my family's cabin."

Sleeping in a warm bed in a cabin is a lot nicer than sleeping in a bag out in the cold. But wait a second, my father and

I aren't going on a vacation; we're setting out on a mission. Nadine completely understands this.

"It's secluded and away from town," she adds. "So you won't be near any people on the very slim chance you do turn into this . . ."

I don't need to finish her sentence, but I do need to thank her.

"That's very nice of you," I say, genuinely touched.

"So you accept?" she asks anxiously.

"Well, I'll suggest it to my father and let you know."

She takes out a folded-up piece of paper from her coat pocket and gives it to me. "It's a map so you can find it," she explains. "There are two cabins on the property, the main house and a smaller one that was the original cabin that my grandfather built."

"Which one should we use?" I ask. "You know, if we decide to take you up on your offer."

"The main house is a lot larger," she replies, then reaches into another pocket of her coat and takes out a key. "Dominy, I really think this is the perfect solution."

When Nadine gives me the key, I could swear she's just handed me a prickly sharp needle, and I flinch. After she leaves I look at my fingers, certain that I'll see blood and a puncture wound. Nothing. Next, I hear a voice in my head congratulating me for following my instincts and confiding in Nadine. She's turned out to be trustworthy, supportive, and generous.

If all that's true, then why do I feel like I've just been stung by a bee?

Chapter 16

"I hate you two!" Barnaby yells from the backseat of the car. "Why can't I go with you guys this weekend?"

"Because you would be bored stiff, and I don't want to hear you complain nonstop for the next two days," my father replies.

We've devised the following plan: My father and I are allegedly going to Iowa to look at a few colleges, and while we're away my brother is going to stay with Arla and her dad. It's totally believable because what little brother wants to traipse around Iowa looking at colleges with his father and big sister? He doesn't even want to come with us, but now that we're pulling up in front of Arla's house, he's getting nervous.

"I won't complain," he protests.

"Barnaby, you're not coming," my father says firmly.

If his words aren't definitive enough, he gets out of the car and slams the door shut.

"This is all your fault," Barnaby seethes. "You're nothing but a BFK."

Whipping around to face him, I ask, "What's that stand for?"

"Best friend killer."

Harsh, vile, kind of clever, and yet, most likely, accurate. It takes me a moment to rebound from that comment. Actually, I take more than just a moment, and I only return from my daze when I hear my father knocking on the window.

"Come on, Dom," he instructs.

By the time I get inside the Bergeron house, Barnaby is the center of attention, like a long lost child instead of an overnight guest. Louis is telling him how he's going to challenge him to an Xbox marathon, first man whose thumbs bleed loses, and Arla is flirting with him. She's only doing it to tease him because she knows he's developed a crush on her since he joined the varsity track team of which she's a starring member, but it's still, oh what's the word? That's right, icky.

Out of Barnaby's line of vision, Arla winks at me. That wink conveys so much girlfriend-to-girlfriend information. *Don't worry; my flirting is completely harmless. Don't worry; your brother is in good hands. And don't worry; you won't want to kill yourself after spending forty-eight hours with your dad.* Well, two out of three ain't bad. By the end of our trip, I may very well want to kill myself, and it will all be because of my dad.

A few minutes later we leave a tongue-tied Barnaby and set off for our fictitious confabs with the deans of several prestigious Iowa colleges. I should be worried that Barnaby might slip and tell Arla or worse, her deputy sheriff father, about what he knows of our lies, but I'm not. I've got too much to think about. Now that it's just me and my father in the car, I don't have to keep up appearances; I don't have to act as if everything is okay and that I'm not scared out of my mind. Surprisingly, though, fear isn't the strongest emotion I'm feeling; it's anger.

When I mentioned Nadine's offer to my father, he flipped out.

"I told you not to say anything!" he screamed. "Dominy, do you realize what you've done?"

"Yes!" I said. "I reached out to my friends for help instead of following your lead and trying to handle it on my own! Look what that's done to you."

He looked so wounded you would've thought I had just told my father that I hated his guts, that I never wanted to be like him, and that everything he's done in his life was stupid and wrong and wasteful. Which is exactly what I did. I betrayed his confidence, but isn't that what he did to me by not telling me about this curse in the first place?

If only the rattling in the trunk would stop, then maybe I could think! My father is actually going to build a cage that he expects me to sleep in, just in case Luba is all-powerful and I become a werewolf. If I wounded him with my betrayal, he has royally screwed me up with his deception.

I look over at my father, youthful and handsome, and I want to scratch his eyes out. If this curse turns out to be true then it is all his fault. He's responsible, and yet he's untouched. I'm the one who suffers because he was reckless and stupid and a really bad shot. The anger travels in my blood like a disease-infected rat that's jumped into a fast-moving stream. It can't fight the current; it can't slow it down; it can only succumb to the journey. I'm about to let the poison that's building up inside of me gush out when I feel the car slow down and see my father's face. He's white.

"Daddy, what's wrong?" I ask.

He doesn't answer me; instead he looks around at the unlandscaped landscape, his eyes fearful but searching for something to emerge from the overgrowth. This must be where it happened. This must be where we were cursed.

"Is this the place?"

"Yes."

His voice is as soft as mine, and it scares me. The farther

we drive from our home, from what I know, from what's familiar, the closer we come to this unreal world where curses rule and werewolves are real. I don't like it here, and if I thought I could convince my father to turn back and go home I would make a plea, but I know any debate is useless.

About ten minutes later the trees and the brush become less dense. You can actually see beyond the first row of foliage to what lies behind it; the sight is like watching fog rise and float away or sunlight creep into a dark room. For the first time since we began our trek out here, I feel a bit hopeful. I don't even care that it might be false hope; I'm desperate for a change, a diversion, so I latch onto it.

Finally, the cabin appears in the distance. It's a solid-looking log cabin resting on the crest of a hill. The land around it is flat and unpopulated, no trees, no bushes, no flowers. It's as if the earth gave away, acquiesced to this intrusion, this foreign structure. My gut instinct—which I still haven't determined is something I should trust or ignore—is that it may not be safe, but it is formidable. Suddenly, I want to get out of this car, put some distance between my dad and me and get inside. I want the sun to set, and I want the full moon to take over so I can know. I'm done with waiting.

The path leading up to the cabin turns slightly, and out of nowhere another house materializes. Almost identical in appearance except this one is smaller, more like a bungalow. This must be the original cabin that Nadine's grandfather built. I'm no architect, but the man must've been pretty handy with a hammer and power tools, if they had power tools back then, because it looks like it was constructed yesterday.

Walking up to the house I can tell that my father is nervous. He's taking deliberate steps, casually looking around, not at the scenery, but in search of intruders. He doesn't trust anyone, not even his sixteen-year-old daughter's friend. He puts the key into the lock and turns it slowly; when we hear the click, he freezes and doesn't push the door open. Maybe he's waiting for our invasion to cause the house to explode?

"Can we, um, go inside?" I ask sarcastically. "It's cold out here."

In response he gives the door a shove, but still doesn't move. Is he once again waiting for something bad to happen? Have I never noticed, but is this how the poor man has spent his entire life? Always expecting danger, always assuming a threat is a clock-tick away? If that's the case I need to learn from example and refuse to live my life like that.

"Excuse me," I say and brush against him as I enter the cabin.

Once I am inside, the cabin doesn't explode, implode, or show any signs of retaliating against unexpected company. It is, however, colder than it is outside. A visible puff of air escapes from my mouth when I breathe, but there's a fireplace in the corner of the main room and a pile of wood, so once we get the fire going, it'll be manageable. And hopefully fending off a night freeze will be our only worry.

Even though there's no heat, there is electricity from a small generator, but of course no Internet or cell phone reception. One of the first things my father does is check the landline, and it is working. I asked him why he was checking to see if there was a dial tone, and he said in case of an emergency. It was the first time we both laughed.

The cabin itself is actually very cozy, really just one large room that's sectioned off into kitchen, living room, and bedroom areas. There's only one extra room, a small bedroom in the back with nothing more than bunk beds and a scuffed-up dresser and, thank God, a bathroom complete with a shower stall. I turn the faucet at the sink and watch with great relief as the stream of rust-colored liquid turns clear after a few seconds. If I didn't have a doomcloud hanging over my head, this cabin would be an enjoyable place to relax in for a few hours.

My father starts a fire in the fireplace, and I plop onto the big overstuffed couch and wrap myself in a multicolored quilt that was folded neatly and propped up against one of the arms like a pillow. I'm swathed in bright swirls of colors in a variety of geometric shapes, and I imagine Nadine, her mother, and her grandmother taking turns working on it as a family project. It's sweet, and it conjures up the impression that her family is close-knit and traditional and loving. Then again the quilt could be store-bought and not an heirloom. Regardless, it's warm.

Kicking my shoes off I'm surprised that the large, oval braided rug in the center of the living room is soft underneath my feet. Guess after so many years of being walked on it's lost its edge. It's learned, like I'm learning, that time is both the enemy and the friend. Just like a father.

"I'm, um, going to build the cage," he says as nonchalantly as possible.

While my father is in the small bedroom putting together the animal cage he expects me to crawl into before the full moon rises, I cling to the last moments of normalcy I may ever experience and make hot chocolate. Just when I don't think I can listen to the clanging of the metal any longer, the whistle on the teakettle blows. I let the whistle continue for so long in order to drown out the commotion inside that my father is the one who turns off the flame.

"You go deaf?" he asks, trying to make a joke.

"Sorry, guess I wasn't paying attention," I mumble.

My father pulls a bag of marshmallows out from his duffel bag and stuffs our cups of hot chocolate chock-full of marshmallows. The man really has thought of everything. Everything except something to say.

Sitting on opposite sides of the couch we sip our hot chocolate as my father steals glances outside, making sure we move into the other room before the moon takes over the sky. Because the cabin is in the center of a clearing, there's a steady, strong wind that travels past the windows, making them buckle and groan. The sound is comforting and fills in the silence that has latched onto the space in between my father and me. There's so much to say, and yet neither one of us can find the will to speak. We just wait. Until he hears something.

"What was that?"

He turns his head toward the front door and mine follows. Uncontrollably, I feel my heart race even though I didn't hear a thing; I was lost in thought, some daydream involving Caleb and the beach.

"I don't know," I answer. "I didn't hear anything."

A few more seconds pass, a few more moments of thick silence. Then the windows rattle.

"Mystery solved," I say.

My father looks at the window suspiciously; he doesn't believe it was the culprit. He's staring at it as if trying to connect with the glass; if he can only make contact, maybe the glass will confirm that it made the sound and my father can stop worrying. I look over at the window as well, not to connect with it, but to watch the light fade. I want to scream at my father that in about an hour we may have something truly important to worry about. But the time to worry comes earlier than I expect when we hear a knock on the door.

Neither one of us can move. My father was right all along; his hesitation to enter this place was justified. It isn't safe; we aren't alone. We're trapped.

The second knock is louder and more aggressive. Whoever's on the other side of the door knows someone is inside and is not happy about it. We feel the same way.

My father puts his index finger to his lips, that cop thing he does to make me keep quiet. This time it's an unnecessary gesture as I have no intention of making a sound, let alone speaking. But then he takes his cop thing a step further and pulls his gun out from his coat pocket, the gun that offers absolutely no solace or protection because it's the gun that he's admitted to me is not loaded. He then compounds what I perceive to be his insanity by waving his fake gun from me to the door. He does this three times until I understand what he wants me to do. He wants me to open the door and greet our unwanted guest.

Without making a sound I move my lips to form one word: *Me?*

Without hesitating, my father nods his head and grabs my arm to give me a jump start. When I'm standing an inch in front of the door, my father flattens himself against the wall to my left, so when I pull the door open he'll be standing behind it unseen. He's going to play cop-without-a-gun, and I'm going to play decoy. Brilliant idea.

Just as my hand is about to grasp the doorknob, I hear another knock on the door. This time it's more pounding than knocking, and I instinctively pull my hand back. Who's out there? No one knows that we're here except for Nadine, but why would she tell anyone? She offered the place to us, as a friend. My stomach churns and my intuition with it. Maybe she isn't a friend; maybe she's a traitor. I don't know whether she's someone I can trust or someone who would betray me.

More pounding. From the other side of the door, from inside my chest, and both are loud and angry. I have no time to turn and make a run for it, for the safety of the bathroom, because my father grabs my hand, places it on the doorknob, and twists it to the left. In a flash the door is open, and before my eyes can register who's standing in front of me I hear words.

"What are you doing here?!"

All I see is dark blue. The sun is gone. Night has come. The truth is only moments away.

"Answer me, Dominy!" the voice shouts again. "What are you doing here?"

This doesn't make any sense. What is Caleb doing here?

How did he find me? "You have to go," I tell him, my voice sounding incredibly tiny compared to his shouting.

"Not until you tell me why you're shacked up here with Napoleon!" Caleb demands.

"What?"

Okay, now something makes sense. Caleb's comment answers my first question; he's here because he's jealous. But why? And how the hell did he know to find me here?

"You lied to me!" Caleb shouts.

I've lied about so many things, Caleb. You'll need to be more specific.

"About what?" I ask. "What are you talking about?"

"I'm not stupid, Dom!" he reminds me. "Bethany College is in Kansas, not Iowa!"

My mind goes blank until I remember the conversation we had about my visiting potential colleges. I was trying to make our faux excursion sound real, and all I did was make a mistake. At least we're getting closer to the truth, *his truth* for being here, but with a side glance at the sky I can see that we're also getting closer to my truth.

"I figured out that you lied to me, so I followed you," he explains. "I can't believe he made you take your father's car!"

The blue in the sky is getting darker.

"Caleb, you're wrong. Napoleon isn't here," I say, my voice starting to shake. "Now go."

"This is his cabin," he replies, his voice solid and strong. "Nadine told me her family has a place near the edge of the hills."

My boyfriend's done being polite, and he bursts into the cabin. He pushes the door open, and because I'm still holding on to it, because I'm afraid to let go of something stationary for fear of passing out, I move with it. My father is less than a foot away on the other side of the door, but I don't see him.

And neither does Caleb as he starts pacing throughout the room.

"Stop being such a douche, Nap, and get out here!"

When Caleb sees the door at the end of the small hallway, he pauses. He thinks he's discovered Napoleon's hiding place.

"So you want me to come and find you? Is that what you want me to do, you coward?!" he cries.

"No!" I scream.

I race in front of Caleb and stand between him and the bedroom door. There's no way I can let him see the cage my father built.

"Get out of my way, Dom!"

"Caleb, I'm begging you! You have to go!"

The way I'm standing—with my arms out to my sides—it truly looks like I'm trying to prevent Caleb from entering the bedroom because I'm hiding someone in there, and that's exactly what he thinks.

"Oh my God," Caleb sighs, completed dejected. "He really is in there."

Seeing his hurt expression, I don't care if he finds out what we're really doing here; I'd rather him think that I'm this disgusting, vile creature than think that I would ever cheat on him with someone like Napoleon. But I don't get the chance to explain what's really going on. My father takes the chance away from me. He comes up from behind Caleb and slams the gun down on the side of his head.

My boyfriend slumps into me, and I stumble back, slamming hard against the door. I try to keep him upright, but he's deadweight, and I'm unable to break his fall. I look down, and I see a bruise start to form on his temple, purple, and I think that it looks pretty against his blond hair, but I know it's going to look ugly when he wakes up. If he wakes up.

"What the hell did you do that for?!"

My father looks at me like I'm some ungrateful brat and points toward the window. "Look outside!"

I don't have to move; from where I'm standing I can see it. The change happened so quickly it was hardly noticeable. The full moon has replaced the sun. One moment it was daylight, and the next it wasn't. Usually it doesn't matter, but tonight is not like any other night. Tonight the moon is going to tell my fate.

"Get inside the cage!" my father screams.

But I can't move; I can't take my eyes off of the moon.

My father opens the bedroom door and starts to drag me inside, desperate to get me into the cage, but I don't want to go; I just cannot go inside that thing. I feel like I'm spinning, like everything is completely out of control; I feel like I'm being dragged to my death.

"Dominy!"

I hear a voice somewhere off in the distance. I think it's coming from a man; it sounds like a man's voice.

"Dominy! Come with me!!"

The voice is lost to me; it means nothing so I don't turn to it. I turn to the only thing that matters. The moon. I look out the window and see the glorious full moon against a backdrop of deep blue. So beautiful, so powerful, so understanding. I have no choice, so I willingly give myself up to the moon as I hear my mother's sweet, angelic voice.

Remember, Dominy, you are blessed.

And then the transformation begins.

Chapter 17

My mother is wrong; her daughter is not blessed.

The pain is excruciating, and the worst part is that it's not the first time I have felt this way. It comes back to me in a blinding flash, a jolt, as if someone snapped an old-fashioned Polaroid camera, and an empty white light is followed by a crystal-clear image. Nothing, then everything. I remember everything that happened on my birthday, the night I killed Jess. I remember everything, because it's all happening again. And because I can remember, I want to die.

Just like before, the pain starts in my stomach, deep inside, where my soul is supposed to be, but I can't have one; there's no way I could feel such agonizing pain if I had a soul. It isn't only physical; it's emotional as well, and I know that my appearance isn't going to be the only thing to change; my mind is going to become altered as well. I am going to become a very bad person. Or to be more accurate, a very bad thing.

From the center of my body, the pain spreads out slowly in four directions and travels down my limbs. It doesn't speed; it takes its time so my mind can assess what's happening, so my mind can be aware and alert and afraid. It's a cruel pain. Vaguely I'm reminded of the one time I had to have general anesthesia when I had my tonsils removed. A few seconds after the doctor put the needle in my arm I felt a burning sensation, and I could literally feel the hot liquid travel underneath my skin. That's what this feels like, only amped up, ten times as hot. But whatever is attacking my body doesn't want to shelter me from the pain; it wants me to be a participant.

I look down at my left arm, and I can see something crawling inside of me, just under the skin, weaving, careful not to linger in one spot for more than a few seconds, but not in a rush. The pain wants to take its time; it wants to play.

I turn my right arm over, and I see the exact same thing, the same pattern, the same rhythm, and I know the same thing is happening down my legs. Wherever this pain is coming from, it's controlled; it's not unruly or disobedient; it has a job to do, and it knows exactly how to do it. I close my eyes because I remember what the next phase of its job is, and I don't think I can stand to see it again.

Screams echo throughout the cabin, and I don't know if they're my father's or mine—probably a combination of both. I lurch forward, no longer able to stand on my two feet, and my hands slam into the wooden floorboards. My face is inches from Caleb's, and I thank God—though his existence at this particular moment is questionable—that my boyfriend is unconscious. At least he doesn't have to bear witness to this revolting transformation.

The screams are joined by cracking sounds, one, two, three, four, and I know that my elbows and knees are breaking, snapping so my joints will bend in the opposite direction. The pain is so intense my body is on fire, and I start to shake; it's like the blood in my veins is starting to boil. I try to shake the heat and the pain off of me, but only end up hurling myself into the wall and quickly crashing back onto the floor. Once again the only thing I'm grateful for is that I feel the cold wood, not Caleb's body, pressing against my face. Underneath me I can feel my limbs scratch the floor, and the sound of sharp nails scraping and clawing and clicking against the wood sickens me, fills me with despair because I know there's no way to fight this; there's no way to turn back; there's no way to remain human.

It's only a matter of time before I'm completely lost within this curse.

Looking up I try to focus on things that have nothing to do with me so my mind can go elsewhere and not have to deal with what's happening to my body. On the mantel of the fireplace I see a photo of Napoleon and Nadine with their mother and a man who I assume is their father. It must be their father; he looks more like the twins than their mother does. It's a beautiful picture filled with sunshine and smiling faces; they're on the beach, maybe at their old home in Connecticut or some tropical island, some place where there's light and hope, some place that looks nothing like where I am right now. I wish I were standing next to them, frozen in time, smiling and basking in the sunlight instead of being devoured by the moon.

Another scream, and this time I'm certain that it's mine because the pain has entered the last stage. It feels like tiny pins, sharp, razor-like, are poking through my flesh, covering my entire body from the inside out. I try to scream again, but I don't have enough energy; every ounce of strength I have is going into breathing. Why can't I just die?! Why won't the angels and saints my mother always prayed to show me some mercy and kill me?! Why won't they take control away from whatever demon is doing this to me and remove my body from this agony?!

Because now it's too late.

Remember, Dominy, you are blessed.

This is NOT a blessing!

My flesh begins to tighten and harden, and when I glance at my arm I see that it's gnarled and knotted like I'm a burn

victim who didn't have the good sense to die. I don't want to
be that brave or stupid or heroic. I just want this to be over.

The razor-sharp pain returns, and I watch as my twisted
flesh is covered by red fur that spreads out across my body
like blood until my skin disappears. Gagging, gasping for
breath I collapse as the nerves and muscles and veins inside
of me acclimate to this vicious takeover. Slowly I adjust, and
the fur covering me, encasing me, no longer feels bristly but
soft and warm like a thick quilt. My new fur is the same
color as my hair was when I was a girl. It's encouraging because it means there's a little bit of Dominy left; she hasn't
been entirely erased. Before she recedes within the animal
I've become, I have to make contact.

My father is huddled into a corner on the far side of the
room, fear etched into not only his face, but every inch of his
skin. I tilt my snout up, aware of how heavy my head has become, and stare at him. Hopefully my eyes look the same and
he can see that it's still me; hopefully he isn't repulsed by
what he sees and he can tell that under all of this is his
daughter, his little girl.

When I hear the whimper behind me, everything changes.
The little girl is ripped away, silenced, and in her place is
something new and different and in many ways better. I notice that the nails on my paws are like curved white ivory,
thick and massive, but tapering to a needle-fine point at the
tip. I know that my body is lithe and muscular, and I feel in-
vincible. I run my long, rough tongue over my teeth, and I
feel that they're large and jagged and hungry. My senses are
heightened, and I can see and hear and smell with more pre-
cision and clarity than ever before. Whatever demon or angel
has cursed me knows exactly what it's doing. And I couldn't
be more grateful. And this boy couldn't be more scared.

Although he's big, he's more child than man, and I can smell
panic wafting off of him like disease on the wind. Slumped in

a far corner of the room, he disgusts me and excites me, and I want to nuzzle my face into his body and rip his limbs from their sockets at the same time. I hear my panting get louder as I stroll toward him, lazily. I'm in no rush; there's nowhere for him to go, and there's no way for him to escape. So there's no reason for me not to take my time.

A puddle of fluid appears underneath his leg and spreads out around him, yellow with a strong aroma that stings my nostrils. It's his fear being released. I like when they're afraid, like the other one was before I killed her. Tasting their fear gives me more power, replenishes me. He looks just like she did, surprised and frightened, and he's wasting his breath begging to be spared. His words, like those of the girl who came before him, are useless.

This one has hair the color of the sun, and it repulses me so much that I can't look at it. Instead I focus on its eyes, brown like the dirt that gets crushed underneath my paws when I walk, much better. He's calling out to me, using the same name the girl did, must be common among these things, a word they use when they beg for their lives, when they don't want to die. Too bad I don't know what this *Dominy* means. If I did perhaps I would spare them their lives.

"Oh my God, Dominy! It's me, Caleb!"

He clings to the wall until he's upright and looking down at me. I sniff the ground, and the acidic aroma makes me dizzy; I shake my head to dislodge the scent from my body and howl. It's a long, thin, high-pitched cry, and it serves its purpose; it shocks the one in front of me so he teeters backwards and loses his balance. Now we're on the same level again; now he's going to find out who's superior, who's more powerful, who will survive.

Swaying my head from side to side I prepare myself, remind myself to lunge for the neck and pierce the flesh where the veins are visible so the blood will flow quickly, stain the ground, and release the life force. So the body can be mine. Now.

I spring forward, feeling my legs extend in front and behind me. I'm completely free, touched by nothing more than the wind that I create, hanging for a brief moment in the air like the moon. We are one and the same.

I lash out with one paw and my nails scrape this creature's arm, tearing away flesh, making blood squirt out in three horizontal lines. I touch down on the ground, only to spring back up, ready to pounce once again and rip more flesh away from the bone. But in midair I hear a crackling sound, what you sometimes hear when lightning flashes, and I turn to the left. The other creature is standing upright holding an object in its hand that's pointed toward me. I've never seen this object before, but I know that it has one intention: to destroy me.

I twist my body in the air and swerve to the left, avoiding the creature in front of me to land on the ground. This time the lightning sound is joined by a flash of light that flies past me and drills a hole into the wall, causing splinters of wood to spray into the air. The sound that comes out of my throat this time is a growl, low and guttural. The last sound that these creatures will take with them to their graves.

"Dominy, stop!!"

The one holding the object cries out to me, but I ignore him. I want the one with the yellow hair. I want to destroy the sun and consume his fear, make him die knowing that he was right to be afraid.

Once again I lunge into the air, my body stretched out, my red fur looking magnificent and sleek. I can see the scared creature under me, his arm shielding his face, one fear-filled eye visible, his body shaking uncontrollably. Then I hear the lightning sprint once more across the sky. It is the last sound I remember hearing before I'm struck by something that makes me fall.

"Dominy!!"

That word again! It's distorted, as if it's coming from miles away, but I know this thing under my weight is the one who screamed. His lips are moving, but I can't hear the words. I see the other one walking toward me but something's wrong with my vision; it's like my head is twisted on its side. The man is walking sideways as if his feet are touching the wall. What's happening to me? Why are my eyes closing? Why can I only see black?

When I pry my eyes open I have no idea how long it's been since I was last able to see. I'm lying on my side, and I can only see two pairs of feet standing next to me. I couldn't have been unconscious for very long; if I had been, these two would have fled. Staying near me means accepting death, and there's not a creature alive that would choose death over life. No, the interval must have been short. Whatever the dark-haired one did to me to prevent me from devouring his friend didn't work.

They're talking again as if I'm not here, as if they think I can't hear them. I don't understand their words, but I can follow their intent.

"Mr. Robineau, what's going on?" the yellow-haired one asks.

"I don't have time to explain," the other one replies.

"But Dominy . . . she turned into that . . . *thing!*" he says, pointing at me.

How dare he call me a thing? I try to lift my head, but I think I only succeed in fluttering my eyes. It's enough though, enough for him to see that I cannot be defeated so easily.

"She's awake!"

The dark-haired one turns to me, and he's holding something else in his hands now. One side is thick and round and filled with a white fluid, while the other end is long and thin and silver. Silver. By instinct, I know that I have to avoid anything made of silver. I don't know why, but I know that it would be a fatal mistake to think that I could survive such an attack. Interesting. I may not be invulnerable, not yet, but I'm wise, and a wise creature knows its limitations. I don't have much time, I'm weak, but I have to try and escape; otherwise I may never have another chance.

I feign exhaustion and drop my head to the floor, keep my eyes almost fully closed, but open just a thin sliver so I can see the dark-haired man approach me.

"What's in the syringe?" the younger one asks. "You're not going to kill her, are you?"

"No!" the older one shouts. "It's only a sedative."

Then for some reason the older one turns around to face his companion. It's a mistake.

"How could you ever think that I would kill my child?"

I am no one's child!

I leap forward, and even marred by fatigue, I'm stronger than him. I flail my arm so my paw slaps him in the back and sends him flying into his friend. Grinning, I watch the two fools fall to the ground into one heap. They're scrambling to break free of each other, screaming at each other and me, desperate to regain control of their bodies. But they're not fast enough.

My paw once again rips through the air and instead of hitting the older one on the back, I allow my nails to rip through the material that covers his flesh and dig into the skin. Body lurching backward, he screams, and I savor the sound, let it wash over me as I see the blood race from the cuts in his back.

"The Taser, Caleb, grab it!"

I don't know what this thing is, but when the yellow-haired one grabs it I see that this Taser is the thing that the other one pointed at me that knocked me out. I cannot allow them to strike me again.

"Shoot!"

The crackling sound slams into my ears. Stupidly, the younger one misses even though I'm less than two feet away from him. His hand is still shaking as he tries to point the object at me again, but I knock it out of his hand and hear it careen across the floor to the other side of the room. They have no weapons, just like me. Finally it's a fair fight.

As I'm about to leap into the chest of the yellow-haired one, I hear another wolf howl outside. I turn toward the sound and feel something tugging at my heart. It's the cry of a male wolf. He could be my companion; he could travel and hunt and sleep with me. Do I give in to the innate desire to connect with my own species? Do I let these disgusting creatures live so I can go in search of one of my own kind?

Yes.

At the open door leading to the outside I turn around and look at the two things huddled together, eyes and mouths wide open, like the feeble prey that they are, and I growl at them. Spit is dripping from my jagged fangs, and I open my mouth wide so they can see my red tongue and my black gums and the power that I possess. I'll return for these two, but for now I need to search for the maker of that howl.

Outside I try and smell the scent, but the wind only brings with it a cool breeze, nothing more. I travel in the direction I believe the sound came from, but after a few paces I stop, unsure. I turn around, then to the left, but I can't track it. It's as if the sound and the smell disappeared into the night, as if they never existed, as if I only dreamed that another of my kind was calling out to me.

But what does it matter? I'm here, free, enveloped by the glow of the moonlight, the glorious moonlight, basking in its radiance. I howl at the moon, a sound filled with pride and thanks and servitude. I am but a humble servant, a glimmer in the eye of the almighty, a meager offspring who must prove its worth.

No! I am nothing but a servant who has squandered a perfect opportunity.

I start to race back to the cabin when my body twitches at

the arrival of a new scent. This is even sweeter, even more precious, even more worth killing. Bowing my head I take a moment to thank the moon for its gift. A blessing must be acknowledged.

I turn to the right and see another house, smaller than the one I was trapped in, from which the intoxicating smell is escaping. Lavender and rain and decay all combined into one delectable aroma that I must revel in. The scent is calling me, and I cannot ignore it.

A foot from the house I stop, the smell growing from a flame into an inferno. I lift my front legs and spring forward so I can pounce onto the door, both front paws pressing into the wood and tearing it from its hinges so it falls flat to the ground. Inside the room I see two more creatures, one a male and the other a female huddled in opposite corners. They're human, like the ones I just left, the ones I just spared, but I no longer feel kind; I no longer feel like exhibiting mercy. Hunger has evicted compassion from my brain, and I want to taste their flesh and drink their blood. So that's what I intend to do.

A sound rips out of my throat, part growl, part howl, filled with savagery and purity and command. I want these two to know what's coming for them. The wood of the door splinters underneath my paws as I walk toward them.

"Dominy!" the white creature shouts.

That word again. I must uncover its meaning.

"Oh my God, it's her!" he cries out again. "She was telling the truth!"

The white creature is shivering, not from cold, but from fear. How majestic his blood will look when it runs like a twisted river down his pale, thin, lifeless body.

"Nadine!"

A new word. I don't like it.

"Nadine! What do we do?!"

Futilely, he reaches out across the room to the female, but

she ignores him. She's moving her lips, but no sound is coming out. If she's speaking, she's doing it silently. She's not like the other one; she's not like anyone I've ever seen before. I can see a layer of silver smoke outlining her body, like a stained halo, that slowly turns to liquid. The vision is really quite beautiful, but the smell emanating from her is rancid. The one who looks like snow is the opposite. He's day; she's night. He's good; she's evil.

"Oh my God, it's Dominy!" he cries out again. "The curse really did come true!"

Still, she doesn't respond, but merely keeps moving her lips, and the smoke around her shifts restlessly and grows in intensity and thickness. Despite the toxic smell living inside the darkness, I sense great power thrives there as well. Power that needs to survive because it's a power that can help make me even stronger, closer to the invulnerability that I know is within my grasp.

A triumphant howl escapes my lips.

I turn to face the creature made of all white. Sometimes deciding which one to kill is such an easy task.

Chapter 18

The man made of ivory is about to be burned.

As I walk toward him I can feel the heat rise in my body and greet the cold air that rushes against my fur. I imagine each strand of red hair acting like an army of flames, extinguishing the cold as it ripples across the length of my body, filling me with fire, fire that needs to spread. I'm a moving torch, and I cannot be stopped.

"Dominy! It's me . . . Archie!"

I hear words coming from the male, but I ignore them because his words no longer have any meaning; only his fear has purpose. Let his mind fall into the abyss of fear that consumes him so I can devour his flesh and remind the world of my strength without any interruption. But when I'm only inches away, when my hot, hungry breath mixes with his cold fear, I am interrupted. By the other one. Her words are different.

"*Orion, souverain des cieux, témoin notre sacrifice.*"

The words seep out of the female's mouth in a whisper, barely audible, but the sound echoes in my ears like thunder. I'm caught in an explosion, and I stumble. Her power is greater than I thought, and if I weren't so hungry it would be amusing.

"*Orion, maître des cieux, voici notre pouvoir.*"

The howl that erupts from deep inside of me is so intense and sudden that it silences her. She reacts exactly the way that I want her to, accepting her fear like her companion already has, giving in to it, allowing it to fill her body like my hunger-heat is filling mine, so I can feast.

The female, now silent, looks at me with a face filled with shock instead of intent. She is staring at me with the awe that is appropriate, and she understands that if I want to kill her there is absolutely nothing she can do to prevent it. She is wise, and I am strong. We understand each other, we need each other, and as I look into her eyes, the color of unattended dirt, I see that she knows I will spare her. This time I'll allow her to live. Her eyes do not offer me thanks but something more important: respect.

Turning away from her I focus on the white male. His body is shaking more violently now as he crawls on the ground. His hands slam hard onto the floor; his knees slide after him, trembling, desperately trying to obey the command of the rest of his body. His eyes dart left, right, searching for an escape that we both know doesn't exist. Good. Welcome the fear, embrace it; the end is almost here.

With each step I take, I can hear my nails click against the wooden floor. With each step I take, I can feel my heart beat faster, and I consciously choose to slow down my pace. I do not want to rush this kill; I want to savor it. I want this time to be better. The last time was like a frenzy, a panic, flesh torn, blood spilt, hunger abated but not quenched. Now I must be in control from start to finish, enjoy every moment and not rush, even though I feel as if I don't have much time left.

My prey is stuck in the crevice of the wall, pushing against the wood as if his slight frame could break through to the other side to reach what he believes to be his freedom. But he will not be free, not until I break through the chains that connect him to life. Not until I decide to open my mouth and plunge my razor-sharp teeth into his flesh and claim what is mine.

His body is a crumpled, shivering mass of white bones. Tiny sounds escape from the mound, whimpers, cries, muffled gasps. Each sound a violation against me and against nature itself. He raises an arm in front of his face as if to prevent me from seeing him, as if he could disappear into the fear that surrounds him, as if anything could stop me from doing what my heart and my mind and my soul are telling me to do.

"Dominy, please," he says, his voice quivering. "I'm your friend."

I have no friends!

For a moment the heat that engulfs me is cooled. I am no longer consumed with fire and rage and hunger; something else fills my body. I have no idea what it is; I have no idea what I'm feeling. It's foreign, and yet it's familiar, but whatever it is, it makes me pause.

I look at this thing huddled on the floor in front of me, and I wonder why I stop. Why have I given in to its plea? Why am I allowing this thing to have an effect on me, to control me when it should have no influence? It is just a thing. And yet this thing has an unexpected power.

"Dominy," it repeats. "It's Archie. I'm your *friend*. You don't want to hurt me."

Trembling words coming out of a trembling body. Weak words coming out of a weak body. I should not listen to them; I shouldn't let them swirl inside my head; I should not let them dictate how I will act. But I do.

My tongue glides across my lips, and I swallow hard, suddenly very aware of my need to drink. The white creature begins to stand to its full height, and he towers above me; he looks down at me, his limbs not still but no longer shaking violently. He is gaining control over his body and over the situation and over me.

"That's it," he says. "You know me, and you would never hurt me."

I look at him, and it looks like he is starting to move, but I realize it is my own vision, my own confusion that is making the entire room start to spin. Dizzy, I turn to the female, the one who understands me, to find my footing, to regain my composure. She is still on the other side of the room, but she is no longer looking at me with respect; her eyes are filled with a mixture of anger and disgust. Quickly her eyes dart from the white one and then back to me, and her lips move to form silent words. I can feel her power; I can feel her desire; I can feel her command.

This time my howl is filled with lust and wild abandon. Not an ounce of caution or restraint or pity is contained within its cry.

I turn back to the white creature, one last look before I kill it. I spring into the air, and my ears are bombarded with sound. My own growls, my prey's cries, and from behind me the sound once again of lightning. All followed by the dark quiet of silence.

Sounds fracture through the silence like sparks of light piercing a black sky. Fleeting, temporary, and then leaving the sky even blacker than before their arrival. I know that I'm surrounded by people. I can hear their voices, but I can't speak; I can't communicate; I can't make any sound of my own. The only thing I can do is listen and wait. An overwhelming sense of sadness threatens to suffocate me since I think this is how my mother may feel. I pray to God that I'm wrong. I pray that she isn't trapped within some dark world just out of finger-reach of ours, someplace where she knows she shouldn't be, but from which she can't escape. Someplace where she can hear our voices, but knows none of us will ever hear her replies. Someplace where I am right now.

When I open my eyes, I'm still connected to that other place. Half there, half here. I don't know how much time has passed. I don't know exactly where I am for a second because my vision is blurry. Then everything comes into focus. The cabin, the morning light, my father, Caleb.

I try to speak, but my throat is parched, dry like a burnt twig. Caleb shouldn't be here. My father and I are supposed to be here secretly, shut off from the world while the full moon loomed in the sky, while we waited to see whether the curse was mere words or something more. I turn my head and can see the sunlight. Whatever the answer is, it's already been revealed. Whatever the truth is, Caleb shares the knowledge. Quickly, I glance at my arms and expect them to be covered in an animal's red fur, but they're not. I look normal. I am normal. But why are my arms tied up with rope?

I try to lift my arm, but it won't budge. Neither will the other one. That's because thick pieces of rope are wrapped around my chest and arms and around my ankles. Twisting from side to side I try to wrench myself free, and despite the rope burning against my skin I don't stop moving until I feel Caleb's hands on my arms.

"Easy, Dominy," he says.

His eyes are focused on the rope and they look beautiful and compassionate and scared. Oh God, please no, please don't let it be true.

"Mr. Robineau, can I untie her?"

My father must nod his consent because Caleb's fingers start to loosen the ropes, and soon my upper body is free. I try to catch a glimpse of his eyes, but he's avoiding me. He can't bring himself to look at my pitiful face. In fact he turns his back on me to untie the ropes around my ankles and doesn't turn around when he's finished.

"Here, drink some water," my father says, taking his place.

Lifting my head to follow my father's command, I feel a burst of pain erupt at the nape of my neck and spread down my spine. When it reaches the end of the bone it doesn't disappear, but spreads out so my entire back feels like it's a twisted piece of fiery metal. I gulp down some water and lie back down on the couch.

Now I'm frightened. It's as if the fear that was living in Caleb's eyes is an airborne virus, and it's leapt into my body, infecting me with the same poison.

"Daddy," I whisper.

I don't have to say another word. My father knows exactly what I'm asking him; he knows exactly what I need to know. I just can't believe he says it out loud in front of Caleb.

"I'm sorry," he says. "The curse is real."

The fire-pain reaches out from the back of my neck and grabs hold of my throat, squeezing, pressing onto my larynx so I can't reply. Then it rises, squirming into my cheeks, my lips, my nose, eyes, forehead, until my entire head is consumed with a blinding ache that no medicine will ever be able to soothe.

"No."

It's a pathetic word, useless, but it's the only one I can think of to say.

I look at Caleb who still hasn't found the courage to look at me, unlike Archie and Nadine standing behind him. They can't take their eyes off me. Wait! What are they doing here too? They shouldn't be here either; I should be alone with my father. He's the only one who can help me; he's the only one who can possibly understand. Why the hell did I say anything to those two? I must have been out of my mind to think that confiding in anyone else would be a good idea.

"Get out!" I shout.

My voice has no power, and no one moves.

"I said get out of here!"

"We're not going anywhere," Archie replies.

"Daddy, please . . ."

It's hard to speak with tears streaming down my face and a twisting pain in my throat, but I have to fight back. I grip the side of the couch to lift my body up to a sitting position. Maybe this way I won't look so feeble. Maybe this way they'll listen to me.

"Please, Daddy, make them leave."

Begging gets me nowhere except on the receiving end of more pitying expressions. What in the world happened? And do I even want to know?

"You heard what Archie said," Nadine interjects. "We're not leaving; we're staying right beside you."

I don't want you here! I don't want anyone to see me like this. My words must be silent because no one responds to my commands. Fine, if they're not leaving, then I am.

Swinging my legs off the couch I try to press my feet into the floor, but I feel like I'm paralyzed from the waist down. No pain, no feeling, no nothing.

"What's wrong with me?!"

"It's the aftereffects of the Taser," my father explains.

The what? My stunned expression is all that's needed for my father to continue speaking.

"I had to, Dom. It was the only way to get you to stop."

I have to ask. I don't want to, but I must. "Stop me from doing what?"

"Killing Archie," Nadine replies.

What?! I have no memory of what I've just been told, but I understand everything.

"The curse . . . the curse turned me into something that wanted to kill Archie?"

"Yes," my father confirms.

First Jess and now Archie. I'm not a werewolf; I'm a murderer.

"Once the full moon appeared," my father continues, "you were turned into a werewolf."

Why aren't they laughing at my father? Why aren't they telling him that he's crazy and needs to book an adjoining room next to my mother at The Retreat?

"I tried to keep you here," my father explains. "I used the Taser on you, but I didn't have it on its highest frequency, so it only knocked you out for a few moments."

Once again I try to remember what I'm being told, but no memory returns. I have to give in to blind faith and trust that what I'm being told is the truth. Just as I have to trust that my father's ripped shirt and bandaged arm are the result of my attacking him.

"We ran after you, but lost you until we heard . . ." Something catches in my father's voice, and he can't continue.

"Heard what?" I ask.

"Until we heard you howl again," my father adds. "We caught up with you just in time."

"Oh my God," I whisper. "I really turned into . . . an animal?"

It's more of a question because I can't comprehend that something so supernatural, something that should only exist in books and movies is actually real.

"Yes," my father answers.

"Well, we didn't see you turn into anything," Archie says, tilting his head toward Nadine. "But we saw you turn back."

Clutching my mouth, I'm not successful in preventing my cry from being heard; the second escapes me and invades the room. I have never felt more disgusting and exposed and vulnerable in my entire life. My father, my friends, and my boyfriend saw me in the most repulsive, incomprehensible state imaginable. How can they ever look at me the same way again?

"We brought you back here," my father recounts. "And put you in the cage. After a few hours you transformed back."

"It was pretty amazing, Dom," Archie adds. "Like watching one of those time-lapse movies where they show a plant growing, but speed it up really fast so it takes a few seconds. You went from wolf to human in about ten seconds."

Ten seconds of witnessing something no human being thought they would ever witness.

"But, you know, when we realized you were naked," Archie says, "we looked away."

"I was naked!"

"Your father was prepared, Dominy," Nadine offers. "We had your clothes ready, and the boys went in the other room while we dressed you."

I grip my knee to stop my hand from shaking. This girl I have known for roughly six months dressed me while I was naked and unconscious.

"Don't be embarrassed," she adds. "I'm used to doing it as a volunteer."

I know her comment is supposed to make me feel better, but it doesn't.

"If it makes you feel any better," Archie says, "Caleb peed himself, which is why he's wearing the sweats I brought with me to sleep in."

Glancing at Caleb I see my boyfriend turn his head away from me. I doubt very much that he can't look at me because he's embarrassed that he wet his pants.

"When it was clear you weren't going to transform again," my father continues, "we brought you out here . . ."

"But tied me up just to be on the safe side," I finish.

My father can't even reply; he just nods his head. So Luba's curse isn't just an idle threat; it's real. And the little bit of humanity that it didn't destroy has now been crushed. Not only am I frightened and disgusted, but I'm humiliated as well.

Luba. This woman I've never known, this woman I'll probably never meet, has taken my life and callously and cruelly damaged it beyond repair. If she wanted revenge, why didn't she bring my father to the police, demand justice for the accidental shooting of her husband? Why didn't she do what a normal person would do? The answer is so simple, it terrifies me.

Because evil exists.

"So all of it's true," I say. "I'm a werewolf because of some Indian woman's curse."

Heartbroken, my father can only muster up the strength to bow his head.

"And I'm the one who killed . . ."

I have to say the words out loud once and for all.

"I'm the one who killed Jess."

This time my father finds the strength because he knows I've lost all of mine.

"Yes."

The sobs overtake my body so quickly I'm not prepared for them. Next the screams come, and I feel something hitting the side of my head. I think it might be Caleb or Archie or Nadine, but it's me; I'm hitting myself, punching my face wildly, without caring what part I touch, as long as I inflict some pain. But I know that I can punch myself from now until the end of time, and it won't equal the pain I inflicted on my friend, my Jess, who I considered my sister, who I loved as much as she loved me.

My father's arms are the first ones I feel around me. I'd know his touch anywhere, his unconditional love and compassion; without it I would be lost, more lost than I feel right now. Doubling over in exquisite pain, I hold on to my father, secure in the knowledge of one thing—that he will never let go. He will never let me fall.

"What have I done?!" I scream. "I killed her!"

"No," my father whispers.

"Oh my God, Daddy, I did it, I killed Jess!"

"No, no!" This time my father bellows, his voice loud and sure. "You didn't do anything."

"It was her."

Archie's voice is like a siren, cutting through the cluster of sounds in the room to create an abrupt silence. I turn to him, but instead my eyes focus on Nadine staring at me. Archie's words repeat in my head: *It was her.* Nadine?

"It was that woman," Archie continues. "It's Psycho Squaw's curse, Dom, so it's her fault!"

Angrily, I flick tears from my eyes. The feeling is starting to come back to my legs, and I have the need to move. Slowly, I get up, swiping at the air when my father and Archie shoot out their hands to help me.

I need their help, but I don't want it.

I lurch forward and grab onto the arm of the couch until I feel steady enough to move on. Wisely, no one comes to my aid; they just watch my struggle, knowing as I do that at some point, I'll be in control of my body again. Finally, I'm able to stand upright, leaning my hip against the table just in case I need support. Now what I need are answers.

"Why are you two even here?" I say, jutting my head in Archie and Nadine's direction.

"We thought we might as well camp out in the small cabin for the night," Nadine says.

"And, you know, rag on you in the morning when you didn't transform into a wolf," Archie concludes.

I can't help but smile.

"Guess the joke's on you two," I reply.

As expected Archie is the only one who laughs.

"And you?" I say, pointing a finger at Caleb.

Immediately his eyes look away and then slowly return to take in my face. "I told you I thought you were here with Napoleon," he informs me.

A vague memory latches onto my mind, and I remember Caleb's yelling at me, accusing me of cheating on him with Napoleon. And then I remember my father hitting Caleb with his gun, but then there's only darkness, a dark, blank slate.

"Is that when I transformed?"

In response to my question, my father has one of his own. "You don't remember?"

I feel like I'm in geometry and I'm being asked a question about the previous day's lesson. I hope that information will miraculously fill in my head, but instead my mind starts to wander. I think about what I'm going to wear tomorrow, what color nail polish I should try next, the last funny thing Jess said to me. Jess. Why did I remember her screams and not Archie's?

"Wait a second," I say. "The last time I transformed, the first time I guess, I distinctly remember hearing Jess's voice, hearing her screams. I don't remember anything else, nothing specific, and I definitely don't remember . . . killing her, but I know that I heard her voice. I was moving toward her to help her. But this time I don't remember anything."

"You were probably fighting it the first time," my father offers.

"You probably had no idea what was happening to you," Archie adds.

"And this time?" I ask.

"Maybe your body has given in to what you truly are," Nadine says.

I know she didn't mean for her comment to sound so harsh and blunt and irreversible, but it does.

"So you think the true me is a werewolf?!"

"I'm sorry, Dom," Nadine starts. "I could sugarcoat it, but what's the sense? This woman put a curse on you before you were born, before you were even conceived."

"So from the day I was born I was cursed," I say, finishing Nadine's theory.

"No," my father barks. "Don't think that way, and, Nadine, please don't fill Dominy's head with such garbage."

"Sorry, Mr. Robineau, it's just how I see it," she says in her defense.

"Well, I don't see it that way, and neither should any of you!" he yells. "This curse is because of me, no one else, and Dominy's an innocent victim."

Am I? Could it be that my destiny is drenched in evil? Isn't it true that some people are born that way? They don't learn how to be evil. It isn't a response to their environment, or a sick upbringing; it's merely part of their DNA. Maybe that's me. Maybe I'm living proof that pure evil exists.

"I might be a victim, Dad," I say. "But I'm far from innocent."

When my father shouts, it's with a new voice. Harsher and angrier than I've ever heard him sound before.

"Enough! What we need to do is find a way to reverse this curse," my father declares. "Before anyone else gets hurt . . . or killed. So Dominy and all of us can put this behind us."

Suddenly I want to feel like an animal, trapped and caged.

"The only way we can put this behind us is to lock me up somewhere!" I shout. "Put me in basement of The Retreat—what's the name of it again? The Dungeon! Yes! Put me there, away from everyone, so I can never hurt anyone again!"

And Nadine is just as quick to lend a helping hand and some rational logic.

"That won't solve the problem at all; it'll only contain it," Nadine says. "Your father's right. We have to get to the root of this spell. And you can count on me to help do just that."

"Me too, Dom," Archie adds. "We'll get to the bottom of it, and then we'll break it. Break it so it can't ever harm another person."

I can't look at Archie any longer. His unrelenting friendship is too much to bear considering that I almost killed him.

"And I don't care what anyone says," Archie adds, as if he can read my mind. "I know you wouldn't have hurt me."

Unrelenting and undeserved.

"How could you know that?!" I scream. "After what I did to Jess!"

Archie doesn't back down from my attack. If anything, it makes him even more certain.

"Because you might have turned into a wolf, transformed into an animal, but your eyes were yours!"

"What?" I ask.

"Your eyes, Dom," Archie says more quietly, but with the same conviction. "They were yours. They were still connected to you as a person."

Half girl, half beast. Isn't that delightful? After a moment I realize it is; I wasn't lost; I didn't completely give in. I am like my mother, always fighting to survive against whomever or whatever is invading my body.

"You weren't going to hurt me," Archie adds. "Right, Nadine?"

Startled, Nadine doesn't answer immediately. But when she does, she agrees with Archie.

"No, I don't think you were," she says. "I think the only reason you attacked is because you got spooked when your father barged in."

My father looks at Nadine like she just stuck a knife in his back.

"I'm not accusing you, Mr. Robineau," Nadine quickly adds. "I'm not. It's just that, well, what other explanation could there be?"

Well, if part of the human me is connected to the wolf me, which one has more power over the other?

"If that's true, then why did I kill Jess?" I ask. "If I could have seen her, I would have never . . ."

"Dominy, you were confused; you had no idea what was happening to you," my father assures me. "I should've told you everything. You could've been prepared, and nothing bad would have happened."

"Don't worry, Dom. From now on we got your back," Archie says. "So nothing bad is ever going to happen again."

If I didn't believe his words, his hug convinces me that I'll never have to question his loyalty or wonder if I'll receive his forgiveness. But I'm not sure about everyone in the room.

"What about you, Caleb?" I ask. "You've been awfully quiet this whole time."

This time when Caleb looks at me, it's without hesitation, and the rest of the people in the room vanish. His eyes are incredibly soft, while the rest of his body is solid and strong and ready for battle. I just have no idea if he's going to fight with me or against me.

"I've been quiet because I want to remember this moment," he says.

"Because it's the moment when everything changed?" I ask.

"Yes," he agrees. "It's the moment when I realized I'm in love with you." He's speaking right to me and ignoring the others in the room. "I thought I was before; I thought that I loved you, but I was wrong. This is love, what I'm feeling right now."

I move closer to the couch and hold on to an arm because I feel my knees buckle. I want his love; I want to feel it drape itself over me, but how can this be true? How can he possibly love me now that he knows what I really am?

"No, Caleb, you don't have to say that."

"Why not? It's the truth," he replies.

"How can you . . . *love* me?" I ask.

"Because I've seen you at your worst, Domgirl," he replies matter-of-factly. "I didn't run away. For a bit there, yeah, I wanted to. My body started to go; I was almost out the door."

"What stopped you?"

"Guess it was our invisible string," he replies.

My tears no longer want to purge my body of shame and

guilt and ugliness. This time they want to celebrate and praise and share the joy that I'm feeling. It's disconcerting to feel so wonderful, so complete at a time like this, but that's how I feel. And fighting against joy, like fighting against a curse, is a losing battle. So I surrender.

"I assume invisible strings are part of a private joke or something," my father says.

Before I can explain, Nadine fills him in.

"From *Jane Eyre*," she correctly surmises. "Jane and Mr. Rochester are connected by a piece of invisible string that is tied from one rib to the other."

"I must've missed that one," my father replies, smiling.

"No matter what happens, Dominy, no matter where this curse leads you, I'll be right by your side," Caleb continues. "Never doubt my words. And never doubt my love."

I can hardly speak, but I have to.

"Thank you, Caleb," I whisper. "I never will."

He kisses me softly on my lips, still not caring that there are others nearby. It's a chaste kiss, a simple gesture to show that we are connected, now and for always. When he wraps his arms around me, I allow their strength to take over, so I can let go of mine. I may be the only one who's cursed, but I know that I can't survive on my own.

Unable to resist, unable to contain their own willingness to help and offer their support, more arms wrap themselves around me. I feel Archie rest his chin on my shoulder, and I feel my father's immensely strong arms embrace all three of us. When he rests his forehead against my temple I feel his tears drop onto my cheek. Our fear, our pain, our joy is all interwoven, one unable to exist without the others, and I'm truly overwhelmed by the feeling of love and friendship and commitment.

It's only when I look up and across the room that I see Nadine staring at me. Understandably, she's keeping her distance. I've known Archie and Caleb for years; my relationship with Nadine is still quite new, and just the fact that she hasn't gone running out of here screaming for her mother or the police is testament that she's an ally. So is the fact that her lips are moving softly, I assume in silent prayer.

I'm about to smile at her when it feels like someone drops a veil over my eyes, obstructing my vision. I blink, and things become clear once again, but far from normal. I see a silver-colored mist ooze out from her body and outline her entire frame. Slowly the mist begins to sparkle and shine and grow until it looks like Nadine is floating within a silver cloud that isolates her and separates her from the rest of us.

I hold Caleb, Archie, and my father tighter around me, not for protection, but as a reminder that unlike Nadine I'm not alone. This time when I smile at her, she doesn't see me, because the silver mist has grown and is covering her face and almost her entire body, trapping her so she can't escape. And I know without a doubt that I'm not the only one in the room who's been cursed.

Chapter 19

A New Day

The honey jar has been refilled.

Everything makes sense. I know it sounds crazy, but there's a part of me that's relieved to find out I'm cursed. I understand my aggression, my physical changes, my anger, even my fascination with the moon—it all fits. Looking at myself in the bathroom mirror—which I've been doing obsessively since the last full moon—doesn't reveal any differences from who I was last week, but I'm not at all the same; I'll never be the same again. And in a completely warped way that makes me feel better, because at least now I know.

I keep examining myself looking for signs that the curse is taking over completely instead of for just one night a month, but I can't find any. Except for that initial hair growth above my lips and on my arms, my skin has been smooth. In fact, my hair is more luxurious than ever before, and the blue-gray of my eyes almost sparkles, so if anything I look better now than I ever did.

There have been other physical changes that I barely noticed at first, but since the last transformation have become more evident. I'm faster and stronger than I used to be, and my senses are sharpened. My vision is improved; I can see farther than ever before. And sometimes I can hear snippets of conversations from a block away. The most dramatic increase of all is my sense of smell. Foods, perfumes, The Dandruff King's body odor, all seem to envelop me. It's like my whole body is doing the smelling and not just my nose.

Emotionally, things haven't really improved. I continue to wake up in the middle of the night, my mind still clutching onto Jess, trying to get closer to her final moments. And then it hits me: I don't want to remember her final moments, because I honestly don't think I could go on living if I did. The will to survive is only so strong. Intellectually I get it; I killed her while possessed by this curse. If there were any way that I could have fought against it, fought against the primitive nature of this wolf spirit that's invaded my body, I would have; I would have killed myself first. In my heart and soul I know that's the truth, so my mind has been able to process the facts. But if the blanks were filled in and I could suddenly see and hear and feel what happened, that would be too much. The curse would win, and I would no longer want to be alive. It really is that simple.

Until then, however, I'm going to have to learn how to live with this thing.

My father is already in stealth mode and has plotted out a calendar for the moon cycle for the next year. He is also trying to figure out the most harmless way to contain me when those full moons come around. Archie and Caleb, true to their word, have immersed themselves in Native American Indian folklore and mythology to see if they can find instructions on how to break a werewolf curse. Good luck on that one. And then there's Nadine.

She's complicated, confusing, and cursed in her own way. I don't know what's hidden in her background, just out of reach from everyone around her, maybe left behind in her old house in Connecticut, but she has her own mystery. Could be huge, could be boring, but she's got something she doesn't want anyone to know about. Whatever her personal damage is, she's still a team player.

Her job has been to pilfer syringes and sedatives from The Retreat, since my father was only able to get one initially and Nadine has much easier access to medical supplies. He thinks a sedative may slow down the change or with any luck prevent it from happening all together, but my dad's decided we're going to use that as a last resort, since there's always the possibility it'll do more harm than good.

It's whacked, but as Archie so eloquently put it in a text the other night, I've got my own Wolf Pack.

My only fear is that one member of my eager band of sidekicks may slip, and then my secret will be out. It would be a hard secret for anyone to believe, but curiosity and suspicion will be rewarded if I'm caught off guard during a certain time of the month. From here on in, according to my father, it's all about the three P's: precaution, prevention, and protection.

Back at school I find out that there's another P to be concerned about: pissed off friends.

"I'm not the one you should be avoiding!"

The book slams onto the lunch table and lands a few inches from my tater tots, knocking over Archie's iced tea.

"Arla!" he shouts, sopping up his spilled beverage with a few napkins. "What the ef?"

"I know that I can be full of myself sometimes and self-involved," she admits. "But when I was nine my mother ran off with some biker chick who looks like Danny DeVito's twin to live in an ashram in New Mexico, so excuse me if I've got issues."

"Your mom likes motorcycles?" Archie deadpans.

Ignoring him and his joke, Arla continues. "I'm quasi-conceited, I know that, but that's no reason to shut me out!"

Plopping into the empty seat next to me, Arla smells like a

fragrant garden. The combination of her perfume and her lip gloss is so floral and pungent, she's like a moveable flower exhibit. There's another scent in there too. She's wearing a blond wig, shoulder-length and feathered, so either she gave it a good washing last night or I smell the shampoo from her real hair.

"We're not avoiding you, Arla," I lie. "I can't speak for Archie, but I've just been, you know, really busy since classes started up again."

Pursed lips and crossed arms don't usually indicate a lie is being believed.

"Busy with Miss Nadine?" Arla asks.

I get so flustered by her comment that I actually toss my hair a little. Totally fake. Just like my response. "I don't hang out with her."

"Me either," Archie says.

He doesn't toss his hair back, but his tone is equally unconvincing.

When my hair gets tossed for a second time, it's only because my head jerks back when Arla points her finger in my face.

"I've seen you with her!" she exclaims. "Huddled together, whispering, changing the subject whenever I walk in the room. I don't know what's going on with y'all, but I've got news for ya: Nadine ain't what she seems."

Uh-oh. Whenever Arla starts dropping y'alls and using bad grammar, we have to brace ourselves, because those are the two major signs that she is channeling her Creole ancestry. And they weren't a nonconfrontational brood.

"I know she comes off a little weird," I stammer. "But Nay's really not that bad."

"Nay?!" Arla shouts. "Now you're calling her Nay?"

"You know, short for Nadine," Archie explains.

"You gave her a nickname?!" Arla spits. "You never gave me a nickname!"

"You didn't like La-La!" Archie reminds her.

"Seriously, Arla, it's not like we're choosing her over you or anything," I say, even though that's exactly what we've done. As Archie pointed out earlier, Arla might be super trustworthy, but she's also the daughter of my father's deputy, which means she's also super risky. We made a pact to keep her in the dark, and now she's starting to see the light.

"Save it, Dom," Arla retorts. "I'm not Caleb; you can't sweet-talk me into believing whatever you want."

Smirking smugly, she gives the book a little push. "Just read this and tell me if you still want to say yea to the Nay."

Archie picks up the book, gasps when he reads the title, and drops it back on the table. The way he's reacting it's as if he accidentally held a slide from biology lab that's smothered with contagious bacteria.

"Where did you get this?!" Archie squeals.

"From my dad," Arla replies calmly.

"What is it?" I ask.

Using only his index finger, Archie gingerly slides the book to my side of the table. When I read the embossed gold title of the book, I understand completely why he's reacting so dramatically.

"You stole police evidence!?!" I say, stunned by the realization that Arla is also super sneaky.

Waving her hands in the air, the red fingernail polish making them look like sparks of flame, Arla shrugs her shoulders and fails to understand why we're shocked. "I borrowed it," she asserts.

"You *borrowed* Jess's diary?" I ask, as politely as possible.

Arla rips the diary out of my hand and starts to wave it, instead of her finger, in my face. "The case is closed. This stuff should've already gone back to Jess's family," Arla says. "But newsflash, my daddy isn't the best cop in the world. He's not even the best cop in Weeping Water and there are what? Four of them on the squad."

Worried that Arla's outburst might warrant attention from nosy classmates, I grab the book and, after a brief struggle, wrench it from Arla's hands. "This is private property," I remind her. "You can't just read it."

Standing up Arla raises her hands over her head, while shouting, "Well, break out the handcuffs and give in to racial profiling, because I am guilty as charged!"

I yank hard on one of the sleeves of her sweater, the same fiery color as her fingernails. "Will you sit down?"

"And stop yelling," Archie adds. "Before you attract any more attention and they start filming *Law & Order: The Two W Edition.*"

"Flip open to page fifty-seven," Arla says in a voice that can barely be described as a whisper.

Rustling through the pages, I don't know which is worse— the fact that I'm violating Jess's property or that Arla memorized which page of her diary had the most interesting kernel of information. When I get to page fifty-seven, neither of those minor betrayals seems important, because right in front of my eyes is my best friend's handwriting. Her words, her thoughts, her secrets. It's like she's right here with me again.

"*July 17,*" I say, reading the entry date on the page.

"Jess's birthday," Archie remembers.

"That's the one," Arla confirms.

I swallow hard, not wanting to continue, but unable to resist.

"*My birthday, sweet sixteen and finally been kissed,*" I read out loud. "*I have nothing to compare him to, but I'm going to put down for all eternity that Napoleon Jaffe is the best kisser ever! Perhaps in the world, but definitely in all of Two W.*"

At some point I lose my own voice and hear Jess reading

her entry out loud, complete with her funny way of always putting a lilt in her voice at the end of a sentence, even if it isn't a question.

"But I think I've made a twinemy."

"A what?" Archie asks.

I don't have to read any further to know exactly what she's talking about; she and I used to love to make up new words. This one clearly relates to the other Jaffe twin, Nadine.

"All night long Nadine stared at me with dagger eyes when I was dancing with Nap. Guess she was jealous that her brother snagged himself a hot girlfriend five minutes after coming to town, and if anyone ever reads this, the hot girlfriend is me!" Archie and I laugh at the same time, but Arla looks like the Nadine Jess was just describing.

"Keep reading," she instructs.

"For whatever reason she was giving Dominy the evil eye too."

"What?!" I exclaim.

"The only reason Dom didn't notice is because she was all over Prince Caleb."

"I was not all over Caleb that night!" I protest.

"You were too," Arla disagrees.

"Archie?" I ask.

"White boy, tell the truth," Arla demands.

"Kind of," Archie relents. "But Caleb's hot so we all understood."

"Oh my God!" I say. "I had no idea I was that type of girl."

"We'll stage an intervention later, Dom," Arla quips. "For now, read on."

"This isn't the first time it's happened," I continue reading. *"I've noticed Nadine staring at us before, mostly at Dom, but I thought it was my imagination. Then I thought about it a little more and realized that Nadine cannot be trusted."*

Sounds like Jess flip-flopped in her judgment of Nadine almost as much as I've been doing. As I read more it's clear that Jess was just as confused.

"*There's something not right about her, but I don't know what it is,*" I read. "*Maybe she's autistic. When I caught her tracing her tattoo with her finger, she reminded me of the O'Brien kid down the block.*"

Hold on a second. "Nadine has a tattoo too?"

"What do you mean *too?*" Arla asks.

"Caleb said Napoleon has a tattoo, way up on his thigh."

"Caleb's checking out Nap's thigh?" Archie snickers.

"Shut up, Archibald," I say. "Isn't that weird that they both have tattoos?"

"They're from the East Coast," Arla reminds us. "My father says things can get pretty wild out there."

"Have you either of you ever seen it?"

"I don't check out girls' thighs," Archie replies.

"Nope," Arla admits. "But Jess must've seen it. Maybe in the gym."

The class bell interrupts our conversation, but I'm not yet ready to give up this new connection to Jess. "Arla, would you mind if I borrowed this for a few days?" I ask. "Just to, you know, read the whole thing and see if there's anything else in here."

Nodding her head, Arla agrees. With one caveat. "Just don't let your father see it," she instructs. "Unlike my dad, yours is actually good at the whole upholding the truth, justice, and American way thing."

The same forced smile appears on both my face and Archie's in response to hearing about how law-abiding and crime-stopping my father is. If Arla only knew.

In my room, I'm devouring page after page of Jess's diary. It's like she's sitting in bed next to me whispering in my ear, gossiping, confiding in me, still treating me like her best friend and not her murderer. The words on the page become blurry, and I have to close my eyes because I feel like I'm going to faint. When I open them I automatically shove the book under my covers because I think I see my father standing in my doorway. I'm wrong.

"I knocked, Domgirl, but you didn't answer."

I smile because it's a lot more refreshing to see Caleb staring at me than my father.

"Whaddya got there?" he asks, jumping on my bed next to me.

I shield the diary from his eyes until I know we're safe.

"Close the door."

"Your father'll kill me."

Head tilt complete with sarcastic smirk. "He brought you into the inner circle and heard all those beautiful things you said to me," I remind him. "He's not going to kill you if you're behind closed doors with his daughter."

Obedient, but wary, Caleb hops off the bed and closes the door. Before he sits back down, I add: "Without reading you your rights first."

"What?!"

"I'm kidding," I say, then add quickly, "Arla swiped Jess's diary from her father's stash of contraband."

His response is exactly what I expect. Out of all of us, Caleb is the most straightlaced when it comes to anything to do with criminal activity or unscrupulous behavior. Sometimes he acts like *he's* the child of a law enforcer.

"You could go to jail for that," he whispers.

When he realizes petty theft would be the least of my crimes, he blushes.

"Sorry."

"Don't be," I say, meaning my words.

We're fully clothed, but I feel incredibly sexy and as if I'm doing something incredibly wrong. Not regarding the diary, but having Caleb in my room. He puts his foot in between mine and the pressure of his leg on my calf makes it difficult to concentrate.

"Arla thought there might be some clues in here to tell us what happened to Jess," I explain. "She doesn't know that we already *know* what happened, but even still, there's some interesting stuff in here."

"Really? Like what?"

Caleb's sneaker rubs against my stocking feet, and I close my eyes because it feels so good. It's like tugging on our invisible string. When I open my eyes Caleb's lips are pressed against mine. One sweet kiss, that's all. For now that's enough.

Clearing my throat and smiling a very grown-up smile, I turn from one page to the next, showing Caleb that Jess was a few shades away from obsessed with Nadine. Whereas I think she's odd and—what's the right word? Melancholy?— Jess thinks she should be a patient at The Retreat instead of a volunteer.

"*I wish twinemy would shut up* . . . Oh that's Jess's nickname for Nadine," I explain.

"Of course it is."

"*I wish twinemy would shut up about her grandmother. All she does is talk and tell stories, my grandmother this and my grandmother that. The woman is old; that's all she's got going for her. I met her once with Nap, and the lady was nassty,*" I pause. "Jess added an extra *s* to nasty in the middle of the word so it spells out . . ."

"I get it," Caleb says, interrupting me. "I didn't know Jess hated Nadine so much."

"Me either. I thought they were friends," I comment.

"Maybe she was just putting on a show to score points with loser twin," Caleb suggests. "Who would be Nap."

"Subtle, Caleb," I remark, tweaking his chin.

"Thanks, Domgirl," he replies, sliding a finger down the bridge of my nose.

Before our play-touching escalates to something my father *would* kill Caleb over, I continue reading words out of Jess's mouth. " *'My grandmother's led an amazing life; I wish I could be just like her.' And that, dear diary, is a direct quote from twinemy's mouth.* "

"What's wrong with Nadine's admiring her grandmother?" Caleb asks. "It's kind of sweet."

"It doesn't add up," I reply. "The few times I've heard Nadine talk about her grandmother, she's always complaining about her, wishing she didn't live with her family. Remember the post-season party at Nadine's house?"

A lightbulb is turned on. "Oh yeah!" Caleb exclaims. "She does hate the old lady."

"Exactly," I say, accidentally placing a hand on Caleb's chest. Feeling adventurous, he leans back against my headboard and puts his arm around me. It feels wonderful, and I lean my head against his broad shoulder.

"Maybe Nadine was simply venting at the party," Caleb says.

"So she didn't come off as some sort of a Grandma's girl?" I add.

Nodding, Caleb agrees. "Yup, plus you know how Jess loved to exaggerate things."

Nobody knows that better than I do. Which means all her diaramblings could be nothing more than figments of her imagination. Then again, why would she harp on Nadine? And if she genuinely disliked the girl, there's enough quirky stuff about her to make fun of; Jess didn't have to go after the grandmother.

Curious, Caleb grabs the diary to get a closer look. He flips through some pages, and when he stops he's not looking at the words, but the pictures.

"Why does Jess have a drawing of Orion's constellation in her diary?"

Orion? I've heard that name before, but where, I can't remember.

"That?" I reply, pointing to the scribble. "I thought it was a doodle."

"Nope, see how the three stars are close together in one straight line," he says, his index finger tracing over the drawing. "That's Orion, the hunter in Greek mythology."

I'm starting to feel nauseous, and it takes me a second to realize it's because the smells in the room have become magnified. Something about what Caleb's saying, something about this Orion is making me sick.

"Orion's a hunter?"

"According to legend," he replies. "Does it mean something to you?"

"I don't know, but according to my own family legend my dad used to be a hunter."

"So's my uncle," Caleb says. "And most of the men over thirty in these here parts."

True, but why do I get the feeling that my father is somehow connected to Jess's diary. "Oops! Sorry, Domgirl, I'm wrong," Caleb says.

Guess not all my feelings amount to anything.

"Jess says here that the drawing is Nadine's tattoo."

Suddenly inspired, Caleb whips around to the opposite side of my bed to face me. He looks like he's had his very own aha moment. "That's why it looks so familiar," he says. "It's Napoleon's tattoo!"

"Twin tattoos?"

It was weird when we thought they both had tattoos; it's downright gross that their tattoos are the same. Reading my mind, Caleb agrees.

"That's really gross," he says.

Actually that's ultra gross. And once again another reason to question what the hell is going on with Nadine. My gut instinct tells me that I need to widen my pack and trust—not doubt—myself. Tomorrow, I'll fill Arla in on everything I've been keeping from her. Another ally will make me feel a lot safer, because dealing with a curse is one thing, but I have a strong suspicion that dealing with a twinemy is going to be a heck of a lot harder.

Chapter 20

For someone whose ancestors gave voodoo dolls to children instead of Barbies, Arla is having a difficult time accepting the fact that I'm now only part human.

"You're a *what?!*" she exclaims, her skin color lightening so it turns dangerously close to Archie's pigment.

"A werewolf," I reply.

Once again Arla looks at me the way we used to look at Jess when she would recite full sentences in Japanese. "A what?!" she repeats.

"The scientific word for the lady's malady is lycanthropy," Archie offers.

"Not helping," I say, slapping him on the shoulder. "I know it sounds like I've lost my mind."

"*Like?*" Arla corrects. "You most definitely *have* lost your mind if you believe what you're telling me."

Trying another tactic, I spell out for Arla how the changes I've been going through these past few months have all been a direct result of the curse. She still doesn't buy it and claims that hormonal imbalance is a more likely culprit than a supernatural hex on my head. Then I confess that my college expedition was just a sham so I would be in a safe setting in case I transformed, which I did, and that despite our precautions things almost ended with a tragic twist.

"Arla, I didn't believe it until I saw it with my own eyes," Archie declares. "It's the truth. Dominy's a she-wolf."

Shocked, I want to tweak Archie's fanciful description of my current physical situation, but unfortunately he's nailed it. As horribly bizarre as it sounds, that's what I am.

"Oh my God!" Arla squeals. "This is a hazing! You guys punked me. Where's the video cam?"

Arla looks around my bedroom in search of something that doesn't exist. She picks up one of Jess's old Hello Kitty stuffed animals and asks it a question. "Did you swallow a video camera, Miss Kitty? Are you streaming my pretty face out to all of Two W?"

"Wow! That is exactly what Nadine thought when you told her," Archie says.

Suddenly Hello Kitty is tossed to the floor.

"Y'all told Nadine?" Arla asks, her voice about an octave lower than normal.

Quickly, I explain how coincidence and circumstance led me to confide in Nadine before telling Arla, and I can see that she is more upset by being left out of the inner circle than she is that my life has been irrevocably changed. But I can't blame her; if the roles were reversed I would feel the same way. It's never fun to be snubbed.

"So that's why you've been buddying up to Ms. Jaffe and giving me the cold shoulder?"

And it's less fun to be misunderstood.

"No, Arla, that isn't it at all," I say firmly. "Nadine happened to be in the right place at the right time and stumbled upon the truth. I *chose* to tell you. Big difference."

And from the way Arla's eyes moisten, I can tell she finally gets it.

"Oh bless your soul. You are philanthropic!"

"Lycanthropic," Archie corrects.

"A she-wolf!" Arla simplifies.

Luckily Arla keeps her always-brightly-colored fingernails short, or else they would dig into my skin when she holds my face in her hands. She's looking at me tenderly, and before she speaks I know that she's channeling her grandmother's spirit.

"My nana is jumping for joy on the other side right now," she says. "You, Dominy, are living proof that the woman wasn't a crazy old banshee like my grandpa always claimed."

As I said, both Arla's parents have Creole blood in their veins, which means Arla can trace her roots back to a heritage of relatives who believed in the paranormal and worshipped magical gods. Clearly, her nana would consider me a patron saint.

All talk of mysticism must be put aside though, and I need to make Arla understand this curse is more than a gift that proves her ancestors sane. I have to admit the role I played in Jess's death. Once again the response to my confession amazes me.

"At least now we know, Dom," she states soberly. "We don't have to invent stories; we know Jess died because of this Luba bitch."

Just like my father, Archie, and Caleb have already done, Arla reminds me that I am not responsible for Jess's death; the true culprit is Psycho Squaw. I've already come to believe this, but it's reassuring to know Arla has joined the club. The only wildcard remaining is Nadine.

"If we're to believe everything Jess wrote in her diary," Arla begins, "Nadine may not be trustworthy."

A mental image of silver smoke wrapping and undulating around Nadine's body pierces my mind.

"I think it's more than that," I say. "I think in her own way Nadine is like me."

"Please, please, please tell me you think she's Lady Dracula!" Archie begs.

This time Arla slaps him in the shoulder for me. "No! But I do think she's full of secrets that she doesn't know how to deal with."

"Then as Nana Bergeron would always say," Arla declares, speaking in her best Creole accent, "let's help dat chile see da light!"

We all agreed that the plot of the first episode of *The Secret Life of Nadine Jaffe* needs to deal with uncovering the truth about the tattoo she shares with Napoleon. There's just something wrong and ickilicious about twin tattoos, and it has got to be a clue to some deeper secret.

After some debate and discussion we decide that the only real way to confront Nadine about her twattoo is to catch her half-naked. (*Twattoo* is Archie's word, not mine, and even though it's kind of gross, it made me smile, because I think he might be a worthy successor to Jess and a new partner in my never-ending quest to bastardize the English language.) But since none of us wants to stray from our innate sexual identity and undress Nadine in private, we're going to have to go public. Or as public as the girls' locker room.

Luckily, Archie hangs out with us there so often he knows exactly where Nadine's locker is. Unluckily, he has a not-so-happy history of spending time in a girls-only facility.

"Before I evolved into the buff gay jock you see before you," he says, "I was the scrawny geek that the older kids in grammar school used to handcuff to the toilet in the girls' bathroom."

His voice sounded brave and not as if he were concealing any repressed pain; it was a period of his life that he's definitely moved on from. But we had never heard this story before and were not prepared for it. Even though Archie had already confided in me that he once thought about running away, I never took a moment to consider the specific events in his life that would have made him come to that decision.

"The first couple of times I just waited until the janitor

found me and broke the lock," he explains. "But when he realized this fad wasn't going to end quickly, he taught me how to pick a lock with a straight pin. Let's just say I've had a lot of practice fine-tuning my lock-picking skills."

At the same time Arla and I reach out and hold Archie's hands. Nobody says a word, and the only response Archie gives us to indicate that he is grateful for our friendship is that he allows his smile to fade and shows us another piece of his true self. He shows us that even though he's cheerful and confident now, he wasn't always that way.

Halfway through our kickball tournament in gym class the next day, our plan was already in motion. While Arla, Nadine, and I were changing into our gym clothes, Archie was telling Mr. Lamatina that he was sick and needed to skip world history to see the school nurse. Lamatina hates interruptions to his daily routine, but he's also a hypochondriac, so Archie was convinced he wouldn't be able to deny him the necessary hall pass to get a medical diagnosis.

After the tournament, which incidentally my team won, we retreated into the locker rooms to undress. En route to the showers, I pulled Nadine aside to ask her if anyone at The Retreat suspected an insider had lifted syringes, while Arla lagged behind the crowd to prop open the back door that leads out to the baseball field. Since the field is unused at this time of day, Archie was planning to have a miraculous recovery about ten minutes before the end-of-class bell rang, tell Nurse Nelson that he wanted to return to class to make sure he got the night's homework assignment, and instead would sneak out of school and into the girls' locker room. Once inside he would break into Nadine's locker, take her clothes out, and hide them. Hopefully, she would be too distracted looking for her clothes, let her guard—not to mention her towel—down, and I'd be able to get a good look at her as-yet-unseen tattoo. It was a risky plan, but since Archie is the unofficial risk taker of my Wolf Pack, we all thought it was a risk worth taking.

When Nadine opens up her locker and screams, I know our instincts were right.

"Who took my clothes?!" Nadine shouts.

The voice doesn't belong to the Nadine of The Retreat, but to the Nadine of her basement. It's loud and angry and pompous. She isn't getting ready to administer some TLC to a needy patient; she needs an answer to her question, and she expects it ASAP. To the surprise of everyone except Arla and me, she doesn't get it.

"Who took my clothes?!" she re-shouts. "You have five seconds to give them back, or so help you, you will be dead."

A few of the girls gasp, others start to snicker, but I remain silent because I've seen Nadine flip out before, at her brother. Unsettling yes, but unpredictable, no.

"Is this yours?"

Standing barefoot in her bra and panties, Rayna Delgado holds up a white polo shirt, the two embroidered W's on the left chest pocket giving it away that it's part of our school uniform. There's nothing on the shirt that identifies it as Nadine's, but since no one else has been robbed, we all know who it belongs to.

"It was sticking out of the trash," Rayna says.

Lunging toward Rayna, Nadine clutches her towel to her chest with one hand, and with the other reaches out to grab her shirt. "Give me that!"

Like a slinky matador, Rayna steps out of the way at the last second and raises the polo over her head like a red cape. "You didn't say if it was yours," she says, "Garbage Girl." Her lips form a triumphant sneer as the crowd cheers the impromptu bullfight.

Instead of answering Rayna's question, which would be the easiest route to reclaiming her clothes, but I guess would also be like admitting defeat, Nadine lunges at Rayna again. This time she forgets about her current attire and flails both arms into the air to retrieve her shirt, the awkward action leaving Nadine not only empty-handed, but empty-toweled too. She's so livid at Rayna's defiance that it takes Nadine a few moments for her to realize she's standing naked in the center of a rowdy group of girls. It takes me less time to see the tattoo just underneath her left hip bone.

Less a cluster and more of a horizontal line, the three stars are in descending size order, the largest being on the outside of her thigh. The tattoo looks exactly like the drawing in Jess's diary and I assume, with mild revulsion, exactly as it appears on Napoleon's body as well. Watching Nadine standing there, exposed and defeated and mumbling, the only thing I find more revolting is me.

Unlike when I acted involuntarily under the control of Luba's spell, this time my actions were calculated. And worse, I made Arla and Archie my accomplices. Together, we reduced Nadine to the broken girl standing in front of me. I can't change what happened, but I can stop it from escalating.

"That's enough!" I shout.

My voice doesn't end the taunting chatter, but it puts a wrinkle in it, so by the time I pick up Nadine's towel off the floor and wrap it around her, most of the girls have gone back to their lockers to finish getting dressed.

"Give me that," I say.

Shrugging her shoulders, Rayna hands me Nadine's shirt. "All Garbage Girl had to do was say that it was hers."

Digging through the trash bin I find the rest of Nadine's clothes that Archie put there. I'm so busy examining them to make sure nothing got stained and I'm so disgusted with myself for what I just put Nadine through that I don't hear Rayna scream until Miss Rolenski barges into the locker room.

"What's going on in here?!"

I whip my head around expecting to see Rayna and Nadine in a catfight on the locker room floor, but instead several feet separate them. Nadine is standing off to the side next to Arla, while Rayna is sitting on a bench, her leg crossed so her ankle rests on the opposite knee to reveal a bloodied foot.

"I cut myself," Rayna says, her face wincing in pain.

"On what?" Miss Rolenski asks.

Looking all over the floor, Rayna shakes her head. "I don't know, but it must've been sharp; look at the blood!"

Our gym teacher is young, but she's tough and was a former all-state softball champion. She's often shared stories of how she got a black eye or bloody nose from a fly ball or a thrown bat, so she's far from squeamish. In fact, she appears to be thrilled that it only seems to be a mild injury caused by carelessness and not the result of a squabble that would require a formal visit to Dumbleavy's office and most likely filling out a ton of paperwork.

"I've seen worse," she says, grabbing a clean towel from the rack and placing it under Rayna's foot.

Turning her back to leave the room, Miss Rolenski orders, "Now put some clothes on and let's get you to Nelson."

While some of the girls help Rayna hobble over to her locker, I give Nadine her clothes back. Watching her pull up her khakis, I remember the real reason we staged this whole break-in in the first place.

"Nice ink," I remark.

My comment comes without warning, so Arla almost drops her wig before securing it on her head. It doesn't seem to startle Nadine though, nor does it compel her to hide the truth. Just the opposite, as she offers more information than I thought she would.

"Oh yeah, it's Orion's constellation," she says, pausing a moment to look at the black stars on her skin before pulling up her pants. "I told you how I love astronomy."

"Let me see," Arla insists as she turns Nadine's body around in case she suddenly gets shy about being exposed. "When did you get it?"

"Defied my mother's orders and got it for my fifteenth birthday," she reveals.

Honestly surprised, I reply, "I would never have pegged you for rebel tattoo girl."

When Nadine laughs, her entire face softens; the silver mist is nowhere to be found.

"Connecticut girls aren't all about pearls and sensible shoes, you know," she says. "Connecticut boys, however, are a bit more predictable."

Instinctively, I know she's talking about her brother. "Napoleon?" I ask.

"A few weeks later he copied me and got the same one."

"Why would he do that?" I ask, hoping my voice sounds more casual than I think it does.

"C'mon, Dom," Nadine replies. "You haven't figured it out yet?"

"Figured what out?" Arla asks for me since my jaw just kind of dropped.

"That brothers are jerks," Nadine says, slamming her locker shut.

Relief fills my body, and uncontrollably I get a fit of gigg-laughs. I haven't laughed like this in a while, so even though it's really not appropriate, it makes me feel good. So does Nadine's comment.

"And, um, thanks for coming to my aid when you did," Nadine whispers. "That was really nice of you."

I think of the time Nadine wiped vomit spittle from my hair. "Just payback."

This time we both laugh. Arla watches us a bit confused, but I'm sure she's as relieved as I am that our spy mission has come to an end. We may not have uncovered any earth-shattering information, but at least we can confirm the tattoo Jess described in her diary is real. Maybe this means the whole thing is filled with facts and not fantasies. Not sure about that just yet, but at least we didn't get caught.

"You dropped this, Nay," Arla says, handing Nadine a card that must have fallen out of her backpack.

"Oh thanks."

Before she shoves it back into her bag, I see the handwriting on the pink envelope.

"When's your mother's birthday?" I ask.

Smiling, Nadine takes a moment to make sure the card is tucked in between two textbooks, so it won't get crumpled, before answering. "This weekend."

"Oh so close," I reply. "My mother's birthday is today."

The entire time we sang "Happy Birthday" to my mother, I couldn't get over the fact that not only do she and Nadine's mother look alike, but their birthdays are a few days apart. Something else they have in common, I guess. We're just about to eat the cupcakes we brought when one of the nurses comes in carrying a bouquet of flowers.

"These were just delivered," she announces.

When she's confronted by three quizzical looks, she immediately replies, "Sorry, they came without a card."

"Weird-looking flowers," Barnaby remarks.

And he's right. A round red vase holds a spray of about six white flowers in various sizes, but each one in the same shape. They look like pinwheels or starfish with five pointy petals that are bent so it looks like they'll spin in a counterclockwise motion. Weird, but pretty.

"What kind are they?" Barnaby asks. I don't know if he's suddenly interested in horticulture or is trying to flirt with the nurse.

"Morning glories I think," she answers.

A strange sensation comes over me; my father's bemused

expression tells me he's feeling the same thing. These flowers smell very much like my mother's favorite perfume, Guerlinade; not as powdery, but the unmistakable scent of fresh lilacs has overtaken the room.

Just as the nurse is about to leave, she stops at the door to say something that extinguishes the happy scent, turning it into a scent that rivals The Dandruff King's natural aroma.

"They have another name too," she says. "Moonflowers."

To Barnaby this new name is a cool piece of info; to my father and me, it's a warning. We're convinced these flowers were not sent by a loved one or someone whose only motive was to share birthday wishes; whoever sent these flowers wants us to know they know our secret and they know about our curse. Or are we just being paranoid?

"They don't look like the moon," Barnaby remarks. "Look more like stars."

The only thing my father and I get a chance to do is exchange worried, anxious looks across my mother's bed before the static from his police walkie-talkie fills the room, the sound immediately followed by Louis's voice.

"Sheriff," Louis barks. "We found the Wizard of Oz."

Despite Louis's cryptic remark, my father remains silent.

"Mason, you hear me?"

Turning his back on the flowers, my father can finally speak. "Yes. Where'd you find him?"

"Ex-wife's house over in Beatrice," Louis replies. "Gonna need you to come down and talk to the locals."

"On my way," he says, clipping the walkie-talkie back onto his belt. "Let's go."

"But we just got here," Barnaby whines, inhaling the moonflower fragrance deeply.

Something in the sound of my brother's voice affects my father as if it's another warning. He's been so preoccupied with helping and protecting me that he's been ignoring his son.

"I'm sorry, Barn, but duty calls," he says.

"Did the Wizard of Oz beat up a munchkin?" Barnaby snaps.

When my father laughs, his face lights up with joy and sadly I feel as if I haven't seen him happy in forever. Funny, how it's sometimes so much easier to embrace the dark than it is the light. He keeps smiling as he speaks; he doesn't want to lose hold of the feeling either.

"It's shorthand, Barn," he explains. "Oz means an ounce of drugs, and the Wizard of Oz is a drug dealer."

"Does that mean Glinda is a happy hooker?" Barnaby asks.

This time we both howl at my brother's risqué comment. Nadine is half-right; brothers can definitely be jerks, but they can also be inappropriately amusing as well.

"No, Barn," my father says in between laughs. "We finally caught him, but since he's been found across state lines I have to go in and make sure he doesn't get away on a technicality."

Makes total sense that we have to cut our birthday celebration short, but it still stinks. Until I figure out how to save the party.

"Dad, you go ahead, and I'll ask Caleb to pick us up."

My father doesn't even have to ask if I'm sure that Caleb will come; he knows he can count on my boyfriend. Just like I can count on my father to do the same thing he does every time he leaves my mother's room: He holds her hand, whispers something in her ear, and kisses her softly on the lips. Neither Barnaby nor I have ever asked him what he tells her; that's a secret between them.

An hour later I can tell that Barnaby's had enough and is ready to go. I'm surprised that he's lasted this long or that he even wanted to stay in the first place, but perhaps as he's getting older he realizes that our mother's coma wasn't her fault. He can't blame her for leaving us; he can only be thankful she's still above ground. However, he still hasn't found the will or the courage to hold her hand and kiss her good-bye. In fact, when I'm finished and ready to leave, Barnaby's already gone.

"Barnaby?"

My voice echoes off the walls of The Hallway to Nowhere, but isn't greeted by my brother's reply. All endearing thoughts of my younger sibling are lost as I walk down the harshly lit corridor in search of him so we can finally leave, and I'm reminded how much of a pest he really can be. And then I'm reminded of something much more important.

"There's a full moon tomorrow night."

The woman standing in front of me, the woman who just turned the corner at the same time I reached the end of the hallway, is old. She's over sixty at least and could be older, with long, straight black hair and pale, unnaturally smooth skin. Her thin lips are pulled back into a wicked smile, but the rest of her face is blank, especially her eyes. Staring at me are two black circles that would look like marbles if they were reflecting any light.

She's wearing a thin hospital gown that hangs on her skinny body, and her hair falls down just above her waist. There's a strong odor coming from her that I can't place; it's more familiar than offensive. When she turns to leave I can see that her black hair covers her entire back like a permanent scar. I want to make her stay, but I'm frozen; I can't move my body or find the words to keep her from leaving. Watching her walk away, I see that the bones in her legs are threatening to jut out from underneath the sheer covering of skin. I can't tell if she looks more like a zombie or a skeleton. To Barnaby she's obviously a friend.

"Isn't she a riot?" Barnaby asks.

I turn around to find him munching on a chocolate bar that he must have just bought at one of the vending machines in the lobby.

"You know her?" I ask.

"Sure," Barnaby replies. "That was Luba."

Chapter 21

Remember, Dominy, you are cursed.

"No!" I scream, turning around to stare at the emptiness that once held Luba's image.

"What's the prob, Dom?" Barnaby asks. "Luba's harmless."

I look around the corner, and no one's there. This is impossible. The woman whose husband my father killed, the woman who put a curse on my head, is the same woman my brother knows? And the same woman my brother is calling harmless?

It feels as if the walls and the ceiling and the floor are starting to inch closer to me, and with every inch they take away a little more oxygen. My senses begin to contract; my vision, hearing, sense of smell, all diminish, and it feels very similar to how the transformation begins. I feel as if I'm starting to lose control of my body.

I start to sway, and I could swear that I'm almost horizontal, but I don't fall. Only because Barnaby grabs my shoulder.

"What's wrong with you?"

The fear in my brother's voice snaps me back to reality. I

can't faint, not here, not in front of him, and not when I'm so close. So close to how it all started.

"Barnaby," I say in a firm, calm voice. "I want to meet your friend."

Guarded, but clearly pleased to play intermediary and make an introduction, Barnaby agrees. "Follow me," Barnaby says, shoving the last bit of chocolate into his mouth. "Luba's kind of like the grandmother we never had."

If I wasn't concentrating so hard on staying conscious, his comment would definitely have sent me reeling to the floor. Grandmother?! Maybe to Satan, but not the Robineau kids.

Barnaby makes a right at the end of the hall. I fall in step behind him and let my fingers graze along the wall, touching the edge of the black stripe, to make sure I stay upright. If Barnaby suspects my request is anything but aboveboard you would never know it by watching him walk; he's practically bouncing down the hall. It could be the sugar from the chocolate bar he just devoured invading his bloodstream, or he's just proud because he thinks I want to meet this so-called friend of his.

We turn another corner, a left this time, and there are so many questions wreaking havoc inside my head, there's no way I can keep them to myself.

"So, Barn, how do you know this woman?" I ask.

"Class project," he replies.

Even if I were in full control of my faculties, I still wouldn't understand what he was talking about. "What do you mean?"

"Sociology."

As if that's supposed to clarify things. "Could you maybe try to answer in a complete sentence?"

A heavy sigh is finally followed by an explanation. "Once a month we have to come here to volunteer and help out. One student gets paired up with one patient," he explains. "And I lucked out and got Luba."

Okay, so that connects a few of the dots. "So she's a patient here?"

Stopping in his tracks, Barnaby turns to face me. "Duh. I just told you it's a student/patient project; if I'm the student, she must be the patient."

I fight the urge to shove my fist into Barnaby's mouth, twist upward, and pull out every bit of information stored in his brain. What does he know about this woman? Has he ever told her anything about our family? Is she filling his imagination with stories about curses and werewolves and boys who accidentally shoot men in the woods? I force myself to smile and keep all of my questions about Luba to myself until I can ask the witch in person.

"Well, then let's go see your classmate," I say instead.

As we continue down the hallway, it finally dawns on Barnaby that this is a very odd thing for a brother and sister to do. "Why are you so interested in Luba anyway?"

Thinking fast, I use what is quickly becoming my go-to technique for when I'm in a jam: I mix the truth with a lie.

"I'm worried about her," I answer. "She looked kind of frail. I just want to make sure she got back to her room okay."

Laughter fills the hall. It isn't mine so it must be Barnaby's. "Oh, sis-dude, Luba may look frail, but trust me, she's anything but."

"What do you mean?"

Finally, Barnaby stops at Room 48. He places his hand on the doorknob, but instead of giving the door a push so we can enter, he turns to me.

"Luba always says, 'Only a fool judges a person's spirit by its surface.' "

I smile even though my mind is consumed with ugly thoughts. Of course Luba would say that; it's because she's living proof that evil can exist in the unlikeliest of places. First my father, then me; I can't believe that she's now gotten to Barnaby too. Well, her influence ends right now. I don't know how, but I've got to put an end to this relationship before she poisons his mind any further.

"It's an old Native American Indian proverb," Barnaby explains.

His words bombard my ears; I hear them, but I can't comprehend what they mean. All I can focus on is the door. It's slightly ajar, and the open sliver of space is illuminated by the same fluorescent lighting that brightens the entire facility. Just on the other side of this door is the woman who ruined my father's life, the woman who put a curse on my soul, and the woman responsible for my best friend's death. Why isn't Barnaby going inside? Why is he looking at me and still talking?

"She's got this other saying too. It's hilarious; it's about . . ."

"Why don't we go inside and let Luba tell us herself," I say, interrupting him. "Give her a chance to spread some of that ancient wisdom."

Yes, I must learn to trust my gut instincts more often; this is precisely what Barnaby needed to hear to motivate him into action.

"Hey, Luba," Barnaby chirps, pushing the door open. "I brought company."

But two people standing in an empty room can hardly be called company.

"Are you sure this is her room?" I ask. I'm back in control of my body, and I'm trying to manipulate my new heightened senses to see if I can pick up a clue as to Luba's whereabouts. Honestly, I have no idea what I'm doing, but it feels better than just standing still.

"Of course I'm sure it's her room," Barnaby snaps, sounding like his old self. "What do you think I am, a 'tard?"

If I want my brother to think that everything is status quo and I'm not freaking out because Luba is still free, I have to sound like my old self too. "Maybe Luba got tired of being your patient and she's in hiding."

"Fat chance," Barnaby replies. "She's the one who chose me in the first place. She told the orderlies that she overheard me talking and liked my sense of humor."

Thankfully, Barnaby walks back out into the hallway, so he doesn't see the look of dread grip my face. It wasn't coincidence that Luba connected with another part of my family; it was intentional. But was it another plot to try and destroy us or was she just trying to prove to us that she's the one in control? There's no way that I can find anything else out tonight without giving my own intentions away to Barnaby. Or is there?

As expected the Sequinox is waiting for us outside with Caleb smiling behind the wheel. Just as we're approaching I toss my bag behind a bush. "Oh I forgot my bag in my mom's room," I pout.

A quick glance at Barnaby then back at Caleb, and my boyfriend figures out I'm lying.

"Want me to drive Barney home and come back for you?" Caleb asks.

"Would you mind?" I say as if that was the sweetest and most unexpected thing I ever heard.

"Not at all," Caleb replies, perfectly on cue. "Okay with you, Barney?"

"It is if you stop calling me Barney."

"Sure thing," Caleb says as he pulls away. "Barney."

Running back, I retrieve my bag and have to consciously slow down so I can appear natural when I reach Essie's desk. Not that she'd even notice; her face is once again buried in some dumb celebrity magazine that doesn't use sentences longer than five words.

"Hi, Essie, I forgot to give you back our passes," I say, pulling out the gray index cards from my bag and handing them to her.

Without looking up at me she takes the cards, looks at their numbers, and places them in the appropriate section of the metal card-holder box on her desk. Then it's back to reading an article about some rich person's divorce or a reality TV star's most recent botched plastic surgery. I know Essie isn't going to be happy, but I have to interrupt her anyway.

"So my brother tells me he's friends with some woman named Luba."

No response.

"Turns out I think she's got a little crush on him, because she's always giving him gifts."

No response.

"I don't think my father will consider it appropriate for one of your patients to be giving an underage visitor some of her medication in return for keeping her company."

Finally, Essie places her magazine on the desk and looks up at me. She's trying to act disinterested, but it's as if one of her tawdry articles just came true in front of her eyes. She's rabidly engrossed.

"Luba's done what?" she asks, pulling her glasses down to the tip of her nose so she can see me clearly.

"Obviously the old lady's confused, and she thinks Lexapro and Prozac are proper thank-you gifts for a minor."

Essie pushes her glasses back into their proper position and then turns her head from side to side to make sure no one is in the vicinity to overhear. "Between you, me, and the lamppost outside, that woman has been trouble since the first day she got here," she spills. "I told Mr. Lundgarden. He's the director here, very nice, but preoccupied with troubles at home. His daughters . . . Well, don't get me started on those two hussies; they are a father's nightmare *if you know what I mean.* And his wife! She spends more money on clothes and Botox than all the women in my magazines combined. I told him that he should get rid of her—Luba, not his wife; it's not my place to interfere in anyone's personal business, but work, that's a different story. Luba's no good; that's what I told him. But what does he do instead? He lets her come and go as she pleases."

It's as if Essie has been saving up her words all these years; she's said more to me just now than she has in the decade I've been coming here. Maybe all it took for her to respond with more than a grunt was for me to engage her in a conversation that made her feel like a person instead of an employee. Whatever the reason, for once Essie's unprofessionalism proves to be beneficial. She's giving me more information on Luba than if I tried to steal the woman's personal records.

"What do you mean 'come and go as she pleases'?" I ask. "Barnaby said she's a patient."

"Honey, she's a patient like I'm a registered Republican," Essie says, laughing at her own remark. "And if you spread a word of that, I'll swear on a stack of Bibles that you're a lying Democrat."

Typically political humor escapes me, just not something I care about, but I'm guessing that Essie is trying to tell me that she's a closet-Democrat and that Luba isn't a real patient.

"So what do you mean? She just shows up and plants herself in an empty room when she feels like it?"

"Not just any room," Essie says. "Always the same, Room 48."

So they keep one room vacant just for the psycho? "But isn't that illegal?" I ask. "I know the red tape we had to go through in order to get my mother moved into a better room. How can a room be kept vacant for someone who may or may not show up?"

"That, my girl, is the $64,000 question."

No, the real question is how much power does Luba really have? "Is Luba holding something over on Lundgarden?"

"You didn't hear that from me," Essie replies. "But it sounds to me like somebody just won a game of Bingo."

It's getting increasingly difficult to follow Essie's turns of phrase, but I think this time she means that I'm right. But how is that possible? This is a state-run facility; don't they have checks and balances in place to avoid corruption and scams like this? Could Lundgarden be a pawn in Luba's game? Or does he just not care that an extra crazy woman is wandering the halls? Well, if Luba doesn't live here full-time, she's got to have a place where she goes home to. And if that's true, there's also the chance that she might have some family.

"Do you have a home address for her?"

"Now, Dominy Robineau, you know that information is classified," Essie says, acting as if she's insulted and sounding, for some reason, as if she's Southern.

"Now, Essie . . . whatever your last name is," I reply. "I thought we were friends. Are you seriously going to act all professional and by-the-book after we've known each other all these years?"

Then I do something I am not at all proud of. I pull out the almost-dead mother card.

"Weren't you on duty the very first day my mother was brought here?"

I can see that specific memory flash right before Essie's eyes.

"Yes," she says slowly.

"And what did you say to me on that day when I was only six years old?"

Mortified, she replies, "That if you ever needed anything, you just ask your Aunt Essie."

I completely disregard the fact that since that time Aunt Essie has morphed into an apathetic stepmother, but it seems that Essie is feeling a bit sentimental. She looks like she's about to cry, and I almost feel bad, but not bad enough to back down.

"Well, the time has come, Aunt Essie, and I'm asking," I say. "How can I find out where Luba lives?"

Leaning forward, Essie gets so close to me I can see the vertical lines all across her lips. They seem to bend and elongate like a picket fence in a windstorm when she speaks. "I don't have an address, but her next of kin is listed as her son," she says. "Thorne St. Croix."

My nose crinkles as if to say "that's an odd name."

Essie must have gone to the same psychic academy that Caleb graduated from; she can read my mind too. "You know those Indians and their crazy names."

I know them better than you think.

"Thanks, Essie, I really appreciate it," I reply. "And don't worry, I'll never reveal my source."

Just as I'm about to enter the main lobby and leave, I'm overwhelmed by the fragrance of the moonflowers. I know my senses have improved, but this is different. This is like the smell is calling me, like there's a hook on the end of it that has latched into my spine and is pulling me toward its source. It's an invitation I can't refuse.

Quietly, I turn around and head toward The Hallway to Nowhere. Essie's hunched over, her face buried again in her magazine, and I quicken my pace. I have no idea where this scent will take me, if it's leading me to Luba or if it's just my imagination getting the better of me, but whatever the final destination, I have to follow the flowery perfume.

At the end of the hall I make a right, then a left. I look into Room 48 to make sure it's still empty, and then continue on until I reach a dead end. The sign on the metal door reads, AUTHORIZED PERSONNEL ONLY. I'm about to turn back when a whiff of moonflowers hits me in the face, rising from the crack between the bottom of the door and the floor. Despite the imposing appearance, the door is rather easy to open, not because of a flaw in its design, but because it isn't locked. Unless the rest of The Retreat's employees have the same work ethic as Essie, I can't imagine someone carelessly leaving this door unlocked. Other forces have to be at work. And by other forces, I mean Luba.

I walk into a long, narrow section of the building that looks to be the medical supply department. Behind locked glass cabinets are tons of shelves housing everything from the syringes Nadine swipes to bedpans to plastic applicator things to oddly-shaped devices made of metal and rubber that I've never seen. One in particular looks like a boat engine with a flexible hose attached to it that ends in a long, thin needle. I pray to God I never have to find out what that one does.

The next section of the room is a huge walk-in linen closet. Towels, robes, dressing gowns, sheets, blankets, and pillows line the walls, all neatly folded, collectively giving off the aroma of bleach that almost overpowers the fresh lilacy smell of the moonflowers that's still tugging at me.

The door at the other end is also unlocked, but this one leads to a stairwell that only goes down. Unusual, but at least I don't have to make a choice. It takes me three flights to reach the next landing and when I see what's printed on the door, I literally take a step back. FIRST WARD. I know that that's fancy jargon for The Dungeon.

The impulse to leave is very strong. I tell myself that I should retrace my steps and go outside to where Caleb has got to be waiting for me, but just before I can give in to reason and common sense, a breeze erupts in the stairwell, creating a small wind tunnel that's jammed with the scent of moonflowers. It's calling me to the other side, but this door looks even more impenetrable. Plus, didn't Nadine say that The Dungeon houses only the most dangerous patients? Even if I could get inside, is it really a place I'd want to be? And is it really a place I want to risk getting trapped in? But it isn't possible to become trapped when there's nothing keeping you locked in.

Like a dream sequence in an old movie, the door begins to ripple and grow transparent, until it disappears entirely. Gone, as if it never existed in the first place. Maybe it's just an illusion, a hologram, but when I tentatively step forward and extend my arm, I touch empty space where the door used to be. If I wasn't convinced the psycho was behind this latest stunt, I'd think it was really cool magic. But soon all thoughts of magic are replaced when the sounds begin.

From within the closed cells that populate this area I can hear muffled cries, sobs filled with anguish and despair, indecipherable shouts, screams that cascade right into maniacal laughter. Nadine wasn't kidding; I don't know how anyone—insane or completely in control of his or her sanity—could spend more than ten minutes in this place without wanting to rip his or her ears off. I'm about to lose my mind, and I've only just stepped foot in here. Then I realize with utter horror that this is exactly what my life has become.

I'm exactly like these unfortunate and unseen souls rotting away in these rooms; I'm trapped just like they are. The only difference is that their cells are made of padding and come with unbreakable locks, while mine is made of flesh and blood. I look around and wonder just how long it will take until this curse becomes unbearable and it breaks me like whatever disease or misfortune has broken these patients and I wind up in a cell next to them.

The only thing that stops me from succumbing to the panic rising in my stomach is that I see something on the floor at the end of the corridor that's bathed in moonlight. I don't know how natural light is getting into this space until I get closer and see a long horizontal window running across the top of the ceiling. It's only a few inches wide, and the glass looks to be inordinately thick, so using it as an escape hatch would be impossible. But the window can be used as a way for the moon to capture my attention.

The moonflower aroma is so thick and pungent I feel like I'm standing on top of ground zero. When I look down I know I am. At my feet I see a spray of moonflowers, exactly the same kind that were in my mother's room, except these have been torn apart. The petals have been plucked and ripped into shreds, the stems bent and snapped in half, and the whole mess has been left in a heap on the cold cement floor. This is why I was brought here? To see some discarded flowers? It doesn't seem worth the effort until something within the pile shimmers in the moonlight. I bend down, and staring up at me amid the floral wreckage are pieces from my father's past: two bullets stained in blood.

Immediately the smell of rotting flesh annihilates every last trace of those freakin' flowers and I know that somewhere Luba is watching me. Somewhere very nearby this evil and demented and vengeful woman is thrilled to know that she has made me travel to the past to hold the truth of my father's crime in my hands.

Out of the corner of my eye I see the door start to ripple, and I know that it's about to return to solid form and truly trap me in this horrible place. My newfound speed comes in handy, and I make it to the other side just as I hear the door slam shut behind me.

I don't know how I get out of The Retreat without being reprimanded or at least seen, but when I jump into the Sequinox I don't see or sense anyone behind me. For now, the old witch is leaving me alone.

When I get home I make sure that Barnaby is upstairs playing video games and bring my father and Caleb into the kitchen so I can convey the details of the past few hours. As expected, once the shock wears off, my father wants to run right out and search for Luba, come face-to-face for the first time in decades with the woman who has waited patiently for her curse to come true.

"And what are you going to do if you find her, Daddy?" I ask.

Without hesitation my father replies, "Kill her."

Caleb is stunned by this response, but it's what I figured he'd say. It's both fatherly and stupid.

"So you want to kill the only person alive who may have the antidote to this curse?"

My father leans against the door leading into the garage for a moment before closing it. When he speaks his voice is more contrite than confrontational. "So what do you suggest we do?"

"Essie told me her son's name is Thorne St. Croix," I explain. "Find *him* and maybe we'll find a way to Luba."

Nodding his head, my father sits at the kitchen table, suddenly weary, and says, "That's a good idea, Dominy."

I sit next to him and hold his hand. I think he's in more shock than I was when I bumped into the old woman.

"I'm sorry you had to see her," he says. "I was hoping to spare you that."

I understand exactly what he's saying, and I wish I had never laid eyes on her either. Seeing her in the flesh and not just in my mind makes this evil all the more real. I'm sure a part of my father never thought that he'd see her again, possibly didn't even think she was alive, but now he knows she's still out there. She's come back to haunt us, and she's brought some of the past with her.

"She made sure I found these too."

The bullets clink when I place them on the kitchen table and swirl in opposite directions until they stop moving and settle into a position that ominously resembles the letter *L*. I don't have to ask my father to know that these are the bullets that killed Luba's husband; I only have to look into his eyes.

This is how he must have looked when he saw the dead man for the first time, when he realized his actions had caused the death of another human being.

He picks up the bullets as if they're pieces of delicate china and not things that were created to kill and examines them. I don't know what he's looking for, perhaps an identifying mark, a company logo, but whatever he's searching for in order to identify these bullets he finds.

"These are from my father's Winchester," he confirms. "These are the bullets that were supposed to kill that deer."

Instead, they killed a man who was married to a powerful woman. A woman who has returned and who may have become even more powerful over the course of time. Interesting how time is a friend to some, like Luba, and an enemy to others, like me. The one good thing that came of my chance encounter with Psycho Squaw was that she reminded me tomorrow night will feature another full moon.

"And the truth is, we still don't know how to deal with this," I say. "We still don't have a plan."

I'm looking at my father, expecting him to have a solution to the problem. But Caleb beats him to it.

"I do."

Chapter 22

And it's Prince Caleb to the rescue. Or more accurately, Prince Caleb's father.

"Remember the old animal protection center?" Caleb asks. "It's the perfect solution."

"How? It went out of business last year," I remind him.

"That's what makes it perfect."

Caleb reminds us that his father used to be head honcho of the Weeping Water Animal Protection Center until, thanks to state budget cuts, it was deemed unnecessary, closed down, and merged with a larger and more modern facility in Lincoln. Now Mr. Bettany is one of three assistants at the Lincoln APC, a demotion for sure, but at least he's still employed. As a result, the center in Weeping Water—complete with a sprawling basement filled with empty animal cages—is vacant.

"Caleb, that's perfect. I forgot all about it," my dad says. "Does your father still have the keys?"

"No," Caleb replies.

Okay, so my prince is pretty, but stupid. How can it be the perfect solution if we can't even get inside the place?

"Because I swiped them."

Yay! My prince isn't stupid or straightlaced anymore; he's a petty thief swinging a bunch of keys on a chain in front of my face.

"I don't usually condone theft of government property," my dad says, "but this time I'll make an exception. Good work, Caleb."

Smiling proudly, Caleb replies, "Thanks, Mr. Robineau."

So one problem solved. Tomorrow night I'll lock myself into an empty cage at the APC so when I transform into a werewolf—a phrase I still can't believe is actually part of my vocabulary—I won't be free to terrorize the locals. That leaves the big picture problem of finding Luba and her son. My father, not wanting to be outdone by a rookie, reveals that he's already on that.

"First thing tomorrow, I'm going to do a search of every state and federal database, so wherever this Thorne St. Croix is, we'll find him."

"You don't think he's right here in town?" I ask.

"I doubt it," he replies, shaking his head. "I know the name of every resident for the past decade, and I've never heard of him before."

Just because someone says something doesn't mean it's the truth. "Isn't it possible that Thorne St. Croix is a fake name?"

My father lets out a heavy sigh; clearly he was thinking the same thing. "Could be, but that's the only lead we have, so we have to pursue it as if it's fact."

"Spoken like a true cop," Caleb jokes.

And my dad follows it up with something only a father would say.

"Tomorrow, I'll stay with you all night, Dominy, to make sure nothing goes wrong."

"We all will," Caleb adds.

"No!"

My sudden outburst startles them both, but I don't care.

The last thing I want is for Caleb and my friends to witness another transformation. It's humiliating and private and painful. As much as they want to help me, I want them as far away as possible when this curse takes over. "Sorry, but I don't want you to see me like that again. Once was definitely enough." Looking in Caleb's eyes I know he's going to protest. "Don't fight me on this, Caleb, because you're going to lose."

"Tug," he says.

What? Maybe he really is pretty but stupid.

"Tug," he repeats.

Oh now I get it. We both hold our invisible string from opposite ends and tug.

"Can you feel it?" my boyfriend asks.

"Yes," I reply, more than a little embarrassed to be standing a foot from my father while kind of flirting with my boyfriend.

"I won't be anywhere near that cage tomorrow night," Caleb says, "but I'll be right next to you all the same."

Before I can thank Caleb, my father says it for me.

"Thank you," he says, clutching Caleb's shoulder. "If anything ever happens to me, it's good to know you'll be there to protect my girl."

"You can count on it, sir."

If the two of them weren't being so incredibly sincere I'd roll my eyes, but I have more important things to do. Like start packing to spend the night in a cage.

Conveniently, Barnaby has a sleepover birthday party at his friend Jody's house to attend, so my father and I don't have to sneak out of the house to spend the night at the APC. A few miles from the police station we see the building, and my father immediately slows the car down as if he's trying to creep up on it. Perhaps he's afraid some animals or homeless people have taken up residence in the overgrown brush that surrounds the place, and he doesn't want to be caught breaking into government property. But can it really be called trespassing, if we have the keys to the front door?

The building is built out of the same material they used for The Retreat and has the same institutionalized look. I guess that makes sense because they were both created to serve the same purpose, which is to take care of the sick and the lost and the lonely. But this one's closed for business. *Well, get ready to open up, 'cause you're about to house a new tenant: me.*

There are a few animal footprints in the snow leading up to the front door, but there's no indication that a person has been here recently. I follow my father's lead and walk backwards down the walkway, dragging a foot over each footprint so our tracks can't be discovered later on. I feel like we're playing some kid game like hopscotch, and I almost start laughing until I'm hit with a wave of nausea. Once we get inside I know why; this place may no longer be in use, but the smell of injured and sick animals still clings to its walls.

My father doesn't seem as affected by the smell, so it's probably me and my super senses. After a few minutes I get used to it, and thankfully it's warm, so I don't think we'll freeze during the night. I guess since the place has been sealed up for over a year it's kept the cold out. But even if the weather dips and makes the temperature drop inside the building, it won't matter, because we've come armed with extra blankets as well as pillows, a flashlight, a thermos of hot coffee for my father, and a change of clothes for me. I put the clothes that I'll change into tomorrow morning on a small ledge about five feet from the floor that juts out from the cage's cement wall. If I leave them on the ground, I risk ripping them to shreds like I'll undoubtedly rip the clothes I'm currently wearing. I may be cursed, but I'm prepared. Until I hear the click of the lock behind me.

The sound makes my body lurch forward as if somebody

punched me in the stomach. I know this is for my safety and the safety of everyone in town, but I still feel like I'm in prison and waiting to be sentenced. It's eerie and final and unfair.

At the same time my father and I see the full moon shining through the window on the other side of the room. He shuts off his flashlight because the moonglow is stronger and smiles at me from the free side of the cage. I know he's trying to share his strength with me, but it has the opposite effect; it breaks my heart. I know this is my father's fault; I know it's because of his recklessness that I'm in this cage right now, but I can't blame him. He would willingly change places with me to bear my newly acquired burden. But that's not going to happen, so all he can do is turn around and give me some privacy.

My first scream makes his body tilt a little, as if the sound of my voice pushes him off center. My second scream makes his hands constrict into two fists, so they look like pendulums as he teeters forward, then back. My third scream makes him drop to his knees and bury his face in his hands. I think I hear him crying, but I'm not sure because my growls are getting louder.

The burning throughout my body, the snapping of my bones, the thick layer of fur replacing my skin is complete, and the girl has lost once again to the primitive spirit within her soul. Dominy is nowhere to be found, and in her place is something better and stronger and smarter than that girl could ever hope to be. I'm superior to her in every way, and how dare she trick me into coming into this cage? How dare she lead me into this dead end?

Leaping through the air, I throw my body, paws first, into the metal bars, and the impact makes me fall to the ground. The stupid man on the other side of this cell is still huddled on the floor like the pathetic creature he is. Our places should be switched; he should be caged, and I should be set free.

That would be the natural order of things; the strongest roam the earth, while the weak wait until it's time for them to die.

Howling, I pace my cage and leap against the bars a second time, the metal barrier that separates me from freedom shaking only slightly. This structure is secure, and my third, fourth, and fifth attempt to rip the bars from their foundation all fail. When I howl again it resembles a wail, plaintive and pitiful, and the sound sickens me. Defeated I bound to the far end of the cage and pace in a circle several times before collapsing into a heap. I need to rest and think of a way out. An hour later, when I'm convinced escape is not an option, I hear a click.

Slowly my head rises, but I keep my snout low. I'm surveying the area with pretended disinterest, but when I see the cage door swing open, I can't conceal my elation. Looking toward the moon I bow my head, showing my gratitude, because I know that it has somehow restored the natural order. I repeat that motion when I get to the door of the cage; my liberator deserves my respect as well.

Outside, the air is brisk and alive and ripe with death. I breathe deeply so I can track the scent and follow it. The snow-covered earth feels good under my paws, crunching underneath me, announcing my arrival, letting the world know that I cannot be restrained, I cannot be caged, I cannot be kept prisoner. My spirit needs to be free, and my body needs to feed, and that's why I can feel my mouth water as the death-smell grows stronger and thick as fog.

Walking past a tree whose collection of branches bears a striking resemblance to a woman, I see what's making that wondrously foul odor. Crouched low to the ground a few yards away is a man who in a few moments will no longer be a man. This one doesn't cry out when my jaw clamps down on his thigh and rips flesh from bone; this one doesn't protest when the blood seeps from his body like a flowing red river; this one doesn't prevent me from taking his life.

The bitter, now-familiar taste fills my mouth, explodes in my throat, and travels throughout my body until my hunger is quenched. I look up at the lady stuck in the tree and howl. If she had a voice she would howl with me to let the world hear her pain, let the world know how her plight of immobility makes her suffer, but she doesn't have that power, so I howl once more, this time for her.

Something about this woman triggers a memory. I've been here before. No, not me—this Dominy has been here; she's the one who knows this land. Maybe if I penetrate her mind a bit further, she'll lead me to a safe place to rest and another fertile hunting ground.

Soon the land starts to change and the buildings are gone, replaced by trees and hills, an open terrain christened by snow that seems to be untouched by humans. The air is colder out here and feels good blowing in my face, across my body, and all along my tail. I come to a clearing and stop; there's something different about the flat stretch of land in front of me. I press my paw onto the shimmering ground and there's no traction; my paw slides out from under me, and my body falls, my stomach flat against the small ice pond. Another memory bites at my brain, and I remember words, something like, *"never judge something by its surface"*; instinctively I know not to walk on this silvery sheath. However, I can't help but stare at my reflection.

Suddenly I'm as frozen as the earth. Gazing into my blue-gray eyes, I don't see a fierce warrior; I don't see a cunning animal; I only see a girl. My red fur blows in the wind, and I wish the tufts of hair were flames so they could melt they ice, so they could take away this vision, but they can't; it's burned into my soul. The girl's fear and horror and sadness are part of me; this is who I am.

This is who I am!

I hear the girl's voice scream somewhere deep within my brain, and I know that she sees my face reflecting back at her as clearly as I see hers. When she shudders, I shudder along with her because I can feel her pain. I know what it's like to feel trapped and alone and ugly.

God help me! Please!! This isn't me!

The sound that bursts out of my mouth is not mine; it's not hers; it's ours. And when I see the ball of light on the other side of the clearing, I know that it's responding to her part of the cry and not mine.

Gliding across the air, the yellow ball moves toward me, growing in size as it gets closer, bringing with it another scent, flowery and pungent, the undeniable smell of cherry blossoms that fills the air as if spring has arrived early. Suddenly, the yellow light contracts and then expands into a long, vertical line, until it spreads apart to reveal its passenger.

The girl standing before me looks to be made of the embers of the sun, her hair, her face, her entire body pulsating with sunlight. She's so different from the moon, I find her appearance to be disgusting, but she possesses a serenity that is calming as she walks toward me. No, not me, toward the lost girl.

"Dominy," she says, a beam of sunlight floating out of her mouth, "it's me, Jess."

Stepping backward, I feel my body shake as a result of the girl's confusion.

"Don't be afraid," she orders. "I told you I'd always protect you."

Slowly the girl, this Dominy, relents, and my body quiets. Jess kneels in front of me and strokes my fur. Her touch is gentle and humbling, because I remember that this is the first girl I took; my first victim has come back to me. But she hasn't come back for vengeance. She has accepted her fate; she understands that I was only doing what I was put on this earth to do. She's merely come back to speak with her friend.

"Look at me, Dominy," she says. "If you want to see who you really are, look at me."

Through my eyes, Dominy looks at the girl kneeling before me, and it's as if we're trying to exchange places.

"Jess?"

The words are unspoken, but I can hear the voice in my brain. The other girl, the one kneeling, her face smiling, her body shimmering, can hear her too.

"I know my hair's back to its natural color," she says, her voice buoyant and light. "But do not tell me you can't recognize me. Didn't I always say I was a walking ray of sunshine?"

"Jess, don't look at me."

Dominy's voice is filled with self-loathing and shame, but the sound is not to be pitied; it's to be admired. She's hardly a coward; this girl is as strong as I am. Jess agrees.

"You think you look different?" Jess asks. "Look into my spirit and you'll see your true self."

I feel my snout rise up, and I know that Dominy is in control; we share this body now. We look into the golden light of this Jess girl, and the layers of shame and guilt and fear start to peel away.

"You're my best friend," Jess says. "Nothing will ever change that."

"How can you say that after what I've done?" Dominy asks, her voice cracking.

The light emanating from Jess explodes into a huge yellow flame, and for a moment she disappears. But then a sound erupts from out of the emptiness, loud and crass and familiar. The sound of deep, heartfelt laughter.

"What's done is done, Dom," Jess says. "It was my time to go; you just made sure I wasn't late."

"I can't believe you've come back to me," Dominy cries from deep within my body. "I've missed you so much."

"I've missed you too," Jess replies. "All this glamour is fab, but not if I can't share it with my best friend."

"Jess . . . I'm so sorry," Dominy says, her voice weeping.

"I know you are," Jess replies. "But it's time we let all of that go and move forward."

I feel drowsy as Dominy starts to take over, as her tears turn to laughter, as she begins to connect with this spirit. Jess touches the top of my head, and a feeling of tranquility spreads throughout my body like a sweet breeze. Together we walk back to the cage, Jess showing us the way, and when I hear the click of the lock behind me, I know that for the first time in months, after all the turmoil and all the suffering and all the pain we've gone through, Dominy and I will finally get a peaceful night's sleep.

Chapter 23

SERIAL KILLER ON THE LOOSE

I'm certain the headline in the *Three W* is referring to me. When I read the rest of the article I'm not so sure. There's no way that I could have killed this Elliot Aldersen vagrant person even though it says that his mutilated body was found near the low hills and several of his limbs were torn off or are missing. Sure sounds like a werewolf's MO, but I spent last night locked in a cage. Unless Psycho Squaw put a curse on some other girl's head, this has to be a super bizarre coincidence.

Thanks to Dumbleavy and his attempts to channel the student body's fear and sadness into a constructive, teachable moment, we have a two-hour assembly during lunch where he and his team of crackerjack guidance counselors remind us not to take candy or a free ride from strangers, so the first time we get to discuss Lars Svenson's latest editorial scoop in private is after school. Collectively, my friends and I decide to rebel and skip our various practices and meetings and walk home instead of taking the bus so we can talk about this latest mysterious death without worrying that anyone will over-hear us and think we're trying to organize our very own Scooby Gang.

"What was Aldersen doing out near the hills last night anyway?" Caleb asks. "It was freezing."

"The hills were his home," Arla answers.

"Like the Waterfall Hills condos? I'd love to live there," Archie gushes. "They have a community center with a pool and an 18-hole golf course."

Caleb sets it up. "Dude, only old men and lesbians play golf."

And Archie hits it out of the park. "Someday, Bells, I may be both."

"My dad said Aldersen was homeless and passing through town," Arla answers, ignoring the boys. "Got citations for loitering and panhandling, but disappeared a few days ago, and when something disappears, Louis Bergeron does not go looking for it. Just ask my mother."

Then Caleb takes the bat from Archie and swings. "Does she play golf?"

Arla and I slap opposite sides of Caleb's head at the same time, my slap followed by a question. "Didn't the article mention that he had a heart condition?"

"Thoracic aortic dissection," Nadine replies. "Which can often lead to an aneurysm that tears the aorta."

"The a-who-ta?" Arla asks.

"The tissuey membrane wall around the heart," Nadine, the wannabe nurse, explains. "Rips it apart without warning, resulting in sudden death."

"So maybe this homeless guy was already dead before his body was dismembered," Archie suggests.

"Or he got too close to some starving mountain lion?" Caleb adds.

"Or a hungry werewolf," I say.

Let's hear it for Debbie Downer! My spoken comment—
which, let's face it, was on the tip of everybody's unspoken
tongue—stops us in our tracks.

"Domgirl, you were locked up last night," Caleb says.

"And your father played watch guard," Archie adds. "If
you escaped to go a-hunting, don't you think your father
would've said something?"

"My father didn't tell me there was a curse on my head for
sixteen years," I remind him. "He's a bit close-mouthed if
you haven't noticed."

Caleb might know my father better than I do. "True, but
he wouldn't keep something this important a secret."

"Is a-hunting like real hunting?" Arla asks.

"Kind of," Archie replies. "Except that you do it in slow
motion."

Archie, like Dumbleavy, is always looking for a teachable
moment, so he turns Arla's question into an opportunity to
demonstrate the art of slow-mo a-hunting. Crouching low to
the ground, stretching out his arms, and taking long strides
as he walks, he scans the area for imaginary prey. With his
white hair and hands jutting out from his silver parka, he
looks like a snowman on the prowl. Picking up a fallen
branch he exclaims, "I found a leg!" Only he would find
humor in death and dismemberment.

He takes another wide stride and karma strikes back as
Archie slips on an ice patch and lands flat on his back.

"Albino down!" he shouts.

It feels amazing to laugh hysterically with the rest of my
friends. It feels like we haven't done this in forever. Together,
we try to help him stand, but of course only wind up suffering the same fate. Sprawled on the ice I look up and see the
sun shining behind The Weeping Lady; she may still be
trapped within one moment in time, but I get the feeling that
I'm about to be set free. Rolling over, I push onto the ice to

stand up and see my reflection. I'm right. The Weeping Lady may be stuck in limbo for eternity, but not me. I remember exactly what happened.

"I killed that homeless man."

And once again Debbie Downer brings the party to a halt.

"Domgirl, not every unexplained death is your fault."

Caleb's words are sweet but ineffective, because last night comes back to me in a flash. I remember the cage door swinging open; I remember leaving the cage; I remember roaming, killing, seeing sunshine in the night, and best of all I remember Jess.

"I saw Jess."

This really quiets my pack. Archie is so shocked by this announcement that he gives up trying to get vertical and plops back down on the ice. Four faces stare at me, begging for me to continue.

"I saw a bright yellow light in the darkness come toward me, and when it got closer it was like the sun was rising in the middle of the night," I remember. "And standing right in that light was Jess."

Arla starts to cry. "It's like Jess turned into what she always was, a ray of sunshine."

"That's exactly what she said!" I cry out. "Before I saw her I couldn't see very well. It was like someone had put a plastic bag over my head. Nothing was clear; everything was hazy and distorted, and my body was moving around, but somebody else was doing it. I didn't know what direction I was going in."

"That's what it feels like when you transform?" Archie asks.

"Yes. I know that I'm moving, I know that I'm alive, but I'm someone else or, I don't know, some other part of me has control. All that changed when I saw Jess."

"Sounds like Jess came to your rescue," Arla says.

Now I start to cry. Could that be possible? "But how can that be? Jess is dead."

"Dom, you're a werewolf," Archie replies. "We've officially made a left onto Supernatural Boulevard."

We can almost feel our friend's spirit join the group as I tell them how amazing it was to see Jess again, to have her pull the plastic bag off my head, make me aware of what was happening to me. I also tell them that it's only because of Jess that I returned to the cage.

"I followed her light back to safety," I say.

"But how did you get out?" Caleb rightfully asks.

"Someone must have opened the door," I surmise.

Archie, Arla, and Nadine have the same answer at the same time.

"Luba."

That name. It's a thousand times worse now that I can attach a real person to it. Eerily smooth, pale face, long, black stringy hair, emaciated body. Evil on a stick. Luba must have let me out of the cage; the only other culprit could be my father, and there's no way he would've done that. I mull it over and realize Luba's actually done something good.

"At least we know the witch hasn't left town," I say.

"Why would she leave?" Archie asks. "She waited how many years for the show to start? Of course she's going to hang around to watch it play out."

Archie's comment leaves me almost as cold as the ice I'm sitting on. How long will this curse play out? How long will I have to hide this secret? How many months will pass, bringing with them yet another and another and another transformation? And how many times will I have to be reminded that I'm not only a werewolf, but I'm a murderer?

Later on in my bedroom I confess all this to Caleb. I don't want him to have to bear the weight of my conscience, but it's becoming so heavy I can barely lift my head. When I do, I see one of Jess's stuffed animals lying on the floor, and it hits me that she's the real reason these questions plague me. More than wanting Luba to remove this curse, I want Jess to be alive. But wait a second? Maybe being able to see her as a ghost or whatever she's become is a small consolation. Then again maybe it will just be a constant reminder that I killed her in the first place.

"Do you think that her coming to me last night is proof that she forgives me?"

"Of course she forgives you," Caleb says. "Now that she's turned into this sunshiny spirit girl, she's got to know all about the hex job and that you had nothing to do with her death."

He's got a point, but . . .

"Even still, Caleb, I really don't know if I'll ever . . . if I'll ever be able to forgive myself."

"Tug."

I'm in no mood to play Caleb's dumb invisible string game, but I stop myself from acting like a mean girl gone totally nasty. "Tug."

"Only you can forgive yourself," he says. "But I can help figure out who's to blame for letting you out of your cage. Next full moon, we videotape."

Will I ever learn to trust my boyfriend as completely as I do my father?

"I knew you'd come up with another great idea."

My father appears in the doorway unexpectedly, the way fathers often do. His sudden presence makes me uncomfortable, and I'm not exactly sure why. Could be because it reminds me that Caleb and I have to censor our conversations in case Barnaby is the one lurking around every corner, but there's something else. It's like when I used to look at the moon and thought it was a premonition, a warning that something bad was going to happen. Maybe my father's like the moon, a living, breathing clue that even more bad stuff is just around the corner. Not a very comforting thought to have about your father.

To the best of my ability I push all bad thoughts out of my head over the next few weeks. I concentrate on cheerleading, try to embrace my increased strength and flexibility by showing off my improved gymnastic skills during practice. Rayna, for one, is incredibly impressed that I can now do a twisting front handspring *and* a Russian split.

"Has Caleb been tutoring you in flexibility too?" she asks after practice one day.

"Unlike you, Ms. Delgado," I reply, "I don't kiss-and-tell."

"Dominy, I think you and your bf have been doing lots more than just kissing!"

I let the girls laugh and think whatever they want. My close friends know the truth—about my newfound athletic prowess as well as my old-fashioned approach to dating—so if the rest of the school thinks Caleb is hitting a homer every Saturday night, makes no difference to me.

I'm improving academically as well. So well that Mrs. Gallagher declared it a holiday last week when I got a B+ on a pop quiz in geometry. I can't imagine that it's a side effect of the curse, but maybe I'm so preoccupied with full moons and werewolves and trying to find Luba and her son Thorne, I'm no longer stressing about school, so my mind can actually absorb the stuff I'm being taught. Whatever the reason, my father put my test on the fridge. It's being held there by a magnet in the shape of our school mascot—the timberwolf—which, I believe, would be the perfect illustration of irony.

Once again luck is on our side because tomorrow Barnaby has a super-early out-of-town track meet at some new indoor arena over in Grand Island, so tonight he's sleeping over at Arla's, and Louis will drive them to the school bus in the morning, so we don't have to worry about leaving him alone while we head over to the old Animal Protection Center for another evening of the watchdog and the werewolf. Which sounds like the Robineau family version of the bee and the butterfly.

On the drive over, my father asks me questions about school, complains about the police-sponsored leap year party in Lincoln tomorrow night that he's not at all thrilled about going to, tells me that he heard some reality TV star checked herself into rehab so she could escape the enormous pressure cooker that is Hollywood—anything to keep the conversation light and convince me that we're just a normal father and daughter trying to make a connection. It has the opposite effect. It reminds me that we're so far from normal we may never be able to find our way back again. But I keep that knowledge to myself and keep up my end of the conversation, so my father thinks he's succeeded in tricking me into thinking we're just going for a drive on a Friday night. To an abandoned building with cages that is now equipped with a video surveillance camera.

"Caleb's father is a techie," I say. "Loves this stuff."

"Looks like his son takes after him," my father adds.

Hidden in the corner of the room in the center of a stack of boxes, Caleb's set up a small video camera aimed directly at the door of the cage. My father got an extra key made to the building so Caleb could come early and have everything ready for us when we arrived. The only clue that he was here is the note taped to the box directly above the camera—*Just hit Record, C.*

"Let's hope your boyfriend's idea works," my father says, hitting the Record button. "Because I have absolutely no memory of what happened the night you got out. It's a complete blank."

And that's why Caleb's idea has to work. We want proof that Luba is the one who let me out of the cage, because if we can catch her on video maybe we can learn more about her and the curse. Maybe she'll do something that we can use against her to trap her. It's a long shot, but at least we'll know for certain that she's working alone and that we don't have to worry about another psychopath.

The transformation feels different this time. It's still excruciatingly painful; I still feel like my limbs are being ripped out of their sockets; I still feel the fur growing from underneath my skin as it envelopes my body, but this time right before I pass out I feel hopeful. I see my father looking at me. His back isn't turned; he's looking right into my eyes, and I can see him forcing himself to remember that I'm his little girl. It's comforting to know he'll always be there for me even when I disappear.

When the plastic bag is pulled over my head, I hold on to the image of my father's face. His compassion and devotion and unconditional love help me remember that I'm not alone, and it gives me strength. This time, instead of feeling like someone has taken over my body and I'm nothing more than cargo, I feel like I'm sharing the controls. This wolf spirit is still stronger than me, still calling the shots, but at least I don't feel as lost, and I definitely don't feel trapped. How could I when the cage door opens with a loud creak to announce my freedom?

A rush of wind passes over me; the front door must be opened too. The plastic bag around my face billows, making it even harder to see. My eyes are cast downward, and I can only see feet as I leave the cage. I look up only once, not to see who's standing next to me, but to try and figure out why there's a red light blinking a few feet away. But just as I do, the smells from outside become too enticing and I'm distracted. Anyway, wrapped tightly within the skin of the wolf, it doesn't matter who came to my rescue or why there's a strange red light nearby; the only thing that matters is that I'm free to feed.

Outside, the air is bitter cold, but I'm on fire. Racing through the open field, the sound of snow-crunch in my wake, I keep moving toward the hills, toward the scent of blood, and stop only when I see the coyote trying to burrow itself into the ground, trying to evaporate into the night to rest or to hide. Silently my mouth opens and my sharp teeth bathe in the moonlight. There will be no resting or hiding tonight, only feasting.

The mixture of flesh and fur and blood fills my mouth and tastes like life itself. It's disgusting and abhorrent and completely natural at the same time. Much more natural than the blinding ball of sunshine floating toward me.

I've witnessed this before so I'm not afraid, only curious. The yellow ball of light hovers before me a few seconds before elongating into a vertical line, and then it spreads out in all directions, brightness taking over the night, shimmering with such intensity that I have to bow my head and avert my gaze. The glow is so dazzling, I could swear that a star has fallen out of the sky. But this isn't a star; it's merely a girl.

"Jess!"

"You know somebody else who's been given the power of the Omikami?"

"What?"

"Google it later," Jess says. "Right now there's someone who wants to meet you."

Swinging my head from side to side I don't see anyone, yet I feel another presence lurking in the shadows. Something almost as powerful as this being Jess has become. A shiver travels throughout my body, not because this presence is cold, but because it's empty. The woman emerges from a black hole, and I automatically step back to get closer to the unnatural sunshine. My instincts are confirmed when Jess introduces this woman.

"Luba is evil," Jess says. "But regardless of all that, she can be trusted."

"How can evil be trusted?" I ask.

"Just because something is evil, doesn't mean it can't speak the truth."

The wolf-spirit is gone, perhaps hiding so I can easily see this disgusting woman who did this to me, who cursed me, and I don't want to hear her speak, I don't want to hear her truth, but I know that I have to. Jess wouldn't allow her here if Luba didn't have something important to say.

"She knows how to reverse the curse," Jess announces.

What?! And she's just going to tell me? After she's finally gotten what she wanted, after her cruel, vindictive plan has succeeded, she's just going to tell me how to get rid of the curse so we can all live happily ever after and make like none of this ever happened? I don't believe it.

"You can believe her," Jess says, reading my mind. "You may not like what she has to say, Dominy, but you can believe her."

I turn my eyes from the pure beauty of Jess's yellow glow to the vile nature of Luba's black light and wait for her to speak. Her long black hair lifts in the breeze like impatient snakes anxious to slither on their way. *Tell me, Luba, tell me what I need to know so I can end what you started.*

When she speaks her voice sounds like oil spilling into a crystal clear lake, smooth, yet destructive. "If you want to break this curse you must kill the original sinner," Luba proclaims. "You must kill your father."

Chapter 24

The sunlight feels wonderful on my face.

It's summer, and we're swimming in the lake. We're shouting and laughing and splashing each other with cool water that dries quickly on our sunburned skin. We're all there, me, Caleb, Archie, Arla, Napoleon, Nadine, Jess. Jess is the happiest of all because it's her birthday, her special day, the first day that she kissed a boy, the first day of the rest of her life. The first day of the rest of her very short life.

Abruptly I open my eyes, and sunlight is still pouring onto my face, but the warmth of my dream has fled and I'm freezing. Because I'm no longer with my friends swimming on a happy summer day; I'm naked and lying on a cold, cement floor.

Without looking over at my father, I cover myself with the blanket that's rolled into a clump at my feet. My modesty is unnecessary because my father is still sleeping in his chair, probably dreaming of a much happier time as well. Maybe the day he first met my mother, when she was driving cross-country and her car broke down on the outskirts of town. She took one look at him and didn't drive another mile. At least that's the story he tells. I suspect if I ever asked my mother she would tell a slightly different version.

Or maybe he's reliving the day he got married at St. Edmund's and thought that he would spend every morning until the day he died waking up next to my mother. Not waking up in a chair after spending the night trying to protect his cursed daughter. But maybe in the back of his head this is the life he always assumed he'd lead. Caretaker to the damned. If that's the case, then why the hell did he ever allow me to be born in the first place?

He should've never gotten married, no matter how much he loved my mother, or he should have simply told her that he didn't want kids. He should've gone to the doctor and had a procedure to make it impossible for him to have children. He should've done a lot of things; but no, he was a reckless child who grew into a reckless adult. The only problem is he's never really suffered from his own actions, while all around him is collateral damage. The proof is written all over his face, such a peaceful expression. Thank God he's sleeping because I can't look at him, let alone speak to him right now!

I don't know how long my privacy will last, so I grab my clothes from the ledge and quickly get dressed. Outside, the clouds must part because the sunlight becomes stronger, and I can feel my face flush from the heat. I don't know why, but I feel like Jess is calling out to me, making me see how stupid I'm acting. Just because my father looks peaceful doesn't mean he's at peace. The anger drifts from me like the dust caught in the beam of sunlight, floating away where it can't harm anyone.

Once I am fully dressed, there's nothing for me to do except wait until my father wakes up. I pull on the bars and the lock is intact, but that really doesn't mean anything. I still could've gotten out of this cage, just like the last time. The only thing that matters is what's on that videotape.

Perfectly on cue, Caleb knocks on the door and uses his key to enter. With him he brings the sunshine. And with the sunshine comes a memory. I wasn't just dreaming of being wrapped in sunshine with Jess, I was remembering the last time I saw her. Last night.

"Morning, Domgirl!" Caleb shouts.

I know that he's shouting because he's scared. It's easier to cover your fears if you yell than if you whisper. But once he hears my father's snoring, he brings the volume down.

"Any news?"

"I saw Jess again."

"Really?"

It takes me a second to figure out why Caleb is so disappointed.

"So that means you got out again," he says, nervously twisting the key in the cage's lock.

Stepping into the main room, I try to remember exactly where I saw Jess, but no images appear in my mind. The only thing I remember is blinding sunshine, which doesn't make sense since I saw her at night.

"I don't know," I reply. "I remember seeing her and talking with her. The details are clearer, but they're still kind of foggy."

"Give it time; it'll come back to you," Caleb predicts, his voice back to its usual calm tone. "Nice to know seeing her wasn't just a one-time fluke."

"No," I say. "I guess our connection never died even though . . . well, even though one of us did."

Caleb grabs the plastic garbage bag my father brought with the other supplies and fills it up with my torn clothes. "Makes total sense. You were best friends practically from the time you were born," he says sweetly. "A connection like that is hard to break."

Smiling, I look up into my boyfriend's face. "I guess that's true. I just wish my mind wasn't such a blank slate."

"Well, if you did get out this won't tell us what happened after you left, but it will tell us who set it all in motion," he says, grabbing the video camera and putting it in his duffel bag. "And my money's on the obvious choice, Luba St. Croix."

The mere mention of her name wakes my father.

"Dominy!"

"I'm fine, Daddy," I say.

It only takes him a few seconds to go from snoring to fully awake, probably a combination of fatherly instincts and cop training, and it doesn't take him long to throw a barrage of questions at me.

"Did you get out last night?"

"I don't know, but I do remember seeing Jess, and just now when Caleb mentioned—"

"Wait a second," my father interrupts. "You *saw* Jess?"

Oops, forgot to fill him in on that piece of information. Quickly I relay the details of my recent Jess sightings to my dad. Instead of being freaked out even further, he thinks it's wonderful.

"You see, honey," he says, his eyes getting teary, "Jess understands what happened and she forgives you."

"I'm not sure I completely deserve it, but yeah, she does."

Now it's Caleb's turn to interrupt.

"What were you going to say?" he asks. "You said, 'When Caleb mentioned . . .'"

For a moment, I can't remember what I was going to say; I'm still thinking about Jess, but then it comes back to me. "You mentioned Luba's name and I remembered seeing her too!"

"Really?" Caleb asks. "Kind of weird that you could see them together since one's a ghost."

For some reason, I start to laugh. "Jess isn't a ghost."

It's my father's turn to laugh. "Honey, if this whole ordeal has taught me anything, it's that nothing is impossible. Jess has come back as a ghost probably to help you get through this."

They don't get it. "Jess is definitely some sort of spiritual being—she was bathed in sunlight; it was beautiful and magical—but she's not a ghost," I say. "She told me what she was, but I can't remember. Why can't I remember anything?!"

"It'll come to you," Caleb insists.

"Don't push it, Dominy. There might be a reason your memory hasn't returned," my father adds, his hands firmly placed on my shoulders to get me to stop shaking. "Jess has been through an incredible ordeal too, so just remember you may not like what she has to say, but you can believe her."

Suddenly my father's hands feel like hundred-pound weights, and I'm being pushed into the floor. I can hear his words repeating and slamming into me like sledgehammers, each strike ripping the plastic bag from my head so I can see clearly. I remember everything that Jess and Luba said to me, and that's why I need Caleb to leave.

"How long do you think it'll take you to watch the whole tape, Caleb?" I ask.

Getting the hint, he picks up his duffel bag. "Shouldn't take me too long, an hour or two at the most, and don't worry, I'll delete the parts when you . . . you know."

I shrug my shoulders. Caleb's seeing my naked body on video seems inconsequential in comparison to what I remembered.

"Come over the minute you finish," my father orders.

"Will do, Mr. Robineau."

Caleb turns to leave, but quickly turns back around to kiss me good-bye. My father coughs awkwardly, Caleb blushes, and I can barely muster a smile. The second Caleb shuts the door, I look at my father, and he immediately knows something is wrong.

"You got out last night didn't you?"

"Yes."

"And you remember what happened?"

"Yes."

"Tell me."

How do I say the words out loud? How do I tell him what Luba told me? I hate myself for the things I was thinking about him earlier. How could he ever know the spell she cast would actually come true? He was just a boy himself. No one in his right mind could ever believe her words would have a future, and no one in his right mind would ever think my father could have such a dreadful past. He's beloved, respected, and admired. He's a pillar of society; he's not a chip in its foundation. Most of all he's my father, and I want him to stay that way, but if I ever want to live a normal life, if I ever want to know what freedom feels like again, I have to lose him.

"Luba told me how to reverse the curse."

Before I say a word, my father reaches backward to feel the back of the chair and sits down. He sits slowly, like an old man afraid of moving too quickly, fearful of the outcome if he falls. My father looks at me bravely, but I know that he's frightened. Or maybe it's just that I'm more frightened than I've ever been in my life, because I know exactly how he'll respond.

"I have to kill the original sinner," I say, repeating Luba's words. "I have to kill . . ."

"Me."

Unable to speak another word, I can only nod. I feel as if by just saying that evil woman's words out loud I've stuck a knife in my father's heart. But to look at him you would never know that I just told him he must die in order for me to live a normal life. The fear that threatened to topple him to the floor a few moments ago is gone, replaced with tranquility; he looks as peaceful as he did when he was sleeping.

"Then that's what you have to do," he says simply.

Oh sure, that's all I have to do. I just have to kill my father.

"What are you talking about?! Didn't you hear what I just said?!"

"I heard every word," he replies. "And I'm glad that it's that simple."

My head crashes into the metal bars as I stumble backward. Pain shoots up, out, and down my body, and I have to grab hold of the bars so I don't fall down. "You think that's simple?!" I scream, the tears falling from my eyes, staining my cheeks. "I have to kill you if I want to end this nightmare!"

When my father wraps his arms around me, I push him away hard, and he falls into the boxes behind him. I don't want his stupid, compassionate arms around me! I want him to tell me that there's another way out of this, even though we both know in our hearts that there isn't.

"Dominy," he says, getting up off the floor, "the curse started with me, so it has to end with me; *it is that simple.*"

Blindly, I start to pace the length of the room, and I feel as trapped as I do when I first step foot in that cage. "You have no idea what you're saying! You have no idea what you're asking me to do!"

Now when my father grabs me I don't have the strength to push him away, but I refuse to look at him. I don't care that his eyes are filled with love and tears and sadness.

"I did this to you! I'm the one responsible for destroying you!" he cries.

I don't have to look at him to know that his mouth his moving, but the sobs that are clutching his throat are making it impossible for him to speak. I know exactly what that feels like. But he's strong, and after a few moments, he wins the fight.

"Dominy, I have tried my entire life to stop this from happening, but I've failed," he tells me. "I can't find where Luba lives. As far as any records can tell, Thorne St. Croix doesn't exist. There's nothing else for me to do except . . . give up my life so you can live yours."

The finality and conviction of his words are like slaps

across my face, wrenching me from my hysteria and bringing me back to reality. He really expects me to do as Luba has ordered.

"Daddy, I can't."

The palms of his hands feel so warm against my cheeks, like his blood is pumping into me, like he's already giving me his life.

"Yes, you can," he whispers. "You have to, baby, because you have no other choice."

The rest of the room fades away. I'm still looking into my father's face, but I'm a little girl, and we're standing over my mother's lifeless body.

"I don't want to leave here, Daddy," I remember telling him. "I want to stay here with Mommy forever."

"Honey, you can't do that; we have to go home," he said. "You have to go to school and play with your friends and teach Barnaby how to be a good boy."

"But how can I do that, Daddy, without Mommy?"

"You have to, baby, because you have no other choice."

He's wrong. I can choose to stay this way forever. I can choose to succumb to this curse and allow it to control and possess and destroy me for the rest of my life or until I can't stand to live any longer. But I know I can't do that; I've only lived with this revolting secret for a few months and already I've caused so much irreversible damage and already my soul feels like it's black as coal. I can't go on like this even if the only alternative means going on without my father.

"Okay."

It's a pathetic word, but it's the only one I can utter.

My father fails even more completely and can only nod his head.

Our embrace seems to last a lifetime and a second all at once. Yet again our lives have been manipulated, and yet again they'll be changed forever.

*   *   *

I've been sitting on my bedroom for I don't know how long, thinking about what I've done and what I'm going to have to do, and I don't know if this is a decision I'm going to be able to adhere to. Maybe I misunderstood what Luba said; maybe I made the whole thing up. Adrenaline pumps through my body at the prospect that it was all a dream, that none of it was real, when I feel something in my pocket.

I start to weep when I see what I'm holding in my hand: cherry blossom lip gloss. It's not mine; it's Jess's, and it's not something she left here or that her mother gave to me. It's from Jess herself, a sign that our connection is alive. Holding the lip gloss tightly in my hands, I remember what she said about Luba.

You may not like what she has to say, Dominy, but you can believe her.

And I know the only way for me to get my life back is to kill someone else I love.

Chapter 25

Remember, Dominy, you are . . .

Oh shut the ef up! I know exactly what I am; I do not need to be reminded! I'm a freak, a mutant; I'm a murderer! I'm the girl whose mother won't talk back to her and the same girl who has to kill her father if she wants any chance at a normal life. I am not *blessed!* I am beyond cursed! I'm one of those people you read about and you thank God you're not them, because if you were you'd just off yourself. Death has got to be more worth living than a life like this.

I smooth out the piece of paper on my desk and look at the picture I drew of my family. Stick figures living within the outline of a house, depicting all the usual suspects—you know, comatose mother, unsuspecting brother, werewolf daughter, and dead father.

The laughter that escapes from my lips reminds me of the sounds I heard leaking out of the padded cells in The Dungeon—demented, wild, and with no chance of salvation. To ensure that my future will have any value at all, I have to either kill my father or myself. Hilarious.

When I hear the knock on my door I crumple the picture into a ball like I've done several times already, but this time I toss it in the trash. I don't need my amateurish artwork to re-mind me of my fate; it's already seared into my brain.

"Caleb's here," my father announces. "Meet us in the liv-ing room."

Sure, why not. The day can't possibly get any worse. Wrong.

"Barnaby's at his track meet, so we don't have to worry that he'll overhear anything."

Two things run through my head when I hear my father mention Barnaby's name as I walk down the stairs. First, his voice sounds lighter than it has in months; I think he actually feels liberated now that Luba has added an addendum to her original spell. And second, if my brother ever finds out the truth about what's been happening to his family right under-neath his nose, he will hate me more than either of us ever thought possible.

Glancing at the time on the cable box I realize it's been more than a few hours since Caleb took the video cam footage from the Animal Protection Center. Just how long does it take to tell us exactly what we already know?

"Did the video pick up Luba unlocking the cage?" I ask.

I can already hear the edge in my voice, but I can't help it. I'm tired of concealing my true feelings, and I'm not my fa-ther; I haven't yet mastered the fine art of delusional thought.

"Sorry it took me so long," Caleb starts. "I burned the digital data from the camera onto a regular DVD so I could show you what was found."

My father nods his head, seemingly impressed with Caleb's diligence and thorough work, but also seemingly ignoring the fact that Caleb has ignored my question. My father is, how-ever, as eager as I am to get to the bottom line.

"Well, son, pop it in, and let's see what we've got."

Involuntarily, a smile materializes on Caleb's face, but it definitely hasn't come from any of his happy places. I know my boyfriend, and I know that's one of his fake expressions.

My father picks up the remote control and turns on the TV from where he's sitting on the couch as Caleb walks over to the DVD player to put in the disc. From where I'm sitting I can see Caleb's hand shake; whatever's on that disc is not going to provide us with an afternoon of family entertainment.

His finger hovering over the Play button, Caleb turns to me. "Dominy, I cut out your transformations and deleted all the original footage," he says.

Well, ain't he sweet. "Thank you."

Then he turns to my father. "So what you're about to see only exists on this copy."

Enough with the setup, Caleb. Start the show!

For a second I think that he's hit the Fast Forward button instead of Play, until I realize he's simply sped up the video; no need to watch me as a wolf circle the cage and howl arbitrarily for hours. Suddenly, the footage slows down, and I'm transfixed; it's like I'm being hypnotized. Right there on my TV is proof of what I've become. And there is absolutely no way I could have prepared myself for the sight. There is no way I could have prepared myself to witness the majesty that I've become.

Despite the grainy imagery the camera has still picked up the red coloring of my fur. It looks . . . Luxurious isn't really the right word; it looks opulent, like a fur that a Russian queen would wear while sitting on a throne. The way the camera's positioned it's looking down at me slightly, so I'm not looking directly into the camera as I walk, no parade around the cell, each step highlighting the muscles and power and strength that lie just beneath the surface, that are just aching to be put on display.

I'm mesmerized as I watch my head turn as if I've heard something in the distance, and then I arch my neck to howl in recognition or response. The sound I produce makes me flinch, and I feel my father's hand on my knee, I can't move to accept or refuse the gesture; I'm as still on the couch as I am on screen.

Another howl pours out of my immense mouth, as clear and solid and strong as a trumpet's blast. When I'm done I look straight ahead and expose my teeth, glistening white and razor sharp, and growl. My power is undeniable, but I don't know if my growl is a warning or a greeting, because the rest of my body doesn't move; it waits.

Until my father gets up and unlocks the cage.

Someone watching the scene gasps—I'm not sure who it is—then someone asks for Caleb to rewind. Silently, he complies, and once again we all watch dumbfounded as my father wakes up, rises from his chair, takes the key out of his pocket, unlocks the cage door, and pulls it open. He steps to the side as I walk out of my holding cell, pausing not to greet my father, but for some reason to acknowledge the video camera. I'm shocked to discover that Archie was right; my eyes are exactly the same. It's like someone dug them out of my face, placed them to the side, waited until I transformed, and then put them into the empty sockets of my werewolf self. It's an undeniable link. And this video is undeniable proof that my father is responsible, as always, for all the terrible stuff that's been happening.

I let my mind fade to black along with the TV screen, think of nothing, feel nothing, wait until someone else begins and then plan to follow his lead. But no one does, not for a full minute, though our collective silence isn't that surprising. What's really left to say? Oops, guess we were wrong about Luba. Or were we?

Caleb clears his throat and speaks first. "Let me play it again."

Holding up his hand, my father answers. "I think once was enough, son."

"Sir, please," Caleb says, his voice respectful, but firm. "I had to watch it a few times myself before I saw everything."

What else could there possibly be to see? How many other ways are there for a father to ruin his daughter's life?

Undeterred, Caleb rewinds the video as my father and I stare straight ahead, deliberately avoiding looking at one another. Soon I'm back on screen, unmoving, but staring at something on the other side of the bars. This time I know what I'm waiting for. I'm waiting for my freedom. Just as my father puts the key into the lock, Caleb hits the Pause button, and my father's image is frozen. If only I didn't know what came next I could fool myself into thinking that my father was just checking that the lock was secure and sat back down, the barrier between me and the rest of the world still unbroken. But once you see something, it becomes part of you that can never be severed, for better or for worse. And seeing my father act reprehensibly definitely qualifies as worse.

"Look at the floor," Caleb orders.

My father and I both hunch forward at the same time, straining to notice whatever Caleb is obviously trying to get us to see. Maybe our eyes are too shocked and scared from the last image, so that they've shut down and refuse to see anything new, refuse to connect to another unwanted sight. But sometimes you have to shut down your mind to see the truth.

"It's a shadow!" I cry.

"Yes!" Caleb agrees.

He hits the Pause button again and runs next to the TV screen. "Right there, it's a shadow."

Bleeding out of the bottom right-hand side of the screen is a shadow that wasn't there seconds earlier. There's no way of knowing exactly who it belongs to, but it's definitely the shape of a person. Someone else was in the building with my father, standing just outside the view of the camera.

"I'll be damned," my father murmurs.

"There's no way to be sure, but c'mon, that shadow's got to belong to Luba," Caleb says. "She used some more magic to get in without being detected. . . ."

"And put another spell on you, Daddy, to open up the cage," I say, completing Caleb's thought.

My father's still staring at the TV, shaking his head, his lips forming a smile. He's not upset; he's amused. "She just won't leave us alone, will she?"

He doesn't have to say another word because I know exactly what he's thinking. It's my thought too. Unless we break this curse, Psycho Squaw is going to keep coming up with ways to mess with our lives simply because it's her life-long quest to satisfy her vengeance. The problem is evil can never be satisfied.

"I know it looks bad," Caleb says, unwittingly uttering the understatement of the year. "But you can't blame yourself. Just like with Dominy, you didn't do a thing, Mr. Robineau. It's this Luba; she's pulling all the strings like some crazy mastermind."

"Thank you, Caleb."

I can tell from Caleb's pout that he takes my father's words and tone as being dismissive. I know otherwise. But since I'm not yet ready to tell Caleb the rest of Luba's master plan, I keep quiet and let my boyfriend think our private screening is over.

"Well, like I said, this is the only copy," he reminds us, handing the DVD to my father. "So you can, you know, do with it whatever you see fit."

After Caleb leaves and we're alone, I can't keep my mouth shut any longer.

"You're thrilled that it's you on that tape, aren't you?"

I have to give my dad props for not arguing with me or trying to convince me I'm wrong.

"It's all the evidence we need, isn't it, Dominy?" he asks in an annoyingly adult rhetorical tone. "Now we know we have no other choice but to break this curse."

We? Seriously? What is he now, a doctor? How are *we* feeling? Are *we* ready to do whatever it takes to get better? No, Dad, it's not *we*; it's *me!* I'm in this on my own. And I'm the only one who gets to make the final decision.

My heart is thumping inside my parka. I actually press down on the left side of my chest to try to calm it down, stop it from beating so hard. After walking a few blocks randomly, I can feel my breathing return to normal, or close to normal anyway. Looking around I can see that it's a gorgeous day, and I try to concentrate on that. Snow is falling from the sky, lightly, lazily, as if the clouds merely had a surplus and didn't feel like holding on to it any longer. Maybe that's what I should do with my pain and my anger—let it go, release it from my body and let it scatter according to the whims of the wind. Wherever it falls, doesn't matter to me, because it's not mine any longer. But it is mine, and when something is yours, even if you don't want it, even if you know that it's destructive and harmful, it can be so hard to let go of it.

The snow crunching under my feet becomes a steady rhythm, and soon that's the only sound I can hear. How wonderful it feels to think of nothing, just one repetitive, comforting sound. I turn a corner and then another and another and find myself, quite unexpectedly, standing in front of St. Edmund's Church. Did I subconsciously bring myself here, or was I just following the sounds of my feet? I have no idea.

I glance at my watch and see that it's almost five o'clock. All the pre-Sunday early bird masses are over for the day, so I know the church will be deserted; might be nice to sit quietly in a pew and reflect. Plus, my fingers went numb about two blocks ago, so I could use a place to defrost and warm up.

The recently shoveled steps have a light coating of snow-dust on them, so when I climb the stairs they creak, but the sound is muffled. Hopefully, my entrance won't be announced; last thing I need is an inquisitive priest asking me to confess my sins. He'd be dialing the Vatican before I'm halfway done with my list.

Sitting in one of the pews in the back, I have to stifle a gigglaugh when I realize there definitely is a hierarchy to organized religion. The pews in the back are wooden, while the ones up front that I sat on during Jess's funeral mass are padded. I guess the closer you get to God, the more comfortable it really is.

I rub my hands together and look around the church in search of something that will replace my cynicism with a surge of hope. Unfortunately, St. Edmund's isn't lavish or ornate; it's an ordinary Midwestern church, with the emphasis on devotion and not design. The floors look like they're made of the same wood as the pews, just a shade or two darker, and their slats are slanted so they meet in the middle to make an inverted *V* shape or an *A* without the horizontal line in the middle. However you look at it, the zenith is closer to the altar than the entrance.

There are a few chandeliers that hang from the ceiling that look like old-fashioned wagon wheels; they used to hold candles before small light fixtures were added when the church converted to electricity. I imagine how beautiful it must have looked on a wintry night, seeing the snow fall through the windows, being huddled together with family and friends underneath the glow of a canopy of candlelight. Even if you don't believe in the scriptures, that sounds like religion to me.

Since it appears that I have the church to myself, I decide to take a walk along the wall of saints. In between the windows on the right-hand side of the church are statues of various saints that all seem to have been carved out of the same block of ivory. They're smooth and are abstract in design, beautiful, but a bit out-of-place with the rest of the church. Regardless I've always liked them, and suddenly I know why. These statues are exquisite because of their simplicity, and it reminds me that not everything has to be complex. Not church, not life, not even important decisions. Keep things simple, and maybe you can get things done.

That's how St. Michael defeated the devil and how St. Joan defeated whatever army was attacking the French and how St. Jess defeated her enemy. St. Jess?!

The statue before me isn't carved from ivory, but sunshine. Jess's golden light is emanating from within her just like it did last night. I grab onto the raised post at the end of the pew behind me and literally fall to my knees. My hope has been restored. I wasn't just dreaming or wishing or hallucinating; I truly saw Jess while I was a wolf, and now I can see her as me. And she looks just as beautiful as I remembered. Just as beautiful as my mother did when the light broke through her lifeless body and we connected.

Can it get any more perfect? Both my mother and my best friend using pieces of sunlight to reach out to me now that I'm this child of the moon. This added meaning makes Jess look even more splendid, downright magnificent.

"I do, don't I?" she squeal-asks.

Perched high atop the regular statue's podium, Jess still has the ability to knock the poetry out of me and bring me back down to reality.

"Jess . . . I can't believe this is happening!"

Like a golden leaf caught in the swirl of an autumn breeze, Jess floats down from her platform until she is standing in front of me. She leans over, and I feel pieces of her sunlight or whatever particles are hovering around her face and body pierce through my flesh; they feel like warm drops of rain. But instead of gliding down my cheek or arm, they cling to the inside of my skin. It's both scary and amazing at the same time.

"It is happening, Dom, but you're the only one who's allowed to see me," she says. "So when you talk to me, act like you're praying or something or else they'll think you're a loon."

Another gigglaugh rips through my throat and echoes off the church walls before getting lost somewhere near the arched ceiling. Jess was a dramatic creature in life, and she's only gotten more dramatic in the afterlife. I shouldn't have expected anything less. Wait a minute; the one thing I don't expect is to be lied to.

"I'm not the only one who can see you," I correct her. "Luba saw you too."

Rolling her eyes she tilts her head back and forth. "Sorry, I didn't phrase that the right way. Humans can't see me."

Stunned, I ask the only logical question I can think of, though it doesn't sound logical at all when spoken out loud. "Luba's not human?"

Leaning her head close to mine and whispering like we used to in geometry, Jess explains the situation. "Even though you sort of straddle both worlds now—the real one and the supernatural realm—I can't really tell you everything. Honestly, I don't know how much I can get away with; I'm still new at this whole spiritual being thing. But I think I can say that Luba's like you."

It takes me a minute to digest and decipher Jess's clue. "So I'm right; Luba's only part human."

When Jess nods her head, a spray of sunshine falls over my face, and I can't help but smile at my friend. I keep smiling when I ask, "What in heaven's name is going on, Jess?"

Her cackle is so loud I turn my head in every direction, convinced a troop of priests is going to run out to see who's disrespecting their house of worship, but none come. I guess I'm the only one who can hear Jess too.

"Dom, I have no idea," she says. "But I'd be lying if I said I didn't love it."

"Me too," I reply. "And thanks for the lip gloss."

Another cackle rips through the church. "You got it?! I

wasn't sure it would work, but I wanted to send you a sign," she admits. "I'll try to do that from time to time, but no promises. Like I said, I'm powerful and all that, but I have limitations."

Tentatively, I reach out my hand, not because I'm afraid Jess won't respond and grab hold of me; I'm just not sure if in her particular state I'll be able to feel anything. When her hand settles into mine, I'm convinced I've witnessed yet another miracle.

"Don't worry, I'm not going anywhere," she confirms. "After all I am an Amaterasu Omikami."

There's that name again. "A what?"

"You haven't Googled it yet?"

"I couldn't even remember it! It's not like it flows off the tongue you know."

"Of course it does, Amaterasu Omikami. If you can master Dominy Robineau, surely you can pronounce my new name."

"Can't I just call you Jess?"

"Well . . . I guess so," she replies, a bit miffed that I don't want to call her by her formal name. "But write it down so you don't forget this time."

Quickly, I search the pockets of my jacket for a pen or a pencil, but come up empty-handed. "I don't have anything to write with."

"Oh must I do everything?" Jess mock-complains.

She pulls out a missalette from the wooden rack hanging from the back of the pew in front of us and turns to the back cover, which has no writing on it except for a stamp at the bottom of the page that reads, PROPERTY OF ST. EDMUND'S CHURCH. Using her index finger as a pen, she writes out the name Amaterasu Omikami, and even though glittery yellow sunshine replaces blue ink, I'd recognize her handwriting anywhere except for one slight change.

"Aren't you going to dot the *i*'s with smiley faces?" I ask.

"Even I have to admit that would be overkill," she replies.

Our gigglaughs and cackles are interrupted when she suddenly throws my body onto the pew and screams, "Get down!"

I flatten myself onto the pew, but that doesn't seem enough for Jess.

"Get lower!" she demands. "On the floor!"

The urgency in her voice is enough to make me follow her orders, but she isn't taking any chances, and I feel her hands lift me off the pew and place me on the floor. Next thing I know I can feel Jess on top of me, and I'm covered in a shroud of sunlight. I want to ask her why she's covering me with her body since she said I'm the only one who can see her, but then I remember her disclaimer; humans can't see her. So if she's hiding, does that mean there's another nonhuman in the house? Lifting my head slightly, I see that it's worse. There's an ex-boyfriend in the house of worship.

I'm not sure where he came from, but Napoleon walks right down the center aisle, past where we're hiding, and then presumably out the front door. About thirty seconds after the door slams, I finally feel Jess lift off of me and sit back down on the pew. She's not only become otherworldly, but overly cautious too.

Sitting next to her I'm not sure what to ask first, so I go with what I think will be the most obvious question. "Is Napoleon human?"

"That I cannot say, Dominy-san," she answers cryptically. "And don't read too much into that. I have rules I have to follow now."

"But you're not sure," I say. "Otherwise why would you knock me to the floor?"

For the first time Jess looks away from me, a bit of her mystical glamour fading. "I may have forgiven you for killing me, Dom, but stealing my boyfriend's heart is another story."

How can she not know the truth? I'm in love with Caleb. I

never once felt anything for Napoleon, and even if I did, I would never have acted upon it.

"I know all that!" Jess scolds, apparently reading my mind once again. "But the fact remains that my boyfriend wanted to be your boyfriend, and while he was kissing me he was probably thinking about kissing you! And you know what, Dom? That sucks!"

It does suck, and I completely agree with Jess, and if I ever needed any stronger proof that this creature sitting next to me is in fact my best friend, I just got it. It's the confirmation I needed that no matter how bad things get, my life is worth fighting for.

"Thank you, Jess."

"For what?"

"For doing what you've always done," I reply. "For saving my life."

Chapter 26

Everywhere you look there's snow, but all I can see is sunshine.

I haven't told anyone about my encounter with Jess. I want to keep it our secret, our connection, our invisible string, but I have to keep reminding myself to temper my good mood so my friends don't think I'm starting to lose my mind. They're adapting better than I expected to the fact that I'm possessed; I'm not sure how they'd react if they thought I was starting to crack under the pressure.

As promised, I Google Amaterasu Omikami and have to clasp my hands over my mouth when I scream in delight. It's absolutely perfect. Jess has morphed into some kind of Japanese sun goddess. Who knows how and who cares why. The beauty of it is that Jess is finally living her dream of being part of Japanese culture, and I refuse to believe that the sun plays an arbitrary part in her afterlife. It has got to be an important clue, since I'm being controlled by the moon, and now my best friend is a deity of the sun.

Everything's going so well that I start to avoid one-on-one conversations with my father. I don't want him to try and convince me that we have to reverse this curse. If I didn't think it was ludicrous before, I definitely think so now. If the curse is broken, not only will I have to go through life without my father, but also without my best friend. It's too much, and I'm not going to do it. We're just going to have to take Operation Big Red to the next level and learn how to defeat Luba at her own game.

Unfortunately, that's a lot easier said than done. A week before the next scheduled full moon comes the first strike against my strategy.

"Bad news," Caleb announces at the lunch table. "My father's found out about us."

"Couldn't you tell us that after I finished my meat loaf?" Archie asks. "How can I enjoy it now?"

"Dude, I thought you guys would want to know."

On either side of me, Arla and Nadine grab my hands, equally stunned by the news that clearly hasn't penetrated Archie's thick skull. "He *knows* about me?" I ask, although my voice sounds more like it's pleading.

"Sorry, Domgirl," Caleb says, grabbing my hands away from Arla's and Nadine's grips from across the table. "He knows that somebody's been using the old APC; he doesn't know why."

"From now on, Caleb, could you lead with the positive?" I ask.

"And never drop a bomb like that again without blowing out the fuse first," Arla adds.

"And, Archie, do you think you could act a little more concerned?" Nadine finishes.

Shoveling a forkful of meat loaf and mashed potatoes into his mouth, Archie is unrepentant. "Above all else this be known, Nay," he says. "My hunger comes first." Turning to Caleb for backup he asks, "Right, bro?"

"If you know what's good for you, Caleb," I say, "the only thing you're going to tell us is what your father's newly acquired knowledge means in terms of the next full moon."

Be careful what you ask for, Dominy; the truth isn't always the easiest thing to hear.

"We have to find a new holding place for you," Caleb responds. "Turns out the state wants to sell the land where the APC is located, so they did a routine walk-through and found evidence that the building's been occupied lately."

"They didn't find anything that links it to Dominy or her dad, did they?" Arla asks.

"No," Caleb assures us. "But they know it's being used, which is why they're tearing it down."

"What?!"

I have no idea whose voice is loudest since we all scream at the same time. The girls at the table next to us turn around, curious if our verbal explosion will lead to something more interesting, but luckily after a few seconds their interest wanes and our conversation can continue.

"When, Caleb?" I ask. "When are they planning on destroying the place?"

"Um, sometime tomorrow."

"Great! So there goes the perfect solution."

"Dom, it was far from the perfect solution," Nadine says. "You got out twice while you were there. Maybe this is exactly what we needed so we could regroup and come up with a better plan."

Logical thinking can be so annoying, even if it leads to the practical application of finding a solution to a problem. After spending a few hours sitting around Arla's living room while her dad is on night patrol, we've come up with a plan B.

"Does your dad still have that small cage he was going to use during the first transformation?" Nadine asks.

"I guess so," I reply. "Unless he sold it on eBay or something."

Ignoring my snarky comment, Nadine continues. "Bring that cage to my family's cabin and transform there. I'll make sure no one decides to make a spontaneous trek out to the place."

"But if Luba can unlock the cage at the APC," Arla says, "what makes you think she won't be able to pick the lock from a cage bought at Home Depot?"

"And what makes you think Dominy won't be able to break out of it," Archie adds. "She-wolf be strong, yo."

"First of all, Archie, don't ever say 'yo' in my presence again," Nadine demands. "And second, we'll finally see if these little suckers will make a difference."

As sort of a voilà moment, Nadine pulls out of her bag a syringe that she swiped at The Retreat. She's been collecting them, but we haven't used them yet. First we thought the industrial-strength cage at the APC would contain me, and then we got too wrapped up in trying to videotape Luba setting me free, so that we sort of forgot. Correction, logical thinking is sometimes exactly what a Wolf Pack needs.

"What's in that thing?" Caleb asks. "I mean, will it be safe on Dominy as, you know, a human?"

"Of course it'll be safe," Nadine chafes. "It's lorazepam. We use it on patients all the time. In fact it's safer than most sedatives because it's a *short-term* benzodiazepine drug."

"Thank you, Nurse Nadine," Archie jokes.

Okay, the inside of the syringe might be safe, but what about the outside. "Isn't the needle made of silver?" I ask.

Smiling smugly, Nadine proves that she's thought of everything. "Nope, stainless steel," she answers. "Even though it's not a bullet, I didn't want to take any chances."

"Nurse Nadine, be smart, yo!" Archie adds, but corrects himself when Nadine jokingly glares at him for once again using the word *yo*. "Sorry, but yo really be smart. And may I also suggest that we throw some rib-eye steaks into the cage as well?"

"What do I need that for?"

Before Archie answers, I sadly figure it out.

"If Nurse Nadine's lorazepammie doesn't do the trick and you wake up in the cage all werewolfy and hungry," Archie explains, "the rib-eyes might satisfy your craving so you don't try to break out."

Push, push, push the bad imagery from my mind and focus on sunshine. It's hard to do especially when everyone around me knows that Archie's suggestion, as gross as it sounds, is really quite smart. But not as definitive as Caleb's final contribution.

"And remember, your dad will have his Taser on him," he reminds us. "So this time nothing can possibly go wrong."

Oh yeah, Caleb, tell that to Mother Nature, who personally delivers strike two.

Just because it's late March doesn't mean Nebraska can't be hit by a severe off-season snowstorm. Just because my father is the sheriff of Weeping Water doesn't mean he can't be called out of town on business. And when those two events happen at the same time, it means that my father will be out of town during the full moon.

"Dominy, honey, I'm really sorry," my father says, his voice as fragile as the cell phone connection.

"That's okay, Dad," I lie. "We've got it all under control."

I had already told my father about our backup plan, and he thought it was the only viable solution. Of course he wanted to project manage the affair, but in his absence Caleb will have to do. In order to make sure no one's parents freak out that their kid is missing all night, we pull a scam that's been working for decades. It's worked in all the old sitcoms I've watched; I hope it works in real life as well.

Caleb told Archie's parents that Archie was going to spend the night at his place and vice versa. Nadine and Arla did the same thing with theirs. I told Barnaby that Arla and I were spending the night at Nadine's and not Arla's in case he decided he wanted to crash the sleepover party and pal around with his track idol, so instead he's going over to Jody's. Since Jody's dad has like a 100-inch flat-screen TV in their basement, Barnaby jumped at the chance to spend another night there.

On our way to the Jaffe family cabin, it seemed like the storm was getting worse every second. Visibility was so lousy I don't think Jess and her godlike sunshine could make a difference. Following Caleb's Sequinox, I drove my father's Bronco slowly, very slowly, in fact, because even though I have driving experience, I don't yet have my driver's license. My father's been letting me behind the wheel—with him in the passenger seat, of course—for years, so I know what I'm doing, but I didn't want to get pulled over for speeding. Unfortunately, no matter how slowly I drove, every bump I went over made the cage rattle in the flatbed. No chance of tricking my mind into thinking I was en route to a fun snowy getaway. Thankfully Nadine's got East Coast manners and kept quiet during the ride; nothing she said would've made me feel less miserable.

It takes Archie and Caleb almost thirty minutes to rebuild the small cage, probably twenty minutes longer than necessary because they keep drinking the hot chocolate Nadine made that Archie's spiked with some chocolaty liqueur, which of course I couldn't have because I was going to be injected with a sedative. Childishly, it reminded me of when Charlie Brown goes trick-or-treating and all his friends get candy and he gets a rock. Instead of drinking a sweet, creamy liqueur, I get a tranquilizer.

But lying in the cage after being injected by Nadine, I don't feel any different. Shouldn't I feel like I'm about to fall into a deep sleep? Shouldn't it be just like when I had my tonsils out? There's no reason that I should still be alert and aware and afraid.

No matter how scared I may feel, it's nothing compared to what my friends are going through. I can't say that I'm used to my human-to-werewolf transformations, not by a long shot, but I know what to expect. They don't.

"Her bones are snapping in two!" Arla screams.

"Her skin! It's disappearing!" Archie's voice dovetails over Arla's.

"Oh my God! Her neck is breaking!" Caleb's cry disturbs me the most. I guess I expected him to have taken a peek at the videotape, but even if he did, it's nothing like seeing it up close and personal.

When the change is complete, when I'm sharing my soul with this other thing, I feel different. Part of me wants to take control; the other part wants this wild animal to lead the way. The only thing my entire body can agree on is how much smaller my space is. I can barely move in a circle without hitting the bars of this cage, and there's only an inch or two of free space above my head. I don't like it, and I don't want to stay here. So I won't.

The cage shakes frantically when I lunge forward, growling roughly, and by the second time it flips over so one of the sides is now on the floor. Screams and chatter fill the air, voices asking what's happening and what should they do, pieces sound like they're shouting in my ears, others as if they're being spoken from a great distance away. They sound exactly like I feel—one second I feel in control, and the next I'm lost within this wolf. I have no idea who is going to end up in control when I get out of this thing. And it's only a matter of time before that happens.

Wildly I pounce onto the bars, howl at my incarceration, ram the cage into furniture, the walls, people. No matter what it takes, I will get free, and I have no idea why these stupid humans haven't figured that out yet.

The first bar snaps easily from the base, and I grip the metal spoke in my mouth and twist it back and forth until it breaks free altogether.

"She's getting out!"

I throw my entire body into the side of the cage and ram it into the wall several times. Splinters of wood shower down on me, the squeak and the clash of metal against wood almost deafening until the next bar breaks apart, this time from what is now the top part of the cage. I stop moving, and these people stop screaming, because we all come to the same conclusion at once. The hole in the cage is now big enough for me to squeeze through.

I take my time making my exit. Why rush it? No one can stop me; might as well make it an event, instill in them the kind of fear that will make their blood taste that much more bountiful. But which one? Which one should I taste first?

The white one, the brown one, the tall one with the yellow hair, or the one with the silver mist clinging to her skin? Such decisions. Opening my mouth I run my tongue over my teeth, and the brown one clings to the one with yellow hair. Yes, I've seen him before, and he's gotten away from me. This time he won't be so lucky.

"Archie," my next meal speaks. "The steaks, they're in the corner."

The one made of pure white skin turns to his right. "She must've kicked them out of the cage."

For a few seconds he disappears from my view, but when I see him again he's holding two pieces of raw meat. Thick and overflowing with blood. I can feel the saliva build up in my mouth like a pool of hot rainwater, and I lick my lips again, this time to wipe away my own juices and not for show.

"Hand them to me, Arch."

Slowly, the meat is handed from one male to the other. I howl as a few drops of rich, red blood fall to the floor, and I watch as the golden-haired one walks across the room. I follow him with my eyes as he stands in front of the door and opens it. They're playing a game with me. I know that; I know what they want from me, but I don't care. I want to taste that meat. I want to suck the blood and gnaw on the bone until I'm weary, until the hunger-need passes through me.

The door is halfway open; the meat is dangling in the air, a long, thick droplet of blood hanging, clinging to the meat as strongly as I'm still clinging to my desire to feed. The blood-drop swings in the air tenuously as the door is opened wider, when suddenly it falls to the floor and splatters into the air. I can smell the blood flying toward me, and I can't wait any longer; I've waited long enough.

Springing through the air, I extend my body, and at the same moment the male flings the meat outside. I swipe the air with my paw and feel my nails slice through the brown one's face, her blood splashing onto my teeth and spraying my tongue. I push the door with my paws, and it easily opens; finally I'm outside, free. As I ravage the first piece of meat, I can hear her screams of agony like wisps of a breeze around my ears. They're recognized, but unimportant. Nothing is as important as my hunger.

I barely look up when I hear the commotion behind me. Two bodies fall into the silver machine next to me, and I watch them start to roll then speed away, making thick tracks in the fresh snow. That means the other two still remain in the house, but in the distance I see a fox getting too close to the other piece of meat. How dare he sniff around my food?

One howl sends him on his way so I can eat my second meal slowly. And when I'm done I can rest in a soft, cool bed of snow.

I don't make a final decision until I walk into Arla's hospital room the next morning and overhear her doctor talking to her father.

"Your daughter's very lucky, Louis," the doctor says. "A millimeter higher, and she would've lost her eye."

"Will she be okay?" Louis asks, his voice trembling.

"She'll have a scar, which should fade, but no, there won't be any permanent damage."

Courageously, Arla smiles when I walk into the room followed by the others. Her father gives her a hug and multiple kisses on her face and leaves the room to avoid breaking down in front of her friends.

On the way over Archie explained to me that after Caleb whisked Arla off to the hospital, I finished eating and spent the rest of the night sleeping outside while he and Nadine locked themselves in the bathroom of the cabin. They found me in the morning naked, but uncursed, so to speak.

"I told my father that I was attacked by a cougar or a mountain lion, I couldn't tell which," Arla explains. "Thanks to Lars and the *Three W*, he believed me."

He believed you because it isn't that far from the truth.

"Guess we'll have to get you a stronger cage for next month," Arla jokes.

I smile along with the rest of them, but I know that next month is going to be different. That's when I'm going to follow Luba's instructions and give in to my father's wishes so I can put an end to this curse once and for all.

Chapter 27

When I was seven years old, my father and I had our very first tea party.

We invited Raggedy Ann and Andy, Winnie the Pooh, Tweety Bird, and Mr. Pinkerton, my stuffed pink elephant. I wore my mother's costume jewelry, her favorite wide-brimmed hat, the white one with navy trim, and a pair of white lace gloves that my father bought for me because he said they looked so lonely in the store window without a little girl's hands to hold.

I remember it was a Tuesday.

"Why are we having a tea party on a Tuesday, Daddy?" I asked. "Shouldn't we wait until Saturday? That's the most special day of the week."

"Tuesday is just as special as a Saturday, Dominy," he said, "when you spend it with someone you love."

I always imagined that my daughter would have special moments like that with my dad too, but she'll have to be content with hearing the stories. That is if I ever decide to have a child. I've come to learn rather quickly that future plans, more often than not, get broken. The people you assume you'll grow old with don't always wind up being a part of your life for as long as you'd like. My mother, Jess, and now my father.

After Arla's accident—let me rephrase that, after I assaulted and almost blinded my friend—it became apparent that this curse will not be contained, conquered, or even controlled. No matter what tactic we try, no matter what approach we take, in the end the spell I'm under proves to be stronger and more resilient. I've given in, and now it's time to give up.

I've tried to deal with it. I've tried to embrace this affliction that's been thrust upon me, and a part of me was starting to believe I could find a balance, that I could exist like The Weeping Lady and straddle both worlds, only to persevere year after year after year. It might not be an ideal life, but it would be manageable. But that was an incredibly unrealistic—foolhardy I think is the right word; yes, that was a foolhardy expectation. So as much as it frightens me, I have no other choice but to agree with my father. The only way to move forward is to sever ties with the past.

I hate letting Luba think she's won, that she will become victorious. What I hate even more is that I'll be losing my connection to Jess.

Having my best friend, my sister, back in my world after I thought she had been ripped from my life forever was a true godsend. It's not something I believed I was worthy of, but obviously someone or something did, because she returned to me. When we break the curse and I become fully human again, we'll be on different sides of the spiritual spectrum, and, according to what Jess told me, communication will be impossible. It's unfortunate, but that's the way it has to be.

And that's why my father has to die by my hand.

He's been resolved to it since the first day I told him about Luba's remedy; it's taken me quite a bit longer. I'm still not completely sold on the idea, but the next full moon is only a week away, and I can't think of a better exit strategy. The only person I've told is Caleb. His immediate silence told me that his heart thought it was the only solution. Of course he tried to come up with another solution and even thought that Jess might be able to intervene. He doesn't know that I've seen her when I'm untransformed, only when I've been a wolf. But I reminded him that she wasn't able to prevent me from hurting Arla, so it doesn't seem like she can get involved in or spoil another spiritual being's agenda.

Trust me, I've thought about everything, and I keep coming back to the simplest solution. And my resolve is getting stronger. It's only when I see my brother watching my father that my conviction falters. Especially when I know that he suspects something.

"Dad, what are you doing?" Barnaby asks.

I'm coming out of the bathroom, and Barnaby is standing at my father's door. I don't have to look inside to know that my father is putting his affairs in order. He's been doing it for the past few weeks, ever since I told him we would do things his way. I've caught him organizing his personal documents, labeling family heirlooms, even separating his clothes into different groupings: clothes that were his father's, clothes to keep for Barnaby or Caleb, and clothes to donate to charity.

"Just doing a bit of spring cleaning, Barn," I hear him say, "getting rid of old junk mail."

"Can I help?"

I step closer to the banister so I can look into my dad's bedroom and see him take a moment before answering my brother.

"Sure, come on in."

Barnaby bounces on my dad's bed, thinking he's going to help our father. Maybe a part of him thinks that this will be a nice memory that they can share when they get older and Barnaby's waiting for his wife to deliver their first child. He has no idea that he's walking into a morgue to have a final visit with a dead man.

A few days later and the roles are reversed when we go visit my mother, just my father and me. I don't want to tag along, but my father insists. Could be that he wants to spend as much time as possible with me before the next full moon? Could be that he needs moral support to visit his wife when he informs her that she'll soon be his widow?

Looks like Essie's got a touch of spring fever; she looks like her younger sister. Her hair's done, she's sporting softer makeup, and she's wearing a cute sweater set in tangerine. Even if my father wasn't preoccupied he still wouldn't notice, but I do.

"Hi, Essie, you look amazing."

"Thank you, sweetie," she replies. "I've decided it's time to change my attitude with a whole new look compliments of my brother-in-law, Chester. He's my husband's younger brother, God rest his soul. My husband, not Chester. My husband's gone seven years this past February; Chester's still alive and kicking and an accountant at Dillard's. He told me it's high time I got out there and snag me another fish before Judgment Day comes and all the oceans dry up. So what do you think? Do I look age appropriate?"

Taking two fire engine-red index cards from Essie's freshly manicured hands, I tell her she's the best-dressed forty-year-old in Weeping Water. Which I hope is an appropriate compliment for a woman her age. By the way she blushes, I trust that it is.

"Sheriff," Essie crows, "you got yourself an angel."

You have no idea how wrong you are Essie.

"Don't I know it," my father says, contradicting my silent thought.

Just as we turn to leave, Essie tugs on my T-shirt. Doing her best imitation of a whisper, she asks, "Any luck finding out more info on you know who and her son?"

Shaking my head, I reply, "Unfortunately not. Seems like they both vanished into thin air."

"Well, I'll keep my eyes and ears open," Essie promises. "And if I hear anything I'll let you know."

I think I know what Dr. Frankenstein felt like. I may have created a little monster in Essie. Oh well, hopefully she'll find a new man and she'll treat me with her usual apathetic charm once again.

I do a little jog to catch up with my father and meet him just as he's entering my mother's room. He grabs my hand like he used to when I was little to give me extra strength and encouragement, and we enter her room together. This time around I think he's holding my hand for purely selfish reasons; he's the one who needs support.

Watching my father sit next to my mother's bed, holding her hand, caressing it absentmindedly, I feel like a voyeur, like I'm intruding on a very intimate moment. Several times I try to think of an excuse to leave, but we both know it would be a sham on my part, and I don't want to disappoint my father; for whatever reason he wants me here. It's only when we're about to leave that I understand why.

Like every other time I've come to visit my mother with my father, he never leaves without kissing her on the lips and whispering in her ear. So when he leans over to kiss her I don't expect anything different until I hear him speak.

"I'm sorry, Suzanne, this has all been my fault."

He presses her hand to his lips and kisses her one more time, then gently lays her hand down on the bed and wipes his tears from her skin. Removing every trace of himself from her body. Part of me wants to turn and stare out the window so I don't intrude, but the other part of me, the part that wins out doesn't turn away. I'm ashamed not because I'm bearing witness to such tenderness, but because I've been a fraud.

Caleb and I joke about having a connection, an invisible string that unites the two of us, but our relationship is nothing compared to the love that exists between my parents. Looking at my father gaze at my mother, I see that it doesn't matter that she can't see him; it doesn't matter that she's barely alive and he's almost dead. Their string is made of a material that will never break. I pray that one day I'll really know what it feels like to have a person tug on the other end of my string like that.

"I love you."

It takes me a few moments to realize that my father is talking to me.

"I don't think I can do this."

Nadine's cabin is solemnly quiet, as if nature has decided to hold its tongue and offer us the gift of solitude. The sky outside is turning a deep shade of blue and in a few moments moonlight will spill into the room and into my soul.

"Yes, you can," my father replies. "Because you know it's the right thing to do."

"How can this be the right thing?! How can this be anything other than a terrible mistake?!"

Looking into my father's eyes is usually like looking into a mirror, but not now. Now I see only peace and acceptance.

"No, this is the only way to *correct* a terrible mistake, my mistake," he says. "I know it's going to be difficult for you, but in time . . . in time you'll understand that you did the only thing you could do, the only thing that I wanted you to do."

I can feel the warmth of the moon on the back of my neck, and I know our time is running out. I don't want to spend the last few moments I have with my father yelling and screaming and trying to convince him to change his mind, because I know it'll be a waste of time. So I make a decision to use the time we have left properly and tell him what I hope he wants to hear.

"My favorite toy is the dollhouse you made for me when I was ten."

The moonglow is burning a hole in my neck.

"My favorite holiday was when I was twelve and had the

chicken pox on New Year's Eve and you let me stay up with you to watch the ball drop."

I can feel the burning fire course through my veins, but I don't think about it; I just look into my father's eyes, wet with tears like a beautiful, calm ocean.

"My favorite memory is when I was fourteen, and you told me I didn't need makeup to look beautiful because I had Mommy's smile."

My body twitches as my bones snap into new positions. There's no more time left; my screams are already turning into howls. I finally find the strength to say the words I should have said to my father a long time ago.

"I love you, Daddy!"

When I wake up I keep my eyes closed because I want to imagine it's all been a dream. Finally, I open my eyes, and I have no choice but to accept the nightmare. My father's lying next to me. His beautiful eyes are still wide open, but the left side of his face is torn off. There's a huge gaping hole where his stomach should be, and I turn away before I can examine his body any further.

Clutching my stomach I wait for the vomit to explode from my body.

But it never comes.

Covering my mouth I wait for the screams to spill out of my throat.

But they never come.

Falling to my knees I wait for the tears to pour down my face.

But they never come.

The only thing that comes is something unexpected and frightening and honest.

An overwhelming sense of relief.

Chapter 28

I don't remember much about my father's funeral.

I'm sure it was well-attended because I was surrounded by crowds of people. I remember being hugged by strangers, shaking hands with men in uniforms, watching two men take a very long time to fold the American flag and then present it to me and Barnaby. Most of the time, I just sat in the front row of the funeral parlor next to my brother and told people that I was okay. I had no idea if I was telling the truth.

At the time I remember thinking that this was completely surreal; it shouldn't be happening, because it couldn't possibly have been his time to die. But then the more logical, rational part of my brain contradicted me. It was his time, and more than that it was the time that he chose. Knowing that made the aftermath bearable.

When my father's body was found it became official, at least in the pages of the *Three W* and according to the subsequent rumor that instantaneously spread through town, that Weeping Water had its very own serial killer in the form of a wild animal. Whether the culprit was a cougar, mountain lion, or a wolf, no one could agree, but as the newly minted sheriff, Louis Bergeron was going to enforce a curfew on the area outside of town especially near the low hills and formally request state intervention and extra funding to find this predator and kill it. He valiantly fought back tears when he told the local TV news reporter that he would avenge his friend's death.

Louis assumed my father had been investigating a disturbance at the Jaffe cabin and had been taken by surprise by this "devil thing" before he could call in for backup. All of that is in the report he filed, including his reference to the "devil thing." I could tap him on the shoulder and whisper "Too late!" but Louis has already rallied a posse to find this killer. I don't think he or anyone would hear or comprehend my comment. For now I'll keep quiet and live under his roof with Barnaby as my father stipulated in his will. Someday the time will come for me to give a full confession to the authorities, but that time isn't now.

Now is the time for penance.

At the repast, my friends and I gathered in my room away from the crowd of well-wishers and would-be bounty hunters. My friends were remarkably kind and understanding. They all suspected what had actually transpired the night of my last transformation, and to spare me the necessity of confirming their suspicions, Caleb did it for me. He's been true to his word and has supported me every step of the way. So have my friends.

Caleb said that once my father knew the only way for the curse to be reversed was for him to die at my hand, he had made up his mind that that's how it was going to be done. Archie and Arla agreed that that's what fathers do; they protect their children at all cost even if it means giving up their own lives. Nadine, ever practical, added that my father felt the need to take responsibility for his own actions.

Archie's the only one who's brave enough to ask me if I remember anything. I don't. We all acknowledge that that's a blessing in itself.

Once that unpleasant issue is brushed aside, the rest of them, including Caleb, do what they always do, which is talk about this werewolf as if it's separate from me, another entity. They don't realize or can't realize or simply refuse to understand that we were joined together; we were one and the same, so this werewolf didn't kill my father; I did. No one, not even Archie, comes right out and says it that plainly, and for that I'm even more grateful, because it's something I keep trying to forget myself.

But I'll never forget it, of course. How could I? It's always going to be there, as strong and as obvious as the invisible string that connects me to my father. Just like the ones that connect me to Caleb and Jess and all my friends. But the interesting thing about an invisible string is that even though it's always there when you need to tug on it, its invisibility makes it very convenient to forget it exists if the connection becomes too painful.

So I accepted their love and their friendship and their honesty, but sitting there on my bed surrounded by them, I had never felt more alone in my entire life. All I wanted was to know that my father was down the hall, and if I couldn't have that, I wanted Jess sitting next to me. But now that I'm rehumanized, I'll never see her again either.

When his casket was lowered into the ground, I do remember being blinded by sunshine, so I'd like to think Jess was nearby, saying her final good-byes.

The Bergeron house is surprisingly big. Louis and his pals converted the attic into a bedroom for Barnaby and bought him his very own flat-screen TV/video game console, and the guest bedroom is now officially mine, separated from Arla's bedroom by a huge bathroom complete with two sinks. Perfect, now I get to watch Arla apply ointment to her scar while I brush my teeth in the morning. As much as my father tried, it's impossible to sever all ties with the past, because the past comes equipped with a perfect handle so you can carry it with you while you travel into the future.

No doubt about it, the transition hasn't been all that smooth, and my father's death has aroused some suspicion. Especially from the dim-witted ex-deputy who may not be so dim-witted after all.

"Dominy, I hate to ask."

That's how Louis began a conversation a few nights ago while it was just the two of us in the living room waiting for Arla and Barnaby to return home from track practice.

"But did your father ever mention that he knew he was going to die?"

He actually orchestrated his own death, Louis. Why do you ask?

"No."

"It's just . . . well, it's just that last week he redid his will and increased his insurance policy," Louis said.

Imitating a shell-shocked, basically orphaned teenager, I nodded my head, keeping one eye glued to the TV. "My dad did like to plan things out."

"Yes, he did. Very meticulous, your father," Louis agreed, grasping onto the straw I threw at him. "I was just wondering if he, I don't know, did he have some kind of . . . premonition?"

No, he was given instructions from a crazy woman.

"From everything he always told me," I reply, "my mother was the superstitious one."

At the mention of my mother's name, Louis nods his head and smiles, his soft green eyes lighting up. "That she was, Dom, that she was," he says. "You know you don't have to worry about her, right? Your father made sure that she can stay at The Retreat for as long . . ."

"As long as she wants," I finish. "I know, he told me once that all that was taken care of."

I also know that there's a fund for my mother's funeral expenses when that time ever comes, and I know that my father has shared this information with Louis, but Louis must've felt he's talked enough about death with me, since he didn't bring up the subject. He told me we'd have dinner when the track stars got home and left the room, leaving behind any suspicions he might have, taking with him only the knowledge that his former boss and friend was a responsible father who, unfortunately, met an untimely end. Barnaby is proving a lot more difficult to appease.

"This is a great room, Barn," I say, sitting on his bed next to him, trying to kill his alien spaceship with my star trooper laser beams.

"I got the biggest TV of any kid in my class," he replies, deftly protecting his spaceship from each and every one of my laser beams.

The kid's as fast on screen as he is on the track.

"It's not so bad here, is it?" I ask.

"No," he says, eyes fixed straight ahead, fingers nimbly navigating the joystick. "The whole thing sucks, like super-sized sucks, but could be lots worse."

I look up to where Louis has hung the American flag my father was given for being a policeman; it is handsomely showcased behind glass in a triangular wooden display case. It belongs to Barnaby now, rightfully so. Now my brother can wake up every morning and be reminded that his dad was a hero. I don't need a physical reminder; I experienced it firsthand. What I do need is a crash course on the finer points of Space Odyssey VII or whatever game we're playing.

My brief distraction proves fatal, and Barnaby's counter-attack is successful. My spaceship is annihilated and bursts into a red cloud that becomes an elaborate fireworks display, ultimately spelling out the phrase *You Are A Loser*. No wonder these video games are addictive; the only way to bypass negative reinforcement is to master the game and keep winning. In that way, I guess it's kind of like life, only much easier.

"Dinner's ready!"

Arla's announcement puts an end to my losing streak for now. Barnaby makes sure I know it will continue. Just as he's about to descend the stairs to the main floor, he turns to me. His body is still as scrawny as ever and his nose is just as big, but his eyes look different; they're clear and bright and focused, like they're the only part of him that's grown up.

"Oh, Dom, I don't know how or why, but I know that somehow you're responsible for Daddy's death," he says casually. "And someday I'm going to figure it all out."

I watch as Barnaby bounds down the stairs, disappearing out of view. My knees start to shake, not a lot, but just enough for me to need to hold on to the railing to steady myself and just enough to remind me that his words are not an idle threat. They're words of caution that I'd be a fool to ignore.

But if I want any semblance of normalcy to return to my days, I have to do just that. Take my father's death, my brother's threat, my unmentionable past and lock them up in little suitcases that for now don't have any handles and tuck them away in my closet. I know I'll have to take them down at some point, but for now, for my sanity's sake, I'm keeping them hidden.

As a result my days do slowly become normal again. Classes, dates with Caleb, cheerleading practice, confabs around the lunch table. It's almost like the horror of the past several months has been erased.

Remnants linger, like the day I accidentally walked home to my old house and saw a FOR SALE sign on the front lawn. For a fleeting moment, I thought if I walked inside and ran up to my room the house would magically become mine again. Why can't my old life return if I wish for it hard enough? Because there are other forces out in the world that more often than not are working against us; they're not our champions, that's why. Turning my back on my old house, I realized that I'm very much like my brother. I've grown up a lot too.

But I still need my mommy.

I hate going to visit my mother on Mother's Day; it's just so pathetic. The doctors and nurses give you that pity look that is completely deserved, but because no one wants to be pitied you smile back as if to say, "Oh that's all right; it's okay that my mom's in an irreversible coma." It's a no-win situation. So that's why I always go visit her on the day before the manufactured holiday. Saves everybody a lot of discomfort.

This visit is very different though. I've often visited my mother without my father, but this is the first time I've come to see her when I know my father will never tag along again, that never again will my mother feel his presence and hear his voice. Hopefully, mine will do.

"Hey, Mom, how are you?"

My question falls flatter than usual because if she could speak, I know her answer wouldn't be one I'd want to hear. If she has any idea what recently happened, the pain in her heart must be intolerable. I pray that she understands we did the only thing we could do. And I pray that she believes the right one got to live.

My father didn't talk about his relationship with my mother very much, but I know they loved each other tremendously. It was one of those whirlwind romances, and against all odds the small-town boy won the heart of the sophisticated European beauty. She gave up everything—her life back in France, the adventures she was planning on having, the outlandish memories she was going to create—all to marry my father and settle down in the middle of nowhere. Theirs was a fairy-tale romance that, I guess, has had a fairy-tale ending. She's Sleeping Beauty, and her Prince Charming was killed by the Big Bad Wolf. When I think of it that way, it almost makes me laugh. Almost.

But any gigglaughs that may erupt are silenced by the sound of squeaking.

"Oh I'm so sorry. I didn't know you were here."

Funny how Nadine looks more normal when she's dressed in her volunteer regalia than when she's wearing her school uniform or dressed up for a party. She really was meant for this place, and she really was meant to come to the aid of people who are lost or sick or who just need a friend.

"I'll come back later," she says, clicking her pen.

"Don't," I say. "We could use the company."

Unlike Jess, Nadine isn't a chatterbox, and that's what I need right now, a quiet companion who will understand I only want her to sit close by so I don't feel like I'm so alone. Nadine gets it and sits in the chair next to the window while I hold my mother's hand. I could stare at my mother for hours and just breathe in her beauty, but for Nadine the novelty wears off after a few minutes. Her long, slow breaths fill the room, and she must be in a deep sleep, because she doesn't wake up when her pen falls out of her hand, clicking and bouncing onto the floor.

It might be the residual effects of when I was inhuman, but without turning around I can sense that I'm not the only person in the room who's still awake.

"Hello, Luba."

She looks as disgusting and sinister as ever; victory hasn't improved her looks. Her pale, unnaturally smooth face is framed on both sides by that long, raven-black hair that falls to her waist. Clad only in her hospital gown, she has, I assume, returned to The Retreat to reclaim her room, but I'm wrong; she's here to reclaim her status as number-one psycho.

"So you think you've won," she hisses.

No, but I'm not going to admit that. "We have," I shoot back, squeezing my mother's hand tightly.

Luba raises her two boney arms and presses her fingers to

her mouth. The movement is grotesque; it's something only a little girl should do. Her hands contain all the wrinkles that should live on her face and are dotted with brown spots that look like a galaxy of dirty stars. Some of her fingernails are long, others short, some bitten off, but all are yellowed and stained. Ugly hands on an ugly woman that do nothing to suppress an ugly laugh.

The sound that drips out of her mouth is thick and gravely at first, but then builds into a series of high-pitched notes. Joy created from evil.

I turn around, and Nadine is still sleeping. She's either the deepest sleeper around, or Luba's cast a spell on her so our meeting won't be interrupted. Good, I don't wish this sight on anyone. I cannot believe Barnaby finds this *thing* entertaining.

Suddenly her laughter stops, and she extends her left hand toward me. Her thumb holds down her pinky so only three spindly fingers are pointing in my direction, inches from my face. No more laughter, but Luba is still feeling the type of evil joy only she can feel, so her thin lips slowly form a smile.

"Remember, Dominy," she whispers. "Once cursed, always cursed."

Chapter 29

"Luba's right."

Caleb tries his best to convince me otherwise, but it's no use. What did Jess tell me? *"Just because something is evil, doesn't mean it can't speak the truth."*

"After everything that I've done," I say, "I'm still cursed."

"How can you say that after what your father did for you?" Caleb asks. "He made the ultimate sacrifice just to break Luba's damn hex."

"And he failed!" I cry. "When it comes to that psychopath, there's no way to win! For the rest of my life I'm going to have to live with this, Caleb. Don't you get it? For the rest of my life I'm going to spend every hour of every day knowing that I took the coward's way out. I killed my father so I could live!"

I don't care how loud my voice is. No one's around; the only one who can hear me other than Caleb is The Weeping Lady, and I'm sure she's heard thousands of secrets in her lifetime that she's never repeated. I can't run from the guilt and the shame and the self-hatred that's festering in my mind. Becoming a werewolf was only part of Luba's curse; her real intention was much larger than that. She wanted to destroy my father's family the same way he accidentally destroyed hers, and she has succeeded beyond her wildest dreams.

"No matter how I try to ignore it and gloss over it, the truth of what I did is still right here," I say, both my hands pounding against my head. "And it's never, ever going to leave me!"

Either the world is spinning around me or I'm going to faint. The trees, The Weeping Lady, the buildings in the distance, they're all whipping around me, making my vision blur. I can't feel the grass underneath my feet. I feel like the plastic bag is back around my head, but this time I don't want it to be ripped off; I want it to squeeze tighter and tighter around my neck so I can't breathe anymore. I want this all to be over!

"Dominy!"

I think that was Caleb's voice, but I'm not sure, because everything is black.

Remember, Dominy, you are blessed.

I know the words, but the voice has changed. It's not my mother's poetic sound; it's my father. His voice is much flatter, much more matter-of-fact, but, undeniably, it's just as compassionate.

How can it be over when it's just beginning?

When I open my eyes, I'm blinded by the sun, and I gasp out loud because I think that Jess is at the opposite end of yet another miracle and has found a way to reconnect with me, but I'm wrong. It's just Caleb. The moment my brain recognizes this fact I hate him, and I love him for being exactly who he is. He's just my boyfriend, nothing more. Despite how much he loves me right now and how much he's already done for me, I know instinctively that someday he'll be out of my life, having moved on to someone else, someone he prefers over me. He's never going to love me the way my father and Jess did. Thankfully, my disorientation covers my disappointment.

But within that disappointment lies hope, because I realize for the first time since my father's death I've truly accepted the fact that I have a future.

"Don't worry," he says. "I got you."

No, you don't, I want to say; you only have me for right now. But maybe that's the lesson I need to learn, the lesson my father wanted me to understand, that all we have is right now, so we owe it to ourselves to make the best of it. If we don't, how can we expect tomorrow and the next day to be any better? He accepted the fact that his time on earth was over because he wanted to make the rest of my days better, unmarred by worry and fear. If I continue to wallow in self-pity, as justified as I think that self-pity might be, then his sacrifice was in vain; it was all for nothing, and evil truly wins out.

Looking up into Caleb's face, made even more beautiful by the sunshine I will forever attribute to Jess, I decide I will never let that happen.

Caleb's lips and tongue taste as soft and sweet as they always do. It takes the muscles underneath his T-shirt a few seconds to relax and let go of the surprise my actions have caused, but soon he's kissing me back, gently, as if each kiss is a reminder of life, a reminder that, thanks to my father, I can still live. Which is exactly what I plan to do.

When Archie first mentioned the idea of having a Full Moon Party in my honor, it was greeted by silence. I could tell by everyone's shocked expressions that they thought it was in the poorest of taste and that Archie had finally crossed a line from which he couldn't return. There was no way he could sweet-talk himself back into our good graces and especially mine after making such a foolish suggestion. That's what everyone thought. Until I agreed that it was a brilliant idea.

I think the word for it is *serendipity*, when all the stars align. The next full moon falls on a Saturday night, the same night Melinda Jaffe has to fly back to Connecticut with her mother to attend the funeral of a distant relative. The price of airfare being what it is today, Mrs. Jaffe made the reluctant decision to leave her twins home alone. Add it all up, and the Jaffe basement becomes the perfect place to have a party for the Wolf Pack plus one. Since it's Napoleon's house we had no choice, but to allow him to be on the guest list.

"Your dip's not as good as your mother's, Nay," Archie declares, chomping on a huge mouthful of the stuff.

"I can see it's preventing you from eating half the bowl," Nadine good-naturedly shoots back.

"I am a growing boy!" he yells.

Caleb slaps Archie's stomach. "Keep growing, Angevene, and the boys are gonna start to look elsewhere."

"Oh really?" Archie asks, smiling mischievously despite a mouthful of artichoke dip. "And you think they're gonna start looking at you?"

"Well . . . the six-pack does speak for itself," Caleb replies, lifting up his shirt to reveal perfect abs.

Not to be outdone, Archie lifts up his own shirt. "Like this wasn't carved from pure white marble!"

"Oh my God!" Arla shouts. "Will you two just make out and get over it?"

"What do you think we do when we're in a huddle on the field?" Archie deadpans.

"I knew it!" Arla shouts even louder. "All that butt slapping is bound to lead to experimentation."

I can't believe how resilient Arla is. After the attack no one would have thought less of her if she had announced her need for a little private time, or more specifically, time away from me. But her reaction was exactly the opposite. She never blamed me for the assault or for scarring her; in fact, as unbelievable as it sounds, she actually thanked me.

"You're thanking me for almost blinding you?" I asked, my voice not accurately conveying how shocked I felt.

"Before this happened," Arla told me, her sky-blue nails gesturing toward her eye, "I thought I was part of your team and helping you because you're my friend."

"And now?" I asked.

"This made me realize I'm helping you because it's the right thing to do," she said.

It doesn't matter that I no longer need my own Wolf Pack, Arla's conviction hasn't faltered.

"I must have inherited my dad's crime-stopping gene, because I'm not going to rest until this Luba is caught and served the punishment she deserves," she pronounced. "No matter what, Dom, good's gotta stomp out evil."

I was so moved by her sincerity I could only shake my head. Until she made me laugh.

"And my pumps with the four-inch heels were just made to stomp out some evil," she declared.

Laughing and hugging her tightly, I added, "So is that lemon-yellow eye patch you're sporting!"

"It's my homage to Jess," Arla explained. "Just a little piece of sunshine to carry along with me while I heal."

Oh how I already miss holding on to a little piece of Jess's sunshine. But she'll always be in my heart. And holding on to two muscular arms isn't the worst consolation prize.

Wrapping his arms around me, Caleb whispers in my ear. "You know I've never kissed Archie, right?"

I let him squeeze me tighter; his chin stubble feels wonderful on my neck. "I know."

"Not since sixth grade anyway."

It's hilarious that Caleb has a higher-pitched laugh than I do. I don't know how long he'll be my boyfriend, but for now I couldn't imagine feeling this way about anyone else. Unfortunately, not everyone agrees I've made the right choice.

"Nice to see that you're up for a party, Dominy," Napoleon says the minute Caleb walks away to get more punch.

"It was time," I reply. "Excuse me."

We both step to the same side at the same time. I don't know if it's deliberate on his part or unplanned, but it puts a glitch into my getaway.

"I was thinking about Jess the other day."

Maybe I'm annoyed that Nap isn't getting the hint that I don't want to have a private conversation with him or maybe the sound of my friend's name coming out of his mouth sounds wrong and irritates me, but I involuntarily channel my inner bitch, who has been lying dormant for several months.

"Seriously, Nap, you don't get to say her name, let alone think about her."

"I'm sorry," Napoleon says, becoming very nervous all of a sudden. "I was just, you know, having sushi and, well, you remember how she was obsessed with everything Japanese."

Of course I do!

"I remember how much she adored Japanese culture because I was there the exact moment she fell in love with Hello Kitty," I explain. "I remember the first time I helped her dye her hair black and straighten it with an iron. I remember the first time we saw Saoirse doing makeup tutorials online, and Jess immediately e-mailed her to tell her that Nakano, her Japanese sidekick, was gorgeous. I remember everything, Napoleon, because I was there. Because I was her best friend, and I loved her. You didn't even like her that much even though you masqueraded as her boyfriend. You're in love with me, and don't think that we didn't know it."

It's just about this time that I realize we have an audience. I didn't plan on it, I didn't want anyone else to overhear, but I have nothing to hide. Everything I said was the truth. So I wrap it up as succinctly as possible.

"So, Nap, you don't get to say Jess's name or remember her or try to make a play for me," I add. "And if you follow by those rules, maybe, *just maybe* I can forget about the past and we can start to be friends."

The only sounds in the basement are the ticking of a clock and Archie chomping on more food. Until Napoleon replies.

"I accept."

I shake the hand he's holding out to me and agree. "Now let's get this party started!"

Somebody turns up the music, and Caleb twirls me around, my hair, my necklace, my skirt spinning with me.

"Domgirl," Caleb says, pulling me in close to him, "I am so hot for you right now."

Grabbing onto his shoulders, I smile. "Well then, maybe we'll have to do something about that later."

Filled with surprise, anticipation, and lust, Caleb can't contain his smile or the little rustling in his jeans. I know he's just about to kiss me when I scream.

No! This cannot be happening!! Not again!!

Out of the corner of my eye I can see the full moon in all its silver glory hanging against a navy blue sky, the full moon that's no longer supposed to pose a threat, the full moon that's making me transform once again into something I was no longer supposed to become.

"No!!!!!!!"

I look down at my arms, and it feels like they're on fire. This was never supposed to happen again; we had made sure of it.

"Help me!!!!!"

Just as I feel my knees about to snap backward, I see Nadine slam a lamp over her brother's head and watch him fall to the ground. Maybe she's being a good sister and trying to protect him from witnessing the horror that's about to be on display. I can't protect anyone, but I can salvage one thing. I rip the necklace Caleb gave me off my neck and throw it at him.

"Caleb, run!"

The rest of my bones snap into place; my skin disappears underneath a cloak of fur; my screams give way to growls, and then one long howl announces I've returned. The curse is still flowing through my veins. I'm still connected to the powerful wolf spirit, and I'm still consumed with the desperate need to feed.

Slowly I walk around the room, taking my time, as all around me is commotion and screams and crying. There he is, the last one I saw before I turned, the one who's escaped me so many times before. This time will be different.

He looks muscular for a human, and his yellow hair is like a crown of sunlight, but he's no match for me; we both know that.

"Dominy, stop!" he cries to me. "It's Caleb. You have to fight this!"

Do not give me orders!!

Leaping into the air I see him cower to the floor, and I open my mouth to show the full fury of my rage. I'm seconds away from tasting his flesh when I feel something burrow into my side and hurl me across the room.

I'm on my back, my paws being held by the one made of pure white, and he's staring down at me. His face carries none of the fear of the other one. How stupid.

"Dominy," he says quietly. "Look at me, look into my eyes. It's me, Archie."

I've seen this one before too. He thinks he knows me; he thinks he's smarter than me. He's another fool. One push against his hands and we flip over. Now he's looking up at me as I pin him to the floor. Our positions are reversed, but he looks exactly the same.

"Dominy," he repeats. "You do not want to hurt me. You don't want to hurt any of us."

There's something in his eyes that I've never seen before, something that makes me remember I'm not alone, that I share this soul with another. Kindness.

"Remember who you are, Dominy, and remember that we're your friends."

I can feel the girl stir inside of me, begging me to let him go, imploring me not to hurt these people. I turn to look at the others, and they're more afraid than he is, but they're all looking at me with the same kindness in their eyes, even the girl surrounded by the silver mist.

Inside of me I can feel the girl become stronger, struggle to take over. I need help; I need more power so I howl at the moon. My sound is long and desperate, but there's no response because the moon has disappeared.

The entire room is pulsating with light, golden yellow and blinding in its intensity. Whatever it is, wherever this magic light is coming from, it's come for the girl, to help her, infuse her with just enough strength to take over, to take control, and to escape.

"Jess!"

I hear the girl scream from deep within our soul, and when her scream is acknowledged, there's nothing I can do to fight it. I feel my body run toward where the moon should be and crash through the window to escape to the outside. The cool air does nothing to change things; the yellow light has followed me, and now sparkles of dust are falling all around me, making me weary, putting me to sleep. I know that this Dominy is taking over, and there's nothing I can do to prevent it. She has too much power on her side and too many allies.

"Jess?"

"I'm right here, Dom."

The voice is finally accompanied by a shape, and Jess emerges from the center of the light, looking the way she did the last time I saw her, as if she's been dipped in shimmering gold, still a breathtaking sight. Thanks to her intervention I'm completely merged with the wolf-spirit now; we've become one, but why? Why did this happen again? Why did Luba lie to me?

"You said I could believe her; you said she was telling the truth!"

"She was," Jess replies.

"That's impossible! If she was telling the truth, the spell would be broken."

"Follow me."

I walk behind Jess, fragments of her light piercing through me, warming my fur, but unable to calm my racing heart. We walk away from the houses and cars, past an area filled with trees and bushes, and only stop when we reach a small clearing. Blinking my eyes to adjust to the mixture of moonglow and sunlight, I let out a low growl when I see the black-haired woman standing in the middle of the clearing, only dirt surrounding her, as if her presence has made it impossible for any life to grow.

"I'm sorry, Dom," Jess says.

I have no idea what she's sorry for until Luba brings her hands up to her mouth and laughs. I've seen her do this before; I remember it clearly. We were in my mother's hospital room at The Retreat. Both of my worlds must be starting to connect, to merge together. Next, I know that she'll raise three fingers of her left hand and point them in my direction. And then she'll speak.

"The original sinner was killed," Luba says, barely able to conceal her laughter. "But not by the original sin."

No! No, this can't be true!

"You tricked me!" I scream.

"No!" Luba rages. "You didn't kill your father!!"

What? That can't be possible. Can it be? I don't remember it, but . . . if not me, then who? "Who?! Who killed him?!"

"Someone who wanted my child's death to be properly

avenged," she hisses. "Someone who believes in vengeance and didn't want my curse to be removed."

Two sounds fill the night—Luba's spiteful laugh and my mournful wail. Both sounds feel like knives slicing through my flesh and my heart, their impact leaving me devastated and so wounded I want to lash out at anything and everything, but I'm too angry to move.

"Now my curse can never be broken!" the witch screeches.

This can't be happening! This can't be real! My father gave his life for me so this curse could be lifted, so it would be over and I could live my life the way my parents always dreamed I would. And now this! It isn't fair!

I don't know if Luba melts into the night or if Jess's blinding sunshine makes her flee, but when I catch my breath, when the shock settles into my body, she's nowhere to be found.

"I'm sorry, Dom," Jess says, sitting on the ground next to me, looking as if she's sitting in a pool of liquid gold. "I couldn't tell you."

Well, tell me now! "Who killed my father?! Jess, please, you have to tell me!"

"I can't," she replies.

"What do you mean you can't?!" I cry.

"I told you, Dom; I have limitations."

Oh my God! I can't believe this is happening! We thought this was over! We thought this was finished, and it's only just begun!

"What am I supposed to do now?!"

Jess doesn't respond right away. She lets me howl and cry and growl; she lets the pain and the anguish settle into my bones. When I appear to be calm, when Jess senses that I'm ready to hear her, she does what she always did when she was alive: She tells me the truth.

"You have to do what I did and make the best of a really,

really bad situation," she says. "How else do you think I got to be a sun goddess?"

That's my Jess. I feel the warmth of her hand travel along my back, and in response I nuzzle my snout up against her leg. It's comforting, like sitting next to my father. My poor father. He gave his life for me and for what? It was all for nothing. No! It can't be. And it won't be, not if I have anything to say about it. There is no way that I'm going to let Luba get away with this. Not her or whoever did her bidding.

But right now is not the time for revenge; right now is not the time for action. It's the time to think about how to fight back and how to overcome this evil for good. I know Jess can't give me the answers I need, I know she can't give me my old life back, but she can give me one thing which I know she always will—her friendship.

Epilogue

Jess's grave is the only one surrounded by cherry blossoms.

"I thought they were a nice touch," Jess says, appearing next to me.

"A little show-offy, don't you think?" I reply.

"That was the point!"

Of course it was.

"Look at me, Dom," she says, raising her arms to create waterfalls of sunshine. "I'm not exactly subtle."

I don't care if anyone's looking; I don't care if anyone sees me and thinks I've lost my mind. I tuck my arm inside Jess's and watch as her sunlight dances and sparkles all around us. Together we laugh like the girls we used to be, even though we'll never be those same girls again.

Where this curse will lead me, I have no idea. It's already brought me to places I never conceived existed, and now that I'm determined to find out who really killed my father, I can't imagine where it will take me next. The bad news: I don't know how much longer I can keep the lid of the honey jar screwed on tight to prevent the honey inside from being scooped out and devoured. I don't know what other secrets I'll need to uncover or what obstacles I'll be challenged to overcome, but against all odds I won't be taking this journey alone. Because there's good news too: All my invisible strings are intact.

I carry my parents' love with me every day, especially my father's. Caleb and Archie have both proven I can trust them with my life, and Arla's stood by me, although she has every reason to hate me, and has even become a surrogate big sister to Barnaby. The jury's still deliberating on the fate of the bee and the butterfly—Nadine and Napoleon—but for now I consider them friends.

My friends. A group that thankfully still includes Jess as its president and now its guiding light. A group committed to helping me and traveling with me wherever this curse may lead us. It's totally *subarashi*.

"Remember, Dominy . . ." Jess starts.

"Yeah, yeah, I know," I reply. "I'm blessed."

And finally, I am starting to believe it.

Dear Reader,

Now that you've read *Moonglow* and have gotten to know Dominy, Jess, Archie, and the rest of their friends, families, and even their enemies, I thought I'd give you a peek at some of the intriguing stuff that's coming up in *Sunblind*, the next book in the series.

Right on page one, Dominy starts to question who she is and why she became a werewolf. She knows the *how*, she knows that Luba set the curse into motion, and as difficult as it's been to grasp, she's coming to terms with her mystical fate. But she can't stop thinking about the bigger picture and the ramifications of Luba's spell. How is being part teenager and part wolf really going to affect the person she is and the person she hopes to become? Will the guilt she feels over her father's death ever go away? And how can she stop Barnaby from wandering over to the dark side? Those are the things Dom wants to know. The problem is she hardly has any time to think.

Turns out, the citizens of Weeping Water are not a quiet bunch. They want to put an end to the terror that's seeped into their sleepy little town, and they've decided to take action in order to rid themselves of this serial killer. Unfortunately, they have no way of knowing what kind of danger they're really in, because Luba isn't working alone; she's got her own army of witches who are almost as powerful as she is. And they're about to unleash even more supernatural forces that threaten to destroy Weeping Water and everyone in it.

Despite all the physical action and drama, there's some happiness too. Relationships are flourishing even while the world seems to be going crazy. Archie, Nadine, and even

Mrs. Jaffe all find boyfriends, and, trust me, you're not going to believe who they are. Even I was shocked when I found out! And don't worry, Caleb continues to prove why he should be crowned Boyfriend of the Year, even if Dominy is afraid and reluctant to fully commit to him.

A lot of secrets are revealed in *Sunblind* too. We learn the true history of what happened on the night Luba cursed Mason and, as a result, Dominy, and how that history is very much a part of the present. Luba is hell-bent on destroying not only Dom, but her entire family. We also find out what's up with the bee and the butterfly—Nadine and Napoleon. Are they good? Are they evil? Are they working together? And, most important, what's the real reason they returned to their hometown?

But through it all, the central theme of this second book in the Darkborn Legacy is the undying friendship between Dominy and Jess. Both girls continue to grow as individuals as they become more acclimated to their newly acquired identities—the werewolf and the sun goddess—but it's as friends that they shine. They become closer, each more in tune with what the other is feeling and thinking, and more loyal to each other than either one ever imagined. The future is nothing like they thought it would be, but it's turning out to be a destiny that they're going to share.

So lives change even more drastically as the harsh light of the sun exposes the truth. But even though the truth is blinding, Dom doesn't become defeated; she doesn't try to hide from her fate. Just the opposite: She embraces the wolf spirit that's living inside of her. And by the end of *Sunblind,* Dominy becomes more determined than ever to use that primal passion and strength to defeat the evil that's lurking within the shadow of the moon.

Thanks for reading—and enjoy!

Michael Griffo

Please turn the page for an exciting sneak peek of

SUNBLIND,

the second book in Michael Griffo's
Darkborn Legacy trilogy,
coming in September 2013!

The morning comes, the moonglow fades
Replaced by what the night forbade.

A relentless light that reveals the worst
Of what I am—
A blessed curse.

Prologue

Which came first, the wolf or the girl?

That's the question I've started to ask myself these past few months, especially right before I transform. Right before my blood turns to fire inside my veins and starts to burn my arms. Just as my legs break and my knees point in the wrong direction, just as I see my skin disappear underneath a cloak of red fur. It should be an easy question to answer. The girl came first, and sixteen years later the wolf showed up. But that's not really the truth. The wolf was conceived long before the girl was born, long before the girl's father even thought of having a child. So doesn't that make the girl an afterthought? Doesn't that put her in second place behind the wolf? A subset instead of the whole package or even some kind of weird descendent to the wolf spirit? I thought it was an easy question, but the more I think about it, I realize it isn't. And now, quite frankly, I don't care. Because right now I'm hungry.

Saliva drips from my mouth like thick water oozing out of a leaky faucet. A low, constant growl drones out of me like metal scraping against stone. There's a dull ache in my empty stomach that needs to be filled, and it needs to be filled now.

I'm trying to control the hunger, keep it from consuming me so I can still be in control, so I can remain languid, but ready to strike. My razor-sharp teeth are exposed and my blue-gray eyes alert, but my soft red fur ripples in the breeze, and my body sways gently with every step I take. Could be out for a stroll, could be out for a hunt, no one can tell. But one thing is clear: Underneath the silver light of the full moon my body looks nothing like that of the girl I was and everything like the thing I've become. A wolf. A wolf that desperately needs to feed.

The problem is, at this very moment, I'm the one who's being hunted.

Behind me are sounds, sounds that shouldn't be heard at this time of night and definitely not in the middle of the woods. These aren't sounds from nature; they're human. Well, part human, because the sounds I hear are coming from one very sick and demented and vengeful woman.

Luba.

When I whip my head around, keeping my snout low to the ground, I can see her right in front of me. I can see her wrinkled face, the skin so pale and thin it looks like it could be peeled away, and her jet-black hair, long and straight, as lifeless as her eyes.

I can hear her laughing, her voice rough and childish and foul, echoing all around me. Instead of dying out the farther it gets from its source, her laughter grows louder until it destroys the peaceful quiet of the night. It's a sound that makes me sick.

There she is, standing before me, her body emaciated, her white hospital gown lifting in the wind to expose bony, scarred knees, her spindly fingers pressed against her chapped lips that form a gruesome smile. I can feel my heart beat faster; I can feel my empty stomach churn, because when I look at Luba, it's like looking in the mirror. We're completely different, and yet we're the same. We both violate the laws of nature. We're both creatures that do not belong in the world. We're wrong, we shouldn't exist, and yet here we are.

Or are we?

I blink my eyes, and Luba's gone. Twisting my head to the left and the right, I scour the darkness, but can't find her. Is she hiding? Was she ever here in the first place? Have I started to hallucinate?! No, she's not in front of me; she never was. I imagined her presence. But she is close by. I know that because I can smell her.

Her anger fills my nostrils like dead flesh. I follow my instinct and turn to run, because her anger is stronger than ever before, and now it's mixed with another emotion that I never expected I'd sense from her—fear.

Why is Luba afraid of me? She's never been afraid before; she's always been confident and vicious and proud. What's changed to make her become fearful? I wish I could waste time trying to figure that out, but I can't because anger mixed with fear is a dangerous combination that makes people do crazy things. And when that mixture of emotions lies within the heart of someone as evil as Luba, dangerous can quickly become deadly.

My slow gait turns into a run, and I make sure to avoid breaking twigs with my paws or overturning rocks. I need to be quiet; I need to remain undetected. I jump over a small puddle filled with rainwater and have to swerve quickly to the right to avoid disrupting a small pyramid of crushed beer cans. The litter is evidence that humans have been here, which means I can never assume the woods are safe. Crouching, I crawl under a spray of low-hanging branches, their mass of leaves tickling my fur as I pass through, and come out to stand on the edge of a clearing. A wide, flat expanse of lush green grass decorated with wildflowers in colors that brighten the night—yellow and pink and orange—colors that turn the earth into a galaxy of vibrant stars. It's a beautiful sight. But one that offers no protection.

How wonderful would it be to lie in this field for a moment, let the coolness pierce through my fur and put out the fire I can feel raging inside of me? But even just a moment is too long to hesitate, to let down my guard. Even just a moment will surely get me killed, especially when Luba's right behind me.

But why is she hunting me? And why does her hatred for me now contain fear? I look up, and it's almost as if the full moon is pulsating, trying to communicate with me in some sort of supernatural Morse code, telling me to use my natural instinct to make sense of a situation that doesn't seem to contain logic. I force myself to hold still, to not breathe, to do nothing but accept the full moon's message. It's a complete waste of time! All I can feel is the painful ache that's returned to my stomach. And then all I smell is blood.

The stench is so glorious I open my mouth to howl, to announce to whomever or whatever is bleeding that I'm coming to feed, but my howl turns into silence. The wolf wants to cry; the girl is cautious. So even though the wolf wants to make a sound, the girl knows that it will only help Luba discover the location of her prey. It's the perfect example of how the wolf and the girl have learned to coexist.

The other thing I've learned is that if I ignore the hunger, there are consequences. The violence and aggression and primal urges I feel as a wolf spill over into my human form after the transformation reverses itself if I don't indulge in wolfen hunger when the feeling overcomes me like it's doing right now. So even though I can hear and smell and sense Luba is approaching and I know I should keep running, I can't. The hunger pains have become more intense, as if a sharp-edged claw is burrowing through my skin from the inside out. I have no choice; I have got to feed.

And only a few feet away is my meal.

A mound of fur and blood. A family of rabbits all huddled

together, clinging to one another as if they're sleeping and trying to keep warm. Except this family is dead and lifeless and bloody. Such a beautiful sight.

A string of saliva drips from one fang and is lifted into the air by my hot, anxious breath. The unmoving bodies are pulling me closer to them as if they're a magnet and I'm a piece of steel. I am unable to resist, powerless to do anything else but take one step toward the bloody mound and then another and another. When I'm a foot away I regain some self-control and begin to circle the carcasses just so I can look at the heavenly display from all sides, my long tongue dripping wet and gliding over my teeth. Halfway around I can wait no longer. The hell with Luba, right now quenching my hunger is more important than guaranteeing my survival.

I lunge forward, but instead of burying my teeth into flesh and bone and blood, I crash into something hard and fall back. I look up, and separating me from my meal is a yellow wall. No, not a real wall, but a huge block made up of what looks like golden marble. Furious, I ram my body into it again, my front paws colliding into the barrier with all my might, only to career back again, my side slamming into the ground.

Dazed, I shake my head, strings of saliva whipping into my snout and my eyes. What the hell is going on?! I turn toward the glowing wall, and my lips form a sneer as a growl escapes from my body. The wall starts to glow with a yellow light, growing brighter by the second, and I try to keep my eyes open, try to see what's creating this display, but the light is blinding. For a few moments darkness replaces the light as if they're joined together, and I can't see a thing. I'm consumed by blackness, utterly alone and utterly afraid.

Until Jess appears.

The yellow wall melts into a thin vertical line that hangs in the air, slicing into the dark night, and then bursts open like a fireworks display, shooting sparks into the sky that twinkle and fall and combine to create something unimaginable, an Amaterasu Omikami, a legendary Japanese sun goddess, or simply the new person that Jess has become. The supernatural being that she became after I killed her. And now I want to kill her again.

What the hell are you doing?!

"Saving your life," Jess replies to my silent cry.

By interrupting my meal?! By making me go crazy with hunger?!

Ignoring my unspoken comments, Jess flicks her wrist, and a piece of sunshine flies into the air. I watch it twist and turn and hover for a second over the dead rabbit family until it falls on top of them, dousing them in golden light, so they look as if they're bathing in honey. The light is immediately extinguished when I hear a loud crash that makes me jump back. The rabbits were huddled together not because they had been sleeping; they were arranged that way so they could conceal a bear trap.

Oh my God, you really did save my life!

Floating several inches above the ground, Jess smiles at me. "I'd say you'll have to do the same for me someday, but it's a little late for that."

Involuntarily I bow my head and scrape the dirt with my front paw. I know Jess doesn't blame me for her death, but still, I am the reason she's dead. I tug at the earth one more time, sending clumps of dirt into the air. My stomach hurts, my head hurts, and now my heart hurts. Enough! I don't have time for this; I don't have time for reflection; I have to focus on the matter at hand—someone has gone to a lot of trouble to try to lure me to my death, and that someone has got to be Luba.

But why? She has amazing powers of her own; she doesn't need to resort to something so basic. Unless, of course, she wants to make it look like it was an accident and not the result of some sick, demonic intervention. Get rid of me and keep her secret safe. Yes, that's got to be it!

"Wrong."

I'm not sure what's more annoying—being contradicted or seeing Jess's smirk.

I'm not wrong. This is a trap!

Sitting cross-legged, but still several inches above the ground, Jess smiles at me. She extends her arm to touch my fur, which I know she loves to play with, but I'm not in the mood to be caressed so I flinch, which only makes Jess roll her eyes at me. Now we're even; we're both annoyed with each other.

"Yes, it is a trap," Jess relents. "But no, Luba wasn't the one who set it."

It takes a second for the reality of Jess's statement to sink in.

If Luba didn't set the trap, that means she has help; she isn't working alone.

"Well, kind of," Jess replies cryptically.

Once again I'm reminded that in Jess's current superior state she is still limited, and she can't tell me everything that she knows. She's bound to a different set of rules that even she doesn't completely understand. But I've learned that you don't have to have the answer to everything to know the truth. I may not know who's working with Luba, but I do know that if Jess hadn't intervened, I'd be dead right now, split into two separate pieces by that bear trap.

Thank you.

"Don't thank me yet," Jess says, looking behind me. "Luba isn't your only enemy."

What?!

I turn around, and I don't see anything, but the noises I heard earlier are back, and they're getting louder. I have no idea what's going on, but now I'm the one who's afraid.

"People are scared, Dom," Jess explains. "And when people are scared, they act foolishly."

I want Jess to tell me more, I want her to explain what she means, but there's no time left; the sounds are getting louder with every second. I'm about to find out just who my enemy is.

"The trap is right up here!"

Barnaby!

The voice is unmistakable; it belongs to my brother. I am frozen in my spot; the only thing I can do is take a deep breath. The smell I thought belonged to Luba is my brother's, and it's the smell of anger and hatred and fear. He's the one who's hunting me; he's the one who set this trap; he's the one who wants me dead. The air around my throat seems to want to strangle me. Luba doesn't want to kill me; my brother does.

"Get behind me!"

Lost in my own thoughts, I can't respond to Jess's command.

"Do I have to do everything myself?!"

Jess disappears into the night, and I'm left alone. Suddenly the air is cold, but it's not actually the air; it's me. It's like the opposite of when I transform; my blood has turned to ice and has stopped flowing through my veins. In the distance I can see shadows approaching and then a light. My brother is at the front of a group holding a torch like the leader of some modern-day witch hunt. Except the witch is a wolf and the wolf is me. I want to run; I want to get as far away as I possibly can, find somewhere safe to hide, but I can't. And anyway, where can I go when so many people are hunting for me?

Maybe this is my destiny: to die at my brother's hand like my father was supposed to die by mine. But I'm not ready to die! I'm not ready to give up! Thankfully, Jess agrees with me.

Just as Barnaby comes into plain sight, Jess appears in front of me and spreads her arms. From her fingertips a wall

of flames erupts, and the sun goddess is replaced by the beginning of a forest fire. The flames spread out several feet on
both sides of me and then turn inward as they start to form a
circle. In a matter of seconds I'm going to be surrounded by
hot, raging fire. Instinctively, I want to break free before I'm
burned to death, and my paws start to dig at the ground, a
high-pitched whimper joining the chorus of crackling flames.
Only two feet remain open behind me; if I don't move now
I'm going to be engulfed, and there won't be any escape.
Crouching low to the earth, I position my body to leap forward, but before I can fly into the air, Jess's voice slams into
my ears.

Trust me!

The two ends of the line of flame connect, and the circular
wall is created; there's no longer any way to escape unless I
want to be burned alive. But wait. . . . Why can't I feel any
heat? Suddenly I realize that the flames aren't threatening to
me; they're not even flames at all. They're an illusion. Once
again, Jess is saving my life. And confusing my brother and
his fellow witch-hunters stuck on the other side of the wall.

"It's a fire!"

But that isn't my brother's voice; it's Louis's! Why in the
world is he helping my brother hunt me down? Or hunting
this animal that they think is terrorizing the town? He's the
police chief, not a vigilante! Could this be the only way he
could think of to avenge the death of his best friend, my father? Could they have figured out that the killings are all connected to the full moon? It doesn't matter; what matters is
that if they find me, they won't know it's me. They'll think
they've found the wild animal that needs to be killed, its dead
body put on display to show the rest of the town that the horror has finally come to an end. Louis won't know that what
he's looking at, what he wants to kill, is Mason Robineau's
daughter, the girl he's agreed to raise as his own child. He'll

only think he's looking at a murderer that needs to be put to death.

The voices are louder now and pull me from my thoughts, which are completely useless anyway. I don't recognize who's shouting; it could be a neighbor, a teacher, anyone who's known me my entire life. But whoever they are, they're just as startled by the sudden, unexpected fire and just as angry that it has interrupted their outing. Once again, if it weren't for Jess, I'd probably be dead.

"Go back to town and get Tourtelot!" Louis screams.

I know that name. Nathan Tourtelot is the fire chief.

"Tell him we've got a fire out here," Louis commands. "He's got to put it out before it gets out of control."

Louis's voice is different from the others. Yes, there's a hint of fear, but mostly there's authority. After years of sitting back, following my father's command, and acting as if he didn't have a decisive bone in his body, Louis seems to have gone through his own transformation. He's become a leader. Which means, to me anyway, that he's very much like Luba. Another nemesis I need to be wary of.

But I can't help feeling that he's also like my father. Protective and strong and courageous. All he's trying to do is keep his family and his town safe, which is exactly what my father tried to do his entire life. Wherever my father is, I know that he's proud of his friend. He may, however, feel a bit differently about his son.

"Look!" Barnaby cries.

Taking a step back, I lower my snout, thinking that this in some way will shield me from my brother's stare. But I have nothing to worry about; Jess's flames are impenetrable. And besides, he's not looking at me; he's found something else even more interesting.

"The trap is shut!" he tells the crowd. "The thing was here!"

Thing?! The word fills me with rage, and if I weren't being held prisoner by Jess's flames, I don't think I'd be able to restrain myself; I'd reveal myself to my brother and Louis and the entire town, show them I'm not a thing! I'm a *werewolf!* It isn't something I chose to be, it isn't something I ever imagined I'd become, but I am! But then I realize with heartbreaking clarity that even if Barnaby and the others knew what I was, knew what I was forced to become, it might not change their minds. They might not be able to separate the wolf from the girl, and they might still want me dead.

"We have to split up," Louis orders. "Half of you go that way; the rest follow me."

I have no idea which directions they're heading into, but I can hear them leave, not retreating, but moving closer to what they hope will be victory. When the flames around me recede, I don't have to look up; I know that we're alone, my enemies have gone, and it's just Jess and me.

"That special-effects display is something I've been working on for a while now," Jess explains. "Just to, you know, test the limits of my skill set."

I nod my head in gratitude, too exhausted and shocked and confused to respond.

"We're very much the same you and I," she adds.

Looking at her splendid beauty, I have no idea what she's talking about.

"We're both works in progress," she says, one hand running its fingers through my fur. "We're both finding our places in this world and in our new selves."

Impatiently, I nod my head. Not because I don't agree with Jess or want to hear what she has to say, but because the hunger has returned. Licking my lips, I walk toward the dead rabbits, unable to contain my joy.

"And that, Dominy, is my cue to leave," Jess says. "I love you, but I cannot watch you eat. It is beyond gross."

Before I can say good-bye, Jess disappears, taking her sunshine with her and leaving me alone in the glow of the moon. The truth, however, is that I'm never alone. I'm never just me. For the rest of my life I'm destined to have a companion, a connection. Like darkness and light, like the sun and the moon, the wolf and the girl will never be separated.

So which came first, the wolf or the girl?

It doesn't really matter, because it looks like they're both here to stay.